NEVER GIVE UP ON YOUR DREAMS!

MY CALL V
THE FINAL SHOWDOWN

MY CALL V

THE FINAL SHOWDOWN

Ronald H. Gray

BLACK WALL STREET NEW DREAM PUBLISHING
Owned by
MY PROVIDER PRODUCTIONS LLC
www.myproviderproductions.com

RONALD GRAY

My Provider Productions LLC
My Call V The Final Showdown
Copyright © 2020 Ronald H. Gray

ISBN-13: 978-0-578-77742-9
Author: Ronald H. Gray
Cover Design/Graphics: Ronald H. Gray
Printed in the United States of America

This is a work of fiction. Any references or similarities to actual events, real people, living or dead, or to real locales are intended to give the novel a sense of reality. Any similarity in other names, characters, places, and incidents is entirely coincidental.

Distributed by Black Wall Street New Dream Publishing
My Provider Productions LLC
www.myproviderproductions.com
blackwallstreetnewdream@yahoo.com

RONALD GRAY

BLACK WALL STREET NEW DREAM PUBLISHING

Revised Edition

My Call

A NOVEL BY
RONALD GRAY

RONALD GRAY

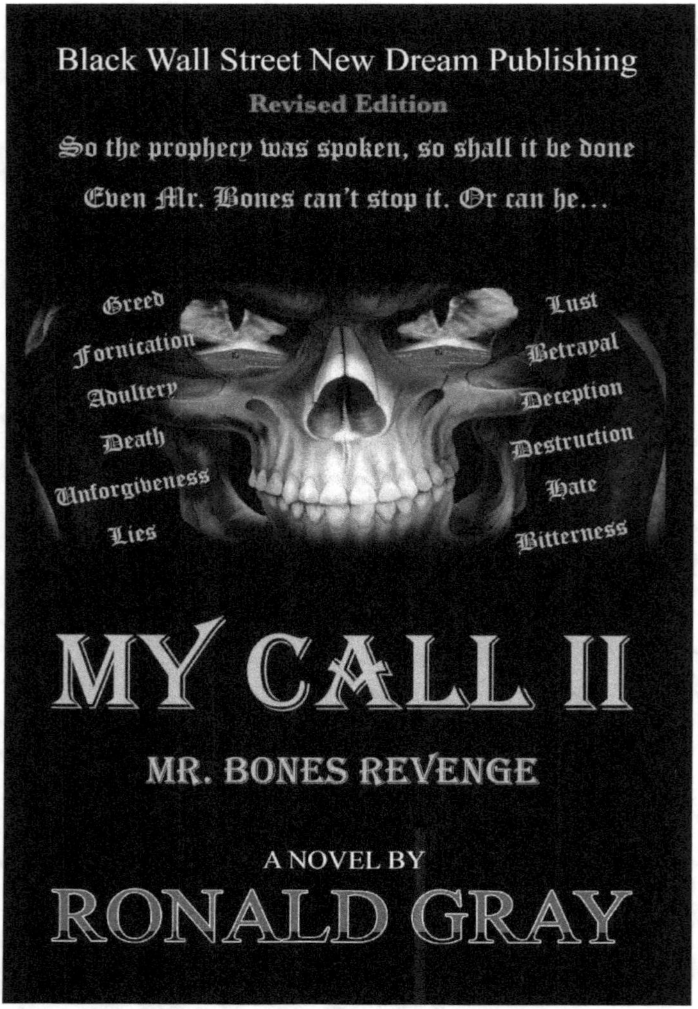

Black Wall Street New Dream Publishing
Revised Edition
So the prophecy was spoken, so shall it be done

Even Mr. Bones can't stop it. Or can he...

Greed

Fornication

Adultery

Death

Unforgiveness

Lies

Lust

Betrayal

Deception

Destruction

Hate

Bitterness

MY CALL II

MR. BONES REVENGE

A NOVEL BY

RONALD GRAY

RONALD GRAY

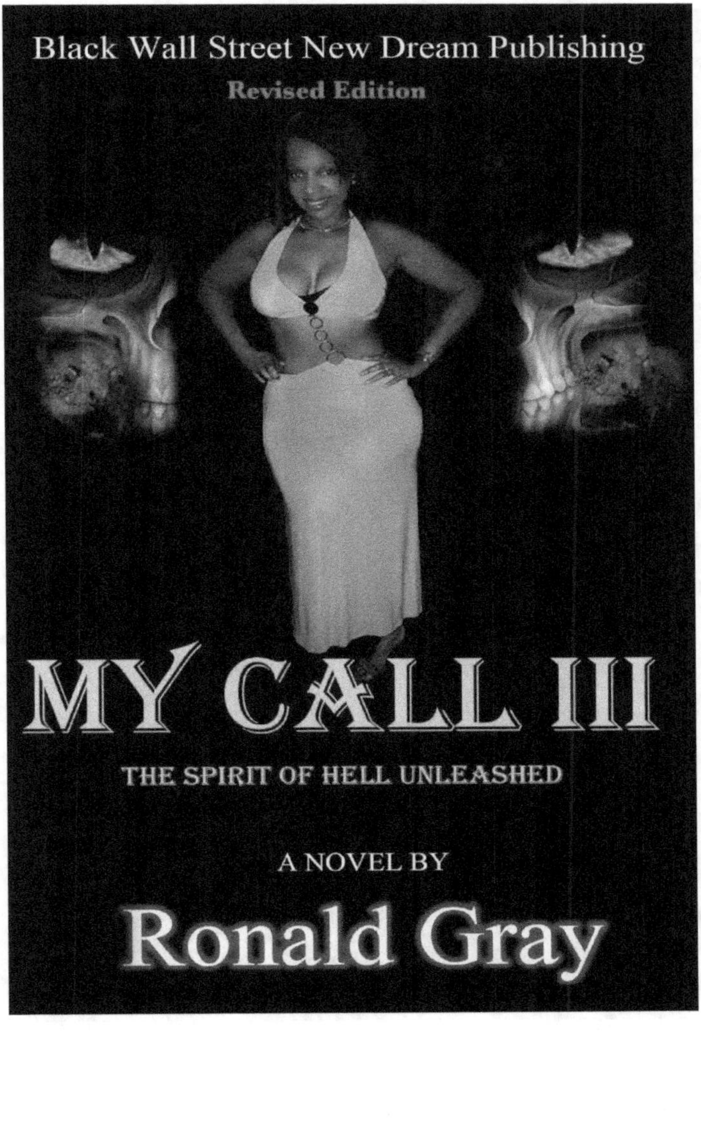

Black Wall Street New Dream Publishing
Revised Edition

MY CALL III

THE SPIRIT OF HELL UNLEASHED

A NOVEL BY

Ronald Gray

RONALD GRAY

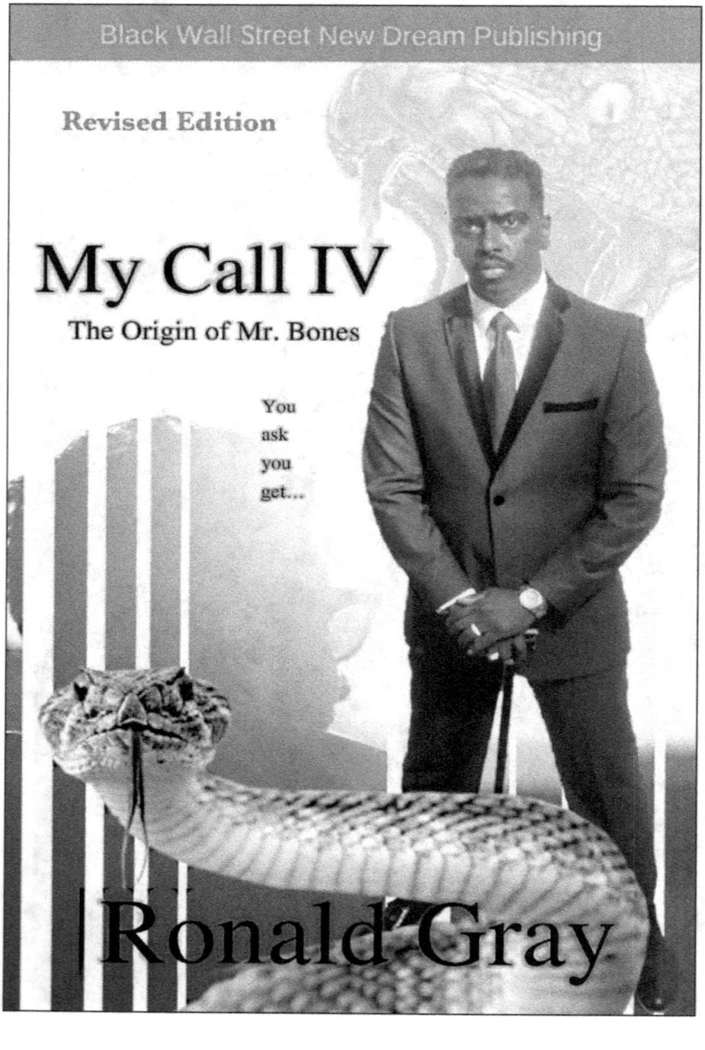

Black Wall Street New Dream Publishing

Revised Edition

My Call IV
The Origin of Mr. Bones

You
ask
you
get...

Ronald Gray

RONALD GRAY

BLACK WALL STREET NEW DREAM PUBLISHING

Revised   Edition

THE MASTER DECEIVER

BE CAREFUL WHAT YOU ASK FOR

A NOVEL BY
RONALD GRAY

RONALD GRAY

Black Wall Street New Dream Publishing

Revised Edition

I don't have much money but I will love you for the rest of your life.

Or

Money for a Lifetime

HAVING THE BEST

REFLECTIONS ON THAT THING CALLED LOVE

BY

RONALD GRAY

RONALD GRAY

DEDICATION

This book is dedicated to my family and friends who have been incredibly supportive of my business. It is the readers who continue to make this possible because of the requests for more of this emotionally powerful series. Thank you very much!

CHAPTER ONE
NOT OVER

Malone Garcia was a quiet man and a loner who lacked ambition. He worked as a cemetery groundskeeper and his attitude was, do your job, nothing less, nothing more. He earned two thousand dollars a month, with a savings of sixty-five hundred dollars in the bank, and lived in a one-bedroom apartment. He is Puerto Rican, thirty-eight years old, six-foot-one, and two-hundred-twenty pounds. Malone remembered the day like it was yesterday.

That day, Malone performed his groundskeeper duties like always during a burial service, but this would be no ordinary burial. The same day the O'Neil family buried Christine O'Neil, their oldest daughter next to her Dad David. Stunningly beautiful Leticia Wilson, the Devil incarnate, along with her animal friends, launched a vicious attack on the people attending the burial. Leticia was finally destroyed in a very violent, vicious, and bloody battle and everyone involved had some degree of emotional satisfaction that she was dead. Especially after seeing all the dead bodies and body parts lying on the ground.

When Leticia and her vicious animal friends attacked the people attending the service, Malone ran and hid at the edge of the woods. He could still see the horror manifesting itself before him. It was something out of a horror movie. He witnessed an earthquake, large black cats coming from the large cracks in the ground, an incredibly beautiful woman turning into a large black wolf, and those black cats ripping people to death.

After all the killings were over and everyone drove away, Malone came out of hiding. You could hear the emergency vehicles in the distance getting closer. Malone walked and looked around, sweating from the intense fear that he had never known. The sight of the awesome carnage lying on the ground caused him to throw up twice. He continued walking until he saw an expensive-looking cane on the ground that belonged to Leticia Wilson. Malone did not know it was hers but felt overwhelmingly compelled to pick it up. He looked around to make sure no one saw him, picked up the cane, and ran as fast as he could.

He fell twice, hitting his mouth on a headstone the second time, which knocked out four of his front teeth. He was dizzy and in pain but stood up quickly with blood dripping from his mouth and looked around making sure no one saw him fall. He wiped his mouth with his hand, brushed his clothes off, and looked around again. He started running with his head up high, mouth dripping with blood, but still holding the cane.

Leticia Wilson's body was destroyed but not the spirit that possessed her. It is the spirit that lays dormant for weeks, months, and sometimes years before it manifests itself. The body dies, but the spirit looks for a new host to inhabit. The O'Neil family had been through so much and suffered greatly, unfortunately, it was not over. This time, it was going to be an all-out war. The deadly spirit of Mr.

Bones desires the total spiritual and physical annihilation of the O'Neil family and anyone close to them. The forces of darkness were determined more than ever to have a final showdown.

CHAPTER TWO

TRANSITION

What a cane it turned out to be! Malone would not be where he is today without the cane and the strange powers that possessed it, as he discovered later while at the *Live!* casino.

After arriving home from the cemetery Malone put the cane on the sofa and looked in the mirror, angry about his missing front teeth. He was in incredible pain, so he rinsed his mouth repeatedly with salt water and called the dentist. Afterward, he laid on the sofa with several cotton balls in his mouth and went to sleep. Two hours later the cane woke him by vibrating against his body and he jumped off the sofa like it was on fire as he watched the cane shake, then it stopped, and he stared at it. Malone thought he was losing his mind and did not know what to do but he wanted to get out of the house, so he decided to visit the *Live* Casino in Hanover Maryland. He showered, rinsed his mouth repeatedly, and put in fresh cotton balls. He then dressed in nice clothes. On the way out the door, he stopped and stared at the cane for several minutes. Not understanding why Malone took the cane with him, he thought it would be cool for walking. He stopped by the bank and withdrew his life savings, of sixty-five-hundred dollars.

After arriving at the casino, he walked around for a while with the cane in his hand and watched people gamble. An hour later, Malone felt the desire to play the dice game craps. Five hours later, he left the casino with two-hundred-fifty thousand dollars in his pocket. He was shocked and drove home ecstatically happy while patting his pockets feeling the lumps of money and kissed the cane as he drove.

The following morning Malone woke in great pain and anger, thinking what happened to him at the casino was all a dream. He sat up in bed and looked around his bedroom and saw his pants on the floor, the cane, and the money lying next to it. He jumped out of the bed and grabbed the money, and held it in both hands, and started dancing. The pain from his mouth made him stop and he threw the money on the bed got his cell phone and called the dentist again. The dentist could not see him today, so he hung up and put his cell phone on the bed, and out of frustration, he kicked the cane. The cane started vibrating and Malone picked it up intending to hit it against the wall but the moment he grabbed the cane, his body started shaking and the cane hit him in the head knocking him out. He fell back on the bed unconscious.

He woke an hour later holding the cane and could not let it go. He sat up in bed and looked in the mirror and smiled. What he saw shocked him. Not only were his missing teeth back, but all his teeth looked great, white, and perfectly straight. Still holding the cane, he stared at it and began kissing it repeatedly.

"Yes, oh yes!" He yelled and started dancing in bed.

Malone put the cane on the bed then showered and cooked breakfast and ate fast with his perfect-looking teeth.

He grabbed his cane and drove back to the *Live!* casino in his old raggedy Impala.

For the next ten days, Malone went to the casino and played craps and blackjack. At the end of ten days, he had eight million dollars in the bank, so he took a break to go shopping. Malone purchased a five thousand square foot, five-bedroom, two-million-dollar, four-car garage home in Silver Spring Maryland. After having his house furnished, he purchased a 2018 Bentley, a 2018 Mercedes SUV, a 2018 Maserati Quattroporte, jewelry, and lots of clothes. Malone enjoyed his new wealth and lavish lifestyle and he started going to the gym and working out hard. It did not take long for his body to become tight and muscular. He dressed well every day, kept himself well-groomed, ate at the best restaurants in town, and spent time with gorgeous ladies. Malone was nice-looking, but he knew the women were only with him because of his money, and he did not care. After three months of this, he became bored and went back to the casino.

Malone had his cane with him of course, and it was as if the cane spoke, telling him what game to play when to play, and how much to bet. This boosted his confidence considerably before he would make any kind of bet.

After four months of playing various games at the casino, Malone won twenty-two million dollars, after taxes. He felt like a king sitting on his custom-designed Lazy-Boy chair in his million-dollar mansion with a beautiful lady sitting next to him. They watched movies in his theater room on his custom-ordered one hundred forty-thousand-dollar Samsung 110-inch Ultra HDTV. He loved watching movies and looking at the beautiful lady sitting next to him. Miss Diana Blackwell wore a see-through gown that made his experience even better.

CHAPTER THREE

THE ORIGIN OF DIANA

Diana Blackwell was an African American woman, forty-two years old, five foot seven, one hundred thirty-five pounds. She is stunningly beautiful with a tight curvaceous body and flawless skin that made her look younger. Diana exercises in the gym five days a week and runs three miles a day, four times a week, and eats healthy. Like many others, she had her share of major heartaches that emotionally cripples people for life, but she has recovered.

Diana was born in Wilson, North Carolina. At two years old, her parents were in a fishing boat accident, her Dad drowned, and her mother was so stressed she gave Diana up for adoption. She was placed in the foster care system. She became rebellious to authority figures when she was thirteen years old. Diana acted out her deep-rooted pains by shoplifting jewelry and this became her obsession. At sixteen Diana was incredibly attractive and possessed a sexy figure beyond her years and she used this to attract attention and get what she wanted. However, she was determined to keep her virginity until she married. She left her foster care parents at sixteen and never looked back. Diana continued to steal high-end jewelry in various states and pawned the pieces along the way. She was caught finally, but this put her on the path of no return.

One day she tried to pawn a stolen expensive necklace to a crooked pawn shop owner. He said it was too much and too hot for him to handle, so he gave her the name and location of someone who could help her. Diana went to an upscale jewelry store and talked to a man named Lamont Thomas. Lamont was Caucasian and Italian, fifty years old, six feet, two hundred thirty muscular pounds. He is handsome but his face has hard features. When she showed him the necklace, he grabbed it quickly and her wrist tightly, so she could not run. Two other men came from the back and one of them locked the front doors and they stood behind her with guns in their hands. Lamont put the necklace in his pocket and released the tight grip on her wrist.

"I don't know how you were able to get this, but it is mine, you stole it from one of my stores."

"No, I did not. I found it." She yelled at him.

Lamont smacked her hard, but she did not cry. Diana stared at him with anger but displayed no fear.

"Liar, you stole it," he smiled at her. "I like you young girl because it took skills to steal this and I see you also have heart, I like that. I have a one-time proposition for you. Obviously, you can steal but I can help you become a professional thief and live that dream lifestyle you desire."

Diana wiped her bleeding lip, looked back at the two men behind her holding guns, then looked at Lamont.

"You have my attention, keep talking."

"Intelligence, I like that. You have heart, some skills, a pretty face, and a slim sexy body with curves. I see the hunger in your eyes to accomplish what you want. All you need is focus and the right guidance and I can provide that and more. My offer to you is this, work for me and get paid a lot of money. Or I call the police now and you get turned out by inmates and guards while in prison and you come out looking abused, old, and ugly. From getting your pussy and ass banged by other women sliding many fingers in you repeatedly and male guards ramming dick inside you as well. What will it be young girl? He stared at Diana and gave her a fake smile.

She held her hand out in front of Lamont and stared at him.

"I need the money for the necklace and then I will work with you, not, for you. Know this, stealing I can do, flirting and teasing men or women, I can do. However, I do not put penis in my mouth, my butt, or vagina, or give up the booty to anyone. I don't lick vagina either." She stared at him.

Lamont looked at Diana and then he and his men laughed.

"You have principles, I like that, however, it is only a matter of time before you spread your legs and give that virgin ass to someone." He reached into his pocket and pulled out a stack of money and counted three thousand dollars and gave it to Diana. "Spend it well young girl. Now sit down so we can discuss details."

From that day forward, Diana became Lamont's protégé. He taught her how to conduct herself as a professional businesswoman and a professional thief in a short time. The merchandise split was always the same, a thirty seventy percent split. Diana would get the thirty percent which she did not like but Lamont provided everything else. Location, transportation, information, drawings for building layouts, tools and he had high-priced attorneys on standby in case she ever got caught. She never did, and Lamont called her, *Ice* because she was smooth as ice in everything she did and emotionally very cold.

At eighteen, Diana was able to pay an attorney to find her real mother and they were building a relationship slowly. Diana had a large upscale three-bedroom condo and expensive wardrobe, and she drove a convertible Corvette. Her legal front to cover her lifestyle was a traveling salesperson for high-end women's clothes.

Diana became frustrated with the money split from her jobs because she took all the risk and getting paid little in comparison to Lamont's payout. She was tired and wanted out of the business to live a normal life, away from Lamont and crime.

Later she did a big jewelry job for Lamont that went well. He gave her a name and address to take the merchandise and Diana exchanged the jewelry for a suitcase. Once in her car, curiosity got the best of her and she broke Lamont's biggest rule, never open the suitcase. She opened the case and was surprised at what she saw, stacks of one-hundred-dollar bills. Diana counted the money, and it was three million dollars. Instantly she started thinking and knew this was her one-time opportunity to get out of this business. She would take this money and run. With three million dollars, Lamont would never find her. She went home, packed, and left town.

Diana was in Charlotte North Carolina living a low-key life but was very bored. One night she decided to go out to a club to have some fun. The one thing she was immensely proud of was she remained a virgin. That night in the club Diana saw this fine-looking young guy walk in and he appealed to her in every way. Handsome clean-cut face with just enough swag not to be cocky. His name was Zechariah Brown. They danced and talked for hours, and their connection was so incredible, Diana went to a hotel with him where they were sexually intimate. She could not believe this was happening, finally losing her virginity, but to a stranger. Diana became very emotional and cried, asking Zechariah to be gentle because she was a virgin. His gentle caressing, kind demeanor, and soft touch helped Diana relax. He took his time to please her, and it was the best thing she ever experienced. Diana was used to pleasuring herself through masturbation, but to have someone else not only pleasingly touch her, but to make her climax several times was incredible.

The following morning Diana felt very guilty about having sex, so she left while Zechariah slept. That same day she got a phone call from Lamont saying he was going to kill her. Diana hung up her cell phone quickly and wondered how he got her new number. She got another phone. Diana knew leaving the state, maybe the country was important, but she started thinking about Zechariah and missed him. The memories of their time together compelled Diana to meet him at another hotel, and they were intimate again and this time was even better. The following morning Diana left again while Zechariah slept.

She moved to Harlem New York and later discovered she was pregnant. A year later, she called Zechariah and told him she had a baby girl, and her name was Diana Brown, and he was the father. Zechariah was shocked and wanted to see her and she said no problem. Later, Diana received another call from Lamont saying, "You can't run or hide from me." Diana was shocked, and she knew the only way to escape Lamont was if he thought she was dead. This was the hardest choice of her life. She left her baby with her mother, Miss Harris, and faked her death in a car accident, and left the country. On the plane to Puerto Rico, she cried the entire trip but knew this was the only way to keep her baby safe and protect herself.

Diana arrived in Puerto Rico with a lot of luggage and a broken heart. For weeks, she had bad dreams of hearing her baby crying and seeing Lamont holding his arms out toward her. For years she prayed every day asking God to reunite her with her daughter and to have a normal life. Diana never gave up hope and believed one day her prayers would be answered. In the meantime, she traveled across the country and never remained in one place too long, for fear of

Lamont one day finding and killing her. She ran for over twenty years to protect herself and her daughter. Unfortunately, along the way, she lost touch with her mother and did not know where she or her daughter was anymore. She took excellent care of herself all these years and remained in great shape by running and working out in gyms across the country. Sadly, she had no real peace and lived with a broken heart.

Diana found out later Lamont and his associates were in prison with life sentences. Her heart rejoiced because she could finally stop running and find her family. Early one Sunday morning Diana was in Potomac Maryland on business. After her business meeting, she felt compelled to attend church. She attended the same church Diana and Ron attended. Diana arrived at church late and received the shock of her life. Although it had been many years, she recognized Zechariah and noticed how closely he was interacting with an attractive woman next to him and a younger lady that would be her daughter's age. After service, Diana found out the attractive lady was his wife and the younger lady was her daughter, Diana. She walked slowly out of church emotionally and spiritually devastated. Her prayers were finally answered but it was too late. In all the years of running, she never lost her love or desire for Zechariah or her need to hold her daughter.

Diana stayed away from her daughter and Zechariah until she could figure out exactly what to do and how to approach them. Unfortunately, her heart once again grew rebellious and cold, and she blamed God for her deep pain and suffering.

Diana was never into gambling but one day she went to the Live! Casino & Hotel in Hanover Maryland, and met a high roller named, Malone Garcia. He was good-looking, playing with a lot of money, and winning. Diana was determined they would get to know one another because she was curious as to how he could win so much money consistently. Spending time together was the only way she could get close enough to learn his secret. The sex between them was good and she was not bothered by their eight-year age difference. However, she wanted so much more than great sex from Malone and was determined to get it, by any means necessary.

CHAPTER FOUR
POWER REVEALED

It was Friday morning and so far, the day had been great. Malone took Diana out for breakfast and then to the Live Casino to gamble for a while and of course, he brought his cane. They saw a stage play afterward at the Warner Theater in Washington DC then went back to Malone's house. He loved watching movies and that night he and Diana laid back in his custom-designed Lazy-Boy chairs and they watched a movie in the theater room. Malone wore shorts and a T-shirt and Diana wore a see-through gown with nothing underneath. He and Diana have not known each other long but they got along well, and he enjoyed her company. She was incredibly attractive, smart, and a great lover.

Diana's sex skills were amazing, and she used this to blow Malone's mind. After a raunchy sex session, they drank wine and relaxed. Diana felt great and looked at Malone and smiled but her heart still ached for her daughter, and she did not want Malone or anyone at this point to call her Diana. It reminded her too much of her daughter every time she heard it, and it was heartbreaking.

"Malone, this has been a wonderful day and I thank you for spending so much of your time with me. I am sure you have other business to deal with."

He took a sip of his wine, put it back on the small table close to the chair, and then looked at Diana.

"Diana, at this point in my life, having pleasure is my business. It is just that simple and hopefully, we can continue to spend time together when we can. I am feeling you." He reached over and caressed her leg and stared at her incredible looking body.

"Thank you for being direct and hopefully we can continue to spend time together, but I need you to do something for me. Do not call me by my first name anymore, it is too painful because it reminds me of my daughter Diana. I miss my baby more than words could ever express." She stared at him with great suppressed emotion but determined to hold back her tears.

"Not a problem and I understand. What would you like for me to call you?"

"Call me Ice. I would appreciate that."

"Consider it done baby but why Ice?"

Diana stared at him getting lost in her memories of so much deep hurt, but she managed to give him a fake smile to hide her pain.

"Just call me Ice, please. Personal reasons and thank you."

"No problem. Now, where do we go from here?"

She smiled at him and repositioned her body on the chair, so he could see more of it.

"You tell me." She looked at him, her body, and then looked back at him.

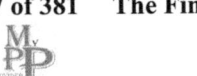

Malone's demeanor changed and he gave her a serious look.

"Why don't we skip all the sugar-coated conversation, and you tell me exactly what you want from me? It is not just sex because you are incredibly attractive and can get that anywhere. It is not money because with your looks and charm, you can find a financial sponsor any day. So, stop wasting time and come correct. What do you want?" He stared at her.

Diana stared at Malone with a blank look on her face because she wanted to tell him where he could go but she was far too smart for that. Instead, she stood and removed her gown and stepped in front of him revealing her beautiful nakedness, and gave Malone a seductive smile.

"Teach me how you win so much money consistently when gambling. In return, I offer you friendship and me! I will be your woman, and satisfy you sexually as you have never experienced in life. My entire body will be yours. I will keep your dick in my skilled mouth, my hot tight vagina, and this great ass of mine would belong to you. Whenever and however, you want me. You watch my back and I watch yours. If not, I will walk out of your house tonight and you will never see me again. Your choice?" She stared at him with confidence as she caressed her inner thigh.

Malone thought hard as he stared at her body. He does not know Ice that well and would not reveal his secret, but he does not want her to leave either. This lady was a true

Full Seven in looks and her bedroom skills were excellent, men and women would get hooked. So, at this point his only choice was, to lie.

"Your offer is a good one and I will take it. Now, come here." He moved off the lazy-boy chair and grabbed her waist, pulled her into him, and kissed her as he caressed her hips and butt.

Ice kissed Malone with passion and then pushed his body away slowly and held her arm out to him.

"Not so fast, my words are true but conditional. First, you talk to me and keep it real, and then we can consummate our new friendship like never before." She placed his hand on her butt. "If you want all this sweet ass of mine and everything else that comes with it, then we become business associates, now." She backed up and stared at his erection and pointed to her vagina.

"Okay." He nodded his head and pointed to the chairs and then exhaled and sat down.

Ice put her gown back on and sat in the chair facing him but spread her legs a little to keep Malone sexually distracted.

"Okay, this is my story. I used to work as a groundskeeper in a cemetery. One day I witnessed an unbelievable horrible event. In the process of running away, I fell and hit my head on a headstone knocking myself unconscious. I woke and went home. That same night, I had visions of winning money in gambling casinos. So, I started gambling and walked around various games until I would get these weird sensations in my body to play. At that time, I knew what to bet and how much. The fall in the cemetery allowed me to make money. I know it sounds crazy, but all the material things I have, speak for themselves. Now, I gamble until that feeling goes away and I never get greedy. This has been the path to my fortune, that's it." He looked at Ice and smiled.

Ice stared at him wondering does he think she was a fool to believe such a ridiculous story.

"Interesting, but I would never believe such a ridiculous story, and tomorrow I will find out the truth because we are going gambling. So, tonight could be your last time being with the best woman you will ever have or one of the many times you taste all this goodness." She caressed her breasts and smiled.

Malone held his hand out and she took it and they walked to his bedroom. He removed his T-shirt, shorts, and underwear and Ice allowed her gown to fall on the floor and stared at him.

"This is not a lovemaking session Ice. This is licking, sucking, and hard dick pumping and I'm greedy." He smiled and stared at her as he stroked his dick.

Ice stepped closer to him.

"You read my thoughts, now follow me to bed and get this life-changing hot ass." She walked to the end of the bed and got on it on her hands and knees and looked back at Malone while her fingers caressed her wetness. "What are you waiting for?"

"Damn!" He held his erection in one hand as he walked toward Ice, placed his other hand on her hip, and slid inside her slowly.

Ice looked back at Malone and smiled while backing her body into him repeatedly.

"That's it baby, slide it in. Act like you want this pussy."

Malone gripped her hips with both hands as he thrust inside her and made fuck faces. He never had any woman this fine fuck him so well.

"This is the best pussy in the world." He slapped her butt and continued thrusting.

Ice gripped the sheets hard for support and she loved how Malone made her feel. She felt her orgasm building and looked back at him, climaxed hard while screaming his name repeatedly.

Malone continued thrusting until Ice relaxed and then pulled out and buried his face between her legs and licked her juices.

Ice gripped the sheets harder and looked at him.

"Baby you are seriously trying to claim this pussy. Ohhhh, my goodness." She moaned, lowered her head, and bit her lip because it felt so good. She thought, *oh my goodness, a hungry man can lick some pussy good.* She continued to grip the sheets and broke a nail in the process but did not care because her next orgasm was so intense. "Ohhhhh Malone, I think you drugged me, I think you drugged me. Ohhhhhh. I am going to climax all over your face."

CHAPTER FIVE
ICE & MALONE

Thousands of people from across the country visit the Live! Casino in Hanover Maryland daily and more on the weekends, and this Saturday night was no different. When Malone and Ice walked into the Casino, eyes followed them, especially on Ice. Malone wore dress shoes, dress slacks, and a dress shirt with his cane in his hand. Ice had a small purse with a strap on it over her shoulder and she wore expensive heels, tight-fitting shorts, and a V-cut top that exposed her breasts. She felt the multitudes of eyes upon her as she walked and Knew her beautiful face and curvaceous body caused men and women to lust, she loved it.

Ice looked at the cane in Malone's hand and shook her head because she thought it was ridiculous but said nothing. They walked around and then stopped and leaned against a crowded Blackjack table. Malone felt the cane vibrate and knew it was time to play. Ice bet five hundred dollars and won three thousand. This was the start of an incredible night for her to win a lot of money. Six hours later they left, and Ice had a three-hundred-fifty-thousand-dollar check in her purse and Malone had a nine-hundred-thousand-dollar check in his pocket. They held hands as they walked through the casino and out the door. Ice had a satisfied smile on her face. Not because of the lustful stares she received, she was used to that, but because of the big check in her purse. Ice still did not believe Malone's story, but her check was proof of something. Malone opened the door for Ice to get in his new Rolls Royce and put the cane on the back seat and drove away. She stared at this man with curiosity as he drove and was more determined than ever to find out the source of his secret. Even if she had to suck his dick every day. A skilled wet blow job beats conversation any day of the week. Forget arguing with a man.

"Baby, this day has been incredible and if I had not witnessed it, I wouldn't believe it. Yes, we lost bets, but the winnings kept coming. Wow! I believe everything you said now about your creepy visions." She leaned over and kissed him. "I'm all yours Malone. So, where do we go from here?" She looked at him flirtatiously and said whatever it took to get closer to him so that he would trust her.

Malone gave her a serious look.

"I will let you answer that. How badly do you want what you want?"

Ice's body stiffened and gave him a fearless look.

"I don't know where you are going with this but do not play with me. It does not matter what you are into, I will fight you tonight until the end if you try anything crazy. Believe that, my nasty lover."

He caressed her thigh delicately with his fingers.

"Relax, you are overthinking this situation," he looked in the back seat and saw the cane vibrating. "My cane is the source of the money we made tonight. I am curious about what else it can do and tonight, I feel compelled to find out."

Ice looked in the back seat and then at Malone.

"Interesting, for some reason that cane has been on my mind all night, and right now, I have a strong desire to visit

a cemetery. I know this makes no sense, but it is how I feel."
She looked down and then shook her head.

Malone gripped the steering wheel tighter and smiled at Ice.

"The cane is speaking to you as well, good. The cemetery we shall go."

They drove for an hour until they reached a cemetery. Malone parked in the front entrance and got the cane from the back seat and then opened the door for Ice. The gate was not locked so they walked in and began walking through the cemetery until they reached a tomb that had a locked chain around the door handles. Malone hit the chain with the cane, and it fell to the ground and the doors opened by themselves. They looked at one another walked in and saw a large casket lying on a table. The casket opened slowly, the tomb doors quickly closed, and Ice screamed and tried to open the doors, but they were locked. She banged on the doors, but they would not open. There was little light in the tomb and when Ice turned around to look at Malone, he stood directly behind her and his eyes were bright red. The cane tapped itself on the ground and one of the tomb doors opened slightly and two black cats walked in and the door closed quickly. The cats suddenly erupted in flames and burned until nothing was left except their bones. Ice screamed for help.

"Shut your hot ass up." Malone yelled and then smacked Ice unconscious and put her body in the casket. He grabbed the cat bones, the cane, and put them in the casket. He mumbled some words and got in the casket and it closed by itself.

An hour later Ice woke up screaming and the casket shook hard and then it stopped. It opened slowly and they got out wearing all black and Malone was holding his cane.

"The spirit of Mr. Bones lives on." They yelled simultaneously.

Ice and Malone touched hands gently and then faced one another and kissed passionately.

"Playtime is over, it's time to destroy the entire O'Neil family, their friends, and anyone else who gets in the way." Ice said to him as she caressed his chest.

They kissed the cane and it floated up in the air, hovered, and then tapped itself on the ground and a large blanket appeared and spread itself on the ground. The cane floated down and laid itself next to the blanket. Malone kissed Ice and they removed all their clothes and laid on the blanket and began having sex. This sexual encounter went on for hours and it seemed as if their bodies moved in slow motion. They had sex on the ground, up against the wall, leaning against the casket, and in various positions. Ice has never experienced anything like that on a sexual level and screamed constantly from intense orgasms. They stopped for a while to stare at one another and performed various rituals. Afterward, they tongue kissed slowly and the sex continued until physical exhaustion took over and they fell asleep on the ground laying close to each other. Hours later, they woke and stared at one another.

"The spirit of the bones speaks. It is time for the final showdown against the O'Neil family. I hate them all, death to them including their seed." Malone said and Ice shook her head in agreement. Their hands caressed each other's body and their passions increased after serious tongue kissing. Malone kissed and licked Ice's body and then got on his knees and buried his face in her butt. His tongue licked her ass with perfection.

"Oh Malone, that's it baby. Stick your tongue in my ass just like that. *Ohhhhh*, damn tongue this ass deep. I am cummiiiing, ohhhhhhh. Fuck me, fuck meeeeee."

Malone pulled Ice down on the blanket on her back, and slid inside her and the sex began as if they were trying to sex each other to death. Ice was on her back with her legs in the air. Malone had her ankles in his hand while on his knees close to her body and thrust inside her with passion. They locked eyes with each other wondering who would give in first. Ice was determined not to allow Malone to fuck her into submission regardless of how tired she was from having so many orgasms. Malone was determined to fuck Ice until she said, *Enough I cannot take any more.*

CHAPTER FIVE

BE CAREFUL OF THE PAST

It had been seven months since the battle in the cemetery when Leticia Wilson and her demonic forces attacked the O'Neil family and others at the cemetery. The hand of God destroyed Leticia and her demonically possessed animal friends. Life for the O'Neil family and friends had been peaceful since then.

It was a beautiful afternoon in Maui Hawaii where Ron, Diana, Keith, and Stacy stayed at the Four Seasons Hotel in two lavish suites overlooking the beautiful ocean. Six of the *Young Wolves* were with them as well and they shadowed their every move. The first day in Maui consisted of Keith, Ron, Stacy, and Diana resting, going for walks, and eating in different restaurants. It was Saturday afternoon and the four of them were playing volleyball on the beach along with the *Young Wolves*, making it ten people on each side. Stacy and Diana wore modest one-piece bathing suits that did little to conceal their gorgeous figures. Ron and Keith wore shorts and tank top T-shirts, and the *Young Wolves* wore shorts and short-sleeved T-shirts to conceal the pistols in their shoulder holsters. Hawaii was a quick getaway for everyone to have fun, relax, and continue to bond as great friends as they have for so many years.

There had been changes in all their lives, especially a greater dedication to the Lord. However, the forces of darkness never sleep, and it was their mission to destroy all, by any means necessary. It was difficult for Ron to know Diana cheated on him with Stacy and he did not believe she had not been with other guys as well. However, he is determined to leave the past behind them, even though thoughts of his beautiful wife being with others, grips his heart with unmeasurable pain at times.

Diana battles with thoughts of her past actions when she thinks about the intense pain she caused Ron. She sees the hurt look in his eyes sometimes. Although he never speaks on her past encounters, she is aware of his pain. Also, Diana deeply regrets Stacy seeing her and Ron having sex and performing a show for her at that time, but Ron was not aware Stacy watched. Now, subconsciously Diana thinks Stacy would like to have sex with Ron, at least one time, or all three of them together. So much regret.

Everyone laughed and had fun playing volleyball not thinking about the past. They were focused on hitting the ball over the net. The ball was hit directly at Diana and she moved quickly to hit it but missed and hit the ground hard. Ron moved to help her get up as Diana pulled her bathing suit bottom from between her butt, Ron brushed the sand from her body. Keith stared at Diana's butt briefly, then looked away and repented for his lustful thoughts about his best friend's wife. Diana was embarrassed and noticed how Keith stared at her. Stacy noticed Keith's lustful look at Diana and his growing erection and walked quickly in his direction. Keith knew he was busted, so he began jumping up and down pretending to be hyped for the game and hoped his erection would go away.

Stacy stood directly in front of Keith and leaned closer and whispered in his ear.

"I saw you Keith, lusting over Diana, and don't play me by saying you did not. She looked between his legs and then at his face. "Your dick got hard in the process," she spoke in anger and stepped closer to him. "Am I not enough for you now? You want some of her ass too?"

Keith stared at Stacy with resentment wondering what to say as he thought about the cheating she and Diana have done together.

He whispered to her.

"No, I do not want Diana, but you would know all about her ass because you had your tongue and face between it." The moment he said those words he regretted it, but it was too late because he saw the instant hurt and anger in Stacy's eyes.

Stacy felt ashamed and Keith's words hit her heart like a knife. She looked down while holding her hands by her side praying, asking God to keep her from hitting Keith in his throat with her fist. She looked at him with tears in her eyes and walked away slowly, realizing things between them would never be the same. They all continued to play for the next hour but Ron, Diana, and the *Young Wolves* felt the tension between Keith and Stacy.

Later that night they all went out to eat at a nice restaurant and then went back to their hotel suites. Keith and Stacy showered and lay in bed together. Stacy wore a thin gown and nothing underneath and Keith wore silk boxers. They laid in silence, each wondering what to say or not to say. Finally, Stacy turned toward Keith with sadness in her eyes and heart.

"Keith, only God knows how sorry I am for my past actions with Diana and others and betraying the bond and trust between us. I am deeply sorry. However, I feel no matter what I say or do, things between us will never be the same. You will never look at me the same or desire me as you once did. My heart aches more than you could ever know." Tears flowed from her eyes and hit the pillow as she looked at Keith.

Keith felt horrible as he looked at Stacy and deeply regretted what he said on the beach. He placed his hand on Stacy's thigh, caressed it slowly, and then spoke softly to her.

"Stacy, I apologize for what I said, and the past is the past. I will not bring it up again, I promise. You know I will always desire you and you should never think differently." His hand caressed her thigh gently and moved closer between her legs.

Stacy placed her hand on top of Keith's to stop him.

"Keith, a man can greatly dislike a woman but still desire her sexually. That is just flesh and hormones. You may never speak of my past actions again, but your heart is another story altogether. Cheating is cheating Keith. Do you want to cheat on me with Diana?"

"No Stacy, I do not." He was trying not to get irritated.

"Do you want to be with other women? Don't lie to me Keith, I can handle the truth, just tell me, please." Holding back her tears.

"No Stacy, I do not want to be with other women. I want you in my life, and only you. You are my best human friend and my wife for life, so please, don't allow the Devil to deceive or trick you into thinking otherwise."

She stared at him and smiled.

"Okay, baby if you say so. Can we pray now?"

"For sure." Keith grabbed her hand and prayed. Afterward, they made passionate love, but both felt each other's mental distance. Stacy tried not to think about her past actions and Keith tried not to think about Diana and how sexy she looked while pulling her bathing suit from between her butt. He repented and focused on making love to his wife.

Ron and Diana's lovemaking was beautiful as always. They laid on their side in bed and Ron held Diana from the back kissing her neck before going to sleep. Having her husband's arms around her was comforting but at the same time, Diana thought about the way Keith stared at her on the beach. She felt his strong lust spirit and now her mind had images of Keith having rough sex with her while Stacy watched. These intense sexual images and thoughts caused her to sexually desire Keith and Stacy at the same time. Without realizing it, she was caressing her vagina slowly with her fingers until she became wet and slid the tip of her finger inside.

This caused her insides and body to jump. She stopped and repented quickly.

"No, forgive me Jesus." She whispered.

Ron raised his head.

"Baby, what's wrong? Are you okay?"

"Yes Ron, I am fine baby. Just praying." She turned her head, kissed him, and pushed her body into him. "I love you Ron."

He hugged her.

"I love you too."

Diana was deep in thought wondering if Ron would still love her if he were aware of her deep sexual thoughts or would it destroy their marriage forever. How long could she fight this battle? Would she one day give in and tell Stacy she wanted Keith? Would Stacy slice her throat, or would they have a threesome? How long oh Lord, would this inner battle last?

The following morning when Ron and Diana woke, they hugged but did not pray together as they normally do. Instead, they kissed each other on the cheek and Ron walked to the shower and Diana kneeled beside the bed in her silk pajamas and began praying. She was emotionally torn and talked to the Lord about her past and what to do. Suddenly, a calm spirit came over her and she heard the voice, *"The battle is not yours to fight."* She smiled and stood.

"Thank you, Lord, thank you." She walked to the bathroom and the sight of Ron in the shower covered in suds as he washed with a washcloth, turned her on.

"Ron, can I join you? Not waiting for his answer, she removed her pajamas.

He turned around and saw Diana standing there naked looking sexy as always and smiled and rubbed his penis.

"No question, come on in." He opened the shower door and Diana stepped in.

Diana turned around in the shower allowing the warm water to cascade over her body and it was relaxing. Ron rinsed and then lathered his washcloth and washed Diana's body from head to toe, front and back until they were both covered in suds. They laughed and rubbed their bodies against one another. After playing, Ron rinsed off and turned away to step out of the shower, but Diana pulled him back in.

"Where are you going?" She grabbed his penis and began stroking it until it was hard. "It would be a shame to waste this. It's hard and hot and I want some morning dick." She kneeled and put his penis in her mouth, sucking him good. Diana did not want him to cum yet, so she stood, turned her back to Ron, placed the palms of her hands on the shower wall, stuck her butt out, and looked back at him. "You know what I want."

Ron was pleasantly surprised by Diana's actions but more than willing to comply. He placed his hands on her hips and slid inside her, slowly and smoothly. Diana loved this slow lovemaking; however, she wanted more excitement before she climaxed. She began throwing her butt faster into him.

"Faster and harder Ron. I need you to fuck me harder. I want to feel your balls slapping against my ass as I throw it into you."

Ron gripped Diana's hips tighter and increased his pace until the slapping sounds of their bodies colliding into each other and Diana's screams and moans were heard. She was about to climax when thoughts of Keith entered her mind and she imagined Keith's hard dick thrusting deep inside her instead of Ron. Diana's orgasm was very intense which caused her to push the palms of her hands hard against the wall and she had to bite her lip to keep from saying Keith's name out loud while Ron was hitting her every spot, repeatedly.

"Ohhhhhh, I'm cumming. Don't stop, fuck meeeeee." Diana could not help herself, she wanted more with each thought of Keith. After climaxing, she turned her head to the side to look back at Ron. "That was so good but don't stop now, lick this hot ass of mine Ron." She stuck her butt out more, giving him easy access.

Ron shook his head because he was surprised by his wife's nasty attitude, but he loved it. Of course, he did not know her attitude and actions were from her thoughts of his best friend sexing his wife and not him. He kneeled and began kissing and licking Diana's butt and then slid his finger inside her wetness, fingering her while he slid his tongue between her butt cheeks.

Diana loved what Ron was doing and the more he did, the nastier she became and wanted more.

"That's it baby, finger this pussy and lick my ass. Ohhhh Ron, it feels so good. Yes, I want it now. My pussy and ass are so wet, fuck my ass baby, I want it in my ass." She was grinding her butt all over Ron's face and pushing against his finger.

Ron stopped, stood up quickly and washed his hands, and looked at Diana like she lost it.

"I'm not doing that and…"

Ron never finished his sentence because Diana turned around and got in his face.

"Yes, you are Ron, please do not deny me now, I want it so badly, fuck me in my ass baby, please. I am so damn horny." She turned around, placed one hand on the wall, reached back and grabbed Ron's dick, and slid it between her cheeks until she felt the tip of his dick against her entranceway. This feeling made Diana crave him more as she slowly backed into him until his dick was in her ass. She felt no pain and began backing into him, slowly at first until each thrust increased her deep burning lust. With each passing second, it pulled her deeper into her erotic fantasies and she slid two fingers inside herself and rubbed her clit with her thumb at the same time. Diana screamed and could not remember climaxing so hard.

"Ohhhhhhhh, Ron, fuck this ass, fuck it Ron. Cum in my ass baby." She was throwing her butt into him.

Ron could not take it anymore and released his seed into her.

"Dianaaaaa this ass is soooo good." He continued pumping into his wife.

They both climaxed hard at the same time. Afterward, she turned around and grabbed the washcloth, and washed herself and Ron. The warm water was relaxing as they rinsed. They kissed passionately and caressed each other's body and then Diana kneeled and put Ron's penis in her mouth. She sucked just the tip, licked both sides up and down, and deep-throated it. She spat on it and did all this repeatedly until his cum hit the back of her throat and Diana loved it. She stood and faced him while holding his dick.

"The next time husband, when I say, in my ass, I mean to put this dick of yours in my ass. It was so good Ron, so good. No, I would not want this every day but when I want it, I want it." She kissed him and walked out of the shower and the bathroom while smiling and softly spoke to herself.

"Stacy, you are not the only one who can be a freak, top that." She got lotion off the dresser and walked to the bed and sat down and began putting lotion on her body.

Ron walked into the bedroom with a towel wrapped around his waist and stared at his lovely wife. Their eyes locked and Diana pushed the bottle of lotion on the floor and spread her legs slowly as she stared at him. Ron walked over, kissed Diana's soft lips, neck, and breasts then licked and kissed her from the ankles to her wetness. He never took his eyes off hers while kissing and licking her body and then buried his face between her legs.

Diana took a deep breath and exhaled when she felt his warm mouth and tongue between her legs. When his tongue dragged across her clit slowly and then sucked on it, her body shook as she climaxed. Diana leaned back and smiled as her body revealed the awesome pleasure her husband was giving her, over and over. She knew things between them were about to change. Not sure for better or worse but for now, she was willing to completely let go mentally, emotionally, and physically. Whatever Ron wanted from her sexually, he would get! Diana was determined from this day forward, to take their sexual relationship to another level. Ron teased her for years to be more sexually expressive, now he was about to receive all that and more. Diana's mental concept was when Ron's dick got hard and she was around, grip it, slip it, slob it, sit on it, or back up on it. Diana would give Ron and herself great pleasure and she wanted a baby. Although the doctor told her she could not have any children, Diana believed, that one day, God would bless her womb.

CHAPTER SIX

JAMES AND CATARINA NEXT LEVEL

The weather was perfect this morning as James and Catarina walked in the park in Potomac Maryland. James wore tennis shoes, shorts, and a T-shirt and Catarina wore the same except her shorts were tight. They played and flirted with one another since they left the house. James slowed his pace to allow Catarina to walk in front of him so he could watch her from the back. She stopped walking and turned around to face him.

"James, I know what you are doing, you are being nasty," she looked at her shorts and then at him. "I can't believe I let you talk me into wearing these tight shorts, the shorts I had on were fine." She stared at him.

James smiled as he looked at Catarina up and down.

"Yes, the shorts you had on were nice, for grandma. You are too young and far too fine to wear those big baggy grandma shorts down to your kneecaps. The shorts you have on are perfect and I appreciate every step you take." He stepped closer and leaned past her so he could see her butt from the back and gently caressed it.

Catarina stepped back and disdainfully looked at James.

"James, do you feel good about what you are doing? You are being disrespectful and stop rubbing my body in public sir." She looked at him defiantly with her arms folded across her chest.

"So, you are not going to act right. No problem, when we finish walking and I get you home, I'm going to give you some, act right." He gave Catarina an intimidating look to make her feel uncomfortable.

"Excuse me! Act right, what is, act right? I am a grown woman and don't you forget it. Speaking of home, why did you purchase such a large house? You live by yourself, so why do you need a seven-bedroom house sitting on three acres?"

"I like space, but God knew one day we would meet, and you would not comply with my desires as you should. So, I would flirt with you, chase you, and then give you some act right. After that, I would have you whenever I wanted."

"What! Again, with the act right statement. That is a caveman mentality, and it is not that easy with me. First, you must catch me, and I am not that easy to catch." She kissed James, gently bit his lip, and then ran off.

James was caught off guard, but he would not allow Catarina to get the best of him, so he ran after her quickly. James prided himself on being in good shape and he was gaining on her. Catarina looked back and saw James was getting closer, so she gave it all she had and increased her speed, determined not to be caught by him so quickly. James was surprised and impressed with her speed which widened the gap between them. He ran regularly for distance and speed and his ego would not allow her to get away. He increased his stride and before Catarina realized it, James was running next to her. They both laughed then slowed down and stopped running. James caressed her hips, kissed her, and then stepped back and started doing jumping jacks to show off his stamina.

"So, what's next dear? What do you have for me? I am ready, are you?" He smiled as he continued doing jumping jacks.

Catarina was impressed with his speed and endurance but was not going to give in and give him bragging rights.

"Okay, you can stop doing jumping jacks now, show off. I do love your stamina," she kissed him. "James let's keep walking because it's so nice out here today and I have something that I want us to talk about."

"Not a problem, and just for the record, you can run sister. I am impressed." He kissed her and held her hand as they walked.

"James, we have run together many times, so stop the drama."

"Yes, we have but today was different because you were thinking about that act right." He kissed her.

"Yes okay, whatever you say dear." She rolled her eyes at him.

They laughed and hugged and walked for a while then stopped at a small café in the park to purchase some water and then sat down on a bench to talk.

"James, we have been through so much in business and our personal life. I would like for us to do something different but fun concerning business. Financially we are extremely comfortable, so we do not have to be involved in anything, just to make money."

"I have been thinking about the same thing lately and I have something you might like getting involved with. Ron talked to me about a movie project he and Keith want to move forward with. I am interested but what do you think?"

"I'm interested and a film project would be fun. We need to set a meeting with him and Keith and get the details." She looked down then stared at James with love in her eyes. "James, how would you feel if I got pregnant? We talked about children but not in detail. Neither you nor I have children and I have been praying about it. If God allowed me to become pregnant, I would cry tears of joy. What about you baby, would you be glad or angry?"

"You do know how to change subjects. Please take my answer the right way Catarina," he exhaled and then looked at her. "At this point in our marriage, I desire for us to have quality time together and focus on just us. Later, if God blesses you to get pregnant, then so be it. Yes baby, I would be happy with no question." He looked at her eyes and saw how his words penetrated her heart and he loved this about their bond.

"I love you James." She kissed and hugged him then leaned on his shoulder and stared into space, thanking God for their great friendship and marriage. She kissed him passionately and Catarina could feel her sexual desires building for her husband. "James, I am ready to go home now, we can finish kissing in private."

"Oh, so now you want some act right." He caressed her thigh.

"You can call it whatever you desire dear." She kissed him, stood, and hit him on the arm. "I will see you back at the car." She ran away.

James ran to catch up with her and when he got close, he patted Catarina on the butt and ran past her.

"I am going to get you for that." She yelled and caught up with him and then jumped on his back and bit his neck.

James loved their fun and playful times.

CHAPTER SEVEN

THE MEETING

A week later the meeting was set at Ron's and Diana's house. All the family wanted to be part of Ron's film project and were eager to hear the details. Ron and Diana decided to have a family cookout while discussing the production of the film and enjoy family and friends at the same time. It was a beautiful sunny day, and you could feel the emotional care and love from everyone. Sheila, Zechariah, James, Catarina, Keith, Stacy, Sandra, Luke, Rick, Cynthia, Derrick, Tonya, Ron, and Diana were all in the backyard. Food was cooking on two large grills and two long tables pushed together had various salads, drinks, and desserts on them and music was playing in the background. Everyone wore shorts, sweatpants, T-shirts, and tennis shoes. Some were talking, throwing a frisbee or Nerf football to each other, playing badminton, and running around the yard having fun. There were hamburgers, hot dogs, smoked sausages, chicken, pork chops, steaks, fish, shrimp, corn on the cob, baked beans, white and sweet potatoes cooking on the grill. Ron and Keith were doing the cooking. The food was finally ready and put on the table and everyone stopped playing, washed their hands, and sat down at the table to eat. Ron said the blessing.

"Dear Lord, we thank you for your grace and mercy for all of us and for allowing us to share this time as a family. Bless this food and make it nourishing for our bodies. In Jesus name, amen."

Everyone said amen and begin to eat. There was a lot of conversation while everyone was eating and enjoying the food. James looked at Ron and hit the table to get his attention.

"Ron, tell us more about your movie project because we are all interested in being a part of it if we can. Do you have a name for the movie yet?"

"Yes, and you all can be part of it. The title of the movie is, *My Call.* The novel has a storyline of the movies, The Ten Commandments, Scarface, and New Jack City combined into one. As well as a major movie, it would make a great TV series, God bless. Anyway, I wrote the book while in prison and recently put it on Amazon and working on doing the marketing so it can achieve as much exposure as possible. I am also going to establish my own film production company to produce my movies instead of waiting for some big Hollywood production company. I have done a lot of research and now I am ready to move forward to the next level."

"Great plan my brother, count me in." Zechariah said.

Everyone else said count me in as well.

"Ron, do you have a production budget for the film project? You know I am great with marketing and would like to head that department for you to promote the book and forthcoming movie." Catarina said with a warm smile and James caressed her arm and kissed her.

"Catarina that would be great and I would appreciate your help along with everyone else. I am no film production expert, but again I have done a lot of research. I want the movie to look professional and have some known actors in it, so I figured it would take about five million dollars for production and another five million for distribution and marketing cost."

"Ten million dollars, Ron that's a lot of money baby which you know I don't have but I will do whatever I can to help, you know that." Sheila said and smiled at him.

"Thanks Mom, much appreciation."

Catarina leaned closer and whispered to James.

"Baby, you know I am tired of dealing with money but how would you feel about us financing the entire film project?"

"I was going to ask you about this later. Yes, let's do it. Thanks baby." James whispered and then kissed her.

"Ron, Catarina, and I were just talking, and we would like to finance the entire film project."

Ron stared at James and Catarina while holding back his tears.

"My brother," he slowly touched his chest with the palm of his hand. "My heart is touched, and I thank you both tremendously." He stared at them.

"Thank you James and Catarina and I know in my spirit the book and movie will do very well financially but it's the deep messages that will have the greatest impact on so many people. I have read Ron's book and it is incredible." Diana said and gave him a quick kiss on the lips.

"Oh James, that is so nice of you and Catarina to offer this. We all thank you." Sheila said as she looked at them with gratitude.

"My brother has always come up with big ideas about things because he is a visionary. He came up with a plan for us to be," he looked over at Ron and shook his head because he was thinking about the plan Ron came up with years ago for them to become drug lords.

Ron nodded at Keith because he knew exactly what he was thinking.

"Never mind, that was the past. Anyway, this film project and film company is positive and will be great." Keith spoke with authority and confidence.

"Yes, it will be. Ron was born a visionary and I will always support my brother. I love you Ron." Sandra said and could not help from getting emotional as she stared at him because she thought about the many things, he and the family have been through.

Ron waved his hand at Sandra.

"Thanks sis, I love you back."

Tears fell from Sheila's face when she looked at Ron and Sandra and then looked at everyone else at the table. Her heart was happy, but she became incredibly sad thinking about how her ex-husband and Christine were killed. All behind forces of darkness and she wondered, *Lord, when will it all end?* Zechariah noticed her mood change and leaned over to hug her. His warm loving touch helped Sheila regroup emotionally and she smiled.

"We all have so much to be thankful for and I thank God for so many things. All of you are my family and don't you ever forget this." Sheila smiled at everyone.

They continued talking and laughing among themselves appreciating the tremendous love and respect they all have for each other.

While the O'Neil family and friends were enjoying the love they all shared, the forces of darkness were being manifested across town.

Malone was in a cemetery dressed in all black holding his cane. He stood inside a circle of pictures of all the O'Neil family and friends. He spat on the pictures and spoke all manner of curses against the O'Neil family.

"I hate all you people. All this happiness and sitting down eating and laughing talking about love. I am destroying love and taking all of you to hell with me, but not before I make you suffer, and then I will destroy everybody." He tapped his cane hard on the ground and he began transforming slowly into a large wolf. The wolf began howling and then pissed on all the pictures and walked away.

CHAPTER EIGHT

COMMUNICATION

Two months passed, and a lot happened in this short amount of time. Ron was working consistently on his film project with Keith, Stacy, and Diana by his side. This business venture was a much-needed project for Ron right now, he needed this distraction from his emotional tug-of-war. He deeply loved Diana, but it was difficult for him not to look at her sometimes and become angry thinking about her being sexually intimate with someone else. When Keith told him about Diana's unfaithfulness (being with Stacy and other women), this hurt his heart and soul tremendously. Although their sex life was great, and he loved his wife's increased erotic behavior, Ron wondered at times was it because of her past actions and if Diana was suppressing her deep sexual desires for freaky sex. He would ask himself how much he trusts his wife right now.

Thursday night they were at home sitting on different sofas in the living room. Both wore shorts and T-shirts. Ron was on the computer writing and Diana was doing the same. She looked at Ron feeling so proud of him and his business focus. Their eyes met and she smiled at him, but Ron had an expression of anger in his eyes, and she felt it.

"Ron, what's wrong baby?"

"Nothing, I'm just thinking about what I'm writing."

Diana knew he was not telling the truth because his writing is a powerful gift from God and he never has to focus that hard, the man can start writing and everything flows.

"Ron, your eyes tell me differently."

He exhaled deeply and then looked at Diana, wondering should he mention how he was feeling.

"You want the truth? No problem. We have been getting along very well and our sex life has been incredible. Your sexual attitude and desires have increased a lot and it causes me to wonder how much more is within you? Do you desire something even more? Are you hiding certain sexual desires and fantasies you do not want me to know about? Is this what caused you to be with Stacy and others? I am not trying to take us backward, but you asked, so this is how I feel at times."

Diana felt his every word and knew Ron was reaching out to her the best he could while dealing with his emotional pains.

"Thank you for being honest, it means a great deal to me. Ron, not a day goes by that I do not regret all I have done to hurt myself, you, and our marriage. However, I pray on this daily, asking God to help us. Do I have sexual fantasies? Yes, everyone does to some degree, but they will not be honest with themselves or their partner. I can assure you that my fantasies are with you and only you. I do not desire anyone else on any level." Of course, she could not tell Ron the absolute truth because it would crush his heart and she had caused him enough pain. "Will I ever repeat my past actions? Never Ron! Yes, I realize you have trust issues with me, but I believe with time, prayer, and love all this will be erased. As far as my increased sexual desires are concerned, I desire for us to have a healthy fulfilled marriage. Sex is just one aspect of it."

"Okay, I appreciate your directness, but I see the way Keith looks at you sometimes."

Diana smiled and then laughed.

"Baby, please don't go there. Yes, you and Keith share this great friendship and bond, the best. However, he is still just a man like all others, flesh. Men will look at women and women will look at men. I see how you look, no, you stare at Stacy sometimes. I cannot blame you because she is attractive and has a great body. Does it bother me? Sometimes it does but I will not allow myself to get caught up in all that because it is natural. Ron, you need to be honest with yourself first and foremost and then me. Do you desire to be with someone else?"

"No, I do not and if I wanted to be with someone else, I would not be here with you right now. I would be with that person." He stared at her.

"Okay Ron, you didn't have to say that so harshly. As if you got it going on like that and I am some charity case." She looked at him trying not to get an attitude.

Ron smiled and then walked over to Diana, kissed her, and got on his knees, and gently kissed her thighs while his hands caressed them, and then sat next to her.

This melted Diana's heart and she kissed Ron and then leaned away from him.

"That was very sweet, but we were talking and…"

Ron kissed her again.

"Be quiet, I don't want to talk anymore." He gently slid his tongue across her lips and then kissed her.

Diana responded by allowing his tongue in her mouth and the moment their tongues touched, she felt his hands move closer between her legs. Talking was the last thing on her mind. It was as if they were reading each other's minds with every movement. Diana stood and removed her clothes and Ron did the same. They stared at each other before moving closer and hugged tightly. Then explored one another's bodies with their hands and mouth. Twenty minutes later they were still caressing and kissing each other all over. Diana lay on the sofa and with a head motion, she called Ron to lay with her. As he laid next to his wife they stared into each other's eyes.

"Ron, make love to my heart and my body will follow. Allow our spiritual love for each other to erase the bad things."

He kissed her soft lips caressed her thighs with the tip of his fingers and moved up until he was gently rubbing between her legs. He felt how wet his wife was when he slid his finger inside her and then licked and sucked the juices off his finger. After sucking his finger, he slid his hard dick inside her.

Tears fell slowly from Diana's eyes.

"I love you Ron so much." She wrapped her arms around him and cried.

Ron loved Diana and could not hold back his tears.

"I love you back Diana, always have, always will."

For the next hour, they made love and cried tears of desire and immense love along the way. Neither of them had thoughts of sexual desire for anyone else. They were connecting in a way far beyond physical or burning lust.

They connected as one with every touch of their bodies and breath. Diana bit Ron's neck and placed both her hands on his butt pushing him even deeper into her wetness as her third orgasm hit. She wrapped her legs around him and sucked his neck hard as her body shook with such intense pleasure.

"Ron, please don't leave me. I love you so much." Her hands dug into his back as she climaxed.

"I will never leave you Diana, you know that." He sucked her neck hard to keep from screaming as he released his seed into his wife.

They pleasured each other to the fullest until falling asleep. Two hours later they woke and walked into their bedroom and showered together. They got out of the shower and pampered each other by putting lotion on one another and gave each other complete body massages. After the massaging, they prayed together and fell asleep holding hands.

CHAPTER NINE

SPIRITUAL DIVIDE

As Ron and Diana slept peacefully Malone and Diana, better known now as Ice, were dressed in all black standing outside in front of their house. Malone and Ice held canes and Malone moved closer to the house and spoke all manner of curses against Ron, Diana, and the house. He spoke death to them repeatedly as he pointed his cane at the house.

Ice was now consumed with hate and other evil spirits. She would never be the same but even with all the evil possessing her, she still loved her daughter and did not want her killed. So, when Malone pointed his cane at the house speaking great evil, she pointed her cane at him speaking curses upon him.

She whispered to herself.

"I don't care how much you hate the O'Neil family Malone; I will not allow you to destroy my daughter. I will find a way to destroy you first regardless of the sacrifice. I will protect my daughter even if it costs me my life."

Malone turned around very slowly as if he heard every word Ice spoke, and then pointed his cane at her.

"Our objective must always remain the same. Kill, steal, and destroy, and do not ever forget that or try and cross me, woman. Do not think for a second because you suck dick as your very life depends upon it, that I love you. Get real woman, you are just a super freak! I love no one. I know you still love your daughter and desire a relationship with her. And you will have that, in hell burning forever," he laughed. "She is a fake Christian, nothing but a closet freak. Your precious daughter has been an unfaithful wife many times. Licking and sucking other women's asses and pussies like it is the best ice cream in the world. Tricking her husband into thinking she is so nice and pure, while her legs are spread wide for someone else when he is not around. Ron knows she cheated now, and it is driving him crazy. I hope he stops praying, emotionally snaps, and chokes the life out of his wife. Sorry no good, ass-licking slut. To hell with your daughter Diana, I will be killing her, slowly. But before I kill that ass licker, I am putting some stiff, evil, demonic dick in her repeatedly. Front and back! Instead of saying oh God, oh God, she will be saying, oh Devil, oh Devil, give me some more of that Devil dick. Then when she climaxes, I will cut her head off." He leaned back and laughed and began dancing. "Kill the slut, kill the slut." He stopped dancing and gave Ice a look of dominance and raised his cane at her. "Now, walk your good dick-sucking lips over here and hug me before I get upset and make a rat bite your toe off while you sleep."

Ice stared at him with unlimited hate but managed to smile and walked closer and hugged him and kissed him on the lips. However, her hug and kiss were a gesture of death to come.

Malone was fully aware of Ice's disdain for him but could care less because she was a pawn to be used only for his gain. He kissed her lips, smacked her on the butt, and looked at her.

"Are you going to continue throwing that sexy ass back on me, sliding your pussy on my hard, stiff, corruptible dick?"

Ice gave him the warmest smile.

"Whatever you want, however you want. I am here to serve you." She kissed his neck and caressed his inner thigh. She thought, *you stupid fool, it is only a matter of time, I will be killing you.*

CHAPTER TEN

GROWING CLOSER

Sunday church service was anointed, and the spirit of God moved greatly as pastor Williams preached. His subject was, *Believe in God regardless of what is going on in your life.* Several people went to the altar call at the end of the service and gave their lives to the Lord. Sheila, Zechariah, James, Catarina, Keith, Stacy, Sandra, Luke, Rick, Cynthia, Derrick, Tonya, Ron, and Diana were all in church. After church service, they talked to each other before leaving.

Sandra and Luke were taking time to get to know each other better and they decided to go out for lunch and then a walk at the park after church. They held hands when walking toward Luke's car. An attractive lady wearing a tight dress that revealed her curvaceous figure walked towards them. Luke tried hard not to look but used his peripheral vision to look at this lovely woman. Sandra noticed this and squeezed his hand hard and then let it go and stopped walking to look at him.

"You couldn't even wait to get off church grounds before you started lusting. Does that woman," she pointed her finger at the lady. "does she look that good to you? Wearing that skin-tight dress showing off the shape of her hips and butt. Oh, never mind, this drives you men crazy. Briefly, I forgot who and what I was dealing with. Men, the real weaker sex because all it takes, is hips and butt to distract you." she grabbed his hand and kissed Luke on the cheek. "Come on, weaker sex vessel." She gave him an accusatory look.

Luke pulled his hand away from Sandra and looked at her.

"I am far from a weak vessel but no problem. Let's go eat and have some fun." He kissed her lips, grabbed her hand and they walked toward his car, got in, and drove away.

They were talking, laughing, and eating at the restaurant. Sandra dismissed Luke's lust Moment because they were having a good time. Later she excused herself and went to the bathroom. Luke stared at her when she walked and Sandra felt his eyes on her body, so she turned to look back at him, and their eyes met. She smiled, shook her head, and kept walking. Her dress was not tight, but you could tell she had a nice figure. When she returned to the table, she kissed Luke on the lips and sat down.

"Luke, I need you to be direct. How do you feel about me, besides desiring to fornicate? Which is not going to happen, so you can forget that." She stared at him defiantly.

"You really are something woman and yes I am attracted to you physically and if I were not, we would not be here now. However, my interest in you far exceeds a fornication moment, as you put it. I like you as a person and want us to spend more time together to build a better friendship." He reached in his pocket and pulled out a small thin case and handed it to her. "This is yours and I hope you accept this conditional gift."

Sandra looked at the box, then looked at him and opened it. The box contained a gold necklace with a heart-shaped charm. She removed the necklace and stared at it.

"Oh wow, Luke this is very nice but what do you mean by conditional gift?"

"Sandra, I am falling in love with you, and I want you to be my lady and wear that necklace. I want us to be in a committed relationship that will hopefully lead to marriage. This is my intention, is that direct enough for you? Coming from a weaker vessel of course." He smiled at her.

Sandra was surprised and caught completely off guard.

"Wow, you surprised me Luke," she held the necklace out toward him. "Will you put it on me, please?"

Luke stood with a big smile on his face and sat next to Sandra and put the necklace on her.

"Thank you, and the answer is yes, I would love to be your lady. No, smart mouth, you are not a weak man, but you did irritate me by staring at that woman." She stared at him, and they leaned over and kissed on the lips. Luke's warm kiss and her feelings for him caused Sandra to open her mouth and allow their tongues to connect. They kissed with increased passion until Sandra felt his hand caressing her thigh and she leaned away from him.

"Okay, it's time for us to go. We are in a public place, and you are trying to get your sexual feel on, and we are not married."

They walked toward the register and Luke paid the bill and they walked out toward his car. As Luke opened the door for Sandra, he leaned over and kissed her.

"You are correct, we are not married, not yet." He kissed her again got in the car and drove away.

"Just for the record Luke, this necklace does not mean we will be fornicating."

"Oh God, here we go with the fornicating speech again." He shook his head.

"I am not finished talking Luke. We are not friends with benefits. No samples, no test rides, none of that. If we are blessed to reach the level of marriage, then and only then will we connect in that way. I am saying this not to be smart but to be very clear so there is no misunderstanding between us, okay?" She stared at him.

"As I said, you are something. Not a problem. Holiness it is. I can wait for your screams and turn you out later." Luke said this to irritate her and have some fun.

Sandra gave Luke a mean look and leaned away from him until her shoulder touched her door.

"What! Do not speak to me so disrespectfully Luke and I mean it. If all you desire is sex from me, then you can take me home and I am telling the Pastor that you are nothing but a wolf in sheep clothing. Like so many other men in the church." As she stared at him her anger increased because he had a condescending look on his face.

They reached the park and Luke got out and opened the door for her. Once she was out, he pulled her gently into him and kissed her lips.

"I am not a wolf in sheep clothing, as you called me. You are incredibly attractive and can talk. Let's walk."

Sandra had no choice but to smile at this handsome man in front of her.

"You think you are smooth, don't you?"

"No, I am me. The rest you will find out in time if you act right." He stared at her hoping for another emotional tantrum.

She was not going to give him the satisfaction of falling for his smart mouth a second time.

"Whatever you say, dear." She kissed him and they started walking through the park.

As they walked an older couple walked towards them holding hands and the man kissed the woman on her cheek.

"You two look lovely together. May God continue to bless you." Sandra said.

The couple stopped walking and so did Luke and Sandra. The woman looked at Sandra and smiled.

"Thank you dear, that was sweet of you to say. We have been married for fifty-three years now."

"Wow, that is very impressive, especially in today's times." Luke said.

"Incredible testimony and blessing. So, how did you manage to remain happy together for so many years?" Sandra said as she smiled at them.

"That's the easy part. Tell them how baby." The older man said as he looked at his wife.

"Very simple, I have been backing my hot ass up on him and sucking his dick for over fifty years," she shook her butt and then pointed her finger at Sandra, but her facial expression looked evil. "And you young lady, you need to be sucking that young man's dick like a lollipop. Slob that dick, spit on it, and then, as you young people say, it's head down ass up, that's the way you like to fuck." She pointed at Luke. "You, young man, fuck her fine ass good. Go balls deep in that pussy and put some tongue in her butt. She will love it. Make her ass hot and fuckable." She and her husband laughed wickedly and walked away.

Luke and Sandra stared at the older couple with their mouth open in complete shock. Never expecting anything like this.

"In the name of Jesus." Luke said as he stared at them walking away.

"Oh my God, in the name of Jesus, what is this world coming to? I felt an evil spirit from that woman as she spoke such filth. Jesus help us all." She and Luke looked at one another and walked away holding hands while shaking their heads.

The older couple was a distance away and stopped walking and looked at Luke and Sandra. They looked around the park and then transformed into Malone and Ice, dressed in all black. Malone kissed Ice on the lips and caressed her hips.

"She is Ron O'Neil's sister Sandra, and the guy is Luke. They are trying to live a Holy life. Not happening because I am going to spiritually corrupt them both with lust spirits so they will start fornicating quickly and get caught up in other negative vices. Drinking, drugs, and all kinds of perverted sex. After that, we are killing them so there will be more fuel for hell."

"I love the way you think. Distraction leads to division and the destruction of the spirit. I love it." Ice kissed Malone passionately and they transformed back into an elderly couple.

A young couple named Finch and Robin were walking toward the elderly couple. They were talking about God and how good church service was today and how they wanted to give themselves to the Lord. The elderly couple walked closer, and the man purposely bumped into the lady and whispered curses to them in an unknown language.

"I am so sorry miss, so sorry, please forgive me for bumping into you. Pray for us, we are old." He looked at them and then looked down.

"No problem, please take care and be blessed." Robin said as she smiled at them.

The older lady stepped closer and gently grabbed both their hands and looked at them.

"May you two be happy together and have fun in life." She leaned forward and whispered curses in an unknown language in Robin's ear and then spoke. "Be happy young lady."

Robin and Finch looked at the older couple walking away and then stared at each other. Suddenly, a strong lust spirit hit Robin and she had never been so sexually turned on as she was at that moment. Erotic thoughts and images came to her mind. She stepped closer and kissed Finch on his lips and then caressed his penis.

Finch jumped when Robin's fingers touched him, and he leaned away.

"What are you doing? Is this some trick or game you are playing to see how I react? I don't play games."

"Relax, I'm not playing games with you, and please don't turn me down. I want you badly and I will do whatever you want, and I promise, this is not a game or test. If you come home with me right now, I will suck every drop of cum out of your dick." She kissed him and whispered erotic things in his ear and spoke in a language she did not understand and continued caressing his penis.

Finch was shocked at her actions but pulled her closer to him so she could feel his growing erection against her body, as they kissed passionately. Their mind and body were being controlled by demonic spirits that compelled them to behave in this manner. One minute they were talking about God and giving their life to him, and now all they desired were each other. Finch was not going to turn down this offer, but he had to find out if Robin were for real and how far she would go.

"Let's go to my car." They held hands as they walked to his car and then got in and he drove to a secluded section of the park and stopped. Finch leaned his seat back and pulled down his pants and underwear exposing his erection and then looked at her.

"Show me you are for real, suck it."

Robin looked at Finch and smiled and then proceeded to give him the best blow job of his life until his body jumped, and he gripped his seat hard as he exploded in her mouth. She had to put her hand over his mouth to keep others who may be walking by from hearing his dirty words of passion. Afterward, she kissed him, and Finch stared at her as if he were in a trance. He pulled his underwear and pants up and lay back on the seat still breathing heavily, feeling as if his heart would burst from his chest.

"Finch, take me to my house and I will feed you a nice meal. Afterward, we can go for a walk and then take a shower together. I will give you a Cialis pill, and we can fuck for the next three days, like dogs in heat." She slid her tongue across his lips and kissed him.

All Finch could do was stare at her and exhaled heavily.

"You are amazing! Yeah, your place it is. Dogs in heat, I got it." They kissed passionately and he drove away.

Malone and Ice walked close to where his car was. They were dressed in all black holding their canes and they started laughing.

"It's so easy to trick these fools. Those two are going to do exactly what I want. Another couple was removed from the righteous path and is now on the corrupt one. Damn, I love it. Just think, they almost got away from my spirit today while in church. All that preaching against sin, people love sin. That is why they commit it so much; they love pleasure more than strict rules concerning what they can and cannot do. My way is easy, give you whatever you want if it is a path away from righteousness and Holiness. By the time people realize how spiritually corrupt they are, it is too late because they desire what they want, at all costs. This has been the way of spiritual destruction for all flesh since creation." He laughed and then kissed Ice. "Come on, let's go corrupt some more souls and take them to hell." They both laughed and embraced each other and disappeared in a cloud of smoke.

CHAPTER ELEVEN

CHAOS

It was Saturday night, Ron and Diana sat in the VIP section of the club. Diana did not want to be here because she never liked the club scene but tonight was important. Keith and Stacy sat with them as well. Ron and Keith wore dress shoes, expensive dress pants, and shirts. Stacy and Diana wore heels, tight jeans, and a blouse. Zechariah was in the club as well since he was head of security. He wore a nice suit but comfortable enough so he could move quickly if he had to. He always watched Diana closely and whenever they made eye contact, she waved and gave him a warm smile. This was a celebration night for Ron because the final editing of his screenplay was finished. He was ready to begin the casting call phase for film production. Ron, Diana, Keith, and Stacy talked and laughed enjoying the fruits of their labor and years of a challenging friendship.

Ice looked forward to this day for many years but now she was nervous as she drove her Bentley to Ron and Keith's nightclub. Tonight, was going to be the day she and Diana would come face to face. Ice knew her daughter would be at the club tonight because she possessed certain spiritual abilities through the demonic forces that she conjures. She drove in front of the club to be seen. Ice stepped out wearing heels and an almost see-through dress revealing her bra and panties and hugged her lovely figure. Ice knew she was an extremely attractive woman and could turn men's and women's heads no matter where she went. Valet service parked her car and she walked into the club with elegance and confidence aware of the stares she received. A tall well-dressed handsome African American man named Ray approached the front door at the same time as Ice, he opened the door for her, and she walked in. Ray was six-feet-three, two-hundred-forty muscular pounds. He walked in behind her and stared at this beautiful woman then lightly touched her arm.

"Excuse me miss, I know you have heard all this before, but you are gorgeous, and your body is incredibly sexy. Allow me to be your escort for the evening."

Ice stopped walking and turned around to look at him. He was nice looking and physically built the way she preferred her men, muscular tight bodies but not too big. She was only here for one reason and did not have time for men and their foolishness but decided to play for a few minutes. Besides, Malone was away on one of his many gambling trips. Ice wanted to intimidate and test this handsome man's confidence level, so she stepped closer and looked directly at his eyes.

"Thank you for the compliment and you don't look too bad yourself. What is your name and please do not waste my time with a lot of talk? You are correct, I have heard it all."

Ray was instantly turned off by this lady now because of her attitude. He disliked women who believed they were all that because they looked good. He was going to tell her where she could go but decided against it, not sure why. Ray was forty-three years old and a successful millionaire real estate investor that felt he could charm any woman, but he was a humble person. Ray was a veteran and was in the Special Forces and always kept his mind and body in excellent shape. He had no children. Ray looked at Ice, smiled, and extended his hand to her.

"You are direct, I like that, and so am I. My name is Ray, and you are?"

Ice felt his confidence and mental strength, this turned her on. She was drawn to this man which made her relax, a little. She shook his hand and his touch sexually turned her on as well.

"Hi Ray, my name is Diana but call me Ice. You seem nice and I would not mind spending time talking with you tonight, however, I am here on business. So, you will have to excuse me, enjoy your night." She gave him a warm smile and turned to walk away.

Ray was now interested in Ice and was not accepting her answer. He stepped in front of her quickly and smoothly.

"Ice, you interest me and very few women do," he reached in his pocket and pulled out a business card, and handed it to her. "I will be in the club for a while to have a few drinks and relax after closing a complicated business deal. When you are finished with your business, give me a call, if I am still here, we can talk. If not, enjoy your evening as well."

It had been a long time since a man stimulated her mind the way Ray was doing now. Malone was a means to an end for her. She wanted to find out more about Ray but now was not the time. She accepted his card with a smile.

"Thank you for such an offer and we will see what happens," she placed the palm of her hand on Ray's chest, leaned closer, and whispered in his ear. "don't go too far, I might be hungry later on." She kissed his cheek and walked away seductively, knowing he watched her every step, as all men do.

Ray looked at her sexy walk and smiled as he walked away.

Ice walked around the club enjoying all the visual attention she was receiving but was focused on one thing, Diana. She looked toward the VIP section and saw Diana sitting with Ron, Keith, and Stacy. The very sight of Diana made her nervous. How could she approach her? What would she say to her after so many years of absence? All Ice could do was stare at her and hold back her tears.

Zechariah was walking when he saw Ice and had to admit she was a fine-looking woman. There was something about her that seemed familiar, but he did not know what it was. He noticed how she stared at Diana and this made him suspicious, and he was determined to watch her every move tonight.

Ice sat down and ordered a drink. This helped her relax a little and she said to herself, *it was now or never*. She stood, exhaled, and walked toward Diana. Zechariah watched her and walked slowly toward Diana as well but kept his distance.

Ice stood in front of the VIP and stared at Diana. She spoke the words that have been in her heart for so many years.

"Hello Diana."

Diana looked at this woman and smiled.

"Hello, do I know you?"

Ron and Keith stood at the same time because of their protective nature.

Zechariah walked toward Ice prepared to do whatever was necessary.

"Excuse me miss, but you will have to leave this area." Zechariah gave her a stern look.

Ice turned to look at Zechariah and smiled at him.

"You look more handsome than ever. Hello Zechariah, it has been a long time. Neither of us will ever forget North Carolina." She turned her head and looked at Diana.

"Lord have mercy." Zechariah leaned back and was astonished at who he was looking at. The love of his life, his daughters' mother, Diana.

Diana and Stacy stood and looked at Ice and then Diana looked at Zechariah.

"Dad, who is this lady you are staring at so strangely?"

"You will never know how much I have desired this day to come," Ice placed her hand on her chest and stared at Diana. "My name is Diana, and I am your mother."

"Lord Jesus," Diana put her hand over her mouth and sat down slowly as she stared at Ice in total shock.

"No way, this must be some sick twisted joke. Lady, I don't know who you are, but you need to step away from here while God is still keeping me." Ron said as he stepped closer to Ice.

"Ron, I am beyond shocked myself, but she is telling the truth. This is the woman that I told you about when we were in prison. The lady I met in a club, shared time with and got pregnant, disappeared and I never heard from or saw again, until right now. Wow, this is unbelievable." Zechariah stared at Ice.

"Wow, how is all this possible, and where have you been lady? How can you abandon your daughter for years and suddenly, show up? What kind of mother are you?" Keith said as he looked at Ice with contempt.

Stacy grabbed Keith's hand gently knowing his temper and capabilities.

"Where have you been all these years Miss?" Stacy said with a serious attitude.

Ron looked at Zechariah.

"Zechariah, is all this for real my brother?"

"Yes, it's for real," he looked at Ice and shook his head. "I could never forget her eyes and the effect she had on me, never." Zechariah looked at Ice from head to toe in a lustful manner.

Ron gave Zechariah a mean look because he thought of his Mom and how Zechariah stared at this woman with obvious lust in his eyes as they were locked on her body.

Keith stared at Ice and was thinking, *Lord, forgive me but this woman is beautiful.* He could feel the blood rushing to his penis and repented quickly so he would not get an erection and have Stacy notice it.

Too late, Stacy saw how Zechariah looked at Ice, and then she turned her head and noticed a bulge rising in Keith's pants. The old Stacy rose in her and she wanted to hit Keith in his stomach. At the same time, she felt her past bisexual desires trying to overwhelm her. She was sickened by her thoughts, but Diana's Mom was very erotic and hot-looking. She repented quickly and then elbowed Keith slightly in his ribs.

Keith winced in pain, leaned closer, and whispered to Stacy.

"Stop, are you crazy?"

Without thinking about it, Stacy stepped in front of Keith and looked him in the eye.

"No, I am not crazy. Are you?" She looked over at Ice and then looked at Keith.

Diana looked at Keith and Stacy like they had lost it because she knew what was going on, and so did everyone else. Keith was lusting over her Mom, Stacy caught him, and now she was angry. She shook her head because these two were something else.

Ice wanted to take advantage of this moment, so she stepped closer to Zechariah and looked at him like he was the best thing in the world.

"Zechariah, have you thought about me all these years? Have you missed me at all?" Giving him a look that only a woman can.

Zechariah knew she put him on the spot purposely and he wanted to scream, *yes, I have missed you,* but he knew all eyes were on him and the past was the past. Truthfully, he wanted to wrap his arms around Ice and hold her for a long time. His heart still loved her, and he felt horrible because he loved Sheila tremendously.

Before Zechariah could respond, Ice moved closer and put her arms around him quickly. His heart betrayed his level of discipline, he hugged her. He instantly felt a strong evil spirit radiating from this woman.

Overlooking the bond he and Zechariah shared, seeing this caused Ron to emotionally snap because he felt Zechariah was betraying his mother.

"Zechariah, let her go." He yelled and his hands were by his side, but he balled his fist up and looked at him with anger and wanted to leap on Zechariah.

Keith had grown close to Zechariah but right now, all that was gone. All he cared about was protecting his best friend, no matter what, or whom. This was a messed-up situation to be in, but so be it. He knew Zechariah was a powerful man physically, but he figured he and Ron could take him. He glanced over at Ron and then looked back at Zechariah with eyes ready to leap.

"Ron, what's up? Talk to me." Keith said.

Diana and Stacy looked at each other with great confusion and knew something had to be done to defuse this situation, and quickly. When Ron yelled, it caught the attention of one of the *Young Wolves* and he communicated with others in the club quickly. Seven of them now stood close to the VIP section. Yes, Zechariah was the head of security, but their loyalty was to Keith and Ron, no matter what. They were all armed and one of them looked at Keith.

"Keith, say something before we start popping. Is there trouble in the ranks right now?" He looked at Zechariah and then placed his hand on his holster and the other *Young Wolves* did the same.

Diana moved in front of Ron and hit Keith on his arm.

"No Ron! Keith stop this right now!"

Zechariah looked around and saw the situation and he knew it was about to go down. Because of his years of

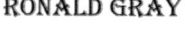

survival in prison, he instinctively pushed Ice gently away from him, stepped back, and raised his hands as he looked at Ron. This was a mutual understanding that he wanted no trouble. He looked at everyone and then Ice, he lowered his head and walked away. This was one of the hardest things he had ever done in his life and it hurt his heart tremendously. But he knew it was the right thing to do, for now.

As he walked away one of the *Young Wolves* purposely bumped into Zechariah and stared at him menacingly.

"You are the man but walking away was a good move on your part, big homie." He patted his holster as he looked at him.

This was all it took, Zechariah snapped because he was feeling defeated and heartbroken. He growled and backhanded this guy so hard he heard a snap before he hit the floor. Zechariah knew he had broken the young man's jaw. The *Young Wolves* did not want to shoot Zechariah, so they jumped him and started beating him.

The heart of a lion rose in Diana and she moved with the grace and speed of a cheetah before anyone could stop her. She managed to grab one of the *Young Wolves'* guns and fired two shots in the air. The *Young Wolves* stopped beating Zechariah, the music stopped, and people ran quickly for the exit doors, there was pandemonium. Ice knew it was time for her exit, so she walked out with the crowd. Her point was made now, they all knew she was alive.

Diana was emotionally hyped, and she knew how sneaky and lethal the *Young Wolves* could be. So, she pointed the gun at all of them, one by one.

"I don't want to, but if one of you takes another step toward my dad, as Jesus is my Lord, I will put a bullet in your head and keep firing." She looked at them with no fear.

"Diana, put that gun down." Ron said.

Zechariah could not be prouder of his daughter as he was right now. She chose him.

Stacy noticed a gun on the ground and picked it up quickly before someone saw it. She did what was natural, protect her friend. She walked over to Diana and stood by her side, pointing the gun at the *Young Wolves* as well.

Keith knew Stacy would pull the trigger with no problem. He motioned for the *Young Wolves* to back away. They did and distanced themselves but remained alert to the situation.

"Stacy, you and Diana need to put those guns down and calm down. No one is getting shot today." Keith said.

Diana looked at Ron as if to say, *what do I do, help me.* Ron saw her look of desperation and walked over to her and held his hand out toward Diana and Stacy for the guns.

"Ron, if you are trying to trick me, we are going to have a major problem." Diana stared at him sternly.

Stacy and Diana looked at each other and then gave Ron the guns. He put them in his waist and kissed Diana. He looked at Zechariah, Stacy, Diana, and Keith. The guy Zechariah slapped was being helped off the floor by one of the *Young Wolves* and he was holding his jaw.

"We all need to calm down, sit down, and talk. This has been an unbelievable night." Ron hugged Diana and kissed her and then walked over to Zechariah and extended his hand to him as a sign of peace, praying he would take it. He loved Zechariah.

Zechariah smiled and shook Ron's hand, thanking God for this. He stepped to Diana and looked at her. They hugged as only a loving Dad and Daughter could do. All five of them walked back to the VIP section and sat down. Ron and Diana sat next to each other, Keith and Stacy sat next to them and Zechariah sat across from them.

"Wow, I don't know where to begin." Diana said as she looked at everyone.

"Zechariah, do you know how this is possible? Any answers my brother will help?" Ron said.

It felt good to Zechariah hearing Ron call him brother.

"At this point Ron, I am in the dark like all of you. Only God knows."

"My Mom. Wow, my Mom is alive." Diana finally broke down and started crying and Ron held her as she leaned into him.

Keith looked around the club and then at Diana as she leaned over, and he looked at her butt. Stacy noticed how Keith stared at Diana which caused her to become instantly irritated. She put her hand on his arm and pulled him back and whispered in his ear.

"No matter what, you can't help yourself can you? I don't care what you say Keith, I know you want Diana." She gripped his arm hard and then dug her nails into it. "Because you keep," she dug her nails into his arm again. "Looking at her ass."

Keith pulled his arm away from Stacy and then whispered in her ear.

"Relax please and control yourself. You need help and serious prayer." He stared at her.

Stacy wanted to hit Keith badly in his chest as she stared at him but prayed to God to keep her.

CHAPTER TWELVE
NOW WHAT

Ray's military experience allowed him to see things most would not notice. When he heard the gunshots, he instinctively hit the floor, as he hit the ground so many times in combat. And then moved quickly out the door like everyone else, but he stood by his car waiting to see Ice come out. Although they just met, he felt protective of her because that was his nature. He leaned his tight muscled body against his white two-hundred-thousand-dollar 2018 Mercedes-Maybach S650 Sedan.

This night did not go exactly as Ice hoped it would, but she felt good inside and looked forward to seeing her daughter again. So much time to make up for. She was deep in thought as she crossed the street and stood on the sidewalk, then she heard someone call her name. She looked down the street and was surprised when she saw Ray walking towards her. His very stride was confident and strong. Now, she had to play her role, but she was glad to see him.

"You are the last person I expected to see after what happened in the club tonight. I don't mean to sound ungrateful but what are you still doing here?" She hugged him and kissed his cheek.

"That should be obvious, waiting for you to come out. An old military habit of protection. Are you alright?"

"Interesting, I am impressed because we just met. Are you feeling me like that already?" She smiled at him seductively.

Ray knew her type and he had to slow her role of conceit.

"Like I said, old military habit." He gave her a, do not get it twisted look.

"Well, I thank you for your concern and I am fine, a little shaken up but who would not be when gunfire goes off in a building." She stared at him hoping he would make a move towards her, but he did not, so she did. "Ray, I am far from some helpless woman, but would you hold me please?"

Ray held her close and the scent from her perfume smelled nice and her tight sexy body felt good in his arms which caused him to become aroused. Ice felt his erection against her body, so she looked up and smiled at him and saw the hardness and kindness in his eyes. She whispered to him.

"Now what Ray?"

They stared at each other until their lips touched and he moved his hands down the small of her back and began caressing her hips and butt. They kissed as if they have known one another for years because they shared instant chemistry. This connection caught Ice off guard, so she pushed Ray away gently and continued to look into his eyes.

"Now what?" Ray wanted this woman badly.

"Ray, I know we just met, and I told you I do not play games. I do not want to mislead you in any way, but I do not want to be alone tonight either. Can we go to a nice hotel please and talk until we get tired, and you hold me until I fall asleep? Valet service parked my car, but I do not feel like dealing with that now, it is just a car. Can I ride with you? If you are interested?"

You could hear the police sirens getting closer.

"Yes, I am interested. Let's get out of here so we do not have to answer any questions from the police. We can go to a hotel if you like or if you feel comfortable, we can go to my place."

Ice looked at him briefly and then kissed him.

"We can go to your place."

He kissed her lips and grabbed her hand walked toward his car, opened the door for her to get in, and then he drove away.

As Ray drove, Ice looked at him and thought, *he is good-looking, fearless, has money, and good taste in cars. Time will tell what this leads to.* She leaned closer and put her head on his shoulder and a hand on his leg.

Ray lived in New York for years but moved to Washington, DC six months ago and purchased a two-car garage, three-bedroom, four-thousand square foot, million-dollar condo in Georgetown. It is a historic neighborhood, a commercial and entertainment district located in northwest Washington, D.C., situated along the Potomac River. He drove up to his garage, the door opened revealing a black 2018 four-hundred-fifty-thousand-dollar Aventador Lamborghini. The garage lights went on and he drove in and the garage door closed. He got out and opened the door for Ice and they walked to the door to his house. Ray put his hand on the panel by the door and it slid open, and they walked in. His home was professionally decorated, and everything was new and expensive. They walked to his large living room where there was a bar and he offered her a glass of wine and they sat down on the sofa close to each other and sipped wine.

"Ray, your place is nice, but I have to ask because a lady needs to know exactly what she is getting into. I am not being materialistic because I am financially comfortable. What do you do for a living to afford such a lavish lifestyle?"

"Fair question to ask. I am a retired twenty-year veteran and have been successful in real estate. I am single, no children, and no women drama in my life. Life is too short to tolerate foolishness. My turn, are you married and what do you do for a living?"

"Not married, no children, and I was involved with someone six months ago but that is over, and I use to be a professional gambler. I made a lot of money over the years and stopped, now my life is simple." She took a sip of wine and leaned over and kissed him. Ice was lying of course but he will never find out because, after tonight, they probably will never see each other again.

"Okay, I appreciate your honesty," he looked at her but knew she was lying about something. Ray grabbed a remote from the table and pushed a button and Jazz music began to play. He put the remote down and leaned closer to Ice. "Forgive my manners but I neglected to ask if you were hungry, I'm a good cook or we can order out, whatever you like."

"Thank you for asking but I am not hungry, but I would like more wine, it's good."

Ray got up to get the bottle of wine and Ice watched his every move because she was drawn to him. He poured the wine for her and set the bottle on the table, and he sat down, and they talked and laughed for hours. It was five o'clock in the morning and Ice covered her mouth as she let out a big yawn because she was getting sleepy.

"I have enjoyed your company. Now you are sleepy, so allow me to show you to your room which has a large bathroom, and the bed is comfortable. You can sleep as long as you desire because I have no plans for the rest of the day, so enjoy my home."

"Thank you and I appreciate you being a gracious host and a gentleman. I am getting sleepy, but I do not want to sleep by myself. Can I sleep with you?" She looked at him to see his visual reaction first.

"Yes, you can." He extended his hand to her and they walked to his bedroom.

Ray's bedroom was large, and she liked his king-size bed.

"I am going to take a shower." He kissed her and then walked into his master bath and closed the door.

Ice looked around his room and then laid on his bed. She was almost asleep when she felt his warm lips on hers. Ray wore a silk T-shirt that fit his tight muscular frame well and silk boxers.

"Hi," she sat up and looked at him. "I almost fell asleep. My turn for a shower as well. You smell good and your body looks great, tight, and muscular. I know you drive the women crazy."

Ray smiled and pointed to the bathroom.

"You will find what you need in the bathroom, so take your time."

She walked into the bathroom and closed the door. Twenty minutes later Ice walked out of the bathroom with a large towel wrapped around her feeling refreshed. She had a bottle of lotion in her hand.

Ray sat on a recliner when she walked out, and soft relaxing music was playing in the background. Ice sat the lotion on the bed and sat next to it.

"How do you feel?" Ray asked as he stared at her.

"The shower was relaxing, and I feel refreshed and sleepy. You were right, you have everything in that bathroom of yours. You must entertain a lot."

"No, I do not. I moved here from New York six months ago and you are the first woman I have allowed in my home. I am particular."

She stared at him while he talked and for some reason, she believed him.

"Okay, will you put some lotion on my legs please?"

"No problem." He got up and began putting lotion on her legs and then sat the lotion on the nightstand when he finished.

"Thank you Ray that was nice," she stood and looked at him. "Ray, I don't like sleeping in clothes, do you mind?"

Before he could answer, she removed her towel and put it on the back of a chair, and got in bed slowly making sure Ray got a good look at her body. Years of consistently working out and running made her body tight. She pulled the sheet over her body once in bed.

Ray stared at her and became aroused.

"Ice, your body is flawlessly beautiful."

"Thank you, now come to bed and hold me, please."

Ray dismissed what she said earlier. He knew what was about to happen. He removed his T-shirt and boxers and got in bed next to her with a full erection. He grabbed the remote from the nightstand and dimmed the lights in the room. Ice snuggled close to him and relaxed. This lasted for about five minutes and then Ray felt Ice's hand on his penis as she began massaging it. No words were spoken, and their chemistry was incredible. For the next hour, they had intense slow sex. Then, the erotic lustful spirit in Ice manifested itself.

"You are so good in bed baby, but I want more. I want us to let go and be ourselves. You can have me Ray, any way you want me. I will give myself to you and please don't judge me, I feel comfortable with you," She threw the sheet off them, and Ice rubbed her fingers across her wetness and then slid two fingers inside her feeling how wet she was and then rubbed them across her lips and Ray's. "Taste my pussy Ray and then slide your hard dick back inside me. I need you to fuck me. After I climax all over it, I will lick my juices off your dick. Then roll over so you can kiss and lick my ass and slide your thick hard dick inside it Ray." She said all this while caressing herself and never took her eyes off Ray.

Ray was surprised by her words and attitude but welcomed it. In the next hour, they did all she asked for and more. He has been with his share of women, but this lady was on another level. He felt something eerie about her but did not know what it was, and at this moment, he could care less. They had sex in various positions on the bed, on the furniture, and against the wall. It was seven-thirty in the morning, and they were sexually exhausted. They showered together and Ray prepared a light breakfast for them. They talked for a while and afterward lay together in bed. Ice fell asleep first. Ray looked at this woman in his bed thinking about all the sexual things they did as if they had known one another for years. He shook his head and moved closer to Ice and thought about all that happened until he fell asleep.

CHAPTER THIRTEEN
A POSSIBLITY

It was one-thirty in the afternoon when Ice opened her eyes, and the sun was shining brightly. She laid in bed looking at the ceiling thinking it was all a dream. She sat up but Ray was not there which disappointed her. She looked around the room and noticed a note on the nightstand. Ray left her a note saying he went for a short run and would be back soon. She smiled and began stretching out her nude body on the bed, then moved to the floor to stretch more. This was one of the daily routines she enjoyed, along with deep meditation. Ice knew she was possessed by strong evil spirits especially after what transpired between her and Malone in the cemetery. She still wanted the power Malone had and thought this was the only way of obtaining it so that she could accomplish her personal goals. Ice has never felt such incredible power in her life and now nothing was going to stand in her way. She would soon find out how wrong she was in her thinking. After stretching she took a shower. When Ice walked out of the shower with a towel wrapped around her, Ray walked into the bedroom wearing tennis shoes, shorts, and a T-shirt. She walked over, hugged, and kissed him.

"Hi baby."

Ray stepped back from her because he was a little sweaty.

"You are a wonderful sight to see wrapped in that towel and I would love to take advantage of this moment, but I am sweaty and need a shower."

"I like you sweaty." She kissed him.

"You are something, but I still need a shower. Let me go so I can handle my hygiene and we can talk when I get out."

"Okay, but there is a problem. I don't have any clothes to put on and you know I can't put the same clothes on from last night."

"You have a point," he walked over to his dresser and picked up a business card, and handed it to her. "This is one of the clothing stores in the area I shop in. Call and tell them what you want, and your items will be delivered to you here. Mention my name and it will be added to my account, not a problem."

"Thank you and you do know how to live well sir. I will take care of this while you are in the shower, and I will return the money to you."

To be playful, Ray took his clothes off in front of her and walked away to put them in the washing machine. He walked back into the bedroom and was massaging his penis when he walked in. He was fully erect now, he hugged and kissed Ice and walked toward the shower. He stopped, turned around, and was massaging himself again as he looked at her.

"Do you like what you see?"

"You are nasty and a tease, go take your shower."

Ray smiled and walked into the shower. Ice loved his confident walk, attitude, and his tight physique. She shook her head.

"Damn, that man is fine. Great looking body and dick, and he can fuck. Oh, can he fuck. Okay, let me focus." She made the call to the store and then sat in the recliner to relax and wait on Ray.

Ray walked into the bedroom wearing a robe and then he got dressed while they playfully flirted with each other. He put on casual dress shoes, pants, and shirt, and a ten-thousand-dollar Piaget Polo S Stainless Steel Watch. His doorbell rang, it was the delivery for Ice. Ray signed the bill, took the clothes, and gave them to Ice. She always enjoyed fashion and looking nice but today Ice wanted to keep it simple and sexy. She walked out of the bathroom wearing casual shoes, jeans that fit her sexy body perfectly, and a nice blouse. She did a turn to show Ray.

"Simple but still sexy. Do you like it?"

"Very much so and those jeans look great on you." He hugged and kissed her and placed his hands on her hips.

Ice smiled and stepped back from him.

"You know I like being in your arms, but I do want us to get out of the house today. If I allow you to continue caressing my body, we will not leave the house any time soon. Also, there is something I need to talk with you about. Can we sit down and talk before we leave?"

"For sure, let's talk."

While Ray was out running, she thought hard about telling him the truth about her life. There was something about this man that made her feel extremely comfortable.

She knew it was taking a big risk but felt compelled to do so. They sat across from each other in his living room.

"Ray, I have given this a lot of thought and realize after I tell you all this, you may not want to see me anymore, but it is worth the risk for me to be honest with you. Please listen and don't judge me."

"You have my attention, and I will not judge you. I have been through wars in my life, real wars, so you can tell me anything."

"Okay, remember you said that. First, let me go back to the beginning." Ice went back to her childhood beginning to the present day. She told Ray about how she met Zechariah, getting pregnant, her daughter Diana, having to leave Zechariah, her jewelry stealing days, being on the run for years, having to be alone for so long, the O'Neil family, meeting Malone, the gambling, and here she is now. She mentioned the creepiness with Malone but omitted her sharing in the evil ritual they did together in the cemetery. "So, what do you think about all I shared with you? Are you going to tell me goodbye and kick me out of your house?"

Ray listened to her every word and was amazed by her very emotional stories.

"Wow is my first response. I appreciate you being brutally honest with me. No, I am not going to tell you goodbye or kick you out of my house. However, I will say this. Much of what you shared with me is your past and how you deal with it now will determine how your present and future life will be. Yes, you need to make some changes in your life now if you want to. All the spiritual wickedness and evil stuff you experienced, will take God almighty to deliver you from. We just met and have connected well, and I am not talking about the great sex we shared. So, my question to you is this. What do you want for your life now and could there be a possibility of a strong friendship with us? Everything starts with friendship and trust."

Ice stared at Ray and had to hold back her tears because she was not expecting to hear that. She had experienced so many negative things in her life, that she was always on guard with people to say and do negative things. She wanted to leap into his arms and hold him tightly and cry a thousand tears of frustration and relief, but she knew she had to maintain her composure in case he flipped on her.

"Your response surprised me Ray and this makes me more interested in you. Yes, I am fully aware I need to make some changes in my life and yes, I desire for us to spend more time together and become close friends."

"Okay, you spoke your desires but let me be crystal clear with you. I want us to become closer as well, but I do not play games and I will not allow myself to get pulled into any foolishness in life. Not for you or anyone and I do not share."

"Fair enough and thank you for listening to me and being direct as well."

"Not a problem, now what would you like to do today and where would you like to go?"

"I have been thinking about that, but I needed to hear your response first. Now I know what would be fun for us. Get something to eat, I am hungry. Hopefully, you like seafood. Afterward, I thought we could do some clothes shopping and then go to a nice park and walk around and talk. Afterward, if we feel like it later, we could see a movie."

"I am hungry now as well and yes I like various kinds of seafood. Clothes shopping is always good, the park is a good idea, and I like movies."

"Great, thank you so much for what could be a new beginning for me," she stood and smiled at him. "Can I have a hug?"

"Always." He stepped towards Ice and wrapped his arms around her body. Not one to miss an opportunity, he bit, kissed, and sucked on her neck gently and caressed her body.

Ice was so comfortable with this man she let out a moan of appreciation and pleasure. She wanted them to remove their clothes and get back in bed, but she was hungry and had to get out of the house for a while.

"I could get used to being in your arms, but you need to stop kissing and sucking on my neck, so we can leave. By the way, just for the record, my neck is my spot. So, don't start something you can't finish." She passionately kissed his lips

"No problem because I start out like I can hold out and I hold out like I started out. You remember that." He kissed her.

"Old school attitude concerning relationships, I like that Sir." She kissed him and grabbed his hand.

They walked to the garage and Ray got the keys to the Lamborghini from the wall and drove out of the garage with the roar of the engine making Ice feel sexy and like a teenager.

He pressed the accelerator, and the car did a hundred miles an hour in seconds. Ray and Ice laughed as he took off so quickly and drove around town. She enjoyed the ride and they talked and flirted with each other a lot before arriving at the restaurant.

CHAPTER FOURTEEN

RON'S HOUSE

It was Thursday afternoon Ron and Diana were sitting in their living room along with Keith, Stacy, Zechariah, Sheila, James, Catarina, and Sandra. A lot of food was on the dining room table. They were talking about Diana's mother showing up at the club.

"Ron, when Zechariah called and told me what happened at the club that night, I laughed thinking it was a joke, but he told me it was not, it all seemed unbelievable. This is amazing on so many levels. Diana, how are you dealing with all this?" James said.

"James, you have been in my life for so many years and seen me through so much, but this is overwhelming. I'm still in shock and if God did not keep me, I would probably be insane by now." Diana sighed.

"No, you would not because I would be by your side praying for your peace as I am now," Ron gave her a comforting hug. "So many questions and for now, no answers." He kissed her lips.

"This is so frustrating for me now that I know she is alive and here in Maryland, truly unbelievable. Where has my mother been all these years and why did she not let me know long ago she was alive? A phone call, a message, or something." Diana wanted to cry but she had cried enough lately.

"Zechariah and I have been discussing this since it happened, and like all of you, all we have are unanswered questions." Sheila said as she looked at Zechariah.

"Diana, many years ago I had so much hope that I would one day see your mother again, but I had to let that go and deal with my life and later, my years of incarceration," he looked at Ron. "Ron, meeting you and getting out of prison was an answered prayer, to say the least. I never thought I could ever love a woman again until I met your Mom and fell in love with her. The day we married was a fulfillment of my heart's desire. Now, Diana's mother has appeared on the scene and I feel very protective of Diana. I need to say this, when she hugged me, I felt a strong evil spirit within her. It was a sickening feeling that made me feel like I wanted to vomit. Diana, you know I always want the best for you, but your mother has been or is involved in some form of spiritual darkness. I can feel it in my spirit." Zechariah had not forgotten that feeling.

Diana looked at Ron and Zechariah lowered her head and looked back at Zechariah with love and appreciation.

"This is extremely hard for me to say because I have been so emotional from all this. When she called my name and said who she was, I was shocked and all I could do was stare at her eyes. Well, in doing so, I saw and felt darkness, but that was quickly dismissed because I contributed what I thought I saw as the shock of seeing my mother alive after so many years of absence. However, I desperately want and need for us to talk." Diana lowered her head again from frustration.

"Diana, I don't want you to get hurt. Personally, let me go ahead and get this off my chest now. I don't trust her." Keith said with attitude.

"Time will tell baby, it always does." Stacy said and kissed him on the cheek.

"Diana, I have no answers but whatever James and I can do to help, please let us know." Catarina said giving Diana a warm smile.

"Well, my wife's safety comes first, in every aspect. James, could you run a complete background check on her?" Ron said.

"We are on the same page Ron; however, this will be extremely hard to do if she is not in the system anywhere. I need something to use for a paper trail." James said and shook his head.

"I can help with that. Not knowing who she was but I noticed her when she came into the club and eventually walked over to the VIP section to speak with Diana. Before that, she sat down and was drinking something. Even after the gunfire commotion and everyone was running out of the club, afterward, I started thinking. I remembered where she sat in the club while drinking and was hoping the glass was still there. I checked, and it was, so I wrapped the glass to protect it and later retrieved her fingerprint from the glass. James, I can give you the print and you can do your thing my brother." Zechariah said as he looked at James.

"Zechariah, you would make a good detective. If the print is clean, this will be enough to do a background check and I will let you know what I find out." James nodded at Zechariah.

"Thanks Zechariah, that was good of you. James, as soon as you find out, please call me." Ron looked at him.

"No problem my brother."

"I know we all have many questions concerning Diana's mother and in the process of doing background checks and anything else that needs to be done. Let us not forget, that she is her mother. Not a day goes by I do not think about my Dad and sister. I miss them both beyond words and would give anything to have them back in my life. Diana, I do not know if this situation is good or bad, but the fact is, your Mom has another chance to possibly be in your life. This is priceless, please keep this in mind." Sandra smiled at Diana and then had to hold back her tears thinking about her Dad and sister and their horrible deaths.

Sheila got up and sat next to Sandra and hugged her.

"You made a good point Sandra and I miss them as well, always will." She hugged her again and had to hold back her tears.

No one talked for a brief period because everyone was caught up in their thoughts and emotions. Ron wanted to change the current mood in the house, so he got up and went to the stereo and pressed Jazz music to play.

"There is plenty of food on the table and I am hungry, so let's relax and eat."

"Boy, you are always hungry and want to eat. I know your wife feeds you." Sheila said and shook her head while looking at Ron.

"Ron can cook, and yes I cook for him and do it well. He has a lot of energy and likes to eat. Ron, do not try to embarrass me in front of your family like I do not feed you.

They all know I do." Diana looked at Ron with a playful attitude.

Ron walked over and whispered in Diana's ear.

"You feed me well and I love to eat, especially you." He kissed her and smiled.

Diana pinched him and walked to the table. Everyone came to the table and sat down, and Ron blessed the food. They all began eating, laughing, and talking about the fun times they have experienced and shared in the past.

CHAPTER FIFTEEN
TOO FAR

For the last three days, James has been busy using his resources to have a complete background check done on Diana's mother. Her mother covered her tracks well, but James had contacts that could find out anything on anyone. James called Ron and told him he had information on Diana's mother and Ron told James that yesterday she called Diana and they talked for a while. The strange thing is, how did Diana's mother get Diana's phone number? This made Ron uncomfortable, and he told Keith about it and Keith assigned several *Young Wolves* to go wherever Ron and Diana went. A meeting was set for Monday morning at the club and Diana's mother would be there, but Ron did not want Diana to go. He told Diana he would let her know what her Mom said later because he did not trust her around Diana. Diana did not agree with Ron, at all.

Sunday night Ron and Diana sat across from each other in recliners in the basement watching a movie. Diana said few words and was quiet all day. She was quiet even in church that morning because she did not want to argue with Ron. They were getting along well, and she did not want this to change but she could no longer remain silent knowing the meeting with her Mom was taking place tomorrow and she would not be there. So, sexual seduction came to mind. Diana wore a T-shirt, no bra, and thong panties after they came back from church to indirectly seduce him into having her way. She noticed he was trying hard not to be sexually playful with her like he always is. He wore sweatpants and a tank top T-shirt.

"Ron, you are being very unfair to me. I should and need to be at that meeting tomorrow, it's all about me anyway."

"This is true my sexy wife, but when I get back, I will let you know everything that happened. I do not trust your mother, so in the meantime, you will stay here, as you should."

Diana gave Ron a mean look and was getting angry because of what he said and how he said it. It was too controlling.

"Ron, I am not a dog, and you can't order me around like I am. If I am not in the car with you in the morning, then when you leave, I will drive my car, I know where the club is. You can't stop me from going, and that's it." She looked at him with much attitude.

"We know nothing about your mother and what she has been involved in all these years. You can be very persistent, but you are allowing your emotions to cloud your intellect. The *Young Wolves* will be here in the morning, and I have already informed them you will remain here and to make sure nothing happens to you. So, please relax and continue looking very sexy in your T-shirt with no bra on showing your nipples, wearing thong panties. Bending over at times unnecessarily and revealing your sexy round butt. You have been trying to seduce me ever since we got back from church. Trying to use your womanly charms and body to sexually distract me, shame on you wife." He walked over to Diana's chair, kissed her, and caressed her leg.

Diana exhaled heavily because she reached that point with Ron. He was condescending and treating her like a child. She slapped his hand hard, and he laughed. Diana stood to face him.

"You think all this is funny Ron. I am your wife, not your slave. Furthermore, I will not be confined in my own home by you, the *Young Wolves*, or anyone else for that matter." She got in his face and pointed her finger at him. "Right now, I dislike you," she moved her face within inches of his. "I…am…going…to the meeting, if you or whoever tries to stop me, it is going to be some furniture moving in this place, believe that." She stared at Ron and then stepped back from him.

"You better keep your finger out my face, now come here." Ron grabbed her waist quickly and pulled her into him and then grabbed her butt with both hands.

"Where do you think you are going? You are so hot and sexy when you get angry with me, and you know it turns me on. I am going to give you what you have wanted all day. I'm going to bend you over this chair and put hard, stiff dick in you." He sucked on Diana's neck and slid his hands underneath her T-shirt to caress her breasts with both hands.

This infuriated Diana and she was not in the mood to be touched or handled by him. They wrestled sexually many times, but Diana wanted nothing to do with Ron right now. She tried to get away from him, but he was far too strong for her. Ron easily picked up Diana and carried her to the sofa. He put her down and she was still trying to get away. He managed to pull her T-shirt up and then lay on top of her kissing her repeatedly.

"Ron stop!" she yelled. "You cannot force yourself on me, stop!" She stared at him.

Ron stopped moving, sat on the sofa, and looked at Diana. The very thought of her thinking he was sexually forcing himself on her repulsed him and he felt bad.

"Forgive me Diana, I was only playing. You know I would never force myself on you. I will leave you alone." He stood and looked at her with sadness in his eyes. He walked away and then stopped and turned his head to look at her. "You can go to the meeting." He continued walking.

Diana saw the hurt in his eyes, she knew Ron would never force himself on her, ever. She pulled her T-shirt down and got up and grabbed his wrist.

"Ron wait, please don't leave. I know you would never intentionally hurt me. Things went too far, and this is all wrong for us. The arguing and yelling, it is not us. You have always been very protective of me and I do appreciate it tremendously, but at the same time, you can't control me."

He looked at the seriousness and love for him in her eyes.

"You are correct, no one enjoys being controlled. I have some thinking and praying to do. I am going upstairs to our room." He leaned forward and kissed her cheek and stepped away.

Diana grabbed his arm and pulled him back and smiled at him.

"Are you going to walk away and leave all this," she pointed to her body. "Don't you constantly say, you finish what you start?" She walked to the sofa and laid down and then waved her finger at him. "Finish what you started, husband." Diana slowly spread her legs and caressed her inner thigh.

He stared at his beautiful wife and became aroused and took his clothes off and laid beside her.

"I love you Diana."

"I love you more. Now, no more arguing and talking. Make love to your sexy wife. I am in the mood for a lot of foreplay all over my body." She kissed him with passion and deep love.

Ron nodded his head and helped Diana take off her T-shirt and panties. He took his time and caressed, kissed, and licked Diana's entire body front and back. He knew when and where to be delicate or firm to every inch of her body. He loved watching the expressions on Diana's face as he pleased her body that he knew so well. Diana loved her husband's touch, but she knew Ron wanted her to start sucking him quickly as all men do, and this made her tease him even more. She eventually grabbed his rock-hard penis and put it in her mouth, deep throating him. She grabbed the base of Ron's penis and began sucking just the head and then licked all over it. She held his balls in her left hand caressing them gently, held the base of his penis with her right hand, and sucked the head. She spat on Ron's dick, sucked, and licked all over it, and then began licking and sucking his balls just the way he loved it, and she continued to deep-throat him.

Ron felt Diana's throat muscles all over his dick and knew he could not take much more of this.

"Diana, that's so good baby." He leaned back on the sofa.

Diana loved his sexual facial expressions. She licked his penis continually and then began sucking his balls again which she loved doing because she knew how much this turned him on. Diana licked and sucked just the tip of his penis until she knew he was ready to explode. She gripped his penis and held it firmly in her hand and smiled at him.

"Oh no you don't, not yet." She got up and lowered herself on his penis and began rocking back and forth. "Not yet baby, don't cum yet, let me ride this hard dick first."

Ron looked at her riding him and tried hard to focus and concentrate so he would not bust because it felt so good being inside his wife. Diana was too hot, tight, and wet for him to last much longer. So, he shifted his body and pulled out.

"No Ron put it back in." She yelled.

"Be quiet!" He put Diana on her back, lifted her legs, and slid inside her so he would be in control. He stretched his arms out toward her. Diana did the same and they locked their fingers together using this to physically support and push at the same time. She had her legs spread wide while she gripped Ron's fingers and their body movements were in perfect sync, matching one another's movement for movement. Diana loved his thrusting and their perfect timing.

"Ohhhh Ron, I'm cummming baby."

Ron let their fingers go, leaned forward, put his arms underneath Diana's shoulder, and sucked on her neck as he continued to thrust inside her. He could not hold out any longer.

"Diana, it's so good baby, pussy's so good."

They climaxed at the same time and pushed their bodies into each other even faster. Ron rose, grabbed Diana's ankles, and looked down, watching his dick slide back and forth inside her. They exploded together and Diana screamed her husband's name as she loved feeling his hard dick penetrate her so well and with great love.

Ron was breathing heavily as he slid out of his wife and laid beside her.

"You are incredible Diana, but I think you need a spanking."

Diana rolled over to face him.

"When you think you can give me one, you let me know husband. I just might like it." She smiled and kissed him.

CHAPTER SIXTEEN
ANSWERS

At nine O'clock Monday morning Keith, Stacy Ron, Diana, Zechariah, James, and three of the *Young Wolves* sat at a large table in the club. Two *Young Wolves* stood outside in front of the club and they all were armed. Everyone wore suits. Diana and Stacy wore heels, a dress blouse, and tight jeans. James handed Ron a folder with some papers in it.

"You can look at the folder now if you want, it contains everything I was able to find out about Diana's mother. I will give you some details. She has had an interesting life, incredibly sad and very painful. During my investigation, her profile came up because years ago she was doing some high-profile jewelry store robbing and was connected to a man named Lamont Thomas. Lamont Thomas had serious connections with some people you do not say no to. He and his crew were involved in drugs, robbery, guns, and counterfeiting and he was making millions of dollars a month for years until he got caught. He and his crew are now doing twenty-five years to life in federal prison. How Diana's Mom got away, I do not know. She has been living a very low-key lifestyle for years and she is highly trained in the martial arts and guns," he looked over at Diana. "no offense Diana but your Mom is a dangerous woman and is not to be taken lightly." James was trying to take it easy on Diana with his words, but he needed to be truthful with her.

"All this information proves is she made some bad choices when she was young, as we all did. The rest is survival and self-preservation on her part." Diana said as she looked at everyone.

"I still don't trust her, and where is she? She's late." Ron said.

Diana looked at Ron and rolled her eyes at him.

"Ron, please don't be mean to my Mom. We all need to hear what she has to say before we put her in the evil category."

"There is something evil about her Diana." Zechariah said as he looked at her.

"Dad please, can we all give her the benefit of the doubt? Good Lord, talk about judging." She shook her head.

"Keith looked at his Rolex watch and sighed.

"She is late and needs to hurry because Stacy and I have other things to do today." He kissed her and began caressing her leg.

Stacy playfully pushed his hand away and then kissed him.

Diana stared at them and shook her head again.

"Is that all you two think about is sex? Oh my God." She said with irritation.

"Don't hate the love Moment baby." Stacy said as she looked at Diana and stuck her tongue out and winked at her.

Ice drove up in front of the club in her Bentley. She got out and walked toward the front doors where the *Young Wolves* stood. One of them lowered his sunglasses and stared at her.

"Damn, she is fine." He whispered to himself.

Ice heard what he said as she approached them. She stopped walking and looked at the young man up and down.

"Don't hurt yourself looking, you could never handle all this."

The *Young Wolves* walked in with Ice next to them. She wore heels, dark blue jeans that looked like they were painted on her body, and a low-cut blouse revealing her ample cleavage. She walked in with an attitude like she owned the club, and she knew all eyes were on her, lustfully. Ice loved it. Stacy looked at Keith as he lusted over Diana's mother, but she was determined to keep her composure this time and not give Keith or this woman the satisfaction. All the guys stood as they approached. Zechariah slowly shook his head as he looked at Ice walk in and admitted to himself how gorgeous she was. Diana stood and so did Stacy. Diana was overwhelmed with emotion and could not contain herself. She walked quickly over to her mother and wrapped her arms around her. Ice hugged her back and it took all her discipline not to start crying.

"I have missed you so much." Ice said as she hugged her tighter.

Ron walked toward them.

"Diana, let's all sit down so we can talk and get some answers." He held out his hand to her.

Diana did not want to but she let her mother go and took Ron's hand, and gave him a mean look. As she walked with Ron she leaned over and whispered to him.

"You promised to be nice to my mother, Ron."

"I promised no such thing but relax." He whispered to her.

They all sat down, and Ice looked at Zechariah.

"Hello, although you are the head of security for this club, you don't have to be so stiff, loosen up baby." Ice said flirtatiously and then smiled at him mischievously.

"Hello Diana, I am fine." His eyes perused her body up and down and said to himself, *you are a fine-looking woman.*

"How did you know Zechariah was head of security?" Keith said.

"It is my business to know things, anyway, can everyone just relax, please? I am not the enemy." Ice looked at everyone when she said this.

"That remains to be seen." Keith said.

"Can we all be adults please? Furthermore, I think this entire situation is ridiculous. I understand everyone's concern for Diana, but I am her mother and would never do anything to hurt my daughter. I have desired for many years to see and hold my baby. We should be able to be somewhere with just the two of us, so we can talk, without all this animosity and judgment going on now. Just the two of us, my daughter and I."

"You made some good points but you and my wife alone, that is never going to happen. We don't know you and after we did your background check, anything is possible with you." Ron said.

Ice was patient with this situation knowing it would be like this, but Ron's words and attitude tested her patience, enough was enough. She stood and pointed her finger at Keith and Ron.

"Are you serious right now? You are judging me, get real. I know all about you Ron and Keith. Ron, your prison time, you and Keith's major drug dealer lifestyle, all the illegal money you two have made for years. The killing you have done and somehow managed to get away with. You two had the best attorneys in the world, for sure. Nevertheless, you are pointing the finger at me, wow. Let me ask you this Ron, Mr. judgmental. How much blood is on your hands?" She pointed at Keith. "And you too Keith Washington. So, do not ever judge me or try to step to me. I have been on my own and in these streets for years trying to survive and I fear no one," she stepped closer to Ron. "And just for the record, I don't talk back, I strike back."

Ron stood quickly and stared at Ice and they both had the look of two lions ready to attack each other at any second.

Diana saw the look in Ron's eyes, and she knew whatever he was about to say or do would be bad, so she had to do something, and quickly. She stepped in between them.

"Both of you stop," she looked at Ron. "Ron please." Her eyes spoke volumes of concern and love, trying to diffuse a potentially volatile situation. She moved to the side as a sign of peace.

You could feel the tension in the air, and everyone was on edge. The *Young Wolves* had their hands on their holsters ready to pull and shoot. Ron looked at Diana with love and then looked at Ice with anger. He stepped closer to Ice and pointed his finger in her face.

"You better watch how you talk to me woman." He was mean mugging her hard and moved his finger closer to her face.

Ice never allowed anyone to disrespect or intimidate her and was not about to start now. She slapped Ron's hand away quickly and he was about to step closer but Ice saw this as an act of aggression. She front-kicked him hard in the chest with power that sent his body to the floor. With the speed and grace of a cat, she did two backflips high in the air and landed on her feet in a boxer's stance. You never heard her feet hit the floor.

Malone walked into the club dressed in all black holding his cane. He pointed his cane at them and yelled.

"What the hell is going on here? Why are you people attacking my woman?"

The *Young Wolves* pulled out their guns and aimed them at Malone. Ron stood up with speed and grace and moved in front of Diana and so did Zechariah. Keith moved in front of Stacy. Ice was surprised to see Malone here and he was the last person she wanted to see right now.

"Ice, it's time for you to leave, walk this way." Malone's words seem to echo throughout the building.

"Who are you supposed to be? You need to run out of here before you get shot full of holes." Keith looked at the *Young Wolves* and then looked at Malone.

"No, this is not what I wanted to happen, I need to spend time with my daughter and all of you are messing it up." Ice yelled.

"Get out of here woman before something really bad happens." Ron said as he stared at Ice.

"You better listen." Keith said.

"Ice, I said walk this way. I will not say it again." Malone said.

"Mom, please don't leave me again, please." Diana was close to tears.

"I am sorry Diana, I really am, but we will talk again soon. Without all this nonsense." She walked toward Malone.

Malone grabbed her butt roughly and kissed her.

"You need to move this ass of yours faster when I speak."

Ice looked at him with hate but had to play her role, for now, to get what she wanted. She stared at Diana and then bowed her head.

"You people have no idea what you are dealing with." Malone looked at everyone and then looked around the room. He hit the floor hard with his cane and every piece of furniture in the room shook and then stopped. He and Ice walked out of the building.

"What in the world just happened?" James said.

Diana started crying.

"No, this can't be happening again, not again." Ron said.

Diana stopped crying, she stared at Ron and moved closer to him.

"This is all your fault Ron. You felt like you had to prove something, as always." She looked at him with such contempt and anger. Her emotions got the best of her and she slapped Ron so hard, spit flew out of his mouth and left her handprint on his face. Diana walked away and Stacy followed to comfort her. As they walked away Stacy turned her head and gave Ron a mean look. She and Diana continued walking and sat at another table. Zechariah looked at Ron and walked over to Diana to talk with her.

Ron looked at Diana with anger that he had not felt in a while. He touched the side of his face, it was hot. He was a little dizzy, his eyes were watery, and his ears were ringing. He was about to walk in Diana's direction, but the room was spinning because his equilibrium was off. All Ron could do was be still and relax until he regained his composure and looked at everyone.

"Okay, I guess everybody is just going to ignore how Diana's mother did an impossible super high double backflip in the air. And her boyfriend or whoever he was, hit his cane on the floor which sounded like thunder, and all the furniture in the room shook. I felt that underneath my feet. We all know by now none of this was on a natural level. That was demonic activity at work, and we all know it. I am tired of going through all this evil stuff. Those two are demonically possessed."

Ron's words angered Diana even more, she stood and pointed her finger at him.

"Ron, I heard you. My mother is not a demon." She yelled.

"Diana, we need to seriously talk." Zechariah said as he placed his hand on her shoulder to comfort her.

CHAPTER SEVENTEEN
REALITY

Later that night Ron was not in the mood to go home but he knew everyone needed to relax. He, Keith, and Stacy were in his living room sitting on the sofa talking. Stacy and Keith sat together, and Ron sat across from them. Zechariah and Diana were in the basement talking. Food was on the kitchen table and three *Young Wolves* were in the kitchen eating.

"What a day, this situation is getting worse and worse. I can't believe Diana put her hands on me." Ron said.

"My brother, she did not put her hands on you, she put one hand on you. She slapped you so hard, that spit flew out your mouth. I saw and felt your pain." Keith started laughing.

Stacy gave him a, *'that is enough'* look.

"Keith that is not funny. Ron, I am sorry all of this happened," she looked up. "Lord, please don't let all this demonic evil stuff be happening again in our lives. Ron, you know how much I love Diana, but I have to say slapping you was wrong. Hitting is wrong, regardless of who does it. Man, or woman, you do not hit each other. Keith, the only one I love more than you is Jesus, but if you ever slap me the way Diana slapped Ron, you will be in the morgue."

He stared at her and shook his head.

"More threats, have you not been delivered from all the threats Stacy? How are you going to talk about loving me and Jesus, and then mention putting me in the morgue, all in the same breath?"

"You are right," she caressed his face gently and then looked at Ron and smiled. "Diana did smack the taste out of your mouth Ron." She and Keith leaned back and started laughing.

"Okay, get your laugh on. As usual, you two have jokes. No problem, laugh all you want but this is a serious situation. Don't forget we saw evil manifested before us, again."

Diana and Zechariah walked into the living room.

"You are right Ron; this is a very serious situation and before we continue to talk will you stand up, please."

Ron stood and looked at Diana.

"Are you going to slap me again?"

"No, I am not," she walked closer and stared into his eyes and then hugged him tightly and looked at him. "Ron, I could say this a hundred times and it would not be enough. I am extremely sorry for allowing myself to become so emotional I got angry and hit you. I may regret saying this to you but, it is the truth. I slapped you hard, and if you had hit me like that or ever do, I would leave you that same day. You and I have been through so much, but we do not attack each other, which I did. Again, I am deeply sorry. Hitting is wrong, no matter what. Please forgive me." Diana hugged him again and tears fell from her eyes.

Ron hugged her tightly and gently kissed her lips and they stared at each other deeply as if they were trying to see if they were still as one. The best of friends. One could hear a pin drop in the room it was so quiet. No one wanted to interrupt this important private moment because Zechariah, Keith, and Stacy knew, these two had to connect again.

"Thank you for being honest and direct. I forgive you and I was wrong myself in some things. Let's sit down and talk."

Diana walked to the sofa and sat down, and Ron stepped away to do the same, but Zechariah stepped closer to him and placed his hand on Ron's shoulder.

"My brother, you have earned a new level of respect from me. You could have gone another way with this which would have been bad for everyone, but you dealt with it with honor, maturity, and discipline. Much respect to you." He extended his hand to him.

Keith looked at Zechariah and was thinking, *no doubt, it would have been bad for you because Ron and I were about to break you down big homie.*

Zechariah's words touched Ron's heart because of the level of respect and love he has for him. The man is disciplined and strong in mind, spirit, and body. He always wanted them to be on the same side. He shook his hand.

"Thanks Zechariah, I appreciate that. We are not just family, but brothers for life, amen."

"Amen!" Zechariah said.

They smiled and walked over to the sofa and sat down on different sides next to Diana. They both hugged and kissed her on the cheek. Diana felt like a queen because she felt so much love from these two and knew both would give their life for her if they had to. She knew God was her best protector in life, but God also uses people, and she had the best two people on both sides of her now.

Keith looked at them and smiled but he could not help but feel left out. He and Ron have been best friends for life and no one or nothing has ever come between that. Not even Diana, Until now! His heart was sad, but he would never show it.

Stacy felt Keith's uneasiness. She was the only person who knew him as well as Ron, maybe better. No words were necessary for her to speak. She leaned over and gently bumped her shoulder into his to get his attention and smiled at him. Keith looked at her and stared into her eyes, they knew. He nodded his head at Stacy with much admiration because he knew she was saying to him, I got you. They kissed and gave each other a pound.

Ron noticed all this between Stacy and Keith. Keith looked at Ron and they nodded their heads at each other. Meaning, I got you, my brother.

"Well, here we are again in a situation with more questions than answers. We all saw the same thing concerning my Mom and whoever that man was. The power of darkness revealed itself again, Lord when does it all end?" Diana looked at everyone.

"Prison is a place you feel and see so much evil, and I have seen years of it. Yes, the guy your Mom was with was evil and she was operating in that same spirit, but I also felt a difference. A spiritual tug of war within herself. Wanting to do good and be loved but operating in negativity." Zechariah said.

"Once again you are right Zechariah, I felt and saw the same." Ron said.

"I did not want to say anything, but I discerned that in her as well. However, if a person is operating in evil but their heart desires to do good, there is hope for them. They can be saved, healed, and delivered by the hand of God. There is hope for my Mom." Diana said with confidence.

"Yes, there is hope for her. The man with the cane called her Ice. I know that term, smooth, and cold as ice. What happened to your Mom Diana to make her this way?" Keith said as he looked at her.

"I don't know Keith, but tonight we are going to find out, hopefully." Diana said and looked at Ron.

"What does that mean Diana, what have you done now?" Ron stared at her as his mood instantly changed to irritation.

Diana did not want to bring Zechariah into this, but she needed his help, and she knew Ron would listen better.

"Ron, please relax and hear me out. Dad and I talked about many things tonight and it was a blessing. The one thing we agreed on was, that communication is the answer to all this. We need my Mom to be able to fully express herself without interruptions and verbal threats," she looked at Keith. "So, I called and invited her to come over here tonight, so we could talk." Diana kissed Ron and lightly caressed his arm with her fingers trying to keep him from emotionally exploding.

"What!" He leaned away and looked at Diana like she was crazy. "Diana, tell me you did not invite this woman to my house with all her evil spirits and that demonically possessed man she was with." Ron's words came out severely harsh.

"We desperately need to talk Ron, and this is not your house. It is, our house, and my Mom is coming by herself." Diana's words were calm and relaxing.

Ron exhaled, looked at Diana, and shook his head. Keith looked at Diana and walked to the kitchen and made a phone call to the *Young Wolves*. He called for more *Young Wolves* to come to the house heavily armed and prepared for anything and he mentioned to the three that were there, company was coming and to post up. The *Young Wolves* went outside to their trucks and suited up. They put on protective wear and body armor and grabbed automatic weapons. Keith walked back into the living room and sat down and nodded at Ron. Ron knew what was going on.

Keith looked at his watch twice as they all continued to talk. Twenty minutes later Diana felt something was about to happen. She got up and looked outside and saw three *Young Wolves* heavily armed and talking among themselves and three more SUVs drove up and six more *Young Wolves* stepped out wearing body armor and carrying automatic weapons. She became irritated instantly and looked at Ron and Keith.

"Keith, what have you done? Why is there so much security out front like we are about to be invaded?"

"You never know, and I like to be prepared." Keith smiled and winked at Diana.

Zechariah walked close to Diana and looked outside and saw the *Young Wolves*.

"Relax baby, all will be well." Zechariah said as he touched her shoulder.

"Exactly my love, relax all will be well." Ron said sarcastically and kissed Diana on the cheek.

"Yes, relax baby." Stacy said and smiled at Diana trying to make her laugh.

Diana looked at everyone and rolled her eyes at them. Two *Young Wolves* walked into the kitchen and sat down and started eating some grapes that were on the table. Ice drove up in her Bentley and stepped out wearing heels and a form-fitting dress. One of the *Young Wolves* escorted her into the house. Everyone stood and Diana greeted her Mom with a hug and she and Ice sat next to Ron and Zechariah. After Ice sat down, she crossed her legs slowly revealing to Keith and Stacy she was not wearing panties. Briefly, they both had lustful thoughts and Ice felt this and loved the fact she was responsible for making them secretly lust and sin, she smiled at them. The *Young Wolves* in the kitchen saw how Ice sat down and the way she crossed her legs revealing she wore no panties. The sight of her naked crotch gave them pause to stare.

"Hello everyone, I know this is a very emotional situation, but I am extremely thankful to be here," she looked around the room and noticed the heavily armed men in the kitchen and thought of the men outside as well. She thought, *all this security just for me. What are they expecting, a hostile takeover?* "Diana, you have a lovely home."

"Thank you Mom. I know you have been through a great deal in your life, and no way can you tell it all tonight, but please, talk to me. What happened to you?"

"Wow, where do I begin?" She started talking about her early childhood, meeting Zechariah, and getting pregnant by him, with Diana. Her jewelry stealing days and having to leave the state because of her involvement with Lamont Thomas and being on the run for many years. Meeting Malone and becoming romantically involved with him and then finding out the secret to his successful gambling. She hesitated to talk about the evil ritual she did with him but felt compelled to tell the truth because maybe they could help her get away from him. So, she mentioned this as well and mentioned meeting Ray. This was the only time she smiled, and her entire face lit up. Everyone could see she liked this man. Ice talked more about her life and wanting peace, but never finding it. "And now, here I am talking to all of you, seeing the two people I have always loved. My baby Diana," she turned to look at Zechariah. "and you Zechariah." She waved her hand in the air. "Relax everyone, I know Zechariah is a married man now and I want the best for him and his wife. I was only expressing myself." She smiled at Zechariah and decided to be mischievous again, she uncrossed her legs slowly, so Keith and Stacy could see her crotch and lust even more. The *Young Wolves* noticed Ice doing this and once again they looked at one another and shook their heads.

Stacy was sexually turned on but became angry as well knowing this woman was playing games with them. She wanted to embarrass her by yelling, *stop spreading your legs showing us your naked crotch*. She held her peace despite wanting to leap across the room and beat her down.

As Ice crossed and uncrossed her legs, Zechariah gave her a mean look and she winked at him and smiled.

"Wow, that is some story Mom. Why did that guy call you Ice? What does that mean to you?"

Ice looked down and then looked at Diana with sadness in her eyes.

"Although we share the same first name, it always bothered me when anyone called me Diana because it made me think of you. This hurt my heart greatly, so I gave myself the name, Ice. This helped me deal with life better because ice is always cold and hard like my life has been for so many years. It helped me not feel something I craved so badly, love."

"Mom, I understand the Ice name, but I will never call you that and you should stop referring to yourself by that name. You are what you speak, please remember that." She smiled at her.

Ice looked at Diana and for the first time in a long time, she cried. Once she started crying, she could not bring herself to stop. It felt like the floodgates of extremely suppressed emotions came to the surface. Ice fell to her knees crying like a baby and it was at this very moment, that everyone in the room felt sorry for her, even Keith. They all have been there and knew this deep-rooted pain and how much it hurts. Tears came to Diana's eyes as she got on her knees and hugged her Mom.

Ron, Diana, Zechariah, Keith, and Stacy began praying for Ice and the *Young Wolves* observed everything going on but never said a word. They knew this was a time for God to do his thing and a spiritual battle was taking place. Ice continued to cry and then screamed very loudly and sighed heavily and then was quiet and motionless. Everyone started clapping their hands and praising God thanking him for deliverance. Ice and Diana stood and hugged each other. Ice had a big smile on her face. But this was a trick of the enemy because she was not delivered from her evil spirits. They all began to hug her one by one. When Ron hugged Ice, he felt something was not right. He whispered in her ear.

"In the name of Jesus, tell me who you are and what you are."

Ice leaned her head back, looked at Ron, hissed and snarled at him quietly, smiled, and pressed her body into his. Hoping to give him an erection. Ron knew she was not delivered, and he was about to react, but God spoke to his spirit and said, *hold your peace.* So, he stepped back from her and smiled. Diana noticed something was wrong but said nothing. Keith and Stacy were the last to hug her. When Stacy hugged her, Ice caressed the side of her face with her fingertips.

"You are beautiful and captivating in every way. Keith is fortunate to have you in his life." She spoke softly.

"Thank you." Stacy smiled and it was the way Ice stared at her that made her spirit uncomfortable. She stepped away but moved in front of Keith to block his path because she did not want him to hug Ice.

Keith looked at Stacy and shook his head and attributed her behavior to possessiveness. He moved around her and hugged Ice.

"God bless you." Keith smiled at her.

Ice hugged him tighter and whispered in his ear.

"Did you and Stacy enjoy looking between my legs seeing my hot cunt? I want to taste Stacy's pussy while my finger is sliding in her ass and then deep throat your young hard dick until you bust that nut in my mouth while she watches." She leaned back and smiled and then walked over to Zechariah.

Keith was shocked to hear Ice speak so nasty, especially after he thought she was delivered by God. He was going to tell Stacy, Ron, and Zechariah what she said as soon as she left.

When Ice and Zechariah talked Ron watched them closely. He noticed how Ice would overtly touch Zechariah's arm from time to time as they talked. This gesture can appear harmless enough, but Ron understood spiritual transfer and seduction well. He stepped toward them, but Diana grabbed his wrist.

"Ron, relax and leave them alone, they are just talking. I do have a question for you. It would be such a blessing if my Mom and I could see each other every day, so I was wondering, could she stay with us for a while?" She gave him an innocent look.

Ron looked at Diana like she lost her mind.

"Not in a hundred million years." He kissed her and walked away.

Diana looked at him and frowned.

It was one o'clock in the morning and Ice was still there talking with everyone. A small cloud of dark smoke appeared on top of Ron's house and when it disappeared, Malone stood there dressed in all black holding his cane. He began tapping it lightly on the roof.

"By the powers of Mr. Bones, I speak death to you all. I am killing everybody and that includes you Ice. I know you are trying to play both sides. Being nice to me, so you can use me, and still protect your hypocrite daughter. Well, no matter what you do, it will not work. I am killing the entire O'Neil family and their friends. I am most definitely giving Diana some of this concrete hard, evil dick of mine before I kill her. Maybe I will save Ice to kill last because her pussy is incredible." He tapped his cane twice and disappeared in a cloud of smoke.

CHAPTER EIGHTEEN
CHOICES

Ice and Malone argued a lot after the meeting. One day in Malone's house they had a heated argument because Ice refused to have sex with Malone, she walked away to take a shower. Ice walked out of the shower with a towel wrapped around her and a smile on her face because she looked forward to spending time with Ray. Malone noticed her spirit of happiness and knew it was not because of him. He felt betrayed which triggered his instant rage. He grabbed Ice by the throat with one hand, picked her up off her feet, and slammed her body against the wall.

"The only reason I don't twist your skinny little neck and break it right now is that you are useful to me in destroying the O'Neil family, including Diana your slut hypocrite daughter. She is a freak, she begged Ron to fuck her in the ass and loved it. Shame on her, closet super freak." He leaned closer until his face was inches from hers. "I'm going to put my straight-from-hell, devil dick in her and fuck that hot pussy and tight ass, better than Ron. Then I will let the rats bite her eyes out and eat her alive." He laughed hideously and licked her lips slowly then put her down.

Ice tried hard to get away from Malone when he had her against the wall, but her skills were no match for his demonically possessed strength. When he let her go, she coughed repeatedly trying to catch her breath, and wiped her mouth, despising his evil touch. She stared at him with extreme hatred and was about to tell him exactly how much she hated his very existence, but Malone pointed his finger at her.

"Don't even contemplate the thought of saying a short breath word to me. I should kick you in your stomach right now and make your intestines come out through your mouth and then cut your head off. Get away from me before I change my mind and kill you now. When I call, your hot ass better come running and kneel before me, with saliva in your mouth ready to suck my crooked dick, like the good female dog you are." He stared at her.

The look Ice gave Malone said it all, and she walked away and got dressed as fast as she could, wearing casual dress shoes, a mini skirt, and a dress blouse, and walked toward the door. Malone grabbed her shoulder and turned her around roughly.

"Don't give it all away, keep that sweet vagina of yours tight and wet so I can rabbit fuck you later." He moved his face so close to hers, that their noses almost touched. "Don't come back here smelling like dick and pussy, you slut. Damn that, I need to smell and taste your pussy before you leave, spread your legs."

Ice always feared Malone's temper and powers but did not desire to be degraded by him now and wanted to talk her way out of it.

"Malone, you know I will please you to your satisfaction. However, I need to get out of the house for a while and go for a walk. So much on my mind." She spoke calmly and looked into his eyes to soften his mood.

"Spread your damn legs," he yelled. "you can't play me fool; I am the master player to the fullest. Now, spread your legs before I call my rats to eat you where you stand." He stared at her.

Ice was beyond fearful of the rats and would do whatever to avoid dealing with them. She spread her legs slowly as far as the miniskirt would allow and turned her face away from Malone.

Malone smiled and put his hand underneath her miniskirt caressing her crotch through her panties and it did not take long until she became wet. He slid his finger inside her wetness and began fingering Ice.

Ice tried hard but once again her body betrayed her and reacted to Malone's expert fingering. She felt her orgasm coming and bit her lip to fight it, but it was too late. Her body jerked and trembled with intense pleasure being released and without being conscious of it, she grabbed Malone's wrist and began moving his hand faster so she could receive more pleasure from his finger being inside her. She was so wet now and exhaled to try and relax from her quick intense climax. She looked at Malone with contempt.

Malone smiled and removed his finger from inside Ice and rubbed his finger across his lips, licked it, and then rubbed his finger across hers.

"Your pussy smells and taste good. Don't you like how good you smell, dear?" Smiling at her.

"Yes Malone, you know I do." Giving him a fake smile and would say and do anything to get away from this man, especially now.

He licked her lips, stepped back, and laughed while stomping his feet repeatedly on the floor. The house shook each time his feet hit the floor.

Ice walked out of the house with a rage waiting to erupt and more determined than ever to kill Malone somehow.

A week later she was on vacation with Ray. They stayed at the five-star Hotel Hesperia Isla Margarita in Venezuela. Their luxury suite gave them a wonderful view of the Caribbean Sea. An hour after eating breakfast they walked along the beach talking. Ice was incredibly happy to be here with Ray and wanted to tease and please him every chance she got on this trip. Ray wore sandals and beach shorts and no shirt. He had no problem showing off his tight muscular physique. Ice wore sandals and a revealing two-piece thong bathing suit with a sarong wrapped around her waist.

"Ray, thank you for inviting me on this trip, your timing could not have been better. I needed to get away to relax and think."

"Not a problem, I am enjoying your company and you look stunning in your bathing suit," he smiled and stared at her body as they walked. "Your body is screaming for my attention."

"It is your attention I desire." She grabbed his hand and they continued to walk.

"Life's beautiful moments. I am glad you and your daughter were able to finally sit down and have a mature calm conversation, a long time overdue. So, where do you go from here, and what have you decided to do about the other guy in your life? Don't insult me and say he is not around."

Ice let his hand go, stopped walking, and looked at him.

"Ray, I do not want to be with him and if I did, I would not be here with you. He is evil and I don't want to talk or think about him," she hugged Ray and looked at his face. "Being here with you is wonderful, so can we focus on ourselves and enjoy each other, please? Life is too short not to enjoy it."

Ray nodded his head, and his hands caressed her hips as he pressed his growing erection against her body while kissing her passionately. Neither of them cared about others seeing them because they were too caught up in their increased sexual passions. Only when Ice felt Ray's hand sliding underneath her sarong and felt his warm hand caressing her butt did she step back from him.

"Your touch is intoxicating but we need to be in private quarters if we are going to continue," she looked at Ray with overwhelming lust and care. "let's go back to our suite and make passionate love."

"You read my thoughts." He kissed her and they walked away holding hands.

As they walked, two attractive women wearing revealing bathing suits walked towards them. When the two women reached them, they stopped walking and one of them spoke.

"You two look sexy. There are many things my friend and I would like to do to both of you." She smiled at her friend and then at Ray and Ice.

Ice and Ray stopped walking and looked at the two women. Ice was sexually turned on already and she thought the timing for this could not be better. She squeezed Ray's hand and smiled at the women.

"Thank you for the compliment and both of you are gorgeous," she looked at Ray and smiled. "Ray, would you be interested in a foursome?" Ice wanted to embrace her instant erotic thoughts."

Ray was surprised once again by Ice and her forwardness. He has never participated in a foursome but since Ice mentioned it, he would not turn the offer down. He looked at the two women lustfully and had to admit they were attractive with tight bodies.

"We have two king-size beds in our suite." Ray said.

"I like your attitude," Ice looked at the two women. "Ladies, would you care to join us in our room?"

The two women looked at each other and then looked at them. One of them stepped closer to Ice.

"I hope you are not the jealous type because after I finish riding his dick, my friend and I are going to turn you out." She leaned forward and kissed Ice on the cheek.

"So you say, let's walk." Ice said with arrogance.

Ray and Ice held hands as they walked, and Ice noticed Ray looking at her peculiarly and became concerned because she wanted to make sure he was not having a change of heart.

"Ray, are you sure you are okay with this? I would not want you to do something you would regret tomorrow."

"I only do what I desire in life, this should be fun. I am surprised that you were interested."

"I'm attracted to men and women Ray, but I prefer to be in a committed relationship with a man. I have feelings for you so doing this will be fun."

"I am learning more about you." He kissed her and they kept walking.

Once they reached their hotel suite, they all sat down, had some wine, and talked for a while to establish a better connection with each other, and then took turns taking showers. The two women showered together first and laid on the bed wrapped in towels. Ray and Ice showered together and when they walked out with towels on, the two women were on the bed in a sixty-nine-position. Ray and Ice stood and looked at one another and then watched the two women pleasure each other. Watching the women please one another so effectively intensified Ray and Ice's sexual desires as they caressed each other while observing them. It did not take long until the women were moaning and screaming from their first orgasms. After calming down, they sat up in bed and one of them waved for Ice and Ray to come over.

"We couldn't wait, come over and us three women will please him first." She pointed at Ray.

Ice looked at Ray and smiled and looked at the women.

"You two spoke my thoughts," Ice kissed Ray. "Lay on the bed baby. I hope you are ready for this."

Ray kissed her as they dropped their towels on the floor and proceeded to the bed. Ray laid on his back, and what followed was a fantasy come true. All three women kissed and licked his entire body front and back. Ice kissed him passionately and then joined the other two. One was kissing and licking his inner thighs, the other licking and sucking his balls, and Ice licked and sucked his dick like no other. Ray had never felt anything like this in his life and was about to explode in Ice's mouth, but she squeezed his dick quickly so he would not cum.

"Not so fast lover, I'm so wet right now and want to ride your face and get it wet." Ice moved forward and sat on Ray's face. She moved slowly at first, but Ray's tongue and mouth were so good, she could not help but scream her first orgasm. Now, Ice desired to feel his hard, big dick inside her. She got on top and rode him hard and fast until she climaxed again.

Afterward, they all took turns pleasing each other in every position and every way possible. Ice climaxed two more times when the two women were kissing, licking, and sucking on her breast while Ray's face was buried between her legs. Ice could feel another orgasm building as each woman's mouth sucked her nipples and Ray's warm wet mouth and tongue were on her wetness. She was so close. Ray's oral skills were outstanding, he dragged his tongue slowly from her pussy to her ass, back and forth. Ice was extremely sexually turned on and wet, and Ray took advantage of this. He used her juices for lubrication and slid his finger in her ass gently while his tongue slid in and out of her pussy. Ice gripped the sheets hard, arched her back, and screamed.

"Ahhhhhhh, I'm cummming." Her entire body shook as she exploded and screamed nasty erotic words as her body absorbed the intense pleasure.

The four of them continued having sex for the next two hours. Three on one, two on two, and constantly changing partners until they had each other in every way. Afterward, all four relaxed for a while drank more wine, and then showered. The two women had clothes delivered to them from one of the clothing stores close by, then they all went out to eat. Later the women came back with Ray and Ice to their hotel suite where the sex continued until the early morning hours until they fell asleep. When Ice and Ray woke, the two women were gone. They showered, ordered breakfast, sat at the table with robes on, and talked while eating.

"Wow, what a night we had," Ice smiled at Ray. "Are you okay Ray because you have a distant look on your face? Do you have any regrets or upset about something?"

"No, not at all. I am sitting here replaying last night's events in my head and how good it was. You were incredible in every way. You were relaxed and had no problem letting go. Last night was unlike anything I have ever experienced sexually. I never would have done that without you."

"Interesting, and we were great together. However, although it was great and extremely erotic, it is not something I desire to participate in regularly. Now I have a confession for you," she lowered her head and then looked at Ray. "Having a foursome allowed me to realize my feelings for you are more serious than I thought."

"Why do you say that?"

"I am far from a jealous woman and even though it was hot and an incredible turn-on to watch, seeing your dick sliding back and forth inside other women bothered me. The extreme erotic passions at that moment helped me suppress my true feelings, but my heart did not like it." She gave Ray a fake smile and continued to eat.

"Thank you for your honesty. Since you mentioned that, in the future, I would rather not share you. Last night was incredible, but I want you for my woman, not anyone else."

Ray's statement touched her heart deeply and all Ice could do was stare at him and control her emotions.

"We have not known each other that long but your words touched my heart. Are you for real Ray?"

"A hundred percent and it's not the length of time you have known someone but the honesty, connection, and quality of what you share that make a big difference." He leaned over and kissed her lips. "I enjoy kissing your warm lips, so relax and embrace what I offer. True friendship."

Ice was feeling him but needed to guard her heart.

"True, a solid connection and real friendship are important, and you know I like your kisses. So once again the question is, where do we go from here?"

"Honesty and trust and take things one day at a time. This works for me."

"Me as well, this breakfast is good. Did you enjoy your food?"

"Yes, the food was delicious and so are you." Ray put a sliced peach in his mouth and then picked her up and laid her on the bed. He opened Ice's robe revealing her beautiful nakedness and slid the sliced peach across her breast. He continued moving the peach around her nipples with his mouth and tongue while his hand caressed her wetness. Then buried his face between her legs.

"You are so nasty, and I love it. Ahhhh, that feels good Ray. That's it baby, just like that. Now suck that clit, ohhhh Ray suck it. Ohhhhhh, you are going to make me climax in your mouth, ahhhhhh, Ray."

Ray continued orally pleasing Ice as he began caressing both her nipples very gently with the tips of his fingers. She arched her back, squeezed the sides of Ray's face with her thighs, and gripped the sheets. Having her nipples touched in this manner increased her pleasure greatly. Ice moaned and screamed her passions as she felt Ray's tongue inside her wetness moving around as his lips sucked her clit. Her thighs pressed the sides of his face again, she leaned her head back further and yelled as she climaxed in his mouth.

CHAPTER NINETEEN
WATCHING YOU

It was eleven-thirty at night and Malone walked on Margarita Beach not far from the hotel where Ray and Ice stayed. He had his cane and wore black sandals, black baggy pants, and a long-sleeved black shirt. He stopped walking and pointed to the hotel where Ray and Ice stayed.

"I hope you two had fun because very soon I am killing you. Ice, I told you not to give my pussy away, but you had an orgy and fucked like a dog in heat. You are a serious freak. After I rabbit fuck your pussy, mouth, and ass, I am going to cut Ray's dick off in front of you with my sword and cut his head off. Your head will soon follow," he laughed and looked around. "Damn, who can I kill tonight? I got a serious attitude." He continued walking until he heard some laughter in a secluded part of the beach. Malone saw two couples lying on the ground having sex on a large blanket. He walked closer without a sound. All four were naked and oblivious to him watching.

"You nasty cheating, low-life dogs! All of you are married to other people but you are here committing adultery, and I love it! This is a hell party because everybody is going to hell tonight smelling like pussy, dick, and ass."

The ladies screamed and everyone attempted to get dressed quickly but it was too late. Malone mumbled some words and waved his cane across the sand. Thousands of large bulldog ants, the most dangerous ants in the world began coming out of the ground and biting them. The ants were extremely aggressive in their attack and injected more venom with each bite. They all screamed and rolled around on the ground trying to get away but to no avail.

"Oh God, oh God. Help us Jesus, help us!" Each screamed this repeatedly.

"Shut up!" Malone yelled. "Now you want to call on God. It is too late; you did not call on God when you were committing adultery. You nasty men had your tongues in these sluts' asses licking it like it was an ice cream sandwich. Everybody licking, sucking, and fucking their way to hell. I love it!" He yelled.

The ants crawled in their mouth, ears, and nose biting them from the inside out. Malone spoke curses and laughed hysterically as the ants were killing them. They crawled inside the women's vaginas and the men's penises biting them to death. They screamed until the ants ate the flesh off their bones and then started eating the bones and dragged small pieces of bones back into the ground as they went. Blood was all over the ground where the couples were killed.

Two armed security guards from the hotel walked toward Malone and shined their flashlights on him. They saw all the blood on the ground and one of them stepped closer to Malone with his hand on his holster.

"What are you doing out here and where did all this blood come from? Don't make any sudden moves." He and the other guard stepped closer to Malone.

These were the last words the guard spoke. Malone pulled his sword from the cane and cut the heads off both guards so fast, it looked like a blur. Their heads fell to the ground, although their bodies were still standing until he cut their bodies into two pieces with one swing. He then mumbled some words and pointed his cane at the water and hundreds of large crabs came from the water and began dragging the body parts back into the water until nothing was left.

He pointed his cane at the hotel.

"That felt so good, I love killing people and taking them to hell. Ice and Ray, I know you enjoyed your freaky sexual event, but your time is coming soon. Sorry no good dogs in heat; ass and pussy licking fornicators." He laughed and walked toward the hotel. "It's got to be someone in this hotel lobby operating in sin that I can take to hell with me tonight. There are fewer Bibles in hotel rooms these days in comparison to how it used to be which I like. I do not want people reading a bible and praying when they come to a hotel. I want everybody smoking marijuana, snorting cocaine, drinking alcohol, committing adultery, and fornicating. I want them distracted by the cares and pleasures of this world for a season. All kinds of sexual perversions, men with men, women with women, oral sex parties, ass parties I do not give a damn. Just keep licking, sucking, and fucking your way to hell." He continued to laugh.

CHAPTER TWENTY

DISCERNMENT

The following Sunday morning Ray and Ice went to Pastor Williams' church. Diana was glad to see her mother again. They sat behind Sheila, Zechariah, James, Catarina, Keith, Stacy, Sandra, Luke, Rick, Cynthia, Derrick, Tonya, Ron, and Diana. All the women wore multi-colored dresses except Ice, her dress was white, and the guys wore different color suits. People continued to come in as the choir sang. The Pastor's sister, Shirley Williams was in South Africa for months for an extended retreat. She was in church today directing the choir. Everyone was seated and Shirley directed the choir to stop singing and sat down. The pastor walked to the pulpit wearing a cream-colored robe.

"Praise the Lord everybody on this blessed Sunday morning. God gave all of us breath in our bodies this morning and woke us up. This is more than enough to praise his mighty name. I want everybody to stand on their feet, clap their hands, stomp their feet, do something to give God some praise. God is and always will be worthy to be praised."

Everyone stood and began praising God until the Holy Spirit took over. The atmosphere changed from what people do in the natural realm to the power of God. His glory was in this place. Pastor Williams knew it was never the tears of people that moved God but a cry from the heart and soul for a change and deliverance. He knew these people wanted something that only God could give them, true peace, and salvation. Fifteen minutes later the people were still praising the Lord and receiving their blessings. The anointing in the church was incredible and Pastor Williams always knew this was how it should be in church and not just entertainment, singing, and no anointing. He stood by the pulpit watching the mighty hand of God touch soul after soul as they cried out for his healing. Twenty minutes later he could feel the anointing of the Lord calming down and he knew it was time to bring forth his message. He raised his hands.

"I thank the Holy Spirit for its healing delivering presence and thank God for all of you here. Since King Jesus has flexed his power, my time this morning will be brief. My message is faith. If you would turn to the book of Hebrew, chapter eleven, verse one. It reads as such, *Now, faith is the subject of things hoped for and the evidence of things not seen.* It does not matter what the present circumstances are, the report of whoever for any situation, or what someone else thinks. If we had all the information and everything we need, then we would not need God and he could not get the glory. We all need more faith right now. No matter how the winds of circumstances may blow in your life, stand on your faith and not what someone may think or say. The words of a human being mean absolutely nothing compared to the unlimited power of God, never forget that. My brothers and sisters hold on to your faith one day at a time and watch the master builder, King Jesus, do his thing. Always keep in mind; it was the spoken words of God that created the world. Can I get an Amen?"

The church said, "Amen."

Pastor Williams made an altar call, and many came forward for prayer. He was always moved in his heart and soul when he saw people moved and transformed by the power of God. That is what the true church is, salvation for souls all over the world.

After church service was over Pastor Williams and Shirley stood outside speaking to people as they left. There was a break in the crowd of people coming out of the church greeting the Pastor. Shirley took advantage of this opportunity and leaned closer to and whispered in his ear.

"Great service my brother, a mighty move by the hand of God, but I have to go back to Africa to do more missionary work, I'm leaving tomorrow. Take care of yourself, I love you." She kissed his cheek and walked away quickly so he would not have time to talk because he would have tried to convince her to stay. It hurt Shirley's heart to leave her brother, but God was using her in various countries in Africa in a mighty way as well. Shirley walked away with tears in her eyes, but she had to go.

When Diana introduced her mother to Pastor, he shook her hand and discerned this woman was dealing with extraordinarily strong demonic evil spirits. The Pastor continued greeting the people and silently praying at the same time. Ron, Diana, Sheila, Zechariah, Keith, and Stacy talked among themselves. Ray and Ice were talking and then walked toward Diana. Diana saw them approaching and smiled from her heart, and then hugged and kissed her mom on the cheek. Ice was emotional thinking about her daughter but to be in her presence now, was satisfying beyond words.

"Hi Diana, hello everyone, this is my friend Ray." Ice said giving them a warm smile.

"Hello everybody." Ray said and then he and Zechariah locked eyes and did what so many men do, size up each other.

Keith, Stacy, and Ron knew Ice was not delivered so they were cautious in dealing with her and Keith gave Ice a suspicious look. Sheila observed Ice and had to admit this woman was beautiful and had a great figure, but she was not intimidated by her in any way. She stepped closer to Ice.

"Miss Diana," she looked at Diana, Ron, and Ice. "Wow, it seems so odd to call you that because you and your daughter have the same name. Anyway, I know all this has not been easy for you to deal with."

"Thank you for your kind words and I see Zechariah made a good choice with you as his wife. It was long ago when Zechariah and I met, we were so young. I was very afraid to tell Zechariah I was pregnant. I loved him so much," she stared at Zechariah with intense lust and did not care who noticed. "It was beyond heartbreaking to leave my daughter and him behind." She looked at Diana. "Having Diana was the best thing in my life, and now I want the opportunity for us to get to know each other. So, no it has not been easy for me by any means."

Sheila and everyone else noticed the lustful way Ice looked at Zechariah and Sheila knew this woman could not be trusted. She hooked Zechariah's arm in hers and gave him a warm smile.

"We both have been very blessed, and I thank God for our union of 'Holy' marriage." She gave Ice a distinctive look when she said, Holy marriage.

"Well, none of us can change the past, so we deal with today. The service was great, we all are here now, so let us go out somewhere nice to eat, as a family." Diana smiled at everyone and stepped closer to Ice and grabbed her hand.

Ice loved this moment and never wanted it to change. She was willing to do whatever was necessary to keep this situation on her desired path. She hugged Diana gently and gave her a big smile.

Ron did not want to spend time with Ice but that would be very selfish on his part, and no matter what, he wanted his wife happy.

"Present time it is, let's go eat." He presented everyone with a fake smile.

They all walked away as Diana and her Mom held hands and Ray walked next to them. Sheila and Zechariah walked behind them. Ice felt the stares as she walked, so to be mischievous and to irritate, she shook her hips and butt extra knowing her tight white dress revealed her curvaceous figure. She wore thong panties, so as she walked it looked as though she wore none, which Ice loved. This caused men and women to look upon her and lust, and Ice loved to be sexually desired.

Sheila shook her head with disgust realizing Ice walked lustfully on purpose and she noticed Zechariah's eyes were glued to her butt with every step she took.

"Do you see something you like and want, husband?" She whispered to Zechariah with attitude.

"Yes, I do, you." He smiled at her knowing he was busted but had to play it off.

"Good answer, very good answer Zechariah."

They all walked to their cars and drove away.

Malone stood across the street dressed in all black holding his cane. He looked at the people coming out of the church and how Ice was mingling so easily with everyone. He became irritated instantly because he planned to walk in this church today and whisper various curses, but the anointing of God stopped him.

"I hate people that walk in the faith of God, I hate them all." As he walked down the sidewalk, he whispered curses to whomever he passed. After he spoke evil curses to any couple he encountered, the couple would immediately start arguing. The woman always smacked the guy she was with and walked away quickly. Malone kept walking and would laugh because he loved operating in the spirit of discord. He thought to himself…*if people would just pray more, I would not be able to defeat them so easily, but I am glad they do not, more fuel for hell.*

CHAPTER TWENTY ONE
HER TRUE SELF

Ice felt proud as she held Ray's hand while they walked. The O'Neil family decided to visit one of their favorite soul food restaurants in Georgetown DC. When they drove into the parking lot, two white 2018 Maserati GranTurismo Coupes drove in the lot playing loud music. Two young men, African American and Latino stepped out of the cars wearing expensive dress shoes, pants, short-sleeved shirts, Rolex watches, and diamond bracelets. They talked and laughed loudly among themselves concerning the new purchases of their hundred-forty-thousand-dollar cars and how successful their three cannabis dispensaries were. The O'Neil family and others could not help but notice them as they began walking in. The two guys walked behind the family and stared at the women. The Latino whistled loudly.

"Damn, will you look at the ladies in front of us? They all look good, but the one in that tight white dress looks like she does not have any underwear on, hips and her fat ass shaking. I would fuck her for days, get my smoke on, and then fuck the rest, especially from the back. Head down ass up." He said this loudly so they all could hear, not caring what they thought, and they laughed.

They all heard what the guy said but Diana was furious at such blatant disrespect. She stopped walking and turned around to face the two guys.

"We all heard what you said, and you have no respect for yourselves and your mouth is beyond disgusting." She looked at them as her anger was increasing by the second.

Ray let go of Ice's hand and turned around to face the guys. The rest of the family turned around quickly, and Ron, Keith, and Zechariah stepped in front of Diana.

"You two need to pray and grow up and learn how to respect other people. Having money doesn't make you special." Ron said while mean-mugging them.

Ice stepped closer to Diana and touched her arm.

"Let it go baby, these two will learn their lesson the hard way in life." Ice stared at the two guys with a smile on her face, but she thought, *if I ever see these two again, I am killing them.*

"Fuck you lady and your entire family. You should be happy I complimented your fat ass. It's not my fault you ain't getting dicked down as you should." The Latino spoke and then raised his shirt revealing a gun in his waist and his friend did the same revealing his gun as well. "It's Sunday people, no need for anybody dying on a Sunday. Besides, Miss tight white dress is shaking her ass good, I know she wants some of this young hard dick." He grabbed his crotch, looked at his buddy, and laughed.

Because of the many things Ray had been through, these two guys talking loudly and displaying guns did not impress him at all. He knew if he wanted to, he could take their lives easily, but this was not his way of life.

"You two are young, and young people say and do stupid things. Thank God for this day." Ray gave them a look that made them realize, he was not one to play with, guns or not.

"Let it go baby." Ice said as she rubbed Ray's arm.

Everyone was furious at the words and attitude of these two, but they knew only God could help them. They all turned around and walked into the restaurant. The two guys looked at each other and laughed and walked in as well.

The O'Neil family sat down at a long table and ordered food and drinks. As they talked, the tension among them began to subside, and they enjoyed their food while eating and talking. The two guys sat at a table across from them. An hour later Ice excused herself and went to the bathroom. She noticed the two guys staring at her. She winked, smiled at them, and nodded her head in the direction of the bathroom as she continued shaking her butt as she walked. Ice was in the bathroom alone standing close to a stall when the two guys came in and locked the door behind them. Ice gave them a seductive smile.

"Good, I was wondering how long it would take you two to man up and come in here. You are right, it has been a while since I had some good sex and I like younger guys because they can fuck. Come in the stall with me and I will spit on your dick, hand slip it, and suck you both and you can take turns fucking me, from the back. I want it hard, deep, and fast. No hugging or kissing, I want balls deep slapping the ass speed fucking until I drain you." Iced gave them a look of seduction.

The two guys looked at each other.

"I knew you were a freak lady, but damn. You can get this young hard dick right now, for sure. Spit on my dick." The African American guy said and laughed.

Ice walked to the last stall in the end because it was the handicapped stall and the largest. The two guys walked in behind her and locked the stall door. They removed their guns from their waist and laid them on the floor, pulled their pants and underwear down, and stood close together. They began stroking their penises.

"Okay freak, start sucking these dicks, and put a lot of spit on them. And lick my balls too." The Latino said and laughed.

Ice smiled, got on her knees, spat on each guy's penis, and took each penis in her hands, and began massaging them at the same time. They looked at her and smiled and then leaned back against the wall and closed their eyes enjoying the hand job Ice was giving them. This is what Ice was waiting on. With years of martial art training, her next moves were smooth. She let the guy's penises go and put her hands underneath her dress and removed two small knives. The guys looked down to see why she stopped stroking them and opened their mouths to scream at what they saw but it was too late. Ice stood up very quickly and stabbed them at the same time in the chest and neck. They were dead before they hit the floor. Ice looked at them, smiled, and then stepped over their bodies as she walked out of the stall. The guy's mouths were opened wide in shock as they lay on the floor dead. She washed the blood off her knives and hands and then put her knives back under her dress. She looked in the mirror to inspect herself and then walked out of the bathroom and walked back to the table, sat down, and continued talking with everyone. She missed a small spot of blood on the top of her dress. Diana noticed it.

"Mom, you have a spot of blood on the top of your dress."

Ice saw it and knew she had to come up with a quick lie.

"Oh, thank you baby. I did scratch myself when reapplying my makeup while in the bathroom." She smiled at Diana.

Stacy noticed Ice's purse on her chair and when she walked back to the table, she did not have her purse with her.

Two hours later they decided to leave. Ice hugged Diana and then she and Ray walked out. Stacy, Diana, and Sheila walked to the bathroom before they left. Ron, Keith, and Zechariah walked with them but stood in the hallway close to the door to wait for them. The ladies walked into the bathroom and they noticed a lot of blood on the floor. They looked around and then opened the handicapped stall door and Diana screamed. The floor was covered in blood and the two guys that spoke to them so disrespectfully lay on the floor with their pants and underwear down and their mouths wide open. They quickly stepped back.

"Oh my God, oh my God." Diana said.

Zechariah, Keith, and Ron heard the scream and ran into the bathroom and saw the ladies staring into the last stall. They walked over and saw two guys on the floor with their pants down and mouth open, they knew they were dead.

"Lord Jesus, what in the world happened to these two? Oh Lord Jesus, so much blood, oh Lord." Sheila said and then put her hand over her mouth.

"Good Lord, I have seen some things, but this is horrible." Keith said

"Who could have done this horrible thing to these two young men? Yes, they were very rude and disrespectful but did not deserve this. Who did this to them?" Sheila said.

Stacy looked at Keith and they said at the same time.

"Diana's mother."

"What! Why would you two say such an evil thing about my mother? She had nothing to do with this. I can't believe you two." Diana looked at Stacy and Keith with disgust.

"Diana, your mother walked to the bathroom, and I saw those two walk behind her, and now they are dead. You noticed a spot of blood on her dress, but she said she scratched herself when reapplying her makeup in the bathroom. But when she came back to the table, she did not have her purse with her. It wouldn't take a genius to figure this out." Stacy said.

"Let's get out of here and talk about this, away from the crime scene." Keith said.

They all walked out got in their cars and drove away.

Ten minutes later Malone appeared in the bathroom in a cloud of smoke wearing all black and holding his cane. He opened the stall door and saw the two dead bodies and shook his head.

"Stupid female, once again allowing emotions to get the best of her. I could care less about these two fools, fuel for hell. I cannot have any negative attention drawn to Ice right now or the O'Neil family and friends. My plan of revenge must be carried out my way, my time. Killing them would be easy, but they all must suffer greatly first." He spat on the floor and tapped his cane on the floor repeatedly until dark smoke covered the entire floor and many rats appeared. Malone pointed his cane at the rats and then the dead bodies. "Eat, my friends, eat it all." The rats began eating the bodies very quickly and all you heard was bones cracking and the rats swallowing bits of flesh. Nothing was left of the two guys, not even blood on the floor because the rats licked it all. The floor looked spotless. Malone looked around and all the rats looked at him for more instructions. "Come my friends, it's time to leave and go eat some more rebellious people." The rats nodded their heads at him, and they all leaped on Malone covering his entire body. He mumbled some words and smoke appeared, Malone and the rats were gone.

CHAPTER TWENTY TWO
MY MOTHER

They all drove to Ron's house to talk. Diana was very upset during the drive home and Ron had to continue comforting her with his words. They all went to the basement to relax. Sheila and Zechariah sat on a sofa together, Ron and Diana on one, and Keith and Stacy on another. They all knew Diana was upset and did not want to say anything to make it worse, but they had to talk. Diana noticed everyone was looking at her.

"This has been another eventful day in the O'Neil family. Ron, you should write this movie and call it, The O'Neil Saga. Anyway, I do not believe my mother killed those two guys. Yes, they had horrible attitudes and thuggish ways and were probably involved in something suspicious. Anyone could have killed them. My mother did not do this, how could she have killed them both at the same time? Okay, yes she's had some martial arts training, but she is not a trained assassin."

"Diana, I read the full report on your Mom, with the training she has received over the years and her survival skills from the street, yes she could have killed them, easily." Zechariah said as he looked at her with compassion.

"All this seems like a nightmare. I have never seen so much blood and they were so young. This is crazy." Sheila said.

Diana heard enough and stood up.

"No, my Mother did not do this." She yelled.

Ron stood, hugged her, and they sat down. Zechariah kissed Sheila and walked away to make a phone call.

"Baby relax, I know all this is overwhelming for you, but we need to know exactly what and who we are dealing with."

Diana looked at Ron with irritation.

"I know this Ron, but don't talk to me like I am some child." Diana rolled her eyes at him and realized he was trying to protect her, but she was not ready to believe her Mom could be a killer.

"Diana, you know we are on your side, however, please consider all the facts. The two guys said some very disrespectful things toward us women, especially your mother. Mom went to the bathroom, the guys followed her, she came back from the bathroom with a spot of blood on her dress, and she lied about applying her makeup, we walked into the bathroom and both guys were dead. All this happened in a short amount of time." Stacy said.

Zechariah sat down and whispered to Sheila. They both shook their heads in disbelief.

"Zechariah, what's going on, do you know something?" Ron said.

"I made a call to a police officer I know in the precinct for that area. I asked discreet questions and he happened to be around that restaurant. No one reported anything unusual happening tonight. No crime or evidence at all." Zechariah looked at everyone.

The buzzer went off at the gate to Ron's house. Ice was at the gate in her Bentley. Ron got up and looked at the monitor and saw Ice. He could not believe this woman was here.

"Unbelievable, Diana your Mom is at the gate."

"Wow, Ron let her in, we need some answers." Diana said.

"Great, the mystery woman appears again. We all saw two dead bodies in the bathroom restaurant, two dead bodies disappeared, and now your Mom appears. She is a walking Houdini." Keith said.

Diana gave Keith a mean look and rolled her eyes at him, but she could not say anything because everything he said was correct.

Ron looked at Keith.

"Keith, do you mind letting Diana's Mom in please?"

Stacy gave Ron and Keith mean looks immediately but said nothing, and then gripped Keith's leg hard before he stood, to give him a message of, *do not get it twisted*. He looked at Stacy, smiled, and walked up the stairs. He opened the gate and Ice drove toward the house. She stepped out of the car wearing tennis shoes, short tight shorts, and a low-cut top with no bra on. Ice dressed this way purposely to irritate and tempt everyone. She walked with a playful bounce in her step and a smile on her face towards the front door because she knew how sexy and attractive she looked. It was always about seduction with Ice. Her tight shorts revealed the contour of her hips and butt and her breasts looked like they would pop out of her top, with visible erect nipple prints.

Keith opened the door, and he could not help but stare because his thoughts were lustful instantly about what he wanted to do to her, which caused him to have an erection.

"Damn!" He whispered as his eyes focused on her breasts and shorts.

"Hello Keith." Ice licked her lips and walked in and stopped, turned around and looked between his legs and then his face and whispered to him. "Your dick is hard baby and begging for my attention. Say it, and I will drop to my knees right now, spit on your dick, and suck every drop of cum out of it. Don't let Stacy see that hard-on I gave you." She winked at him and kept walking.

Keith was very embarrassed and repented of his thoughts as he adjusted himself. He closed the door before turning around and walked into the living room. Ice looked around the room and turned around to look at Keith.

"So, where is everyone Keith?" She spoke like she owned the house.

"We are downstairs, follow me."

"No, I know where the basement is, you follow me." She walked slower so he could lust over her body longer. When she reached the doorway to the basement, Ice stopped walking and bent over in front of Keith to pretend she was tying one of her shoes. Her shorts rose and exposed her butt cheeks revealing she was not wearing panties. While bent over she turned her head to look at Keith and rubbed between her butt cheeks slowly with her fingers. "I know you want to bury your face and dick between my legs and ass." She stood and turned to look at Keith and gave him a look of, *I know you want all this.*

"You are very twisted and foul. You may have Diana fooled but not me, and I know you killed those two guys in the restaurant. I don't know how you got rid of the bodies, but you killed them."

Ice stepped closer to Keith blew her breath in his face and whispered to him.

"You watch too many movies dear. However, soon my breath will smell like Stacy's pussy because her legs will be wrapped around my face. Then your hot wife will come home and kiss you in your mouth with my pussy scent on her lips and breath." She smiled at him, rubbed her nipples to make them more erect, and turned around to walk downstairs.

Keith had an image of kicking Ice in her back extremely hard and watching her fall down the stairs headfirst. It took God to prevent him from doing just that because he was beyond angry. He began calling on God as he walked downstairs to keep from possibly committing murder.

Ice walked downstairs with an arrogant attitude as she displayed her gorgeous figure. Her nipples stood at attention, her breasts looked ready to pop out, and the fabric of her shorts gripped her hips and butt tightly, revealing her profound sexiness.

When Diana saw how her mother was dressed, she was embarrassed and everyone else stared at Ice. Diana walked over and hugged her.

"Hi Mom," she hugged Ice and then whispered in her ear. "Why are you dressed so slutty?" Diana looked in her face and saw darkness in her eyes which caused her to step back slowly.

"Hello Diana, I am glad to see you as well." She gave her a fake smile and then walked to a sofa and sat down slowly, purposely sticking her butt out more than necessary just to sit down.

Sheila looked at Ice with disgust knowing the guys stared at her lustfully. Diana sat next to Ron who stared at Ice as well.

Keith walked over and sat next to Stacy, but she felt his anger and noticed the angry look on his face and so did everyone else.

"Keith, what's wrong baby?" She whispered to him.

"I will tell you later, but Diana's mother is the Devil." He whispered to her and then looked at Ice. He could no longer keep his thoughts to himself. "Diana, ask your mother why she killed those two guys at the restaurant?" His words were spoken with venom and he could care less at this point what anyone thought of what he said, even Ron.

"Keith, are you crazy?" Diana yelled and stared at him.

"This is why I had to come here tonight, to clear up some things. I do not want any of you to think negatively about me. My daughter means everything to me and what she thinks of me is important. We are all family and I care." She looked at everyone.

"You ain't my family," Keith waved his hand toward everyone else. "*This* is my family; I do not know you and do not want to. You have Diana deceived but not me," he stood and stared at Ice hatefully and pointed his finger at her. "You are evil, and I don't want to get to know you, ever. Stay away from me and my wife, or there's going to be some problems." His eyes were locked on Ice with an increased rage, and everyone knew it. He stepped to walk away and turned around to look at Stacy. "Let's go baby."

Diana knew something was wrong with her mother but what Keith said about her was disrespectful and it made her angry.

"Keith, you don't have to be so rude and mean. Give my Mom a chance to talk." Her words were cold.

Keith threw his hands up in the air.

"Fine, let the Devil speak." He walked back and sat next to Stacy and stared at Ice.

The tension in the room was building and Ice knew she needed to express herself quickly before this situation got out of hand.

"Keith, I am not the Devil. This is what happened tonight at the restaurant. When I walked out of the bathroom stall, those two thugs were standing there. They said some very nasty filthy things to me, and I tried to walk around them, but they grabbed me, pushed me back to the big stall, and locked the door. Then they grabbed my clothes and body and put their hands underneath my dress. I screamed for help, but no one came. I thought they were going to rape me, so instinctively I reacted and defended myself. It was not my intention to kill them, but they were strong and kept coming at me. In seconds they were on the floor dead, I was shocked. What was I supposed to do, let them rape me?" She lowered her head and began crying hard.

Diana sat next to Ice and hugged her as she cried. Ice looked at Diana with tears coming down her face.

"One of them turned me around to face the wall and then pushed my body against it. Then…they…pulled their

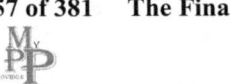

penises out and were trying to force themselves on me. One of them…pulled my dress…my dress up and the other was trying to pull my underwear down. No one came to help me." She began crying hysterically while looking down.

Diana held her closer and began crying as well thinking about what she would do if this happened to her. She looked at Keith with anger because of what he said about her mother before he even knew the truth.

"Keith, you were so wrong, so very wrong. You need to apologize to my mother for the hateful things you said about her, without knowing the truth." Tears flowed from Diana's eyes.

Keith looked at Diana like she lost it and was not about to apologize to her because he did not believe that fairy tale she just told. Stacy gave Keith a look of, *do the right thing*.

"Diana, what you experienced was horrible…"

"Zechariah," she interrupted him. "Thank you for your spirit of compassion. I know you mean well but please call me Ice; I prefer that."

"I will never call you that. Your name is Diana, just like your daughter. Do not allow the past to corrupt your future. My heart goes out to you concerning this extremely horrible event that happened to you. So, what happened to the bodies?"

"Good question, what happened to the bodies, Ice?" Keith gave her a look that said, *I do not believe a word you said*.

Stacy pinched Keith.

"Keith, please listen baby." She kissed him but did not believe her story either.

"No, I understand the doubt. I have made a few connections in my lifetime. So, I made a phone call to someone I know, and they got rid of the bodies and cleaned the scene." Ice knew only one person could have gotten rid of the bodies so quickly and thoroughly, Malone. She was not about to tell them that.

Keith stared at Ice and then stood up.

"It's a good story but I am not into fairy tales. I have heard enough, she is lying, and I am out," he turned to look at Stacy. "come on baby, I am tired of listening to the Devil for one night," he looked at Ice with cold eyes. "I meant what I said, stay away from me and my wife, and get yourself delivered."

"Keith, do you have to be…"

Stacy never finished her sentence because Keith gave her a look, she had seen many times before, she knew he was serious.

"Stacy, I said let's go." He held his hand out toward her.

Stacy felt he should not have said this in front of Ice, but she did agree with him and would always stand by his side. She grabbed his hand and they walked away, and Keith gave Ice a look that said, *do not cross me*. He nodded at Ron and he and Stacy walked up the stairs and left.

"Wow, Ron your friend is direct and cold." Ice said and looked at Diana for emotional backup.

"Mom, please forgive him and give him time. He will come around." Diana hugged her.

"Keith is direct but he's not cold. He trusts his instincts." Ron looked at Ice and thought, *and so do I,* but he was not going to say this to Ice because he knew Diana would verbally and emotionally attack him and he did not want this between them.

Ice knew they did not fully believe her story, so she wanted to have some fun before she left the house tonight. She leaned on Diana as she forced tears from her eyes.

"No matter how hard I try to walk in peace, people seem to attack me. How long do I have to keep praying and keep waiting for peace? Haven't I suffered enough?" Her tears continued to flow as she leaned back on the sofa holding Diana.

Ice spread her legs a little wider intentionally so everyone could get a better look. Her nipples were erect, and her shorts were so tight it revealed her camel toe, and she knew this.

Zechariah and Ron could not help but look at her breasts and between her legs and repent repeatedly. Diana was not aware of what was going on until she looked at a large mirror they had on the wall and saw the reflection of her mother and how she sat on the sofa. Diana saw the lustful looks Zechariah and Ron had on their face. This angered her instantly and she saw the angry look Sheila had on her face as well, knowing her husband and Ron stared at Ice directly and lustfully. Diana leaned toward Ice.

"Mom, close your legs please." She whispered to her.

Ice heard Diana but waited a few seconds until she complied, giving everyone one last look between her legs.

"I am so sorry about all this. I need to go home and pray for comfort and peace. Diana, where is the bathroom? I would like to rinse my face before leaving."

Diana pointed to the bathroom and Ice arched her back as she stood, making sure her shorts exposed her butt. When she walked away her butt cheeks were on display and she loved it because all eyes were on her. Inwardly she laughed with each step while making her butt shake.

Diana was embarrassed and shook her head in disgust when she looked at her Mom walk away shaking her butt unnecessarily and revealing so much of herself. She and Sheila saw Ron and Zechariah's eyes locked on her every step.

The moment Ice closed the bathroom door, she put her hand over her mouth and burst out laughing.

"That was so much fun causing Ron and Zachariah to lust so hard as they stared between my legs and my ass. My daughter and Sheila hated every second of it, but I know Ron and Zechariah desired to fuck me badly. If I could get my hands on Zechariah, the things I would do to that man. Ron could get this hot ass of mine too. I love my sweet daughter, but I know she isn't fucking him right." She laughed quietly.

Diana looked at Ron, snapped her finger to get his attention, and then stood and stared at him.

"Ron, your eyes were lustfully locked on my Mother's body, and don't deny it because I saw you. You were lusting over my Mother. How disgusting can you be? You want a MILF now? So very disgusting. You should be ashamed of yourself." She gave him a disgusted look.

"Diana, what is a MILF?" Sheila said.

Zechariah lightly touched Sheila's arm.

"I will tell you later baby."

"No, I want to know now, what is it?"

Ron tried hard not to, but he laughed and then stopped when he saw the look on Diana's face.

"Mrs. O'Neil, your son is being disrespectful and disgusting right now. A MILF stands for, Mothers…I…Like…to…Fu…" she waved her hand in the air. "You know the rest of that word. I am so embarrassed by my Mother. Oh my God, Ron." She stared at him with more disgust.

"Oh, my goodness. Ron, have you lost your mind?" Sheila yelled and stared at him.

"Mom, you and Diana are making too much out of this, and she is…"

He stopped talking when Ice walked out of the bathroom and her shorts still revealed her camel toe and butt cheeks. She stood next to Diana.

"I thank all of you for listening to me. I am going home to pray. Diana, give me a hug baby before I go, please."

When Diana hugged Ice, Sheila leaned closer to Zechariah and whispered in his ear.

"If you hug her, there will be a problem in our house." She kissed him, smiled, and then gave him a serious look.

Ice held her arms out toward Ron for a hug and then smiled at him. Diana gave Ron a look of, *don't you dare* and looked at Ice with contempt.

"They are tired, time to go Mom."

"Bye Ron, Sheila, and Zechariah." She hugged and kissed Diana on the cheek and then walked up the stairs slowly making sure they all got one last look at her round derriere. She laughed when she walked out of the house.

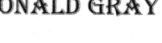

Zechariah and Ron tried hard not to look at Ice when she walked away but they could not help it. This woman was gorgeous from top to bottom. They looked at her and quickly looked away.

Diana stepped in front of Ron and put her hands on her hips.

"Ron, are you still lusting over my Mom? Had to get one last lustful look, unbelievable." She shook her head and walked over to Zechariah and hugged him and whispered in his ear.

"You were lusting over my Mom and Mrs. O'Neil is angry with you. You are in trouble." She kissed his cheek.

Zechariah hugged Diana and gave Ron a salute walked toward Sheila and touched her hand. Sheila looked at Zechariah and then at Ron.

"Pray hard tonight son." When she and Zechariah walked up the stairs, she looked at him. "We will be doing some serious praying tonight, husband." They walked out of the house.

Sheila was not upset with Zachariah because she understood, men will be men and Diana's mother is gorgeous. However, she had to play the role. It keeps men on their toes. Her mindset was, *so what, he looked at a good-looking woman displaying her body. But I am his wife, and we are going home together, and I will be the one making love to him.*

Diana stared at Ron waiting for him to apologize for his disrespectful ways, but he had this silly grin on his face which only irritated her more.

"So, you have nothing to say? What's wrong Ron, I do not wear my shorts tight enough for you now? You want my butt cheeks hanging out when I walk? She walked away from him and up the stairs.

Ron stared at Diana and her every step turned him on. He knew she was upset with him, but he wanted to play.

"No, I don't want your butt cheeks exposed in public Diana. However, you are beautiful, and your body is all that. Yes, in the house, I want to see your butt cheeks, camel toe, and nipple print. And wear some crotchless panties as well." He laughed.

Diana stopped walking, gave Ron a mean look, and then kept walking. He walked behind her and wrapped his arms around Diana and kissed her neck.

"I love you baby." He kissed her neck again and pressed his body into hers so she could feel his erection.

Diana pushed him away and ran up the stairs to get away from him. She made it to the living room when Ron caught her, picked her up, and put her on the sofa. He lay next to her and started kissing her and moved his hand up her dress.

"Your skin is so soft," he bit her neck and sucked on it. "don't fight the feeling baby." He laughed and slid his hand between her legs.

"Stop it Ron, I am not playing with you. Get your hands off me. You got a hard-on from lusting over my mother, not me. You are disgusting." She squirmed hard trying to get away.

Ron continued sucking her neck and moved his hand inside her panties and caressed her wetness then slid his finger inside Diana. He fingered her slowly while talking dirty to her.

Diana tried to resist but her husband knew her body too well and she was wet and close to climax. Ron expertly caressed all her spots with his finger.

"Ahhhhhh, Ron I'm cummming baby." She leaned her head back. He continued fingering Diana while she climaxed and then removed his pants and underwear and slid inside her.

Diana loved her husband's slow thrusting no matter what, so she held on to him tightly, enjoyed every second of this pleasure, and wanted more. She knew Ron was close, but she wanted to be in their bedroom on the bed. So, she stopped him.

"Ron, let's go to the bedroom so we can make love in bed." She kissed him passionately.

"No, we can stay here, and you can let me finish what I started, and then you can go to bed and go to sleep if you want. But right now, it's dick stroke time." He pushed Diana's legs back and held her ankles and continued thrusting while saying nasty things to her as he increased his pace.

"Ohhhhh Ron, your dick feels so good and I know you want to cum now but please stop and take me to the bedroom so we can make love, please baby. I need it."

Ron did not want to stop but he pulled out of his wife and then picked her up and carried her to their bedroom and they made love for the next two hours. Diana cried as they made love because of the connection and love between them. They climaxed at the same time.

CHAPTER TWENTY THREE
THE RIGHT TOUCH

After Ice left Ron and Diana's house, she knew there were things she should not have said or done, but it was too late for that now. Her heart desired to have a relationship with her daughter, and no one was going to stand in her way. She had a lot on her mind and needed some peace and had no desire to deal with Malone, so she decided to stay at the Sheraton Hotel in Silver Spring, MD. When Ice drove in front of the hotel in her Bentley and stepped out of the car, the men and women working valet stared at her and wanted to park her car just to get a closer look at this beautiful woman. Ice handed her keys to one of the valets and walked inside knowing all eyes were on her. Her gorgeous face and tight shorts revealed her curvaceous body just the way she liked. One young guy stopped walking and stared at her.

"Wait, please stop walking for one minute, damn."

Ice stopped walking and looked at this handsome well-dressed young man.

"Lady you are so fine. I know you have heard all the games. True story, I played the lottery two weeks ago, the DC Keno, and won one million dollars. After taxes, six hundred thousand dollars in the bank. I am still celebrating, and I got ten thousand cash in my pocket right now. No disrespect, no games, direct and to the point like you women say you want. So, help me celebrate. I would lick your entire body, two times. Eat your booty like groceries, lick wine off you, and dick stroke you any way you like. I am not playing." He stared at her and smiled.

Ice could not help but smile and then gave him a serious look.

"You don't know me, and you want to put your mouth on my body," Ice shook her head. "Thank you for the compliment and congratulations on your win, but I am very busy right now, and take my word for it, you don't have enough money baby." She waved him off and walked to the front desk.

He stared at this gorgeous woman and walked away with a look of disappointment on his face.

"She missed out, I would have paid serious money to taste that, licked the pussy, licked the ass, and fucked her in several positions, repeatedly. Dick and balls slapping, I am a freak like that." He walked away irritated.

After checking in Ice walked to her room. She looked around and laid on the bed to relax and thought about Keith and how he stood up to her which she liked because it revealed he had heart. This turned her on mentally and sexually and so did Stacy. Ice felt the fire in Stacy along with her deep inner struggles concerning her suppressed desires for women. Tears began to run down Ice's face because she felt her struggles of wanting to be spiritually clean and walk in peace. There was also the desire to walk selfishly and cause others pain if they got in her way. Ice knew she needed God in her life completely but how could she surrender to someone who allowed so much suffering to transpire in her life? How could she let go and fully trust God, who in her mind, let her down so many times, how?

Ice was very frustrated, and she knew the one person to call to help her relax. She got her cell phone and called Ray.

"Hi baby, I am at the Sheraton Hotel in Silver Spring because I needed to think. Can I come over and get a hug and spend the night? Thank you...I will see you soon." She smiled and hung up the phone.

Ice felt better instantly. She took a quick shower, put her clothes back on, walked out to her awaiting Bentley, and drove away. She did a lot of thinking while driving to Ray's house and could not wait to be in his arms. She pulled into his driveway, got out, and rang his doorbell. Ray answered the door with no shoes or socks on, just dress slacks and a silk T-shirt.

"Ice, come on in."

She stepped in, closed the door, and immediately wrapped her arms around Ray, and he hugged her back. For the next three minutes, Ray held her and said nothing because he knew she had a lot on her mind, and this was what was needed. It was impossible for him to not notice how incredible she looked in her low-cut top with no bra on revealing her full breasts, nipples, and tight shorts. He became aroused.

Being in Ray's arms touched her emotionally and she wanted them to remain this close for years to come, however, Ice felt his growing erection pressed against her body. She looked up at him.

"I have missed you Ray."

"The feeling is mutual, and I am trying to stay focused, but you smell so good, your body is on display and you are wearing those shorts, you are a gorgeous woman." He placed his hands on her hips.

Ice laughed because she thought about what the young guy said and how he reacted as she walked into the hotel. No woman ever tells it all.

"You do know how to make me laugh and thank you. Can we go to your room and lay down and talk for a while?"

"Absolutely!" He turned to walk away.

The moment Ice saw his wide thick muscular back, a playful spirit came over her. She hopped on his back and kissed his neck.

"It has been a long time since I had a back ride. Come on Ray, take me for a ride?" She laughed and held on tightly.

Ray laughed and walked to his bedroom feeling good that he was able to help Ice smile and be playful. When he got to his bed he turned around and sat down, so Ice could easily fall back safely. She did and giggled like a young girl because she had another playful and sexual thought. Ice removed her clothes quickly and sat up to look at Ray.

"Ray, will you get naked please, and lay down with me on your back?"

"What man in his right mind would say no to that request." He removed his clothes and placed them in a chair and laid on his back.

Ice smiled and moved her body over his and straddled his face.

"I want to have multiple orgasms while I am grinding my pussy and ass all over your face."

Ray tilted his head up so she could hear him speak.

"My kind of woman." He put both hands on her butt and began moving his head up and down as his lips and tongue moved slowly across her wetness.

If anyone walked by Ray's house, they probably heard Ice's screams of passion as Ray pleased her and this continued until Ice climaxed three times and screamed Ray's name loudly and repeatedly. What started as playful sex, turned into so much more. After laying on the bed to relax for a while, Ice went to the kitchen and brought back a bottle of honey. She crawled on the bed with the honey in her hand.

"I have to ask, what are you going to do with that? I am not into all that freaky stuff." He gave Ice a half-serious and playful look.

"Relax, you are in wonderful caring hands and you will like everything I do." She kissed him.

Ray lay on his back and Ice licked and sucked his penis until he was fully erect and then put small drops of honey on his lower abdomen, balls, and penis. Her tongue spread it all over his penis with each slow lick until she deep-throated it.

Ray felt her throat muscles tighten on his penis and knew it would not be long before he exploded in her mouth.

Ice knew he was close, so she grabbed his penis firmly and sucked the tip. She applied pressure with her hand, slowly eased up, sucked the tip, and deep-throated it repeatedly, then held it in her mouth.

"Ahhhhhh, damn," Ray exploded hard in Ice's mouth, but she never stopped sucking. His body jerked because he was cumming so hard. "ahhhhh, damn, damn. Let it go, you are trying to kill me, let my dick go."

Ice laughed on the inside, but never stopped sucking until she sucked every drop, and his body still jerked from her great oral skills. She finally let Ray's penis slide out of her mouth and moved her body up and kissed him.

"Hi baby." She gave him a playful mischievous smile.

Ray was breathing heavily as he stared at her and was trying to get his body to relax but this woman had him in total sexual euphoria.

"Hi baby! Is that all you can say after trying to give me a heart attack? Wow, oh my goodness, damn that was good, so good. I do not think I have ever cum like that in my life. My heart is racing, oh my goodness. You tried to kill me."

"Relax baby," she rubbed his chest gently. "You will be fine and please stop saying, I tried to kill you because I would never do that. So, did I please you darling?" She gave him an innocent look.

Ray looked at Ice like she lost it.

"Are you kidding me? If you tried to make a point, I got it, and you are incredible, damn you are good."

"Thank you sir." Ice kissed him and looked at the man she had fallen for in such a short time. She kissed him passionately and moved her hand to his penis and caressed it.

"Stop, don't touch my dick. Don't touch it." He moved her hand away.

Ice laughed and kissed him.

"Is something wrong Ray? Are you alright? She moved her hands towards his penis again as she continued to passionately kiss him until her hands caressed the inside of his thighs. "Am I too much for you?" She spoke with a playful attitude.

"You can be smart mouth and say whatever you want but I do remember how you squirmed and pushed my face away from between your legs and backed away from me, quickly." He kissed her.

"Oh that, Well I had a leg cramp at that moment." She smiled at him.

"Okay, so you tell it." He grabbed her and they began wrestling playfully on the bed.

CHAPTER TWENTY FOUR
HOLD ON

Rick and Cynthia were in Georgetown shopping. Rick wore casual dress shoes, dress pants, and a long-sleeved dress shirt that revealed the contours of his muscular physique. Cynthia wore Christian Louboutin shoes, tight jeans, and a top. Rick carried all the shopping bags as they walked toward the car.

"This is a typical shopping scene for a man and woman. There are six shopping bags in my hand but only one bag has something in it that belongs to me, and I am carrying all the bags! Why is that?"

"Baby, you know how it goes. I give you what you want, you give me what I want, and we are both happy. Don't go against the grain, keep carrying the bags." She walked in front of Rick to use her body to flirt with him. "Do you like what you see, bag carrier?" She turned her head and looked back at him while shaking her butt as she walked.

Rick loved Cynthia deeply and was very satisfied with what they shared as husband and wife. Yes, she was extremely attractive, but it was much more about her that he loved. She teased him about their twenty-one-year age difference at times, but Rick was confident within himself and their tight bond.

"Yes, I like what I see but I am more attracted to your heart and spirit." He stepped quickly to walk beside her and put his arm around her waist and kissed her lips.

They stopped walking and Cynthia looked into his eyes.

"I thank God for allowing us to get married and continue to grow in friendship day by day, and I love you being so nasty in bed." She laughed and kissed him passionately.

Two well-dressed African American young guys walked past them and one of them shook his head as he looked at Cynthia's body.

"Damn, look at the body on that lady, hips, and ass for days. Pretty in the face with tight jeans on showing all that ass." He and his friend laughed but kept walking.

Rick stopped kissing Cynthia when he heard what the guy said and was about to say something to him for being so disrespectful, but Cynthia pulled his arm.

"Baby just ignore the comment because we are too mature to allow silly comments to cause us to miss our blessings."

"True and I am getting hungry, so let's go eat after we put the bags in the car, with all, your things in them."

"You are such a good husband." She winked and kissed him.

They talked, laughed, and flirted with each other while walking to the car. They reached the car and Rick put the bags in the trunk then picked Cynthia up playfully from the front and she wrapped her legs around his waist and began passionately kissing him.

A black van with tinted windows slowly approached them, and suddenly four men with masks jumped out of the van pointing guns at them. Two of them hit Rick in his neck and head with their guns and Rick fell to the ground but he was still conscious.

Cynthia screamed.

"Rick, are you okay?" She yelled as she looked down at him.

Another masked man slapped Cynthia hard, and she fell to the ground and screamed.

"Stop all that stupid screaming and get your hips in the van. Now move your ass." He said sternly and pointed his gun at them and to the van.

One man patted them down and found their cell phones and stomped them on the ground. Two men helped Rick up and threw him in the van roughly and another man easily picked Cynthia up and put her on his shoulders and rubbed her hips as he put her in the van. The van door was closed, and all four men got in and the van drove away quickly. Two men sat upfront and three were in the back. The man who put Cynthia in the van leaned forward and rubbed her leg and breast. Rick hit him twice in the face and knocked him out and the other two jumped on Rick and began beating him with their guns. Cynthia yelled for them to stop and she smacked one of them. He smacked her back and Cynthia fell back against the van wall. The two men beat Rick unconscious and then pulled Cynthia by her legs across the van floor unsnapped her jeans and unzipped them. They tried to pull her jeans down, but she held on to them tightly, kicking, and squirming hard. They managed to pull her jeans down below her hips revealing her thong underwear and butt as she continued to squirm.

"Stop, you sick rapist!" She screamed at them and continued kicking.

"Shut up and stop all that stupid screaming. Girl, you got thick thighs and ass with these sexy tight panties on. We do not have to wait, let's run a train on this fine-ass woman right now. Snatch off her tight jeans and panties, and we can take turns fucking her. Damn, she got ass." One of the men said with a gravelly voice as he rubbed her hips and butt.

The men in the back laughed and the driver of the van turned his head to look back at them.

"Leave sweet hips alone. We have business and I am not letting you perverts mess up this deal. If you want some ass, when we are done, get a prostitute. Until then, hands-off unless you want to catch a bullet to the brain." He turned his head back around and continued to drive.

The guys in the back stared at the driver and then leaned away from Cynthia.

Cynthia pulled her jeans up quickly, snapped them, and exhaled. She felt bad for Rick and worried about him because she had no idea how hurt he was because he was unconscious. She was afraid but had to remain strong for herself and Rick, but she wanted answers.

"What is going on and why did you idiots kidnap us? You all made a mistake, we are not rich, and you kidnapped the wrong people, stupid fools. All of you are a bunch of sick rapists riding around in a van kidnapping people. If you want pussy that badly, go buy some. There are plenty of women out here selling ass. Stupid fools. I hope you catch a disease!" She yelled at them.

One of the men put his gun against Cynthia's head.

"You got a smart mouth. I do not care what the driver said, if you call us fools, rapists, and idiots one more time, I will jam this gun in your mouth, breaking all your front teeth. And still make you suck our dicks with bloody gums and all, now sit your ass back and shut up." He tapped her in the head with his gun.

Cynthia only saw his eyes because of the mask, but she saw the evil in them, and this was enough for her to know he was serious. She leaned against the van wall and began praying to herself.

The man who Rick hit and knocked out woke up during the ride and he stared at Rick thinking, *when this is over, I am stabbing you repeatedly.* An hour later the van drove into a large dark warehouse and stopped. The warehouse had a small office in the corner, several old sofas in different places, and a large flat-screen TV on a stand. Rick finally woke up and he was in great pain and dizzy, but he had to remain focused to allow all his years of being a detective to kick in. His lip was busted, and he knew he had a few broken ribs from the men beating him. Thank God he was in great physical shape to withstand such a beating. Cynthia saw his eyes blinking and knew he was awake. She hugged him tightly, and Rick groaned in pain.

"Rick, I am sorry baby, are you alright?" She had to hold back her tears because she loved him so much but did not want to give these men the satisfaction of getting the best of her.

The five guys got out of the van with their masks on and guns in their hands and pointed them at Rick and Cynthia. They put handcuffs on them and made them sit on one of the sofas. The largest of the five men turned the lights on in the warehouse and then approached Rick and tapped him on the head with his gun.

"It's knowledge time for you two. I talk, you obey. If not Rick, you get to watch my men run a train on your beautiful sexy young wife Cynthia. These men will never get a woman as fine as your wife, so you know how nasty they will be with her."

"What do you want and how do you know our names?"

The man tapped Rick on the head again with his gun.

"Wrong Rick, you don't talk unless I say so. Last warning Detective Rick, we talk, you obey, and your wife does not get banged out. At least, not now anyway, but she will get it later, as fat as that ass is. Oh, we all got to get some of that." He looked at his men and they all laughed. "You know the saying Rick, it ain't no fun, unless we all get some," he and his men laughed hard. "Now Rick, back to the business at hand. I know everything about you Detective Rick because we have been watching you for some time. You were responsible for getting some associates of mine life sentences in federal prison. In doing so you have some valuable information pertaining to these individuals that I now want. You do not even know what you have but I do. This information is worth over one hundred million dollars and you are going to get it for me, plain and simple."

"I have no idea what you are talking about. I have no information worth that type of money. You have the wrong man. My detective days have been over years ago and I sent a lot of evil people to prison a long time ago. I can't help you." Rick looked into his eyes to learn all he could through his mask.

The leader tapped Rick on the head again with his gun.

"Wrong Rick, you do have what I want. I am going to mention one name to you, Victor Augular, the world's biggest drug lord. Now, do you know Rick?"

Things begin to make sense to Rick. It was rumored years ago that Victor Augular had millions of dollars stashed away in secret accounts across the country. The information on the locations of these accounts was on flash drives that no one seemed to have, and they were never located. Rick was thinking, *could I have these flash drives somewhere in one of my many boxes of files in storage? And if so, how would these people know about it now after all these years?* Even so, he needed to play dumb to give him more time to figure a way out of this mess.

"Of course, I know who Victor Augular was, but he is dead, and I was one of the many detectives on that case. We are talking about hundreds of people from various departments involved in bringing him down. Local police, DEA, FBI, IRS, Treasury Department, and many more. We are talking about years of work in his case. Why me? I was only a local detective at that time. I never had any access to secret files or a high-security clearance. Again, you have the wrong man." Rick stared at him.

The leader stared at Rick and then shook his head and looked at Cynthia and then looked at Rick again.

"I thought you loved your sexy wife, but you want to play games with me. Okay Rick, we can play games. I came prepared," he looked around the warehouse. "Three Legs," he yelled. "Three Legs come over here."

A large heavy-set African American man walked out of the office with a limp. He stared at everyone and then walked toward them. He was six feet ten, three-hundred-eighty pounds. He was fat but very muscular as well. He wore black boots and blue jeans overalls. The leader pointed to him.

"This man helps people with their memory. We call him, *Three Legs,* and you about to find out why," he looked at Three Legs. "Three Legs, show Rick and his sexy young fat ass wife, why they call you, Three Legs." He looked at Cynthia and smiled.

"No problem boss." He walked closer to Cynthia and stared at her and then unsnapped his coveralls and they fell to his feet, showing his nakedness and the largest penis anyone had ever seen. He looked at Cynthia as he stroked himself and now held his fully erect sixteen-inch hugely thick penis in his hand. He pointed at Cynthia. "Are you ready for all sixteen inches of my large penis, sexy lady?" He smiled revealing his yellow-stained crooked teeth while stroking his penis.

Cynthia looked at this man with horror and wanted to run. She had her experiences with well-endowed men before, but this guy was massive, what you would call a horse dick. He would destroy her vagina and kill her in the process of trying to insert that thing inside her.

"Oh, my Lord Jesus, help me. You are not getting anywhere near me with that thing. You are deformed." Her insides shook because she was so afraid, and tears began flowing down her face and she looked over at Rick pleading with her eyes for him not to allow this to happen to her.

The men laughed, and the leader tapped Rick on the head again with his gun.

"Three Legs is going to help you Rick with your memory. This is what is about to happen. We are going to strip the clothes off your hot wife, bend her over one of these sofas, and tie her down. Then, Three Legs over here is going to begin inserting his third leg inside your wife. All sixteen horse dick inches, not a pretty sight Rick. Lots of screaming and pain." He smiled at him.

Rick did not want to think about this freak of a man violating his wife, but he did not know the exact location of the flash drive either. He stared at the leader.

"You are one sick twisted evil bastard. If you touch my wife in any way, there is nowhere in this world where you could hide, and I do not find you. I will hunt you down to the end of the earth. What you are asking for is impossible. I have collected years of files, how am I supposed to know what is what? I am talking about hundreds of thousands of pages and various disks. There is no way I could know what is on all those pages and disks at this point. You are asking for the impossible." Rick yelled at the leader.

"I am disappointed in you Rick. I thought you were a smart man, and you loved your wife. I guess she does not mean that much to you. Okay, it's playtime." He looked at his men and Three Legs. "Strip the wife, and Three Legs, get your oil."

Two of his men grabbed Cynthia from the sofa and Rick tried to intervene but one of the men hit him in the chest with his gun and pushed him back on the sofa pointing the gun at him. Cynthia fought the men as hard as she could. Kicking and screaming but it did no good. They took the handcuffs off and removed her clothes, bent her over a sofa, and tied her down with handcuffs. Cynthia looked at Rick the entire time while kicking and screaming.

"Rick, help me please Rick. Do not let them do this to me. Oh God please help me, Rick help me. He will kill me, Rick." She screamed and cried hysterically.

Three Legs got a bottle of oil from his jean pocket and put some on his penis and began stroking it and it grew even bigger. He walked over to Cynthia and stood behind her. He tapped the tip of his penis on her butt.

"You are a fine-looking woman, and your butt looks so good. You got one of them, eat the booty like groceries butt, but I ain't into licking no butt, I am Three Legs. However, for you, I think I would lick it. Too bad I got to mess you up." He laughed, leaned forward, and licked Cynthia's butt slowly with his big tongue.

Cynthia's body jerked when she felt Three Legs' tongue on her body, it was extremely repulsive to her. She was sweating and felt like she was going to have a heart attack because her heart was beating so fast, and her entire body shook because she was terrified. She would rather get shot in the head than allow this man to put his monster size penis in her.

"Rickkkkkkk." She screamed with every ounce of energy left in her.

This very sight made Rick feel like he was about to throw up.

"Wait, just wait," he yelled. "I have some information that might help you but I'm not sure. Please stop." He yelled again.

The leader waved his hand at Three Legs to stop. He frowned and rubbed Cynthia's butt and then stepped back and held his penis in his hand.

"A miracle, your memory came back. Talk and make it quick Rick." The leader said.

"I have a storage room that has my old computers and many boxes of paperwork and files in it. As God is my witness, I have no idea what is written on those pages and it would take months to go through all that stuff anyway." His eyes pleaded with this man for mercy.

"Good Mr. Rick. Allow me to fill in the blanks. On your computer is a file marked Augular, but it is spelled backward. That file is encrypted but do not worry about that. In that encrypted file is another encrypted file with the location of a safe deposit box. That box has a flash drive with encrypted files as well. Those files have the locations of Victor Augular's secret account locations. Now, all I need from you is the location of your storage bin." He smiled at Rick.

Rick shook his head and told the leader the location. The location was a two-hour, one-way drive from where they were now, but Rick did not know this.

"May God have mercy on your soul because when this is over, I will not." Rick's eyes were full of hate.

The leader smiled and smacked Rick hard busting his lip even more.

"Shut up before I let Three Legs have another taste of your big butt wife. This is the situation, three of my men and Three Legs will remain here. My other man and I will go to the address you gave me. If it is the wrong address, I will call my men and Three Legs will do his thing to your wife," he tapped his gun on top of Rick's head. "and he might do you as well. He does not care; he is sick and freaky like that." He smacked Rick again and laughed.

Three Legs looked at Rick and smiled revealing his crooked yellow stained teeth.

Rick's lip was bleeding badly but this was the least of his concerns.

"Will you cover up my wife please before you go?" He looked at the leader.

He looked at Rick and then walked over to Cynthia and caressed her hips, butt, and breast, and then snatched a dirty old sheet off one of the sofas and put it over Cynthia. He smiled and kissed her hard on the lips.

"Very nice."

Cynthia spat at him twice and the second time it would have landed on his leg, but the leader moved his leg quickly.

"You nasty female dog. Save some of that spit." He smiled at her and then looked at Rick.

"Your wife has fire in her and she is absolutely beautiful Rick, curves for days and soft lips. However, I changed my mind Rick, since she spat at me twice, I am going to, as the young people say, tap that ass good when I get back. And then my men will run a train on her." He and his men laughed hard, and he turned to walk away but stopped and looked at his men and then Rick. "Rick, your wife hurt my feelings, I do not like being spit on, and since she was a rude nasty mouth slut and spat at me twice, when I get back, I am going to watch each of my men put dick in her mouth and shoot cum down her throat. And in case she gets any stupid ideas like biting the dick, I will be holding my razor to your throat while she is getting faced fucked, repeatedly. She bites the dick, I cut your throat and she will watch you bleed to death, real fast. Simple Rick, your big butt pretty wife gets gang fucked, sucks dicks, and swallows cum and you both live." He looked at his men and they all laughed. Then he and the other man got in the van and drove out of the warehouse.

Rick looked over at Cynthia.

"Hold on baby, just pray and hold on. I love you."

"I love you too Rick, God help us." Her tears flowed down her cheek and she prayed to herself harder than she had in life.

Occasionally each of the men walked over to Cynthia and spoke nasty derogatory things to her and rubbed her body. This was done to create more fear in her and because they could.

Rick prayed equally as hard to himself. At the same time, he felt rage toward the men, knowing if the opportunity presented itself, he would kill them all, with no hesitation.

CHAPTER TWENTY FIVE

HELP

Sheila and Zechariah were home listening to music and relaxing. Early that day Rick and Zechariah talked, and Rick mentioned he and Cynthia were going shopping and invited Zechariah and Sheila to join them for lunch in Georgetown.

Rick told Zechariah he would call him with the name of the restaurant where they were, but Zechariah never received a call, and his spirit was not at peace for some reason. He called Rick several times but there was no answer which made him more uncomfortable. Sheila felt his disturbed spirit and asked what was going on, so he told her, and her spirit felt uncomfortable immediately as well. Sheila went to her bedroom to pray, and Zechariah called Keith and Ron and explained what was going on. Keith called Rick and Cynthia several times but no answer. They all knew something was wrong, so Keith called the *Young Wolves*. Ron, Keith, and six of the *Young Wolves* arrived at Zechariah's house in a stretch Benz limo and they all wore suits. The *Young Wolves* always made Sheila nervous because she knew what they were capable of and knew there would be serious trouble.

Ron had his attorney contact Rick's car dealership to track it. Sheila hugged Zechariah and kissed him and then hugged Ron and Keith and told them to be careful. Ron, Keith, Zechariah, and the *Young Wolves* got in the limo and drove to the location of the car.

Rick sat on the sofa in pain, deep thought, and prayer. Suddenly he remembered the tracking device that was put in the watch he wore. He needed to push the button on the side of his watch without being seen, this activated a signal that revealed his location. Ron and Keith knew of this device and this signal would be seen on their cell phones as well because it was programmed that way. Rick watched the men carefully as he pushed the button on his watch. He sighed heavily knowing help would come, but would it come in time?

The limo reached the location of Rick's car. Ron, Keith, Zechariah, and the *Young Wolves* got out to look at it.

"Something is wrong, I can feel it." Ron said.

Zechariah looked around the place and noticed a camera on the corner of a building and the camera had a clear view of Rick's car. He pointed to the camera, and they all looked at it. The *Young Wolves* looked at Keith and he nodded his head at them. They all walked inside the building and Ron offered the head of security five hundred dollars to view the tape, but the guard said no. The *Young Wolves* unbuttoned their jackets revealing two shoulder holsters; the guard had an instant change of heart and took the five hundred dollars. They all watched the tape and it showed Rick and Cynthia being kidnapped the guard wanted to call the police, but Ron paid him another five hundred dollars not to. They walked back to the limo and stood next to it.

"Lord have mercy, who and why would anyone kidnap Rick and Cynthia." Ron said.

"I don't know partner but remember, Rick was a detective for years and he helped put a lot of people in prison. This had to be something from his past that has reached out to him." Keith said.

"Well, be that as it may, we have to find them and get them back. No matter what." Zechariah said as he looked at everyone.

"True that my brother. So how do we handle this?" Ron said.

Suddenly Ron and Keith's phones beeped, and they looked at their phones at the same time and smiled because they both knew what it was.

"Great, this signal is from the tracking device in Rick's watch. Hopefully, Rick, Cynthia, and his watch will all be in the same place. Let's ride." Ron looked at them and stepped forward.

"Wait," Keith held his arm out in front of Ron. "We have no idea what we are about to walk into." Keith looked at Ron.

"I was about to mention that. You can't win a battle if you don't know your enemy and its sources." Zechariah said with years of wisdom.

Ron gave Zechariah a condescending look, but he knew he was right, as usual.

"Both of you are right, we need to think about this for a minute," he stared out into space and then shook his head. "One name just came to me, but it makes no sense, Victor Augular." Ron said as he stared out into space.

"Victor Augular, that man is dead, thank God. However, it does make more sense now. Rick was the lead investigator in that case, along with many others. Victor Augular was the biggest drug lord the world has ever known, due to the help of the evil Mr. Bones. You don't get that big without having some friends in powerful political places across the globe." Keith said.

"Very true, this could be some associates of Victor's that reached out to Rick for some reason. You can believe it is not just about revenge, this must be about money and a lot of it." Zechariah said as he looked at everyone.

"Keith, we are not the same anymore and we can't operate in that old spirit," Ron stared at Keith and spoke with a calm voice. "Whoever is behind this is about money and power and killing people in the process means nothing to them. I know time is not on our side and calling the police would make matters worse. God will always be our protector, but God gives us wisdom. We would need an army to help us with this because we don't know what is on the other side of that door." Ron said with much concern in his voice.

"Then, an army it is," Keith stepped away and got his cell phone out and made a call. His conversation was brief, and he put his phone away and walked over to them. "Help is on the way, and they will be here in thirty minutes, suited and ready."

Ron gave Keith that, what did you do look.

"Keith, who did you call?" Zechariah said.

"Good question, who did you call Keith?" Ron said.

Keith smiled and then looked at the *Young Wolves* and one of them stepped closer to Ron.

"He called some of our friends." He spoke with no real expression on his face and full of confidence.

Thirty minutes later, four black vans with blacked-out windows drove up with the words, Private Security, written on the side. Seven heavily armed Latino men dressed in all black stepped out of each van, and then a black Bentley Mulsanne drove up next to the vans. Two well-dressed Latino men stepped out and walked over to Keith. One extended his hand to him, and they shook hands and he looked at the men dressed in black and looked at Keith again.

"Mr. Keith Washington," he pointed to the men in black. "will this be enough? More would not be a problem." He stared at Keith.

"Mr. Mateo, once again I thank you. You have come through like you always do."

"For sure. You and I have history my friend and you would do the same for me."

"No question." Keith stared at him.

"Take care my friend and be careful." He extended his hand to Keith.

"I will." They shook hands.

The two Latino men walked back to the car and it drove away.

"Keith, twenty-eight heavily armed men in thirty minutes, and who is Mr. Mateo?" Ron said.

"I will tell you about him later, now is not the time. Zechariah and Ron let's go find Rick and Cynthia," Keith waved at the guards in black. "Follow us."

Ron, Keith, Zechariah, and the *Young Wolves* got in the limo and the guards got in the vans and they all drove away.

Rick and Cynthia continued to silently pray since the two kidnappers left. The other three stuck their tongues out at Cynthia making disrespectful gestures but they never took their masks off. Cynthia was extremely uncomfortable bent over and tied down to the sofa. Her constant pleading to the kidnappers finally paid off and they allowed her to sit on the sofa next to Rick with handcuffs on. She was naked but a sheet covered her body. Rick was in excruciating pain but managed not to pass out because he was overly concerned about Cynthia. Three Legs walked around the warehouse with his coveralls pulled up talking to himself. Occasionally he stepped close to Cynthia and pulled his penis out and began stroking it. He did this once and the other kidnappers laughed, this made Cynthia angry, so she spat on Three Legs. He slapped her so hard she fell off the sofa. They put her back on the sofa and covered her body slowly with the sheet to look at her nakedness longer and her entire face was red and swollen. She looked at the kidnappers with contempt and defiance, but her heart was very afraid. Cynthia leaned on Rick for emotional support, and she continued to pray. Rick wanted to do so much to protect his wife, but he could not, and this made him feel helpless. He would sacrifice his life to protect his wife.

The other two kidnappers retrieved the information from Rick's storage and were on their way back to the warehouse. All the files were decrypted, and they had the locations of Victor Augular's secret bank accounts and safe deposit boxes on one encrypted flash drive. The total amount of money was seven- hundred million dollars, and all of it was in cash in various places across the globe. An hour later they drove into the warehouse and got out of the van with their masks on and walked over to Rick and Cynthia. The other three walked closer to them and one of them approached the leader.

"So, don't keep us in suspense. How did things go?"

The leader reached inside his pocket and pulled out a red flash drive and held it up.

"Everything went well, and much more than we thought. Seven-hundred-million dollars in cash, in various places across the country. The easy part is they all are no-name accounts, just account codes, and passwords which are all on the flash drive. All we need to do is go get it. I'm about to be super rich, half is all mine." He gripped the flash drive hard and waved it around in the air and then put it back in his front pants pocket.

"You got what you want, now let my wife and I go." Rick said as he looked at the leader.

"You got your money, now let us go and I pray God has mercy on your souls." Cynthia said.

The leader leaned over and snatched the sheet off Cynthia rubbed her breast and then kissed her roughly on the lips. Cynthia rubbed her lips across her shoulder and spat on the ground.

"You nasty dirty bad breath walking dog. Men like you are cowards and weak. The only way you can get a woman is by force or pay her a lot of money to compensate for your two-inch baby dick, and that's when it's hard." She stared at him coldly.

The other kidnappers laughed hard at what Cynthia said but her remarks made the leader angry. He smacked her and pulled out his gun and aimed it at her head.

"No, please don't shoot her." Rick yelled.

"Your smart mouth just got your big ass in trouble. First, I am going to finger fuck you and find out how you taste." He moved his body quickly between Cynthia's legs and spread her legs apart using his legs and moved his hand between her legs with his finger extended to insert inside her.

The next sound you heard was a loud gunshot. One of the kidnappers walked behind the leader and shot him in the back of his head. Blood and brain matter splattered all over Cynthia's face and body and his body fell on top of her.

Cynthia screamed and kicked the body off her and it fell to the floor.

"Oh my God, Lord Jesus. I got blood all over me, oh God." She was beyond frantic.

Rick grabbed the sheet quickly and gave it to Cynthia, and she wiped the blood from her face.

"Relax baby, just relax." Rick helped her wipe off the blood.

The kidnapper that shot the leader kneeled removed the flash drive from his pants pocket stood up and held it up in the air.

"Stupid fool, look at you now. Your brain is on the ground. How are you going to claim half the money? No one steals from Mr. Patrick Elizar."

There was a loud explosion, and the warehouse doors came crashing in. Ron, Keith, Zechariah, the *Young Wolves*, and the Latino guards rushed in with guns in hand. A bullet hit the kidnapper holding the flash drive in his forehead and he was dead before he hit the ground. The flash drive fell to the ground and Rick saw it and a shoot-out erupted, Rick and Cynthia moved quickly to the floor. Cynthia looked at the sheet on the sofa and wanted it badly to cover her nakedness but did not want to risk getting shot in the process. The kidnappers pulled their guns out and started shooting back. Three Legs fell to the ground close to Cynthia and seeing her lying on the ground naked and helpless, turned him on. Bullets flew, and people were getting shot and killed but all Three Legs cared about was looking at Cynthia. He crawled on the ground slowly getting closer to her.

"I am coming, I'm coming to get you sweet butt. Three Legs is coming for you." He said this quietly and repeatedly as he crawled closer to Cynthia, breathing heavily, and sweating because of his large size.

Rick heard what Three Legs said and watched him get closer to Cynthia which infuriated him. Although he was in great pain, he managed to kick him in the face as hard as he could, hoping to knock him out. This only made Three Legs angry, and he grabbed Rick picked him up, and slammed him hard on the ground knocking him out. Cynthia screamed and crawled toward Rick, but Three Legs grabbed Cynthia's legs and pulled her toward him. She kicked and hit him hard several times, but he smiled because this turned him on more.

Three Legs stood and picked up Cynthia and put her across his shoulder and walked toward the office. He did not care about the gunfire taking place, he only cared about having his way with Cynthia.

All the kidnappers were on the ground dead except one, he was on the side of a van about to shoot Zechariah.

"Zechariah, lookout." Keith yelled and raised his gun to shoot the kidnapper.

A hail of bullets flew past Keith's ear and hit the kidnapper's body. He hit the ground dead because Ron shot him. Keith turned around and Ron was behind him with his gun in hand. He and Keith nodded their head toward each other, they heard Cynthia scream and saw this huge man carrying her naked body across his shoulder like she was a sack of potatoes. They both ran closer and shot Three Legs in the back. He stopped walking and turned around slowly facing them and gently put Cynthia on the ground.

"You can't kill me, I'm Three Legs." He unsnapped his coveralls and it fell to his ankles and then he started stroking his penis with both hands making his penis hard in seconds. He smiled revealing his crooked yellow-stained teeth.

Keith and Ron looked at each other and looked at him.

"Good Lord, what kind of freak are you?" Keith said.

"I'm Three Legs, I got the biggest dick in the world. Sixteen inches and I was in a circus, but they kicked me out. Now, I got to put my dick in this pretty young thing on the floor. I am going to put me a Three Legs baby in her and then we can be a family, I want a family to love." His body was bleeding badly from the gunshots, but he continued stroking his penis.

Cynthia was on the ground hearing this crazy man talk and noticed an old rusty piece of long thin metal on the

ground close to her. She grabbed it and jumped to her feet and swung it as hard as she could at Three Legs penis. His penis hit the ground and blood poured from his body.

"Ohhhh, ohhhhh, you cut my dick off, you cut my sixteen-inch dick off. My dick is gone, Three Legs dick is gone. Ahhhhhh you cut my dick off. Now I got to kill you." He screamed and moved with a speed that Ron and Keith did not expect, especially since he was losing so much blood. He reached over and grabbed Cynthia by the neck with both hands and easily picked her off her feet.

Suddenly, a long sharp piece of steel came through Three Legs' stomach. Rick had shoved a piece of sharp rebar through his back. Three Legs let Cynthia go and turned around to look at Rick. He looked at the steel sticking out of his stomach, coughed up some blood, and pulled the steel slowly through his body, and threw it on the ground, and then he hit the ground. Cynthia was on the ground coughing and crying. Rick was dizzy and in great pain, it took all the strength he had to jab Three Legs with that piece of rebar. He fell to his knees barely remaining conscious. Ron and Keith moved quickly to Rick and Cynthia's aid. Rick was very embarrassed for Cynthia because she was still naked and when Ron helped him stand, he looked around for something to cover her. Keith helped Cynthia stand. She was in pain and extremely embarrassed about being so exposed in front of everyone. Now she had no choice but to lean on Keith for physical support realizing her breasts were pressed tightly against him. As Keith held her, he noticed her body looked incredible and he prayed hard to himself, *don't get hard, don't get hard.* Once again, his body betrayed him, he felt the blood rush into his penis until he was aroused. He desperately tried to hide it by maneuvering his body in a certain way, but this proved to be a big mistake. When he shifted his body, Cynthia did also to support her weight, and this caused Keith's penis to rub hard against her thigh and this friction caused his penis to become fully erect.

Cynthia felt Keith's erection against her body, and this caused her to have sexual thoughts of her past desire to be with him. She moved her leg purposely against Keith's penis to feel it better. She repented quickly of her thoughts and actions, looked at Keith, and shook her head.

"You know I can feel your hard penis rubbing against my leg Keith. I understand because we are all human, so relax, this never happened, but it could have long ago. However, I am too much for you, too hot." She whispered to him and smiled.

Keith looked down because he was embarrassed and surprised by her words.

Rick saw an old sheet on another sofa and pointed to it.

"Ron, I can stand on my own, will you get the sheet off that sofa please, and cover my wife."

"Absolutely my brother." He looked around and noticed the shooting had stopped. He moved quickly but cautiously to the sofa and retrieved the sheet and ran back to Cynthia. He gave the sheet to Keith, and he helped Cynthia cover herself and he exhaled praying hard to himself repenting of his lustful thoughts. Cynthia was a gorgeous woman from head to toe.

Three Legs' body shook, his eyes opened, and tears flowed from them.

"She cut my dick off, all I wanted was a family. Now, no family." He spoke softly to himself and then sat up and pointed his finger at Cynthia. "You cut my dick off, now Three Legs is only two legs." He moved slowly as he stood and saw his penis on the ground and pointed to it. "That's my dick, that's Three Legs' dick."

Ron, Keith, Rick, and Cynthia turned to look at Three Legs with shock.

"You have got to be kidding me." Rick said.

"No baby, no family, and now how am I going to make my money? I got to kill everybody. My dick is gone." He yelled.

Four *Young Wolves* ran towards them and saw Three Legs and they dropped to one knee and shot him multiple times. His body shook from the hits, but he was still standing.

"Oh, oh you got me now. You can kill me now because I am no longer Three Legs. I got no dick. You got me."

The *Young Wolves* looked at each other and then shot him multiple times again. He shook and fell backward, and his body made a loud sound when he hit the ground.

"No more Three Legs." He spoke softly before closing his eyes.

The *Young Wolves* walked closer to them and one of them looked at Keith.

"Who was that crazy-looking big dude with the missing penis? Damn, how could anyone take all those bullets and still stand?" He shook his head.

"He was the Devil in disguise, and I am glad he is dead." Cynthia said.

Zechariah and other guards walked over to them.

"Is everyone all right?" He looked around and saw the bad shape Rick and Cynthia were in and regretted asking such a stupid question.

"Let's get out of here." Rick said and walked toward Cynthia. He stood in front of her and all he could do was stare at her in great sorrow because, in his mind, he failed to protect her.

Cynthia felt his thoughts and hugged Rick tightly, but it was important to hold back her tears because she did not want him to feel any worse.

"Oh Rick, I love you baby." She squeezed his neck and kissed him repeatedly.

"I love you too, but you are hurting my neck." He grimaced in pain.

"Oh my God, I'm so sorry baby." Cynthia kissed his cheek and they all walked away.

When they got close to the area where the kidnapper was shot in the head and dropped the flash drive, Rick looked on the ground. He saw the red flash drive close to the kidnapper's dead body. Ron supported him to walk but Rick managed to walk away from him and picked up the flash drive and put it in his pocket and then walked back to Ron for his assistance. Ron, Keith, and Zechariah noticed the flash drive as well.

"It must be some important data on that drive my brother?" Ron said as he looked at Rick.

"Yes, and I will tell you about it later."

They continued to walk out of the warehouse and saw police cars and ambulances in the parking lot. Zechariah spoke with the police briefly and then Cynthia and Rick got in separate ambulances while Zechariah, Ron, and Keith got in the limo, along with several of the *Young Wolves*. The Latina guards got in the vans and left. The limo followed the ambulances to the hospital. Ron looked at everyone in the limo.

"Thank you, Jesus, we all are alive."

"Amen!" Everyone in the limo said.

Three Legs' eyes opened, and he looked around and saw his penis on the ground. Tears flowed down his face, and he coughed up blood. He managed to crawl very slowly toward his penis and held it in his hand and then placed it on his chest.

"They got me, they cut my dick off. No more Three Legs. I know I got mental issues but all I ever wanted was a family, I got no family. I am all alone. Lord please, I do not want to go to hell. Don't let me burn up please Lord, please."

A police officer walked over to Three Legs and stared at him.

"Sir, I am dying and all alone. Don't let me die alone, help me have peace."

"You are not alone," he kneeled and laid his hand on Three Legs' head and prayed for him. "Lord Jesus, search his heart and deliver his soul into your kingdom. Thank you, Jesus."

Three Legs looked up and smiled.

"I am not alone anymore. I got a family now."

"Yes, you have the best family in the world."

A dove flew into the warehouse and landed on Three Legs. The dove rubbed its head against Three Legs face gently. He smiled, his heart stopped beating, and he died. Tears fell from the police officer's eyes, he smiled and stood, and walked away. The dove flew out of the warehouse.

CHAPTER TWENTY SIX
HEALING

After going to the hospital and getting checked, Rick stayed two days in a private room because of his injuries and Cynthia stayed with him. After leaving the hospital they spent most of their time at home. Cynthia's facial wounds healed perfectly with no scars, but the doctor told Rick it would take six weeks for his ribs to heal. Seven weeks passed since the kidnapping of Rick and Cynthia, and they spent a lot of time praying and reading the bible together which helped bring them closer. Cynthia noticed Rick was not as affectionate as he used to be. When she flirted and sexually played with him, he always pulled away and this bothered her a lot. Rick would not even allow her to perform oral sex on him to relieve some of his stress. One night after a meal, walking together, a workout at home, and then a shower they sat in the living room on the sofa listening to music. They wore shorts, and T-shirts and were in a good mood, so Cynthia felt this was a good time for them to talk.

"Rick, can we talk about something?"

"Always, what's on your mind?"

"I know the kidnapping and the details are not easy for either of us to discuss but you have been very distant from me ever since. Is it me, have I done something to cause you to be distant?"

Rick stared at Cynthia, looked down, and then exhaled because he was in deep thought. He was aware it was only a matter of time before this would come up and he knew exactly what Cynthia was referring to. A day had not gone by he had not thought about the kidnapping and how he was knocked unconscious. Then he woke up and saw that huge freak of a man carrying his naked wife over his shoulder. Every day since then the same questions came to his mind about Cynthia. What happened to her while he was unconscious in the van? What did she have to do to protect herself? Was she raped by the kidnappers when they were in the van? Did the large freak man do something sick to Cynthia before he put her on his shoulder and carried her away? Rick had a natural protective spirit, but he could not protect his wife, and this affected him a great deal emotionally and mentally. Also, Cynthia never discussed what happened to her in detail. She would always say, *God was working it out.* He looked at her.

"As a man and your husband, I know I let you down. I did not protect you and this bothers me greatly and I think about this every day. I blame myself for you being sexually assaulted and I pray daily for your forgiveness." He stared at her, and tears came to his eyes, but he held them back.

"Oh Rick, baby I have nothing to forgive you for. No woman could ask for a better husband or protector. Rick, I know you would give your life to protect me. I would never want this to happen, but it does make me feel good, it would make any woman feel good. Besides God, you are my best protector."

"But I could not protect you from being sexually assaulted. I could not protect my wife from being raped." He looked at her and tears flowed from his eyes.

Cynthia stared at Rick and shook her head and tears came to her eyes. She now understood why he had been so distant. Rick thought she was raped.

"Oh my God Rick, I am so sorry you have been dealing with and carrying such an emotional and spiritual burden. Yes, I was touched at times, slapped a few times, and repeatedly threatened but I was never raped. Baby look at me," she placed both hands on the sides of his face gently and stared at him. "as painful as it would have been if that happened, I would have told you. No sweetheart, I was never raped, thank God. Please, please believe that. I would never lie to you about something like that." She continued to stare into his eyes.

For the first time in weeks, Rick smiled from his heart and soul. He felt a heavy burden lifted immediately from within. Not overlooking all the crazy things that happened to them, but knowing his wife was not raped made a huge difference. Rick shook his head and wiped the tears from his face and hugged Cynthia and never wanted to let her go.

"I love you so much." He whispered in her ear.

Cynthia felt his deep love and felt his heavy burden lifted. She knew it would take time for them to be healed completely from what they went through, but this was a huge step. She kissed his lips gently and for the first time in weeks, he did not move away. Their kissing turned to passion and Rick began caressing her thighs, stomach, and breast. He did not want to make Cynthia feel uncomfortable, so he stopped and leaned away from her.

"Rick, it's okay baby, I won't break. I want you, so let's go to bed." She kissed him, stood up, and held her hand out to him.

Rick grabbed her hand and they walked to the bedroom together and kneeled next to their bed and prayed.

"Lord, we thank you for your grace and protection over our lives and for keeping us as one." Rick said.

"Thank you Jesus for allowing us to see you are the answer to all things and for bringing us closer." She kissed him.

They stood, removed their clothes, and got in bed, and began kissing and caressing each other. Cynthia stopped kissing and looked at Rick.

"Rick, I pray we can talk to each other about anything because communication and prayer will always keep us close."

"I agree, communication and prayer are the glue to a strong friendship, relationship, and marriage." He kissed her passionately and they began making love.

They made love many times, but this time was different. All their love, emotions, and passions were slowly building spiritually. Their every touch melted each other's hearts because of their deep love. They moved slowly in all they did to please one another, and time was not a factor just their love for each other. Their lovemaking was beyond beautiful.

Cynthia lay on her back and Rick was on top thrusting slowly inside his wife knowing her body well. His lovemaking was so satisfying, and his hard dick felt so good inside her until she exploded with an intense orgasm.

"Ohhhh, Rick you feel so good, don't stop, keep fucking me. Ohhhhh, my goodness Rick, I am cummiing." She continued pushing her body into his. Cynthia loved when Rick would pull out after she climaxed and suck him until he exploded in her mouth, but not this time. She placed the palms of her hands on Rick's chest and stared at his face.

"Rick don't say anything, please. I do not want you to pull out and cum in my mouth, I want to feel your seed inside me, I want a baby Rick. Get me pregnant, I want us to have a family.

CHAPTER TWENTY SEVEN
A MENTAL TOUCH

Derrick and Tonya felt like newlyweds and their actions showed it. They were affectionate constantly, attentive, and respectful to each other. Many relationships start out this way but unfortunately, in a short period, things would begin to change. Such as taking each other for granted, saying rude and mean things to each other, being disrespectful, and not putting each other first. Then the physical neglect and not allowing lovemaking to be a priority in the relationship. All this and more creates a communication bridge in the relationship. Next comes lies, deception, and cheating. They vowed not to allow this to happen to them and embraced the saying, *start out like you can hold out, and hold out like you started out*. The emotional, spiritual, and sexual chemistry between them was intense and they worked out together regularly. Which gave them tight bodies and they were very attracted to each other. They moved into a two-car garage two-bedroom condo in Silver Spring, Maryland and they worked for the same large advertising company in Washington, DC in the marketing department. They had a combined annual salary of one hundred ninety-eight thousand dollars. They had put in a lot of overtime hours at work on a big advertising campaign and they needed a break.

It was eleven o'clock Sunday night when Derrick and Tonya arrived home from the gym. After showering they sat on their bed put on lotion and afterward got dressed. Derrick put on sweatpants and no T-shirt because he wanted to show off his tight abdominals to Tonya. Tonya put on a satin top and loose-fitting satin shorts. She would bend over in front of him at times pretending to stretch. Derrick leaned back on the bed to relax and when he sat up, Tonya was directly in front of him, bent over and stretching. He laughed and pointed at her.

"You are something else. Ever since you got out of the shower you have been bending over in those baggy shorts, supposedly stretching. Baby, I like your thin shorts but what size are they? They are big and baggy, they might fit me." He leaned back on the bed and laughed then sat up and pointed his finger at her shorts.

Tonya stared at him and became irritated instantly because she liked the shorts and wanted to be sexually playful with her husband.

"That's not funny Derrick."

"I am not laughing at you; I'm laughing at those big baggy shorts you're wearing. Circus clown shorts." He continued to laugh.

"Okay, so according to you I am not sexy unless I am wearing pants hugging my hips or tight shorts revealing my butt cheeks." She looked at Derrick and wanted to push him on the floor.

"Now that's what I am talking about. Tight booty shorts revealing butt cheeks and camel toe." He looked at her and licked his lips.

Tonya stepped closer to the bed and stared at him.

"I am glad my confidence level is high, and Jesus is my Lord because I could smack you right now for being so disrespectful to me." She turned to walk away.

Derrick grabbed her hips, stood up, and pulled her into him. He kissed her and began rubbing her hips.

"Stop playing, you know how sexy you are to me and how attracted I am to you." His hands moved inside the back of her shorts and rubbed her butt.

She pushed him back.

"Oh, so you like my shorts now. Now you want to feel all over me. I wonder why, oh I know, easy access. You will learn my husband, you will learn. Women like to be chased sometimes and all clothes on a woman do not have to be revealing or skintight, Derrick. I will be in the kitchen; I need a snack." She stepped back and Derrick tried to grab her, but Tonya pushed his hands down and stepped away quickly and walked out of the bedroom towards the kitchen.

Derrick knew what he said and how he spoke to his wife was wrong. He walked into the kitchen, and they stared at one another. Tonya had an expression on her face of, *I am waiting for your apology.* He kissed her on the cheek and began making chicken salad and sweet tea. They ate in silence and looked at one another periodically and then went to the den to listen to music. They sat on different sofas relaxing and wondering who would be the first to give in. Derrick knew they needed a change of scenery for a while, a vacation would be the answer.

"Tonya, I know you have to work hard to get what you want in life and we have been working extremely hard at work on this big campaign, but we need a break, and soon.

Let's take a vacation and get away for a while." He smiled at her.

His words touched Tonya's heart deeply and caused her entire demeanor to change.

"Derrick don't play. Do not say something because you know it is what I want to hear so you can have your way with me. You know how badly I want to take a vacation."

Derrick walked over, kissed Tonya, and sat next to her.

"Two things my dear, one is, I am not playing. And two, I married you, so I will always have my way with you, eventually." He leaned forward, kissed her neck, and sucked it while his hand moved up her thigh.

Tonya took a deep breath and exhaled, feeling her entire body and mind relax. She loved her husband's touch, and he knew it. However, she wanted to hear more about the vacation but did not want to make Derrick feel she was rejecting his touch or kindness. She turned her face toward his so their lips and tongue could touch, and they kissed passionately. This is what Tonya called, a mental touch. Standing your ground, but still allowing the man to feel accomplished. After they kissed passionately, she leaned back and looked at him.

"You know how to turn on my body Derrick, you always have. Let's talk more about this vacation we need."

"Okay!"

After discussing places to go, they finally agreed to Barbados and stay at the Sandals Royal Resort. They would leave next Sunday and stay for a week.

"The timing for this vacation could not be better and I am looking forward to being someplace tropical with a cool

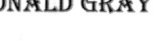

breeze and having some husband-and-wife alone time. So, no business talk on this trip, Derrick." She kissed him.

"Consider it done, and now, back to where we were." He placed his hand inside her shorts and began caressing her thigh and placed her hand on his penis so she could feel his erection.

"It's amazing the effect a pair of loose-fitting shorts has on a man." She spoke sarcastically and began massaging his penis.

"Yes, and you have made your point about your baggy shorts. For the record, it is you in the shorts that stimulate me so much. When a man is really into a woman, in love with that woman, and she has his heart. That is where the real power is, not just tight shorts. I am in love with you." He leaned forward and kissed her cheek softly.

Tonya could only stare at him, and tears fell from her eyes because his words and spirit touched her heart.

"I am in love with you also Derrick." She kissed his lips and stood up and looked at him. "Don't move, I will be right back." She walked to the linen closet and removed two pillows, sheets, and a blanket, and walked back to the den. She spread the blanket on the floor, the sheets, and the pillows. "I know we have to be at work in the morning, but we can get an early start on that vacation, here and now." She licked her lips and seductively caressed her thigh as she looked at him.

"I like the way you think." He got up and stood next to Tonya and walked slowly around her body looking at it up and down. He stopped directly behind her and removed his clothes while kissing her neck. And then pressed his body into hers so she could feel his erection pressed against her butt.

Tonya removed her top and they laid on the floor and began caressing and kissing each other passionately but she still had her shorts on. She moved her shorts to one side and Derrick slid inside her.

"Ohhhh Derrick, you feel so good." She slid her tongue across his lips and began rocking her body against his. They made beautiful love on the floor in various positions and Tonya never removed her shorts. An hour later they lay next to each other on the floor on their side facing each other completely satisfied sexually.

"That was amazing baby, you are incredible, and you still have your shorts on." He kissed her.

"That is something, husband. The benefits of baggy shorts." She said this condescendingly and kissed him.

CHAPTER TWENTY EIGHT
WHAT TO DO

A week later after Sunday church service Rick talked to Ron, Keith, Zechariah, and James and asked them to meet at his house that afternoon so he could discuss something important with them. Sheila, Diana, Stacy, Cynthia, and Catarina agreed to go shopping in Georgetown. Rick knew the guys would be hungry, so he ordered crabs, shrimp, and lobster. Everyone arrived at his house dressed in their suits from church saw all the food and sat down. Rick said the blessing and they began to talk and eat.

"Rick, we appreciate all this good food, but you did not ask all of us here just to eat, what's going on?" Keith said.

"Always direct, I like that about you my brother. First, let me say no words could express how much Cynthia and I appreciate everything you all did to rescue us; you saved our lives. I will always be forever grateful. This brings me to why all of you are here now. James, to start this conversation, I have a legal question for you."

"Ask away, if I can answer it, I will."

"If you found a lot of drug money, what would you do?"

"It's not a simple answer Rick because there are variables and situations to where the money was found, who it belongs to, is the case under investigation, and many other variables."

"Okay, a lot to deal with. Well, let me get directly to the point. When Cynthia and I were kidnapped one of the kidnappers retrieved a flash drive from my storage room that I did not know I had. Anyway, after he got it, he mentioned it had the locations of Victor Augular's alleged hidden secret accounts."

"Victor Augular, that is a name none of us will ever forget. I think I know where this is going but please, keep talking." James said.

Hold on, I am getting there. During the shootout, the leader of the kidnappers was shot in the head, and he dropped the drive. On the way out, I saw it on the ground and picked it up."

"I remember seeing you pick up that drive Rick." Ron said.

"Yes, you did. The flash drive was encrypted but I was able to take care of that," he paused and exhaled and looked at everyone. "The drive contains all the locations of Victor's secret numbered accounts across the globe. The total amount is seven hundred million dollars, all in cash and I know how to get it."

"Good Lord." Zechariah said.

"Now that is some serious loot." Keith said.

"No doubt about that." Ron said.

"If I did not trust everyone here with my life, I would walk out now and pretend I never heard this conversation. Wow, that is some serious money. Okay, I will give you the short version. Victor's secret money accounts have been a rumor for years and no one believed they existed. However, the mere fact you have it, proves someone does know it exists or you and Cynthia would have never been kidnapped Rick." James shook his head.

"This is true, and now I know this question will lead to the bad part. The drug dealer that was allegedly killed by Victor Augular named Elizar, was mentioned by one of the kidnappers." Rick said.

"I know that name well and the case. Mr. Elizar, a young lady named Michele who was with him that night in his bed, and all his security guards were brutally killed years ago. Their bodies were dismembered in a horrible scene. During the investigation of that case, Michele's profile came up in an FBI large credit card scam. She was linked to a professional team that made millions through credit card fraud. She had a cousin named Martina who vanished after Michele was killed and was never heard of again. I remember seeing the profile on Martina, she was stunningly beautiful with a mixed heritage like Michele. African American, Italian, and Puerto Rican. Now the weird part to all this is I recently found out that Elizar had a brother named Patrick who was doing two life sentences in Federal prison. He was scheduled to go back to court in a month to have his case overturned. Two days after your kidnappers were killed Rick, Patrick was killed in his cell."

"Wow, all this is becoming more and more complicated. People from our past still affecting our lives today." Ron said.

"Yes, and now back to the seven hundred-million-dollar thumb drive. Whoever knew about the alleged secret accounts of Victor probably now thinks it was either a rumor, destroyed during the shootout, or never found."

"Which is good but what would you do with the drive James?" Rick asked.

"As tempting as it would be to take my time and go get all that money, I think it would be a situation of opening Pandora's Box of evil and mayhem. If it were brought to the light the secret accounts exist and that much money is involved, there would be a finder's fee for sure of at least ten to twenty percent. That is seventy to one hundred forty million dollars clean clear money. You could turn it in Rick and allow me to handle all the paperwork for you or destroy it and forget you ever had it. Your choice." James looked at him and everyone else.

"You are right it is very tempting to go get all that money, but my wife and I have been very blessed, and we do not want any more negativity in our lives. So, I will let everyone here help me decide what to do. Do I go in the garage and put a hammer to the flash drive or give it to James and let him do his thing?" He looked at everyone.

They all looked at each other and then looked at James. They agreed to give the flash drive to James and let him get the reward. Rick gave the drive to James.

"Do what you can my brother but let me say this. No amount of money is worth losing yourself over. So, in the process of doing what is needed, if you discover along the way the drive is causing you too many problems, let it go, it's not worth it." Rick said as he spoke to James seriously.

"I like that and thank you. I will do what I can and will keep everyone informed."

"Great, and now I am still hungry and there is more food in the kitchen."

Catarina, Sheila, Diana, Cynthia, and Stacy walked into the house.

"I smell seafood. I hope you men did not eat it all because we are hungry." Cynthia said.

All the men greeted their wives with hugs and kisses, and they all sat down to eat and talk.

CHAPTER TWENTY NINE
VACATION

Derrick and Tonya were enjoying the first day of their vacation in Barbados. The Sandals Royal Resort was beautiful, and they were booked in the *Love Nest* suite. It was large with a king-size bed and a wonderful view overlooking Oistin Bay beach. They unpacked and sat on the balcony looking at the clear water and the people having fun below. The temperature was eighty-two degrees with a light breeze, exactly what Tonya mentioned she wanted. After being on a plane for over ten hours because of a connecting flight, they were tired and decided to take a nap and then get up and eat at a nice restaurant. They laid on the bed in shorts and T-shirts and faced each other. Derrick kissed Tonya and caressed her legs, and she knew where this was going.

"No Derrick stop, you said we would take a nap and then go eat. Besides, I am tired baby."

"Oh Lord, not you. After you marry them, the sex gets less and less. You hear the phrases, *not tonight baby I got a headache*, or *not tonight baby I am tired*." He looked at her with an attitude.

"Derrick stop the verbal drama. I satisfy you consistently very well and you know it, so do not play. However, I will give you a quick blow job so you can relax and release some stress, and then we can take a nap." She smiled at him.

"What! I do not want a quick blow job or quick sex. However, since you did mention a blow job, if you are going to do it, you may as well do it right. Take your time with plenty of tongue foreplay. Put some spit on the dick, slob it good, lick my balls too. Lick my dick up and down on the sides and do that thing you do with your mouth, you know, how you suck just the tip, and your mouth makes that popping sound. Wet up the dick good baby and then deep throat it, so I can bust in your mouth, and please keep sucking every drop." He kissed her.

Tonya stared at Derrick hard and shook her head.

"Derrick, you have watched too many porn movies in your life. You can be so nasty and no, I am not doing all that, at least not now. Maybe later, right now, go to sleep please."

"Okay, but can we have quick fast-moving rabbit sex?"

"No Derrick," she yelled at him. "Baby, please go to sleep," she spoke calmly. "I will take care of you later, I promise. Thank you and I love you." She kissed him and closed her eyes.

"Wow, well B. B. King said it best years ago in his song, *The Thrill Is Gone*. My thrill is gone." He exhaled as he looked at her.

Tonya knew he was trying to make her feel guilty, so he could have his way, but it was not going to work, not this time. She opened her eyes and looked at him, shook her head, kissed him, and closed her eyes.

Four hours later Derrick and Tonya sat in one of the restaurants at the resort enjoying a nice Caribbean meal. Derrick wore casual dress shoes, dress pants, and a short-sleeved shirt and Tonya wore flat casual shoes and a multicolored Caribbean dress that was a little tight in the waist. Derrick loved the dress and how it flowed as she moved.

"Have I told you this evening how lovely you look in that dress?"

"Yes Derrick, you have, and I thank you for the compliment. Although I am a little surprised you like this dress so much since it's not skintight." She gave him that look.

"Baby, I thought you knew. Everything you wear does not have to be tight. Loose-fitting clothes serve their purpose, especially shorts, easy access." He smiled and winked at her.

"You are something, and yes, loose-fitting serves its purpose, always will." She winked back at him and sipped her wine.

They talked and flirted with each other throughout the meal. A Jamaican song began to play they both liked, and several couples got up to dance. Derrick and Tonya did the same and they moved well together. Tonya was feeling horny and wanted to tease her husband in a classy way. While dancing she turned around and backed up to Derrick and began slowly winding her body on him until she felt his erection and then turned around to face him.

"Hi baby, are you ready to handle all this?" She dropped down slowly and came back up, never taking her eyes from his.

"The only thing stopping me from putting you on one of these tables is witnesses. Does that answer your question?"

Jamaican songs continued to play, and people continued dancing.

"Maybe, maybe not," She backed up and then took short steps toward him while winding her body and doing other sexually teasing dance moves. She was inches from his face and whispered in his ear. "I will let you do anything you want to me Derrick, as long as you don't hurt me. Lick your dick, and suck it good," she backed up and danced provocatively while staring into his eyes. Tonya moved closer and whispered in his ear again. "Let's go, I am ready for my husband to make me scream. I want your lips, tongue, and dick." She kissed him.

What Tonya said made Derrick stop moving and stare at her with a look, that said it all. They walked back to the table, Derrick paid the bill, and they walked away and caught a taxi back to their hotel. The moment they stepped into their hotel room and closed the door, Derrick pushed Tonya gently against the wall. He kissed her passionately while lifting one of her legs and slid his hand between her legs.

"Baby, wait, I want to talk to you." She pushed her leg down.

"What? Are you kidding me?" He gave her a look of you must be kidding.

"Please, I need us to talk, it is important." She kissed him to try and calm him down.

He placed her hand on his penis which was fully erect and made her squeeze it.

"You feel how hard my dick is and you still want to talk? This is human concrete ready to go to work, and you want to talk."

"It will come back, now let's talk." She kissed him and sat on the bed and looked at his irritated expression.

Derrick looked at Tonya and shook his head and sat next to her.

"This better be good," he adjusted his penis and stared at her. "Go ahead and talk while I sit here with a serious hard-on. I hope I don't get blue balls and become dizzy." He stared at Tonya.

"Always with the verbal drama. You will not get blue balls or get dizzy Derrick, so relax. I will take care of you, I promise. Please do not interrupt me Derrek, it is so hard in life to meet and find a compatible husband or wife, and it becomes even harder to meet a Christian mate who genuinely loves and lives for Jesus. This is the crucial part, it is easy to fall in lust and love, but liking a person is equally important. Not what they can do for you or any of the material things they may bring to the table but do you like the person? Remove the stuff, and all you have left is the real person. I prayed for years asking God to bless me with a man that likes me. We have great emotional, mental, spiritual, and physical chemistry. A Christian marriage is so much more than quoting scriptures. It is important to sexually desire your mate, and lovemaking should be wonderful between both. The church needs to stop the teaching of restricted sexual practices between husband and wife. For example, if you say this during sex, you are going to hell. If you do this during sex, you are going to hell. If you have sex in certain positions, you will become demonically oppressed. All this is beyond stupid. Yes, as Christians we all need to be careful what spiritual doorways we open in our lives. However, a woman desires to be sexually satisfied just like a man does. It is okay to want your husband or wife to rock your world in bed."

"Tonya, I got it…"

"Don't interrupt me, I am not finished. You respect me in every way. You never call me that B word regardless of how angry you may be at me, or anything negative, and you always respect me in public. You call me your queen, which is nice but what makes your words have such a strong impact on my heart is you treat me like your queen. I am your Christian queen who is in love with her man, and I love your open and very sexually expressive attitude and all the freaky sexual things you do to me. I am far from offended when you talk sexually dirty to me. It turns me on, and you know it, even if I do not talk dirty back to you. I love my freaky, sexy, dirty-talking husband. Thank you for listening to me, I am finished now." She kissed him.

Derrick looked at Tonya as she talked and, in the beginning, he was irritated, but the more she talked, he felt blessed for the connection they shared. It touched his heart Tonya felt comfortable enough to talk to him so openly.

"Thank you for being so open with me. This degree of communication so many couples do not have. They can talk to their best friends about anything but not their husband or wife, and this is sad. This means, your husband or wife is not your best friend, and they should be. I thank God for us." He put his arm around her waist, held her hand, and looked at her with such emotional attachment.

"I am proud to be your queen." She leaned forward and pulled her dress up and placed his hand on her thigh.

Derrick caressed Tonya's thighs until she relaxed more and then slid his finger inside her panties rubbing between her legs until she became wet. He slid his finger inside her moving it around the way she loved and turned her on even more. He pulled his finger out, licked, and sucked on it while he looked at her.

Tonya leaned over and used the tip of her tongue to caress Derrick's neck and then removed his finger from his mouth and put it back inside her. She moved it around more and then licked his finger all over slowly and lightly bit it and sucked it.

"I love tasting my juices," she stood and removed her clothes, and leaned back on the bed. "I am all yours."

Derrick stared at her while he removed his clothes and was fully erect and wanted to be inside Tonya badly. Their lovemaking was always special, but Derrick desired to cater to every inch of his wife's body, and for the next two hours, he did just that, it was all about her. Not one inch of Tonya's body went untouched by his hands, mouth, and body. He put different kinds of fruit on her body and licked and ate it. Tonya had five orgasms from her husband's wonderful touch. After her last orgasm, Derrick exploded inside her, and they laid next to each other hugging and kissing passionately. The bed was a mess, and they took a shower together, put robes on, and called room service for a linen change. With clean bodies and fresh linen, they laid on the bed for a while and then prayed until falling asleep.

The rest of their vacation consisted of tours, water sports, eating at various restaurants, lots of lovemaking, and sleeping. When they boarded the plane to come back, they sat next to each other, and looked at one another, and smiled. They felt energized, refreshed, in love, and at peace. They kissed, leaned back in their seats, and went to sleep. This was a positive distraction and a dream vacation for them.

CHAPTER THIRTY

MARTINA

Martina lived in Costa Rica for the last six years until she moved to Nevada recently to a three-bedroom condo. She is thirty years old, five feet eight, one-hundred-thirty-eight curvaceous pounds of beauty. She has an extremely attractive face and beautiful tight body and mixed heritage of African American, Puerto Rican, and Italian. She is Michele's sister, who was killed by Victor Augular's assassin, Mr. Case, some years ago at Mr. Elizar's house. Mr. Case cut Michele's head off the night she was in Mr. Elizar's bed in the process of sexually satisfying him.

Michele worked as a high price escort for a few years. Martina and Michele were always close but argued constantly about Michele's lifestyle. Martina was a middle school teacher and she hated what her sister did for a living and told her constantly she was far too smart to be selling her body to strangers. Michele's response would always be the same. You teach school for fifty-seven thousand dollars a year. At times you meet men, talk for a while and they eventually spend money on you doing various things, and then you have sex. For what, except satisfying each other's hormones? I make sixty thousand dollars in a month because I work for myself, travel around the world, and date men for a minimum of five thousand dollars a night. I date only four nights a week and I decide when, who, how, and how much. This conversation repeated itself over and over with them.

Martina kept her condo but now lives in a two-car garage, four-thousand square foot five-bedroom house in Las Vegas Nevada. She was in the fitness room finishing her workout and was tired and hot and drank some water and sat on the bench to relax and think. She thought about how she got to where she is now in her life. Martina remembered it all like it was yesterday, her mind did a flashback…

When Michele was killed it affected Martina so much, that she left the country and moved to Costa Rico. She had no problem getting a job as a middle school teacher and she kept busy but cried every day because the loss of her sister was heartbreaking.

Later her world came crashing down when she lost her job as a teacher. A female student in one of her classes became jealous of Martina tutoring a male student she liked. She convinced the guy to lie by giving him a blow job in the boy's bathroom one day after school. She told him to say Martina made sexual advances toward him and rubbed his penis when tutoring him. Martina had no blemishes on her work history but was fired anyway and no school would hire her after that. After depleting her savings, she was not able to afford her two-bedroom apartment, so she moved in with a girlfriend. This lasted for a year until her friend kicked her out because her friend's boyfriend constantly flirted with Martina and wanted her badly. Martina's friend accused her of flirting with her boyfriend and asked her to leave. The fact was, Martina's raw beauty and erotic look caused her girlfriend to become jealous and in her mind, she figured it was only a matter of time before Martina and her boyfriend had sex. So, she had to go but gave Martina some money before she put her out.

Martina put all her things in storage and stayed in cheap nasty hotels that hookers used regularly because she had nowhere else to go and that was all she could afford. She hit rock bottom when she lost all her things in storage because she could not pay her rental fee. Martina had no money and nowhere to go. She sat in the hotel lobby one night dressed in flat shoes, a blouse, and tight jeans, and felt defeated. One of the older hookers walked over and gave her a cold soda and a club sandwich. This woman had a worn-out and abused look like she had been in the business for a long time. She watched Martina because she assumed she was a hooker as well and with her beauty, she would soon be taking her customers and other ladies' customers that worked the area as well. She sat in a chair next to her and Martina told this stranger her story. The older hooker discovered she was wrong, and Martina was trying to survive. The hooker smiled at Martina and shook her head.

"Wow, that is some story, but we all have stories, and some far worse than yours. I do not feel sorry for you at all because you are a walking gold mine. You're also a blind fool at the same time."

"Why do you say that?" She spoke with anger because the lady called her a fool but continued to eat the sandwich and enjoyed the drink.

"Look in the mirror honey. You are young and incredibly beautiful with a great-looking body. Men and women would pay top dollar to spend time with you. It is an old saying but still true, you use what you got, to get what you want. You are smart and pretty, with a great body. Stop with the pity party, feeling sorry for yourself, and get off that great-looking ass of yours and use it to get paid."

"You mean have sex with strangers, that is so disgusting." Martina was repulsed by the very thought of doing such a thing.

"So, you wonder why I call you a fool? When I say men and women would pay top dollar for your time and your sexy body, I mean top dollar. I know for a fact you could make three to five thousand dollars a night easy. There are a lot of rich lonely men and women in this world. But I am not going to lie to you, your good looks will only take you so far. You will have to perform sexually eventually. Hand jobs, sucking dicks, licking pussy, and giving up some pussy and that round ass of yours. That is a fact of life."

Martina felt like she would throw up imagining what this woman said to her and immediately thought of her sister Michele.

"My situation is really bad, but I couldn't do that, I just couldn't."

"It's your life and you are in a state of survival. Survive or die, your choice," she walked away and then stopped and got a card from her pocket and walked back to Martina and handed it to her. "Here, in case you change your mind. Call the number on the card and this person can get you started today. The soda you drank and the sandwich you ate will only hold you for so long. Go get paid, pretty stupid fool." She winked at Martina and walked away.

Martina took the card and watched the lady walk away. She sat in her chair thinking about everything the woman said and her current reality. She thought about the many conversations she had with Michele concerning her escort lifestyle and how degrading and dangerous of a life it was, which eventually caused her death. How could she consider walking this same dangerous path? She thought of how her life got to this point. A student lied on her and she was fired. A friend accused her of something that was not true, and she was kicked out and now homeless. All because of her looks. Her looks got her into this situation and her looks could get her out, but at what price? She leaned back deep in thought and fell asleep.

Martina woke up when she felt a tap on her shoulder. It was the hotel manager. He was tall and decent-looking.

"Miss, you can't sleep in this lobby. You have to go."

Martina looked at him with sleepy eyes.

"I have no money and nowhere to go."

"Well, you can't stay here. If you do not leave, I am calling the police and you will be arrested for trespassing."

"Please, I need some rest. I am so tired." Giving him a pleading look.

"Miss, you are too fine to be broke and homeless," he looked around the empty lobby, and then looked at Martina. "I tell you what, I will give you a clean room for one week and five hundred dollars if you spend one night with me. Afterward, we never had this conversation." He stared at her.

Martina looked at him like he was crazy because she knew what he was implying, it is what all men want from women, sex. She thought of her situation and realized what she had to do, regardless of how disgusting it would be. She looked around the lobby stood up and held out her hand.

"Room key to a clean room, five hundred dollars, and I will spend time with you."

He gave her the biggest smile and then stepped closer.

"Just so you know, this will not be a conversation date. You are beyond fine, and I want some of that fine ass of yours, tonight."

"Okay, I got it," she spoke with attitude and then held her hand out again. "Room key and five hundred dollars. And I need time to shower and take a nap because I am very tired, so give me five hours before you knock on my door. Oh, and bring a condom."

"Baby, I got condoms, all kinds of dick pills, marijuana, cocaine, and any kind of liquor you want. Yes, we will be fucking a long time tonight." He smiled and walked to the office and retrieved a room key and five hundred dollars and walked back. He gave Martina the key and money. "See you in five hours, I need to shower and get my stuff." He kissed her on the cheek and walked away with a big smile on his face.

Martina could not believe what she was about to do but felt like she had no choice. Drugs have never been her thing but thought if she could smoke some weed and drink enough, she would be numb to what she was about to do. She looked at the room key and the money in her hand and walked to the room. Once inside she looked around and had to admit the room and bathroom smelled good and was clean. Martina felt disgusted, but life goes on and she was determined to make it. She exhaled, removed her clothes, and walked into the bathroom to take a shower. The hot shower felt good, and she walked out of the bathroom with a large towel wrapped around her and laid on the bed and fell asleep.

Five hours later Martina was awakened by a knock on her door. She sat up and looked around the room and made sure her towel was wrapped tightly around her body before she answered the door. The hotel manager stood there holding a backpack in his hand.

"Hi sexy, can I come in?"

"Sure, come on in." Although she was disgusted with all this, Martina made up her mind to at least be nice to the guy, especially if he did not act like a total idiot. Hopefully, he would only last about five minutes and she would put him out of the room and then take a long hot shower, again.

"Thank you," he stepped in and closed the door behind him. He put his backpack on the table and stared at Martina. "I know you have heard all the pick-up lines before, and this ain't no line, but damn woman you are fine. Standing there wrapped in that big towel with no makeup on, but still the finest woman I have ever seen in my life. I don't want to offend you, but you are a walking gold mine for yourself."

"Thank you and that was sweet of you to say. So, what is in the backpack, and what is your name?"

"My name is not important, but you can call me HM, short for, hotel manager and I will call you Money Fine. So fine, you walk like money." He laughed.

Martina had to laugh, and it felt good to be wanted, even for money.

"I have it all in my backpack, we are going to have a great time tonight. Money Fine, I have seen a whole lot in my life, and I know this ain't your thing and probably your first time. You are in a bad situation trying to get out and probably hate yourself for doing this. Relax, I am a nice guy and will be gentle with you. Let's start this night off with some wine and go from there."

"Thank you for understanding," she thought, *if you were nice, you would help me out and not demand sex from me, but life is not like that, nothing in life is free and everybody must pay in some way.* "Wine it is." She smiled at him.

HM, got the wine and glasses out of the backpack and they shared their first drink. After a few drinks, Martina felt good and enjoyed his company. This went on for a while and they drank more, smoked weed, did some cocaine lines, listened to music, and finally had sex.

When Martina woke up, it was early morning and HM was gone and she had a serious headache. She laid in bed naked and then sat up and replayed the entire night in her head, what she could remember of it. She did remember the sex was good because there was a lot of foreplay, he took his time and caressed her entire body, instead of sticking it in and humping her like a dog. She even remembered climaxing twice and it was intense. However, Martina felt dirty and ran to the bathroom and vomited. After brushing her teeth and rinsing with mouthwash, she took a long hot shower and walked out with a towel on, laid on the bed, and cried like a baby. Thirty minutes later she walked toward the table and saw a note and ten one-hundred-dollar bills. The note was from HM and it said, *thank you for a great time and you have the best lovin' I ever had in my life. Take care, HM.* Martina smiled and counted the money.

"Fifteen hundred dollars for a few hours and the loss of my dignity. Okay, I got it. There is a whole lot of money in this world, and I am going to get my share and find out who was responsible for killing my sister, no matter what it takes." She did not have a change of clothes, so she washed her clothes by hand and hung them up in her room to dry. Took a nap and later put her clothes on and went shopping and never looked back.

Martina came back to the present and took another drink of water. She looked around the beautiful home that she worked so hard to get.

"Yeah, that was the first time selling my ass for money, but far from my last. I have traveled across the globe and met more people than I care to remember. I eventually connected with Mr. Elizar and became part of his criminal organization and serviced many international clients. Later I found out Victor Augular and his organization were responsible for Michele's death. Elizar and Victor Augular are dead now. I was able to get next to Elizar's brother, Patrick Elizar, and was able to get some valuable information from him. Unfortunately, he was a liability to me, and I had to have him eliminated in prison. I cannot afford any loose ends. I found out about Victor's secret money accounts and almost had the location of the accounts, until the stupid crew, I hired to kidnap Rick and his wife Cynthia, messed up everything. Now, because the crew is dead, thanks to the O'Neil family and friends, I do not know if the information is forever lost or what happened to it. It doesn't matter, I am going to find out, even if I must wipe out the entire O'Neil family and anyone else who gets in my way. I do remember Michele calling me a week before she was killed, saying she was sick of the business and wanted out. She never got the chance." She walked toward a desk in the room opened a drawer, pulled out a case, and sat it on top of the desk. She removed two Smith & Wesson Model 500 Magnum handguns, capable of firing a 50-caliber bullet. Martina pointed the guns at a mirror on the wall and stared at her reflection. She lowered her arms to her side holding the guns. "If God does not stop me first, revenge is coming. The money will not bring my baby sister back, but I can make sure her death was not in vain. I have read and learned so much about the God-protected O'Neil family and associates. The chosen one Ron, a real prophecy-walking miracle man. Prison could not hold him, bullets could not kill him, and he cannot be destroyed. I will find out if that money exists and if it does, I will get it. No one better get in my way, including you miracle man Ron. If so, I will find out if your body can withstand these fifty-caliber bullets coming from my two cannons right here." She pointed the guns toward the mirror again. "I can stop a tank with these and Ron, you ain't no tank. Seduction, sex, and death here I come. Damn, when God created the woman, he created the most powerful weapon in the world. Pussy! Hot, tight, wet pussy. Men and women will argue, fight, and kill over some pussy! Damn, what a powerful weapon. Something so small but so dangerous." She smiled hard.

CHAPTER THIRTY ONE
DEAD BONES

When James and Catarina arrived home from the meeting at Ron's house, he kissed his wife and went directly to his office and got on the computer and began making calls. After three hours of not being disturbed, Catarina walked into James' office wearing a thin long gown with thong panties and no bra. She stood in front of James' desk to get his attention and wanted to talk because she saw how distracted he was. Catarina desired for them to spend quality time together tonight because James was gone all day.

"James, I know you are busy, and you have been busy all day, but you do have a wife who desires to spend quality time with her good-looking husband. If it's not asking too much?" She said condescendingly.

James exhaled with irritation and looked at his wife as she stood in front of him looking beautiful and sexy as always. His attitude instantly changed, and he smiled at her.

"You look gorgeous in that thin gown and..."

Catarina extended her arm out to James and waved her hand in his direction. A signal for him to stop talking. She turns around so her back would be to him and turned her head to look back at him. Catarina spread her legs and did a deep squat very slowly, caressing her butt with both hands at the same time. When she stood back up, she bent over, placed her hands on her butt and spread her butt cheeks, and then stood up and made her butt shake and smiled at James.

"Wow, you did all that so well, and I love it. And no, it is not asking too much but I am in the middle of something particularly important right now. So, if you will give me about," he looked down and began typing on his computer. "Give me about another hour, or two, and I will be all yours," he looked at her. "I can assure you I will take my time and appreciate you putting on that sexy outfit, and your sexual display, thanks baby." He continued typing on the computer.

Catarina was not a woman to get upset easily but James' words and nonchalant attitude bothered her. She walked in feeling good and sexy, desiring to be romantic, but her husband was being distant and secretive, and this was not working for her. She stepped closer and closed James' laptop with an attitude.

"James, we need to talk."

"Catarina, I am busy right now and this is very important." He stared at her.

"I understand that, but I am more important, and when did you start hiding things from me. We always talk about everything James, remember?"

James exhaled and stared at his wife because he knew she was right, they always talk. He stood and moved closer to her, then kissed her passionately and began licking and sucking the tip of her nipples through her gown. His warm breath and tongue felt good to Catarina, and she wanted more, but they needed to talk. She knew James was being sexual so he could go back to work and then go to sleep. This was not happening tonight; they were going to talk first. She was about to push his head away, but James put both hands around one of her breasts, massaging it and his lips formed a firm suction on her nipple. Between his warm breaths, licking her nipple, massaging her breast, and now having his lips locked on her nipple made Catarina pause on pushing his head away because everything felt so good. She leaned her head back and moaned. A minute went by of this great feeling, but Catarina was able to mentally regroup and gather more discipline, and then pushed his head slowly away.

"No James and you are smooth, but I can't let you have your way right now because we need to talk," she knew how fragile a man's ego could be, so she kissed him passionately and then stepped back. "Come on, let's sit down and talk." Catarina was turned on and walked to the sofa seductively to tease James and then gave him her trademark innocent look after she sat down.

James stared at his wife's beautiful silhouette as she walked, he desired her and was irritated at the same time, but he knew he had no choice but to listen to her now. He adjusted his erection and sat on the sofa across from her. Knowing James was aroused and irritated turned Catarina on even more, but she had to remain focused.

"James, tell me what is going on and what's the deal with the secret meeting you had at Ron's house. Please, can I get the short version and not the long-drawn-out attorney story?"

"No problem, short version it is." James began telling her about the flash drive with the locations to Victor Augular's secret money locations and Rick had it, but he gave it to him to turn in for the finder's fee. He told her the amount was seven hundred million dollars.

Catarina agreed Rick keeping the flash drive and going to get the money himself was a bad idea. She mentioned to James to please be careful and to speak with someone he trusts, before making it known to the authorities that he had the flash drive. James nodded at her.

"You reminded me of the person I do trust and can call." He retrieved his cell phone from his desk and made a call. "Lawrence, what's up my friend, this is James…yes I know it has been a while…can we meet and talk tomorrow, it's important. Great, I will see you tomorrow." He put his phone on the sofa and looked at his sexy wife. "I thank you for your help, as always. I could not have been blessed with a better friend and wife." He got on his knees directly in front of her and placed the palm of his hands on top of her legs.

"James, what are you doing?"

"Relax and I will show you." He leaned forward and pulled her gown off her shoulders exposing her beautiful breasts and began licking, sucking, and biting her breasts gently and slowly. This was the beginning of a wonderful lovemaking session for them. There were lots of moans, sexy talk, and screams of passion for the next hour. James' face was covered with his wife's juices because his face was between Catarina's legs for some time, giving her three orgasms with his great oral skills. Then he penetrated his wife in four different sex positions before he erupted inside her. Afterward, they showered and prayed together before going to sleep.

At seven o'clock the following morning James sat on a bench at Haines Point Park in DC with his friend Lawrence who works for the Department of Justice. They wore running attire so as not to stand out in any way. The weather was a cool 70° and great for running. James told him the complete story about the flash drive and the kidnapping of Rick and his wife Cynthia. Lawrence did not know James had the flash drive in his pocket. When James finished talking, Lawrence gave him a very stern look.

"James, you came to me because you trust me, so let me give it to you straight. I know you have heard the term, dead bones. Well, this is one of those situations that fit this story. Some bones should never be dug up once they are buried. Revealing Victor Auglar's secret money accounts would open a Pandora's Box of tremendous greed and evil in people. Many agencies would have their hands out to collect some of that money and there are corrupt people in every organization. There would also be exposure for people that would not want to be exposed. This is a dead case, let it remain dead. My advice to you my friend, we never had this conversation, and I would destroy that drive and never speak of it again. You do not want this box opened, ever. This is not only great advice for you but also a warning. Some people would get involved in this case once it was made known, who would make you and anyone else involved, disappear if they had to. Remember my friend, dead bones." He stared at James and walked away and then began running and never looked back.

James processed every word Lawrence said especially the extremely concerned look on his face when he gave him advice. He sat on the bench and then removed the flash drive from his pocket and stared at it.

"It's amazing how something so small could cause so much damage and suffering in the wrong person's hands. Well, I can't let that happen." He put the flash drive back in his pocket and stared out in space as he thought hard about his next move.

Malone sat on a bench at Haines Point as well dressed in running gear and wearing dark shades with his cane in his hand. He watched James and his friend the entire time. Before this meeting, Malone continuously sent oppressive spirits to Martina's mind to visit Washington DC.

Martina's mind and spirit were bombarded with thoughts of visiting Washington DC, but she did not know why. However, she felt compelled to fly to DC yesterday and stayed at the Watergate Hotel. Martina enjoyed running and once again her spirit compelled her to come to Haines Point this morning to run. She wore grey and white tennis shoes, tight grey spandex running shorts, a sports bra, and a grey tight-fitting T-shirt. Even with no make-up on, Martina looked great, and her spandex shorts and tight T-shirt revealed her incredible figure. As she ran and got closer to Malone, he stuck his cane out in front of her. If it were not for Martina's great reflexes, she would have fallen trying to avoid his cane. She stumbled and then stopped and looked at Malone like he was crazy.

"Sir, unless you are blind, I am getting ready to cuss you out because you almost made me fall sticking your cane out in front of me." The look on her face revealed how angry she was.

Malone removed his shades and stared at her. His eyes were black except for the yellow dot in the middle.

"Be quiet and sit your hot ass down before I cut your damn head off, nasty dick sucking fornicator. Listen to what I am about to tell you and hope I do not change my mind and rip the heart from your chest. You are a seed swallowing, taking dick in the ass slut, but I like that." He stared at Martina.

Martina looked at this man and trembled inside because she had never felt such evil in her life and was terrified. She sat down quickly and being this close to him made her skin crawl and she felt sick immediately.

Malone began telling her about Victor Augular's secret money accounts and the flash drive that James had and he briefly pointed to James when he talked.

Martina's fear was great, but curiosity was getting the best of her, so she had to ask.

"Can I talk now?" She looked at him and then lowered her head.

"What's your question? You multi-national ass licker"

"How do you know all this and who are you?" She never looked at his face while talking.

"What I am, is far more important than, who I am. This is all you need to know. However, I know everything about you. So, shut up and listen. James is going to start running and so will you, and you will purposely bump into him. After you fall, you will use your pickpocket skills and my help, of course, to get the thumb drive out of his pocket. Do not get distracted because you will be on your back while on the ground, this is not dick-taking time. Say a few words and then keep running and do not look back. I will be in touch with you very soon and instruct you on what to do when to do it, and how. If you do what I say, when I say, and how I say, you might live a little longer so you can keep sucking dicks. Which you do very well. Oh, I will let you know when I am coming by so you can slob on my long, fat dick. I have seen you suck dick, and you suck it damn good, spit all on it, I love it. By the way, I want some ass too." He smiled at Martina and then his eyes turned red. "Now, go get the thumb drive, baby swallower." He laughed and stared at her.

Martina stood and felt physically weak and sick. She saw this large rock on the ground and wanted to pick it up and bash this man in his head, but fear gripped her entire being. She felt compelled to do everything he said. She walked away and then turned her head to look at him, but he was gone. That sent chills to her body, and she ran toward James.

James was going to do exactly what Lawrence suggested and destroy the flash drive. But first, he wanted to get a short run in, since he was already here. He started running and was feeling good and then he noticed Martina running ahead of him and he had to repent. His thoughts were of her flesh and what he wanted to do to her. She was gorgeous in every way a woman could be. Beautiful face and incredible looking body and if he were not married, he would talk to her now.

"Lord, forgive me for my lustful nasty thoughts about this woman. She is fine. Forgive me Jesus." Somehow, he did not realize how close he was to her.

Martina knew now was the time, so she drifted in front of him to make it appear like an accident. James ran into her, and they both fell and rolled on the ground. While they were on the ground, Malone was nearby watching, and he tapped his cane on the ground and spoke curse words at James. Martina was able to slip her hand inside his pocket and get the thumb drive and he never felt a thing and she put it inside her bra. When they stopped rolling, James was on his back and Martina made sure she was on top of him. After she sat up, she purposely pressed her body down and moved her butt gently into his pelvic area and felt his growing erection.

"Oh my God, I am so sorry. I did not notice how close I was to you before realizing I had to stop and tighten my shoelaces." She stood up and brushed her clothes off in a seductive manner and then looked at James' eyes to make sure he noticed she stared at his erection.

James had never been more embarrassed as he stood up and wiped off his clothes trying to lose his erection. Being this close to her body made his erection more visible and the print easily showed against his sweatpants.

Martina stepped closer and noticed his wedding ring and the bulge in his pants. She knew this was a perfect time to embarrass him further.

"I noticed your wedding ring. You must have been in deep thought about your wife when running and missed her because now you have a hard on," she pointed between his legs. "Your size is nice because I felt it pressed into my butt when I sat on you. Make sure you tell your wife you got a hard-on staring at another woman and grinding your body against her. Shame on you," she smiled at him. "You are a nice-looking man and if I were your wife, we would go to the car right now, and I would slob all over your hard dick until you bust that nut in my mouth." Martina moved closer and leaned forward to whisper in his ear. "Your wife would never know, let me suck you off in your car."

James was shocked at what she said and leaned away from her.

"What!" He stared at her.

Martina reached down and grabbed James' penis quickly and squeezed it.

"Hot and hard, just the way I like it in my mouth, pussy, and ass." She squeezed it again and then ran away from him.

All James could do was watch her run away and thank God.

"Thank you, Lord thank you. That woman was fine." He stared at Martina as she ran and had more lustful thoughts of her. He had to repent again and bent down to tighten his shoelaces and ran in the opposite direction of Martina.

Malone was still close by and watched the entire scene unfold and laughed.

"I understand how you feel James. As fine as Martina is and her voluptuous body, you cannot help but have lustful dirty thoughts. Please, keep lusting and sinning so you will remain distracted. Less bible reading, less praying makes it so much easier to trick people into hell. I love tricking souls into hell." He continued to laugh.

CHAPTER THIRTY TWO

DEEP THOUGHTS

Later that night Sheila and Zechariah were home relaxing. Sheila approached Zechariah earlier to make love, but he was not in the mood, and she noticed he was far away mentally. Sheila prepared dinner and they sat in the dining room to eat but the conversation was dry and short. Zechariah washed the dishes, and they showered and kneeled on the floor next to their bed to pray. They wore tan-colored silk pajama pants and tops. After praying they stood, hugged, and kissed each other, and then Zechariah lay on the bed and stared at the ceiling in deep thought. Sheila knew something was seriously bothering him because he was not his usual spirited self. She noticed his attitude changed since Diana's mother showed up and Sheila wondered if Zechariah had thoughts about being with his daughter's mother. Yes, they discussed this, and he assured Sheila his heart was only with her. Sheila was aware the heart of a person can change when the circumstances change, and this was a huge change. His first love, his child's mother is back on the scene. Any person would have thoughts of what if. Zechariah was cheated in the past of having a relationship with his daughter and her mother. Sheila thought about this every day since Diana's mother showed up and anyone would have these thoughts under the circumstances. And there is the obvious, the woman is extremely attractive with a great-looking body. Sheila was not jealous of her presence, but she was concerned about her husband's heart's desire. The lovemaking between Zechariah and Sheila was always good but lately, Sheila felt his distance during sex, and no matter what a man says, a woman who is into her man can feel the difference. The physical contact can be good but the mental and spiritual can be off. Was Zechariah having second thoughts? Sheila stared at him lying there while she was in deep thought as well. She got a bottle of lotion off the dresser and sat on the bed to put lotion on her elbows and knees. She set the bottle on the dresser and looked at Zechariah. She needed answers but also wanted to make love to her husband now. Sheila got on the bed and laid on top of him and began kissing him slowly while rubbing his penis, but there was no response from him. Zechariah pushed her off his body slowly and then kissed her forehead and continued to stare at the ceiling. Now Sheila was irritated.

"Zechariah, what is bothering you?" Her tone was a little louder than it should have been, but it revealed her attitude. "Zechariah, you have been quiet and distant for a while, and please don't insult me and say, you have not. I understand you have a lot on your mind concerning Diana's mother being back in her life. I am a woman and a wife who pays attention. That woman is a freak walking and if you gave her half a chance, she would have sex with you in a heartbeat, any place, anywhere. I mean no disrespect, but Diana's mother is nasty. The way she was dressed at Ron's house and how she sat on the sofa purposely spreading her legs like a dog in heat. You stared because I saw you, but you are a man, and it is normal to look at a woman who exposes herself like that. She would have dropped to her knees and sucked all you men off if you allowed it. She is a nasty dirty dog." She stared at Zechariah with attitude.

Zechariah could not help but laugh at what his wife said and how she said it. This irritated Sheila even more.

"You think this is funny Zechariah?" She wanted to hit him but never would.

"Relax baby, I am only laughing because of what you said and how you said it. We already had this conversation but let's talk. Yes, I have been a little distant because of everything that has happened recently. I have been thinking, how do I continue to have a loving relationship with my daughter when her mother is back in her life? Her mother is emotionally and spiritually very damaged. What happened to Diana's mother was horrible and of course, she deserves a chance to have a relationship with her daughter, no question about that. And yes, anyone with a discerning spirit can feel Diana's mother's strong lust spirit. Yes, she is incredibly attractive, but I do not want her. I only want who God has blessed me with, my wife, you," he kissed her. "Forgive me for being distant but I need the wisdom of God to guide me concerning the right thing to do. I want Diana's mother to be happy and at peace, but I do not want anything to do with her, nothing. I think she is trouble waiting to happen. It is my job to protect my daughter but if I push her mother away or be mean to her, Diana will resent me for it, and this will damage the relationship we share. What do I do?" He shook his head and exhaled in total frustration.

Sheila stared at Zechariah and felt bad now for being irritated with him after hearing what he had to say. She felt the pain in his troubled heart and spirit. Zechariah was in a tough situation, and it would be easy to say, show love to your daughter and all would work out. She also knew Diana's mother was trouble. She kissed him and gently caressed his face with her hand.

"Zechariah, thank you for sharing all that with me. Your situation is a tough one. Know this, what affects you, also affects me. God will lead and guide you in the right direction as you continue to pray and seek his wisdom. He has not brought you this far in your life to leave you now. We will continue to pray for his wisdom and protection. In the meantime, you need to pay attention to your wife and keep your eyes off Diana's slutty mother. There is nothing she can do for you that I cannot do, and better. You need to remember that when you stare and lust over her body. You get a pass because she was physically so close to you and others when she sat on the sofa doing all that fake crying and spreading her legs in those tight revealing shorts. Anyway, skip all that for now because I am horny and desire my husband to make love to me, so you can do all that nasty stuff you know I like." She kissed him.

"It will be my pleasure." He kissed her lips softly and their passions increased as their tongues tasted each other, and they began making love.

Zechariah explored Sheila's body with only his hands and mouth, and she had three orgasms from his oral skills and fingers alone. She lay on her back and loved everything Zechariah did, and every orgasm was more intense than the previous one. After looking in Zechariah's eyes, she knew he was only going to continue, and it was too much. Her body was raw nerves, and she could not take any more regardless of how great it was. Five minutes after her last orgasm, Zechariah began licking her ankles and moved toward her thighs and she knew where he was going. Sheila moved her body away from him and got off the bed and looked at Zechariah.

"Sheila, what are you doing? Get back on this bed and stop running from me. You are standing there naked, looking like you are ready to run at any moment." He laughed at her.

Sheila laughed as well and then shook her head at him.

"No, I am not getting back on the bed because you are trying to make me pass out. Yes, I am running from you."

Zechariah got off the bed and tried to grab Sheila, but she was quick and jumped on the bed in a stance ready to move at any second. She smiled at him and was having fun but was serious about not allowing him to get his hands on her.

"Sheila, stop running from me. We are not teenagers, we are husband and wife, so lay back down." He tried to grab Sheila again, but she jumped off the bed and looked at him, and smiled.

"No, I am running from you, and you can say all you want but I am still running. I cannot take any more orgasms right now. I need a break." She knew this was silly but did not care and laughed along with him.

Zechariah tried to grab Sheila repeatedly, but she ran around the room or jumped on the bed to avoid him. They both laughed while playing this cat-and-mouse game. Sheila's evasiveness caused Zechariah to desire her more. He finally caught her and pulled her back on the bed and held Sheila down playfully while he kissed and caressed her body. Sheila laughed while trying to get away from him and they tossed and turned on the bed until Zechariah's touch got the best of her. She desired to satisfy her husband but needed a break. They relaxed and kissed passionately until she felt his erection pressed against her leg. Sheila moved on her back and Zechariah put her legs in the air and moved his body on top of hers and she saw an intense sexual look in his eyes. She knew he was ready to penetrate with purpose which caused her to be apprehensive and his penis was so hard.

"Zechariah, you are going to just put the head in, right?" Giving him her schoolgirl smile.

"What!" He moved his body off hers and started laughing and looked at her. "Put the head in, just put the head in? Are you serious? This is not our first date Sheila. I am going to do more than, just put the head in! I am going dick and balls deep in you, repeatedly." He laughed.

Sheila slid her body away from him and shook her head.

"You are talking about banging. Oh no, there will be no banging, none of that. My body is too sensitive, you are not going to beat my stuff up." She stared at him, and they started laughing. After playfully exchanging words back and forth they remained in this playful state for a while.

"That is it, I am not in the mood now. You messed it up, I don't want any lovin." He laughed at her.

"Yes, you do want some lovin. I needed to make sure what you were going to do because I saw a hungry sex look in your eyes and I knew you wanted to do some serious fucking. So, I said to myself, oh no, he is not banging my body. There will be no banging tonight." They both laughed hard. Sheila loved her husband and did not want him to go to sleep unsatisfied. After more laughing and playing they relaxed, and she kissed Zechariah passionately and then wrapped her lips around his penis. It did not take long before Zechariah erupted in her mouth.

"Ahhhhhhh it's good baby. Keep sucking that dick, suck it, ahhhhhhhh Sheila." His body shook hard, and he tried to slide away from Sheila so she would let his dick go because it was so intense. "Baby that's enough, let it go, you are trying to bust my brain. Let my dick go." He was breathing heavily and had a look of total amazement on his face.

Sheila continued sucking until she drained him, and loved his satisfied reaction and powerless state, and her feeling of complete control. She used her throat muscles to suck every drop of his cum and then finally let his dick slide slowly from her mouth and stared at him.

"Think about that when you are lusting over another woman, husband. Your dick is attached to your body, but it belongs to me." She smiled and kissed him.

Zechariah was overwhelmed with satisfaction and breathing heavily when he looked at Sheila.

"Yes, it's your dick. All your dick, you are incredible."

"I know, and you remember that. Okay, catch your breath and relax so you can bury your face between my legs."

"What!" He looked at Sheila like she was joking.

"You heard me, I want to feel your warm lips and tongue on my clit and bury your face between my legs until I wet your face with my juices, but I need you to take your time and go slow."

He stared at her.

"For sure, you are nasty!"

"And you love me this way. Now relax so you can handle your business."

"Not a problem." He looked at his wife and smiled and instantly decided to do to Sheila what she did to him. Zechariah moved his body down on the bed and began kissing and licking Sheila's legs slowly while working his way up between her legs. He teased her wetness with tender slow licks and soft kisses, knowing she was close. Sheila gripped the sheets hard and arched her back as her orgasm hit and then Zechariah sucked her clit and would not let go.

Sheila was screaming from such an intense orgasm and tried to back away from Zechariah, but this caused him to suck her clit more and grip her legs tighter, and hold on as she squeezed the side of his head with her thighs.

Zechariah continued sucking as she was twisting her body to get away from him and screaming at the same time.

CHAPTER THIRTY THREE
ITS MY TIME

After Martina got the thumb drive from James, she spent the next two days working out in the fitness room at the Watergate Hotel. She got help from a past friend who was good at decoding encrypted files, but Martina was not dumb enough to send him the file. He explained exactly what to do, and she did it from her laptop and agreed to pay him five hundred thousand dollars. Martina told him he would get his money once she decoded the file and took a trip out of town. After two days the files were completely decoded and what Martina saw made her mouth drop open. Ten different locations across the globe with Victor Augular's secret money accounts totaling seven hundred million dollars. The money was in banks in New York, Florida, Las Vegas, Maryland, Belize, Cayman Island, Bogota, Columbia, Switzerland, Tahiti, and Hawaii. Martina made a copy of the decoded file and then laid on the bed tossing, turning, and laughing.

"Yes, I am coming for the money," she continued laughing and playing on the bed and then sat up and stared in space wondering was her anger toward the O'Neil family justified. The fact is, they had nothing to do with her sister's death, they were not around yet. She was angry with the O'Neil family and friends because she had to go through them to get her hands on the thumb drive and it was not easy. Martina could get the money and leave the O'Neil family and their friends alone and leave town and never look back. Time would tell she thought because it depends on how hard it would be to get all the money from the banks. Hopefully, she will not have to kill anyone in the process. The first bank for her was the closest, a bank in Silver Spring, Maryland. Martina sent a copy of the bank's locations to her phone and added fingerprint protection to open her phone. Later, she went to the exercise room to work off some stress. An hour and a half later, she was back in her room, showered, and in bed looking forward to tomorrow. The first day of her bank journey.

The following morning Martina walked into the bank wearing an expensive but conservative pants suit. She looked nice but did not want to bring too much attention to herself. Thirty minutes later she walked out of the bank with five million dollars in cash from several large safe deposit boxes. All she had to do was use the password and code from the encrypted file and the money was now in her hand. No picture ID was needed. There was a large duffle bag in one of the safe deposit boxes to put the money in. An attendant carried her bag and Martina wanted to scream with joy but kept her composure. A taxi waited for her, and the attendant put the duffle bag in the taxi and Martina gave him a hundred-dollar tip. She got in the taxi, and it drove away.

Martina sat on the bed in her hotel room staring at some of the money she pulled from the duffle bag.

"What am I going to do with all this cash now that I have it, wow. Five million dollars in cash sitting on my bed and I know it is only the beginning. Where do I put all this money and the rest to come?" She thought for a minute and a plan came to her. She would purchase a motor home and have a large safe put in and disguise the safe as a cabinet. She would then drive the motor home to various states as she traveled so her movements would be hard to track. Next, establish an account with a private jet company so she could travel across the globe and take the cash with her as it was acquired from each bank. A taxi to each airport, a private jet to where she needed to go, and another taxi to the bank. A taxi from the bank with the cash, and then to her awaiting private jet, and travel to wherever her motor home was at that time. Martina went over this plan in her head several times until she was finally comfortable with all the details, and then she went to work.

The following morning Martina's new journey began. She called her friend who helped her decode the file and told him the five-hundred-thousand dollars she owed him could be found in a backpack under the bed in the hotel where she stayed. Martina left the hotel but paid for the room for two more days to give him enough time to get there. She purchased a five-hundred-thousand-dollar forty-foot motor home. She had some items removed from the motor home to make room for two large safes that were custom designed to look like cabinets. After that, her travels began. Her next three stops were banks in New York, Florida, and Las Vegas. Martina was in Vegas now and had three hundred million dollars in cash in her motor home safes. She knew people in Vegas who would help her get anything done for the right price. She wanted a bigger house, so she purchased a two-level eight-thousand square foot six-bedroom, four-car garage house in a gated community in Vegas for eight million dollars. The house was fully decorated in three weeks. There was plenty of space to park her motor home on her property. Martina did not want to leave a paper trail, so she paid cash for everything to the right people who knew how to make anything look good on paper. Everything was going well for her and now she needed rest, so she worked out at home, ate, showered, and laid in bed wearing a satin nightdress and nothing underneath.

Martina was unaware Malone watched her every move along the way and he admired her aggressive behavior. Even now he stood at the foot of her bed dressed in black holding his cane. He tapped his cane on the edge of her bed and mumbled some words and a mist appeared underneath her bed and then dissipated, leaving behind a pack of rats. Malone hit the bed hard with his cane.

"Wake up woman." He laughed.

Martina opened her eyes, sat up quickly, and looked at Malone. She could not believe he was in her bedroom and never heard a thing and this surprised her because she always felt good about her sharp senses.

"What!" She yelled. "You again, are you crazy and how did you get in my house fool?" She turned and grabbed a gun from her nightstand and pointed it at Malone. And then stood up on the bed. "I don't know how you got in my house, but you've got five seconds to get out or I will shoot you in your head, and I am a great shot. Now, get out of my house you creep."

Malone tapped his foot on the floor several times and then shook his head.

"You should be careful how you talk to me and put that gun down, or my friends will eat you from the inside out. That would be a shame because you are a beautiful woman with fantastic sex skills. So, relax because I came here to talk, taste you, and yes, fuck you, from the back." He smiled at her.

"Go to hell, you think I am playing with you, I said get out of…" Martina never finished her sentence because she noticed her bed was covered with rats. She screamed and frantically began shooting at the rats.

"Stop shooting at my friend's fool!" He yelled and smacked the gun from her hand with his cane and it fell to the floor. He hit the bed hard with his cane and mumbled some words, and the rats ran under the bed. One of the rats grabbed the gun with his teeth and pulled it underneath the bed. "Stop all that stupid screaming and calm down before you have a heart attack."

"Oh my God, oh my God. Where did all the rats go and who in the hell are you?" Martina was very scared, but she had to find out if the rats were still under her bed. Her body trembled as she got on her hands and knees and leaned over slowly to look under the bed. The rats were gone, and Martina's nightdress was pulled up on her back revealing her butt because of the position she was in. Malone stared at her derriere.

"Damn, look at all that fine body. You got hips on you and all that round ass in the air. I am going to enjoy banging that from the back." He laughed.

Martina was so frightened by all the rats she was not aware of how exposed she was until Malone's nasty comments. She reached back and pulled her nightdress down quickly to cover her butt and then stood up on the bed to face him.

"I don't know what kind of sick magician you are, but you better get the hell out of my house before I kick your teeth out." She got in a fighting stance.

Malone laughed and then leaned forward and blew his breath on the bed, stood up, and pointed his cane at the bed.

"You hurt my feelings, and now I am going to watch my friends eat you alive. You smart-mouth slut."

Martina looked down and noticed many small humps moving underneath her covers on the bed. She kicked the covers off and saw a pack of rats moving around and then they all stopped moving. The rats stood on their hind legs, looked at her, and began snapping their teeth.

"Oh my God," she screamed. "Oh my God, please don't let the rats get me, please, please. I will do whatever you say, please help me. Oh my God." Martina was so scared her entire body trembled and she felt like she was seconds away from having a massive heart attack.

"Typical, like so many others, you call on God when you need his help. Any other time you are licking and sucking balls and backing that ass up on some dick. However, I know you ain't thinking about no dick now, are you? Unless you are the super freaky type, and you want a lot of little rat dicks poking you. Forget that, I got the big one," he grabbed his crotch. "Now, take that thin nightdress off and give me some pussy before I make the rats eat your ass off. You'll walk around with a flat chewed-off ass." He laughed hard.

"Oh God yes, whatever you say." Martina did not know how he was doing all this and did not care. She would do absolutely anything to keep these rats from eating her alive. She removed the nightdress, threw it on the floor and stood there shaking from fear.

The rats jumped on the floor and dragged the nightdress underneath the bed. Malone laid his cane on the chair and smiled at Martina and removed his clothes and stared at her. The last thing on her mind was sex but when she looked at Malone and his tight body, she was attracted to him and he was well endowed. He kept making his penis move up and down and this caused her to desire him, in a sick twisted way. Malone grabbed his penis and waved it at her.

"You know what it is, come put your fat lips on this dick and start sucking. And do not act like it is your first time, because we both know you have been sucking dick, and licking pussy, and ass a long time. Put some spit on it and start sucking and I need to feel it in the back of your throat then maybe we can talk later." He continued to wave his dick at her.

Martina was repulsed at what she was about to do but knew this feeling all too well. This was different, and she would suck twenty dicks in one night instead of being eaten alive by rats, to hell with that she thought. She moved off the bed slowly and then looked under it and saw no rats or her nightdress. She stood up and shook her head and stepped closer to Malone and looked at him.

"I hate you beyond words, whoever you are. But right now, I am going to suck your dick so good, I hope you have a quick heart attack and die, in great pain." She looked at him with venom in her eyes.

Malone put his hands on Martina's hips pulled her into him and stared into her eyes. His nose and mouth almost touched hers.

"I don't give a damn how you feel about me. Just get your mouth wet and start sucking and then we are fucking, believe that." He kissed her lips hard and aggressively.

Martina felt horrible but kneeled in front of him and grabbed his penis and began sucking it. She wanted to bite his penis as hard as she could but something in her said, do not do it. Martina knew her oral skills were highly impressive, but no matter how hard she tried or what she did, she could not make Malone cum. However, something was happening on the inside of her, and she hated this feeling. She became wet and horny, and this disgusted her, but she could not help it.

Malone had to admit this woman could suck a dick, maybe better than Ice. He was always in control and wanted to have some fun with her first. So, he reached down and stood Martina up and put one hand on her lower back and lifted her up with one hand and carried her to the bed. For the next twenty minutes, Malone caressed Martina's body slowly while mumbling various erotic curses.

Martina could not figure out how he was able to lift her with only one hand like she weighed nothing. She had experienced getting a massage many times in her life by different people but what she was experiencing now was unlike anything she ever experienced. His touch was warm and penetrating and it felt as if other hands were touching her body at the same time. It was incredibly relaxing, stimulating, and an extreme turn-on. Martina could not remember being so turned on in her life as she was right now. She turned over on her back and began fingering herself. Slow at first and then faster and deeper as her passions increased by the seconds. Then it happened, she had an explosive orgasm, and the pleasure was very intense.

"Ahhhhhhhh," she screamed while fingering herself and felt many hands massaging her at the same time and she tossed her head from side to side repeatedly.

Malone turned her over and began licking her butt while his hand was underneath her and slid two fingers inside her. He buried his face between her butt cheeks and made his tongue firm and probed her anal entrance with it. His fingers and tongue were too much for Martina and she could no longer hold it in, she screamed her deepest sexual desires.

"Ahhhhhhhh yes," she screamed. "in my ass, slide your tongue in my ass. Fuck me in my mouth, pussy, and ass. Just fuck meeeeeee." The moment Martina said this she felt Malone's warm tongue trying to penetrate her butt, and it felt so good. It felt like another person's mouth was licking and sucking her wetness at the same time. Her mouth opened on its own and she felt a hard penis sliding inside and sucked it with passion. Martina climaxed so hard that she felt Malone's hard dick slide inside her wetness. He fucked her with slow, long, and deep thrust. All this was beyond wonderful, and her pussy erupted with her juices coming out. Malone continued thrusting slow and long.

"Ohhhhhh I am cumming so hard." She screamed.

Malone increased his pace and exploded inside her and leaned forward to stare into her eyes.

"Your pussy will always be mine and I am turning your hot ass out." He kissed her lips and continued thrusting inside her.

Martina could not take such intense pleasure anymore and she passed out, but her body moved back and forth with Malone's penis still inside her. Two hours later she woke up feeling drained and exhausted but sexually satisfied in every way possible. She noticed how clean she felt and smelled, and she had a different night dress on. Malone sat in a chair close to her bed fully dressed holding his cane. She sat up and looked at him.

"What happened and what did you do to me? Did you drug me? How did I get so clean and fresh?"

"Relax, you got what you wanted and it's just the beginning. And no, I did not drug you. After you passed out from all that good lovin I put on you, I carried you to the tub and washed you and put lotion on your body. I also went to your dresser drawer and found another night dress and put it on you as well. Oh, I changed your sheets because they were wet from all your sweet love juices and you rolling all over the bed." He smiled at her.

Martina stared at him in bewilderment trying to figure all this out in her head. How much of what happened to her was a dream or real? Deep inside she knew it was all real and her body told her that. She had never felt this good after sex in her life, minus the soreness between her legs.

"You show up out of nowhere in my life while I am running in the park and told me things you should not know.

Then you show up in my bedroom, and somehow you give me the best sex I have ever had in my life, by far. Who are you really and what do you want from me?" She was thinking, *he can't be here to kill me because I would already be dead. What does this crazy man with strange abilities want from me?*

"My name is Malone, and I am here to help you get the rest of the money you seek from the overseas banks. You have done well so far, but you will need my help. You called me a magician, I am that and so much more. I can do anything at any time. I do not want money and I can get sex any time I want, so do not flatter yourself. Although you are exceptionally good in bed and a freak, just the way I like it. Now, back to the business at hand. You may think so, but the O'Neil family was not responsible for your sister's death. Her profession got her killed, sucking all those dicks, and getting her pussy and ass banged out regularly." He laughed and said this to irritate her.

Malone's harsh words about Martina's sister caused her to become angry instantly. She sat on the edge of the bed and stared at him with hatred.

"Don't mention my sister's name, you disrespectful bastard. Be glad I did not bite your dick off when I sucked it. If I had a knife in my hand right now, I would stab you in your forehead." Her eyes said it all.

Malone waved his cane across the floor in front of her.

"Oh, how the truth hurts. You know you love sucking dick, just like your nasty dick-sucking sister. Two nasty dick-sucking tramps, you need to get checked medically.

Do not forget my friends, the rats. Now shut up and don't interrupt me again."

Martina's heart started beating fast and she looked quickly on the floor and her bed for rats.

"Okay, I won't interrupt you." Her facial expression revealed her intense fear.

"I thought so. I will help you get the rest of the money. Giving you a total of seven hundred million dollars in cash. You could build your own empire with that much money. In return for my help, you will get next to the O'Neil family and their friends and help me destroy them all. I have my reasons and I could kill them in a day if I wanted to, but I want them all to suffer greatly before they die. Especially, that so call chosen one, Ronald O'Neil. It is about divide and conquer. Keith is Ron's best friend, but Ron and Keith have freaky wives who like licking pussy," he pointed his finger at her. "just like you, and they do it well too. You will get next to the wives and cause doubt. Yes, they all gave their lives to the Lord and are supposed to be Christians now, but I am going to change all that," he stood and pointed his cane at her. "I got the power of Mr. Bones!" He yelled and began transforming slowly into a large black wolf.

Martina screamed and her heart felt like it would explode, as her fear paralyzed her. She began sweating, and could not move a muscle, and her body trembled. Her eyes were locked on this horrible creature in front of her.

The wolf stepped closer and sniffed her and then moved its face between her legs and sniffed her again. It backed up, shook its head, sneezed and looked at her, and growled.

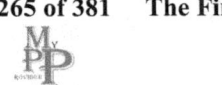

She looked at the wolf and her intense fear caused her to urinate on herself. Martina was thinking, *oh God please do not let this wolf kill me, help me Jesus! Oh God help me!*

"Jesus help me!" She screamed as loudly as she could.

The moment Martina screamed the name Jesus, the wolf stepped back, raised its head, and howled, and then transformed back into Malone. He stood in front of her holding his cane and his facial expression revealed his serious attitude.

"I hate that name. Now you call on God to help you. No matter, if you do not do as I say, I am going to rabbit fuck you, cut your arms off, and then let the rats eat you alive." He laughed and sat down.

Martina trembled from fear and could not believe what she just saw. She raised her shaking arm in the air.

"Please don't kill me but can I talk now?"

"Hurry up and talk, before you piss on yourself again." He laughed.

"I will do whatever you say, how you say. But, when I am finished, will you let me live so I can get as far away from you as possible, please." Her words were spoken in tremendous fear.

"Sure, why not, but just for the record, I can reach out and touch you from anywhere in the world. Do what I say, and you will be free to live your life as you please. Oh, there is someone I want you to meet." He waved his cane in the air and smoke appeared. When the smoke cleared, he was gone.

Martina felt extremely exhausted, mentally, and physically. Nothing in her life prepared her for what she just experienced. She wondered, how could such things be possible, no magician could be this good. Could all this be magic or was she dealing with the powers of darkness itself?

"Oh my God, oh Jesus." Martina leaned back on the bed and was sweating. She began crying and began praying asking God to help and protect her.

CHAPTER THIRTY FOUR

MARTINA, ICE, & RAY

After Martina cried for an hour, she finally got off the bed and looked around her house for any sign of rats. She was very scared and did not know what to do at this point except hurry and take a shower. Martina could not believe she urinated on herself, but intense fear will make your body react. Martina felt a little better after the shower and sat on her bed wearing a silk gown and in deep thought. She was curious as to who this person was Malone wanted her to meet, but now she was hungry and tired. She went to the kitchen and prepared tuna fish and iced tea. She ate two tuna fish sandwiches with sliced peaches and drank some tea. Afterward, she walked around the house one more time looking for rats, and then walked back to her bedroom, laid on her bed, prayed, and cried for mercy.

The following morning Martina was awakened by the sound of her doorbell. She went to the bathroom to quickly brush her teeth, gargle, and rinse her face and answered the door. Malone and Ice stood there. Malone had a fresh haircut and wore dress shoes, a white dress shirt, and a dark blue three-piece suit, and his cane was in his hand. Standing next to him was an extremely attractive lady wearing heels, a tight dress revealing her cleavage and curvaceous body, and had a small purse in her hand. Martina had to admit, this lady was beautiful.

"Good morning Martina, may we come in and talk." He said this in a businesslike manner.

Martina stared at this woman and then looked at Malone and thought, *I do not know what kind of game he is playing. Like he was not over my house yesterday trying to fuck me to death. He must be trying to impress this woman he is with. I don't give a damn, anything but the rats and that wolf.* She motioned her hand for them to enter.

"Good morning, please come in."

Malone and Ice walked in, Ice showed such grace and confidence as always. She had to admit Martina was extremely attractive and was drawn to her, but this was business and she needed to remain focused. Martina closed the door and they walked to the living room and sat down. Malone and Ice sat next to each other on the sofa and Martina sat across from them. She felt uncomfortable wearing only her nightdress in front of them with no panties or bra on, but it was too late now.

"Martina, I know we disturbed your sleep, but we will not be here long," he pointed to Ice. "Martina this is Ice, Ice this is Martina. You two will be working together to destroy the O'Neil family and whoever else gets in the way. They are all going to hell soon anyway."

Martina and Ice noticed when he spoke, all the professionalism was gone from his voice, and they saw evil in his eyes. However, Ice was fully aware of who he was and what he could do. Ice looked at Martina and smiled.

"It is nice to meet you Martina, you are lovely, even when you first wake up." She stared at her and looked directly between her legs.

Although Martina was attracted to Ice, the way she stared made her feel uncomfortable, so she crossed her legs and leaned back on the sofa, trying to be professional.

"Thank you for the compliment and you are attractive yourself," she looked at Malone. "Malone, what do you want us to do, exactly?"

"You and Ice will get next to Ron, Keith, Stacy, and Diana and seduce them, and I don't care how you do it, as long as you get it done, and soon. I will help you of course. Martina, Ron's wife Diana is Ice's daughter, and she will be yours to seduce and destroy. She is an undercover sexual freak pretending to be a Christian like so many others these days. So, it should not be difficult for you to seduce her. I want you two to meet and then go to a hotel and get freaky, and secretly film it so Ron can see his precious Christian wife getting fucked in the ass and pussy by you with a dildo or wearing a big thick strap-on. Make sure you fuck her good and deep because she loves it that way." He leaned back and laughed knowing Ice would be angry at his words.

"No!" Ice yelled and stood and looked at Malone with anger.

Malone looked at Ice with eyes black as coal and grabbed her wrist. His very touch was hot to her skin.

"Sit your slut walking ass down, just because you have been fucked in the ass repeatedly does not make you tough. You must have forgotten who I am. The next time you sit on the toilet, I will make rats come up from the water and bite through your ass and out your mouth. Now sit down, and act like you know who I am."

Ice was incredibly angry but his words and the image of what he said sent chills to her body. She had no choice but to obey, for now. She sat down, lowered her head, and then looked at him.

"I am sorry Malone. What do you want me to do?" She spoke calmly and gave him a fake smile.

"Oh, now you want to pretend because you walk and talk classy, you don't know who you are. Do what sluts do, shake ass, spread ass, and work hips, lips, and fingertips. This is not new to you, so play your part and you might not wake up screaming with your bed full of rats." He looked at Martina and winked at her.

Martina saw the evil look in his eyes when he spoke, and she could not help but shake for a second, thinking about what she went through concerning the rats.

"Malone, when do you want Ice and I to start?" Martina asked.

"As soon as you get back from your trips and as I mentioned with my help, it will not take you long. Now, I need to go and take care of some business," he looked at Ice. "Ice, you stay here so you and Martina can talk and get to know each other better. She will take you home," he stood holding his cane and then looked at them. "Don't you two get too freaky while I am gone, save that spirit for me." He laughed and tapped his cane on the floor hard and smoke appeared surrounding his body, seconds later, he and the smoke were gone.

Martina and Ice put their hands on their chest and spoke at the same time while looking at each other.

"Oh my God."

"Ice, you have known him longer than me. How does he do what he does? Is he one of those evil magicians that sold his soul to the Devil as people often say?" She stared at her.

"Trust me when I say this, you do not want to know who he is." She sat next to Martina, stared at her face, leaned forward, and kissed her lips.

During the kiss, it was as if they read each other's thoughts. They continued kissing with more passion and then leaned away from each other.

"Are we on the same page?" Ice said.

"Yes, we are. Do what we have to do and then find a way to get away from Malone."

"There is no getting away from him. The only way to get him completely out of our lives is to kill him but I have not figured out how to do that yet." Ice shook her head out of frustration.

"We will, but for now let's talk. Tell me about you and how you got involved with this very evil man."

"Okay, it's a long story but I will make it short. I will start with meeting the love of my life. My real name is Diana but call me Ice please."

Ice began telling her story starting with meeting Zechariah, getting pregnant, having to leave him. Faking her death and leaving her baby Diana behind with her mother. Her life of crime, being on the run for years, Zechariah going to prison. Seeing her daughter Diana for the first time in many years at church with Zechariah and his new wife. Meeting Malone Garcia at the *Live! Casino* in Maryland. Learning all about the O'Neil family because her daughter was now married to Ronald O'Neil. Wanting to have a loving relationship with her daughter but none of the O'Neil's like her. Meeting a wonderful man named Ray and desiring for them to have a relationship, and so much more, Ice could not believe she told this woman who she just met her life story. When she was done, tears were in her eyes and flowing down her face.

"Wow, that was incredible," she hugged Ice and held her until she stopped crying and then leaned back and looked at her. "Well, let me get my story over with." Martina did the same and told Ice everything concerning her past. From her sister Michele's lifestyle, her getting killed, to where she is now, and everything in between.

"So much heartbreak and sadness. We both have very horrible stories and so much pain. Now, we can work together and hope for the best. Malone mentioned you were taking a trip. Are you okay?"

"Yes, I am fine, but this trip is necessary. I will be traveling internationally going to Belize, Cayman Island, Bogota Columbia, Switzerland, Tahiti, and Hawaii. Not necessarily in that order but it must be done." She thought about telling Ice why she was going to all these places but changed her mind.

"That sounds like fun. When will you be leaving?"

"Tomorrow afternoon and Hawaii will be my first stop." She thought, *should I tell Ice the truth*?

"I would like to go with you if you don't mind."

"Okay, your company would be great, and we could talk and get to know each other better." She kissed Ice on the lips. "However, there is something you need to know first about this trip."

"I understand and thank you, but I know you are going to get the rest of Victor Augular's money from his secret bank accounts. Malone mentioned this to me. Relax, yes money will always be important, but I am not motivated by money like I used to be. I just want my daughter and I to have a loving healthy relationship."

"Okay, so much for that. We travel and watch each other's back." They both smiled at each other.

"Great, and I have a thought. My friend Ray and I have not shared much time together. If you are in the mood to meet him, I will call Ray now and see if he has the time to fly from DC and come to Vegas. He can take a private jet and be here tonight. I am sure you are tired so if he can come, we will not be here long."

"I don't mind meeting Ray, but I would not want him to do all that."

"No problem for him and he loves to travel. Besides, I am sure he misses me as much as I miss him. He is very handsome and got it going on in the bedroom and I desire for us to make love tonight. This would definitely take my mind off all this madness going on and give me an intense orgasm, which I need." She kissed Martina. "Unless you, want to make me scream." She caressed her leg.

"You need to call your man." She pushed her hand away.

Ice gave Martina a quick kiss and then got her phone from her purse and walked away to call Ray. They talked for five minutes and afterward, Ice sat next to Martina with a big smile on her face.

"I had to get off the phone, that man started talking nasty to me, and I am already horny. Anyway, he will be here tonight. You two can meet, and talk, and then we will go to a nice hotel."

"As big as this house is, you don't have to go to a hotel."

"Thank you but to be very direct, Ray and I have wild sex sometimes and tonight is going to be one of those times. I would not want our noise to keep you awake." She stuck her tongue out at Martina.

"Okay, but the invitation is still open. Now, I am going to get a quick workout, shower, and lay down for a while. Please make yourself at home and there is plenty of food in the refrigerator. If Ray gets here before I wake up, come and get me." They both stood and Martina hugged Ice.

"Would you like me to join you in the shower?" Ice gave Martina a mischievous smile and kissed her.

"You are something, but you could not handle me. You need to save all your energy for Ray. Please, make yourself at home." Martina hugged Ice again and walked away seductively.

"That's what your mouth says." She watched Martina walk and knew it was only a matter of time before they connected sexually.

Seven hours later Martina was awakened again by screams. She sat up in bed thinking she was having a bad dream but heard the screams of a woman. Now she remembered Ice was in the house and her friend Ray must be there as well. They were in one of the bedrooms upstairs. She heard more screams, and moans, and then she heard the voice of a man as he screamed in passion. Hearing all this turned her on. All was quiet after that, and Martina laid down and relaxed for a while and then got up wearing her nightdress. She brushed her teeth, gargled, washed her face, and then went to the kitchen for a snack. She cooked some bacon and then made a bacon, lettuce, and tomato sandwich on wheat toast and a glass of orange juice. Thinking Ray and Ice might be hungry later, she cooked more bacon and made two more sandwiches for them as well.

Ice and Ray showered together and put lotion on each other then sat down to talk.

When Martina sat down at the kitchen table to eat, Ice walked in wearing a large white T-shirt with nothing on underneath. A minute later this good-looking muscular man walked in behind her wearing burgundy silk pajama pants and a T-shirt to match. Martina stared at him for several seconds and thought, *damn this man is fine.*

"Hi, you must be Ray. Ice said you were a handsome man, well she did not lie. Please, have a seat. I made a BLT sandwich and one for each of you if you like." She stood and extended her hand to Ray.

"Hello Martina, it is nice to meet you. Please forgive me if we woke you. It was my intention of going to a hotel once I got here but," he turned to look at Ice and then looked at Martina. "Someone was very persuasive in having her way and I was taken advantage of." He looked at Ice and smiled.

"Well, you are a big man and if Ice can take advantage of you, what can I say."

Ice stepped closer and hugged Martina and then Martina whispered in her ear.

"I heard you two having sex."

Ice looked at Martina and smiled and then kissed her on the lips like it was an everyday thing. Ray was surprised at this but said nothing.

"Forgive me, I could not wait, so I jumped him. However, Ray and I like BLT sandwiches, so this is great, and thank you." She and Ray sat down and began eating.

"Martina, thanks again for the sandwich, it's good! The bacon is crisp the way I make my sandwiches." Ray took another bite and kept eating.

"Girl, this sandwich is good, thanks again."

"Martina, Ice mentioned you will be traveling internationally, and she will be going with you. It is up to you, but I have the time and if you want, I do not mind traveling with you. There is safety in numbers and the three of us going together would be good, if you are interested?"

"Well, since you mentioned it, I was not sure at first, but I get a good vibe from you Ray. Having a man with us will be good. Did Ice mention why I am going?"

"Yes, briefly but your business is your business. I would like to go along to make sure your travels are safe. I am a combat veteran and trained to do many things. We can have some fun along the way." He looked at Ice.

"We sure can baby." She kissed him.

Martina stood and looked at them.

"Yes, I would like that very much, and thank you, hold on I will be right back," she walked to her bedroom and retrieved a suitcase on wheels from the closet and walked back to the kitchen, and put the suitcase on the floor. She opened it and it was full of cash. Martina counted two million dollars and put it on the table, closed the suitcase, and then pushed one million dollars each toward Ray and Ice.

"I don't know your situation, but this is for you both, for going with me. One million dollars each and I am not trying to insult either of you but please take it. I want you to have it." She looked at the surprised expressions on their faces.

"Martina, I do thank you for such a grand gesture, but you don't have to pay me. I am financially comfortable." Ice said.

"Same here Martina, I am not on welfare either, but damn. One million in cash, wow."

"I am going to take a risk and say this to you both. I never in my life expected to be in a situation such as this. It comes with a big price, and that price is Malone. I want him out of my life, by any means necessary, and I do mean, by any means necessary." she looked at Ice and then Ray. "Now, changing the subject, the screams of you two having sex woke me and I must admit, it turned me on. I do not have anyone special in my life right now," she looked at Ice. "Ice, will you share yourself with me? I am not asking for a love thing, but great company and lots of nasty sex on our travels for the next week and a half." She stared at them both.

Ray looked at Ice waiting for her to respond because he was not about to speak about this situation. Ice stood and grabbed Martina's hand and she stood as well. She kissed Martina passionately and then Ice motioned her head at Ray to come over. Ray stood and stepped closer to Martina and kissed her and then stepped back.

"No Ray, kiss her like you kiss me."

Ray stared at Ice and wondered if this was a setup, but Ice nodded her head in Martina's direction.

"Ray, it's okay. I want this to happen, it will help us become closer. She had a good vibe." Ice smiled and stepped closer to Ray and put her hand on his shoulder.

Ray moved closer to Martina and then kissed her with passion as he rubbed her back. For the next two minutes, they were kissing each other. Martina grabbed Ice's hand and they walked to her bedroom and Ray followed them. They removed their clothes got in Martina's bed and began having sex. Everything was slow for the first hour, with lots of hugging, touching, kissing, and tasting each other all over. Then, their actions became erotic as their passions increased tremendously. A lot of nasty talking and sex in many positions, all three of their bodies were so intertwined, that they look like one.

Malone stood across the street dressed in all black pointing his cane at Martina's house and saying all manner of curses against it.

"That's it, do it. Fornicate, sexual perversion, nasty talk. Suck dick, eat pussy, lick ass, anal sex, do it all," he tapped his cane on the ground. "I love people that have turned their back on God. I am taking everybody to hell with me. We all are going to spend eternity burning." He laughed and then disappeared into a cloud of dark smoke.

CHAPTER THIRTY FOUR
CLOSER TO THE PRICE

For the next two weeks Ray, Ice, and Martina were either aboard a private jet, riding in a taxi, or staying in luxury hotel suites with two king-size beds and the best hotel concierge services. They had a simple and direct system for the banking situation. Martina would go in dressed conservatively with the private password and code for the bank boxes. Ice walked in behind Martina but acted like she did not know her to watch Martina's back. If anything went wrong, Ice was prepared to shoot whoever she had to as she and Martina ran out of the bank in the awaiting car with Ray driving. However, they were not aware Malone was always close by performing his evil rituals, so they never had any problems. He would point his cane at the bank and speak curses in the language of the country they were in and then disappear. They got up early to eat breakfast every morning, worked out in the hotel fitness room, and then went to the banks. Martina and Ice walked into the bank, Martina walked out with a duffle bag full of cash and Ice walked behind her and they got in the car and Ray drove away. They ate in the best restaurants, went to clubs sometimes at night, and then back to the hotel to have sex. The next day they would get on the private jet with the cash and travel to their next destination. This was their behavior for two weeks, until Martina had it all, another four hundred million dollars. Now, the total was seven hundred million dollars, in cash, minus money spent.

When they arrived in Vegas, Ice and Ray helped Martina put some of the cash in the safes in her motor home. The rest was put in several large safes hidden in Martina's house. She gave Ice and Ray ten million dollars apiece, although both were reluctant to take it, Martina was very persistent. Ray and Ice stayed in Vegas with Martina, and they partied hard for a week until all three were physically and mentally exhausted from not enough sleep, too much drinking, and very intense sex. Martina wanted a sexual fantasy of hers fulfilled, so she paid two attractive women ten thousand dollars apiece to have sex with Ice while she and Ray watched. They joined in on the fun and it was the freakiest sex scene you would ever see, you name it, and they did it. Ray and Ice promised to stay in touch with Martina and they left.

Martina had never been happier in her life than she was right now. She stood in her motorhome in front of the safes with the doors open, looking at all this cash and thinking about the rest of the cash in the safes in her house. Three weeks later she became sick and was throwing up a lot, so she went to Sunrise Hospital which is the largest acute care facility in Nevada. She was diagnosed with a severe case of food poisoning, pneumonia, syphilis, and gonorrhea. She called Ice and Ray to inform them of her sickness and to get checked. The doctors gave Martina a fifty percent chance of survival and walked out of her room. She prayed harder than any other time in her life. She lay in the hospital bed one night crying hard and looked at the ceiling.

"Lord, I have experienced horrible pains and suffering in my life. Now I have safes with over six hundred million dollars in cash, all mine, but now I am in this hospital probably dying. What good is all my money now Lord?" She grabbed the bible from the nightstand and held it close to her heart and cried herself to sleep.

CHAPTER THIRTY FIVE
FAMILIAR SPIRITS

It is seven-thirty at night and Ron was home sitting in his basement with Keith and Stacy. Stacy and Keith sat on a sofa together. They were all dressed casually, and Diana was upstairs in her bedroom getting dressed to go out with her mother.

"Ron, when James called me two weeks ago and told me what happened, I tried not to laugh but I could not help myself. He got pickpocketed by some woman he ran into and lost the thumb drive. She must have dug in his pockets while they rolled on the ground. James said she flirted with him once they got off the ground, and then she ran away. The woman must have been fine for James to get distracted like that because he got that fine wife at home. In any case, the brother got taken because he got distracted by the big booty." Keith leaned back on the sofa laughing.

Ron could not help but laugh as well until he saw how Stacy looked at Keith and she became more irritated by the second because he was laughing so hard.

"Is it that funny Keith? How do you know she was attractive or had a big booty? All you men are something else, no matter what you have at home and how good a woman she is, you will always look at other women and think dirty nasty thoughts about what you would like to do to her. I know, pretty in the face, slim in the waist, hips, lips, and a big butt and you men lose your mind." She hit Keith's leg hard with the palm of her hand and gave him a mean look.

"Stop hitting me Stacy and I am not playing! God supposedly delivered you from all your violent ways, so act like it and stop hitting me, and keep your mind on the Lord." He looked at her.

Keith's words irritated Stacy more because of the hypocrisy of his actions sometimes. She turned her body at an angle to look at him and slid her body back on the sofa.

"Let me ask you something Keith. When you and I are out having fun and you see a nice-looking woman and your eyes are locked on her body and glued to her butt, are you thinking about the Lord then? No, you are not. You have nasty dirty thoughts on your mind, so do not play me and come at me like that. Don't make me have a flashback, Keith." She leaned closer and stared at him.

"You know what, all the years I have known you two, some things have not changed. Can't you two for one day act like you are not about to attack each other, please? God has delivered us all, so let us walk in his love and power."

"Very true, preacher Ron." Keith looked at Ron and then Stacy. He hugged and kissed her.

"Keith, my home is yours and Stacy's. However, since you two have been blessed with a nice home of your own, save all that hugging and feeling all over each other for your own house."

"Straight up hater baby, just a hater." Stacy looked at Ron and smiled. "Ron, it's good Diana has been spending more time with her Mom, because at the end of the day, you only have one mother."

The doorbell rang and Ron stood to answer it, but Diana stood at the top of the stairwell and looked down.

"Ron, I got the door, it's my Mom." She yelled and walked away.

When Diana opened the door, Ice stood there smiling. They hugged each other and Ice walked in.

"Mom come on in, it's good to see you. I get emotional every time I call you Mom." She hugged Ice again and held on to her.

Ice's heart melted seeing her daughter but physically holding her was emotionally overwhelming and she had to hold back her tears.

"You are going to make me cry and mess up my makeup." She wiped her eyes to get rid of her tears. "Anyway, where is your husband?"

"He, Keith, and Stacy are downstairs. Come say hello before we leave."

Diana walked to the basement door and Ice was behind her pretending to be happy to see them, but she was not because she knew they did not like her.

"We are coming down baby." Diana said as she and Ice walked downstairs but Ron, Keith, and Stacy were in for a surprise.

Diana wore heels, a long red form-fitting dress with a long slit in the front that stopped one foot before her crotch and was low cut in the front revealing a lot of cleavage. Ice was dressed the same, but her dress was black and a little tighter. They both had small purses in their hands. When they reached halfway on the stairs, all eyes were on them, and Ron immediately began calling on Jesus repeatedly to himself to keep from going off. Stacy and Keith stared at them and was seriously lusting. Ice loved the way they all looked at her and Diana, so she purposely walked down the stairs in such a way they could see some of her panties in front because of the long slit. She wore crotchless panties, so she knew what they all saw. Not being conscious of it, Diana walked the same way down the stairs which revealed her panties in front as well. She smiled hard at Ron and then noticed his mean look and building anger, but she was not about to allow him to spoil her mood with her Mom. She also noticed the way Keith and Stacy looked at her and she could see and feel their lust spirits. Immediately a mischievous spirit came over her, so she stepped and moved purposely the same way Ice did, so they saw more of her crotch area as well by the time she got to the bottom of the stairs. Keith looked directly between her legs and Diana saw his stare but for some reason, it did not bother her, she liked the attention. They both turned around once they were at the bottom of the stairs to show their dress and figure. Tight dresses revealing the crotch area, cleavage, hips, and butt. Ron was furious.

"Hi everybody, don't we look nice tonight." Ice said and smiled knowing Ron was about to go off just from the look on his face. So, she stepped closer to Diana and pointed at her. "Ron, don't your wife look gorgeous in her beautiful dress?" She gave him a fake smile.

"Wow, I did not know you two were going to a nightclub." Stacy said sarcastically.

"Neither did I. So what club are you going to?" Keith's penis was rock hard, and he noticed Stacy giving him a mean stare as if she knew he was aroused.

"We are not going to a nightclub; we are going to a concert and a jazz show as well." Ice said.

Ron stood and looked at them with a controlled demeanor, but his anger was building by the second.

"Miss Diana, I mean no disrespect for what I am about to say. You are a single grown woman and can dress however you want and go where you want, that is your business. However, my wife is a Christian woman, and she is not going out of this house looking like some high-price call girl selling booty," he took one step closer to Diana and stopped and stared at her. "Diana, are you crazy? Showing all your breasts and crotch area to the whole world. Go change your damn clothes." He yelled and was so angry his fist was balled up by his side and he was grinding his teeth.

Keith, Stacy, and Diana were shocked at Ron's reaction. They had not seen him this angry in a long time, and he used the word damn, he never said that. Diana jumped when Ron yelled at her and she was a little scared at what he would say or do next, but she was not going to back down now.

"Ron don't yell at my daughter like you are a madman. If you have anger issues, you need to go and pray or talk to a counselor. You are her husband, not her slave owner, so do not try and control her like one." She looked at Ron and felt his rage but did not care because she was going to spend time with her daughter with or without his blessing.

As Ron looked at Ice, he never wanted to slap a woman so badly, but he continued to pray to himself to have peace.

"Diana, your mother can dress like a slut all she wants, but you are not leaving this house dressed like that."

"What! Ron, I cannot believe you called my mother a slut. You know what, I am so done with you tonight. I am leaving, come on Mom." She turned to walk away.

Bad move on Diana's part. Ron moved quickly grabbed her arm tightly and pulled her back.

"You are not going anywhere." He stared at Diana.

Without thinking about her instinctive behavior and training, Ice hit Ron hard in the nose with the palm of her left hand, hit him with her right hand on the side of his neck with a ridge hand blow, and then front snapped kicked him in the stomach. Ron hit the floor hard and landed on his back and his nose was bleeding badly.

"Don't you put your hands on my daughter." Ice was in a fighting stance as she looked down at Ron.

Ron was surprised at Ice's speed and strength, but now all he felt, was anger. He laid on his back looking at Ice but jumped to his feet with one move and stepped toward Ice. Keith moved quickly and grabbed Ron's arm pulled him back and stood directly in front of him.

"Remember who you are my brother, don't let the Devil use you. You can't win this right now, let Diana leave before this scene becomes worse." He spoke calmly to Ron to diffuse this situation.

Stacy walked next to Ron and looked at Diana and Ice, not believing what just taken place and how Diana was acting. She knew Diana was so wrong in what she was doing and was surprised to see this very arrogant and defiant attitude from her. She looked at Ron.

"Ron, please calm down and let Diana leave." She looked at Diana and shook her head and wanted to say so much but held her peace.

Diana never intended for all this to happen and now she felt bad and did not want to go. She walked over to Ron and put her hand on his arm, but he pulled his arm away from her.

"Don't touch me. You want to go out so badly, you and your Mom go do your thing. But remember this, you picked the wrong side." He stepped back and stared at Diana and then looked at her mother and wiped the blood dripping from his nose.

"I am so sorry about all this. Ron, please forgive me, but I was instinctively protecting my daughter as any mother would do, please forgive me. I will always protect my daughter from anyone no matter what." She gave him a stern look and then a sorrowful one but did not mean it.

"I am not picking the wrong side Ron. You are my husband, and she is my mother who is finally in my life. I am spending time with my mother Ron, you need to get used to it, it's that simple." She looked at the anger in his eyes and turned away. Diana grabbed her mother's hand and they walked up the stairs together.

Keith looked at them, lusting hard. Stacy looked at Keith's very lustful look as he stared at Diana and her mother going up the stairs. She was angry but now was not the time to say anything. Ron watched them walk away and it hurt him greatly to see Diana walk out of the house dressed the way she was and the words she said to him. He walked to the sofa and sat down with tears in his eyes because his heart was broken. Stacy and Keith saw Ron's pain. It bothered them greatly to see someone they loved and cared for so much be hurt by his wife. Keith walked over and put his hand on Ron's shoulder.

"Hold on my brother, God did not bring you this far for nothing."

"Amen to that Ron." Stacy sat next to Ron and put her arm around his neck to comfort him.

Keith became angry seeing his best friend disrespected by his wife. He ran up the stairs and caught up with Diana and Ice before they opened the front door to leave.

"Diana!" He yelled.

They both turned around and stared at Keith.

"What Keith! Stop yelling at me. I have had enough yelling for one night." She looked at him with a nonchalant attitude.

"Diana, I can't believe after all the things you and Ron have been through, you are going to disrespect him like this."

Diana stepped closer to Keith.

"I am not disrespecting my husband Keith, and you need to mind your own business and pay more attention to your wife, brother." She turned to walk away and then turned around and stepped closer to Keith. "Just for the record Keith, I see the way you look at me and I feel and see the burning lust in your eyes, and I have seen you adjusting yourself." She looked between his legs and then looked at his face. "Your dick is hard now and I see how you look at my mother, lusting over her. I noticed you adjusting your erections when you stare at her like you did tonight. You and Stacy lusting over my mother, you two should be ashamed of yourself." She leaned closer, getting in his face. "I know you want to be intimate with my mother, Christian Brother. Correction, I know you want to fuck her, but you are not going to, ever." She whispered in his ear. "I know you want me Keith, but you will never get this hot pussy of mine because you can't handle me. So, go fuck your wife." Diana turned to step away and then turned back around and stared at Keith. She grabbed him quickly by the back of his neck with one hand and grabbed and squeezed his penis with the other. She kissed him hard on the lips, and walked out the door defiantly, shaking her hips and butt.

Ice was shocked by what she witnessed her daughter do and say, but she loved it. She stepped closer to Keith.

"Wow, they say the fruit does not fall far from the tree. Like mother, like daughter." She put her hand on her dress close to the slit and spread her legs farther apart revealing more of her crotch. She rubbed between her legs with her fingers while looking directly at Keith. "When you think you can handle this hot pussy and ass, call me. I will give you the fuck of your life, believe that." She smiled at him and walked out of the house.

Keith stared at her and shook his head and adjusted his penis because he was hard. What he did not know was Stacy walked up the stairs to check on him and she heard and saw everything Diana and her mother said and did. Stacy was so angry and hurt tears were coming down her face.

Keith turned around and saw Stacy standing at the top of the staircase and he could tell by the look in her eyes and the tears, that she heard and saw everything.

"Stacy, it's not what you think."

She walked over and stood in front of him and reached down and grabbed his penis. It was still hard. She let it go stepped back and stared at him as her tears flowed.

"You know what Keith if you want Diana and her mother so badly, you can have them. Go fuck them both. I am tired of all this relationship drama, I have had enough, I am done. I am leaving you Keith. You know me very well, so look into my eyes. If you touch me, if you do anything to try and stop me from leaving here, I will fight you until one of us is unconscious."

Ron stood at the top of the staircase dealing with his hurt and pain but surprised at what he saw between them now.

"Keith, what did you do." He yelled.

Stacy and Keith turned around and saw Ron standing there.

"I am so sorry Ron, so sorry. I can't do this anymore." She ran out of the house crying.

"Keith, what did you do?" Ron yelled.

Keith lowered his head and then looked at Ron with tears in his eyes.

"The devil my brother, we all are being attacked by the devil. I do not know about this one Ron. I just don't know."

CHAPTER THIRTY SIX
A CHOICE

It is two o'clock in the morning and Diana and Ice were at the jazz lounge. They had a good time at the concert and were having a better time now. They sat at a table with two well-dressed good-looking men who they talked and danced with since they arrived at the lounge. They never told the men they were mother and daughter. Diana's friend was Barry and Ice's friend was Mark. Diana had too much to drink and was being flirtatious with Barry. When they danced together, she pressed her body on him and welcomed his hands on her hips and butt, something she never allowed anyone to do except her husband. Ice did the same with Mark but always kept a watchful eye on her daughter. They drank, talked, and laughed while sitting at the table like they had known each other for years. Barry's hand was underneath the table on Diana's leg, and she did not move it, so he slid his hand inside the slit in her dress and caressed her thigh.

Because of Diana's mental and spiritual state, she allowed Barry to do this and his warm hand caressing her thigh felt good. Ice knew exactly what was going on underneath the table with them because she allowed Mark to do the same thing to her. However, she opened her legs wider and put her hand underneath the table on top of Mark's hand guiding it inside her slit and up her leg. She rubbed his fingers on her crotch area, so he would know she wore crotchless panties.

Barry kissed Diana on the cheek moved his hand between her legs and caressed the outside of her panties until he felt a wet spot. He moved her panties to one side with his fingers and rubbed the outside of her wetness. This made Diana jump and brought her back to her senses as she moved his hand quickly from between her legs, leaned away from him, and looked at her Mom.

"Ice, I need to go to the lady's room, will you come with me please?" She gave her a look of, YOU better come with me.

"Not a problem, I need to go myself." She moved Mark's hand from between her legs and stood. "Excuse us gentlemen."

Ice and Diana grabbed their purses and walked to the ladies' bathroom. There was no one there but them.

Barry put his finger close to his nose and sniffed it and smiled.

"Diana smells good, I almost had my finger inside her, and she was wet." He looked at Mark and shook his head.

Mark smelled his finger as well and smiled.

"My brother I can relate. I was so close to putting my finger inside Ice, damn." He shook his head.

Ice looked at Diana when they were in the bathroom.

"What's wrong baby, are you okay? You have been drinking a lot tonight and I can tell you are not a drinker."

"Yes, I drank too much but it's more than that. This night is all wrong for me, I should not be here, and I feel bad for the way I treated my husband tonight. On top of all that, I am a Christian married woman, and I allowed this stranger to hug and feel all over me. Mom, I allowed his hand to caress the inside of my leg and crotch and I enjoyed it. It made me wet, and he was about to put his finger inside me." She grabbed both sides of her head with her hands. "God, I must be going out of my mind, Lord help me." She stared out in space with her hands on her head.

Ice stepped closer and hugged Diana then stepped back.

"Baby girl, relax. You have dealt with a lot for a long time, and I can tell you have a controlling husband. You are not going out of your mind; you need to let go and do the things you want and not what someone else says you should do." Ice hugged her again and kissed Diana on the cheek. "Look at me, I am your mother, but I am also a woman. Tell me the truth, when Barry caressed your leg, did it feel good? When he was caressing your crotch, did it feel good? When he was about to put his finger inside you, did you stop him because you wanted him to stop? Or did you stop him because of the guilt others have put upon you for years? Tell me the truth."

Diana looked at her mother.

"I am a Christian married woman mother, not some slut walking the streets looking for a good time."

"Okay, I got that, but you did not answer my question. Did it feel good, and did you want him to continue?"

Diana looked at her mother and felt so confused. She lowered her head and then looked at her in shame.

"Yes, his hand felt good between my legs and yes, a part of me wanted him to continue, but that is flesh and because something feels good to you, it does not make it right. A lot of things we do may feel good, but it could destroy us in the process."

"You only live one life Diana, and I can't make the choices for you, but I do want you happy and satisfied. Does your husband satisfy you in bed?"

"Mom, I am not answering that, it's too personal."

Ice leaned back and laughed.

"Oh, my goodness, my daughter is shy and a prude. Child, I am a grown woman, and every woman in her right mind desires to be sexually satisfied. Damn, all this political politeness. Does Ron keep his face buried between your legs and ass and does he keep hard dick in your pussy and mouth? Yes or no, damn all that niceness."

Diana did not want to answer her mother.

"Not like he used to. We used to have freaky hot nasty sex, but not anymore. I do not know why, but my sex drive has increased a lot, and sometimes I do not want Ron to be so gentle. I want him to fuck me like he used to and talk dirty and nasty to me like he used to. I know things change in all marriages and become dull at times. Maybe it's me."

"No, do not fall into that marriage guilt. It is both of you. You need to talk to your husband and tell him exactly what you want and how. I saw the way Barry looked at you all night. He has a strong lustful look in his eyes that is waiting to be released on the right woman. Girl, that man would lick and suck your ass and pussy repeatedly and fuck you good, if you let him."

"Oh my God Mom, you are so disgusting. Truth be told." She looked down. "I need all that right now." She looked up. "Anyway, forget all that. Let's get out of this bathroom and tell those two men goodnight. I need to go home to my husband. I feel so bad about all of this."

"You will be fine daughter but let's get out of here."

They walked out of the bathroom laughing.

What they did not know was Malone was in one of the bathroom stalls when they were in the bathroom. He was dressed in all black holding his cane.

"I am going to turn you out tonight Diana. I spoke erotic curses upon you." He mumbled some words and spat repeatedly on the floor.

Keith stayed and fell asleep on the sofa upstairs when Diana and Ice left. Ron went to his bedroom, fell on his bed, and cried out to God for help. After praying for a while, he felt the powerful anointing from the Holy Spirit and God revealed where Diana was. He changed clothes quickly and grabbed his gun from his dresser drawer woke Keith and explained everything to him.

"Say no more partner, what do you want to do?"

"I am going to get my wife and I pray this night that no one gets in my way. Call the *Young Wolves* and have them meet us at the Jazz Lounge."

"We are on the same page." Keith got his cell phone and made the call.

Malone was still in the bathroom stall speaking demonic curses against Diana and Ice and the spirits were oppressing them greatly.

Diana and Ice sat at the table talking to Barry and Mark. The plan was for them to leave but Malone's evil spirits were influencing them. Diana continued to drink and all four of them were drinking, talking, and laughing all over again. Diana was more turned on now and Barry whispered erotic things to her, saying everything she wanted to hear from Ron. Ice allowed Mark to finger her underneath the table and she was close to climaxing. Barry's hand was between Diana's legs rubbing her crotch on top of her wet panties. She spread her legs further apart because Barry said and did all the right things causing her to desire more. He moved her panties to one side and his fingers caressed her wetness. One finger pressed against her outer labia. He was close to sliding his finger inside her when he heard this click sound and felt something hard and cold against his head.

Eight of the *Young Wolves* stood close to the table, and they were all dressed in black gear and had guns in their hands by their side. Ron held a gun against Barry's head and Keith had a gun in his hand close to his side. Barry, Diana, Mark, and Ice looked up in total shock as they stood there.

"Oh my God, Ron!" Diana said and moved Barry's hand quickly and closed her legs.

"Diana don't say one word. Stand up and step away from the table, and I pray you have panties on." Ron said with controlled rage.

When Diana stood her legs were shaky because she was afraid of what Ron was about to do.

"Ron, I don't know who you think you are, but you are not about to manhandle my daughter." Ice was afraid as well, but she would never show it.

Keith looked at one of the *Young Wolves* who stood close to Ice and nodded his head at him. He bent down and whispered in Ice's ear.

"Lady, I have no ties to you, so if you don't close your damn mouth, me and my friends will drag you out of this place and pistol whip you in the back alley and leave you on the ground bleeding to death."

Ice looked at this young man and saw the seriousness in his eyes and did not say another word.

Ron looked at Barry with anger controlled by the hand of God.

"The only reason you are walking out of this place alive is God is on your side. You and your friend stay here until we are gone."

Ron, Keith, Diana, and the Young Wolves walked out of the Lounge, but Barry, Mark, and Ice remained seated. Barry was so scared when they left, he pissed on himself. Ron's Bentley was parked in front of the Lounge, he opened the door for Diana to get in and nodded at Keith and drove away. Keith got in the car with one of the *Young Wolves* and they all drove away.

As Ron drove home Diana was afraid and did not know what to say to him, or if she should say anything at all. So, she said nothing. Ron looked at her and was beyond angry, but God kept him.

"I am going to ask you something and you better not lie to me. Do you have any panties on?"

"Ron, stop treating me like I am your property, and you are my pimp. Of course, I have panties on. What is wrong with you?" She said with attitude.

"Spread your legs and let me see."

"What! I am doing no such thing." She stared at him with defiance.

"I said spread your damn legs!" He yelled and looked at Diana with great anger.

Diana jumped when Ron yelled and the look in his eyes made her afraid. She spread her legs revealing her panties.

"Are you satisfied now, pimp husband?" She was being smart and trying to hide her fear.

Ron looked at her with increased anger but was trying to remain calm.

"Did you have sex with the guy you were with at the Lounge?"

"No Ron, I did not." She looked at him with more defiance.

"You have been drinking a lot, I can tell. People do stupid things when they drink. Did you kiss or have sex with anybody tonight? Did you suck any dick, lick any pussy or ass?"

She wanted to tell him where he could go but was afraid he would do something crazy.

"No, I did not, and you know I didn't, so stop talking crazy to me Ron. Stop interrogating me. I am not a slut."

Ron slammed on the brakes bringing the car to an abrupt halt and it made Diana's body jerk forward. It was a good thing no cars were behind him. He pulled the car over to the side of the road and put it in park turned to face Diana and then put his finger in her face.

"Then you need to stop acting like a slut. I don't know who you are anymore." He yelled.

Diana put her hands up.

"Ron don't hit me, I will tell my Dad and the Pastor."

"I would never hit you Diana, so stop being dramatic. You are something." He stared at her then put the car in gear and drove away.

Ron drove up to his driveway and opened the car door for Diana to get out. As they walked to the front door, they looked at each other with mixed emotions. He opened the front door and let Diana walk in first walked in behind her and closed the door. He stared at her body when she walked, and thought, *I can't believe her but damn she looks good in that dress and her body is so sexy.* He replayed in his mind all she had done and that brought him back to reality.

Diana stopped walking and turned around to face Ron.

"Ron, I know you are furious with me and want to talk like you always do. But I do not feel good, I have a bad headache, and I am tired. All I want to do is take a relaxing hot shower and go to sleep. We can talk tomorrow."

"No, we are talking tonight!" He yelled.

"Stop yelling at me Ron, I told you I have a bad headache. Now is not a good time for us to talk at all and you know it. You are far too upset and not thinking rationally and all you are going to do is ask me question after question and yell at me some more. Talking tonight is not going to accomplish anything. I need a hot shower, Ron. I will talk to you in the morning." She turned around and walked away.

The way Diana dismissed him fueled his anger. He stepped in front of her.

"Get your butt back here, we are talking now. Your choices put you in this situation, your choices." He moved closer and sniffed her body, and then stared at her. "Why do you want to take a hot shower so quickly? Trying to clean up, wash the sex scent off? Do you think I am stupid Diana? You fucked that guy, didn't you?"

Diana looked at him like he was crazy and threw her hands up in the air.

"Ron, you are allowing your emotions to get the best of you, and for the last time. I did not have sex with anyone. And stop using that F word."

"You must be joking about my language right now. I am not stupid or blind Diana. When I approached the table where you sat, I noticed the guy had his hand underneath the table. And I saw the shocked expression on your face when you saw me just before I put the gun to his head. You were enjoying whatever he was doing to you." He got in her face. "He was fingering you, wasn't he? You let some strange dude put his dirty nasty hand between your legs and finger fuck you." His eyes became small and tight as he stared at Diana and the muscles in his face twitched because he was so angry.

What Diana saw in her husband's face right now caused her to step back from him.

"Ron, you need to go pray because you are scaring me." Her head hurt badly but she would not say anything about taking a shower and going to bed. Ron had this crazy out of his mind look on his face.

"I noticed you did not answer my question, you let him violate you. I know he was fingering you when I walked up." He was so angry you could hear him grinding his teeth.

"Stop attacking me Ron, I am not the enemy." She threw her hands up. "Fine, you want to talk Ron, let's talk." She walked quickly to the living room and sat on the sofa.

Ron enjoyed seeing her shake her hips and butt when she walked away, but his facial expression never changed as he walked into the living room and sat on the sofa across from her.

"Answer my question Diana and don't lie. Did you let him finger you?"

Diana was trying so hard to keep her composure, but she felt her anger building.

"I am not on the witness stand Ron and you are not going to interrogate me. I did not have sex with anyone and no, he was not fingering me." She looked at him and thought, *no way would I tell you he was about to.* He was so angry and at this point, she would try anything to distract Ron and make him calm down. So, she leaned back on the sofa in frustration, exhaled, and nonchalantly spread her legs to possibly tempt him.

Ron looked between her legs and loved the sight, but he knew what she was trying to do, and it was not going to work, not this time.

"Interesting gestures you do. I know how you dance Diana and I know you were grinding your body all on that dude and you kissed him. You spread your legs well. Did you spread your legs like that for that dude? I am sure you did, you and your mother. Both of you left here dressed like escorts looking for money and some dick. Nasty slut spirit."

Diana's heart felt like it skipped a beat when she heard those harsh words come out of Ron's mouth. He called her and her mother a slut and this caused Diana to emotionally snap. She stood up and pointed her finger at him.

"I am not a slut Ron!" She yelled at him. "Don't you ever call me or my mother a slut again." She looked at him coldly.

Ron stood and stared at her.

"Don't dress and act like a slut and you won't get called one."

That was it, Diana had enough. She removed her earrings, took her heels off, and stepped to Ron, and got in his face.

"I made some serious mistakes tonight for which I am deeply sorry for, and I apologize for hurting you and I ask for your forgiveness. Like I have forgiven you for your negative deeds in our marriage. But, if you call me a slut one more time, it is going to be some furniture moving in this house, believe that." She pointed her finger in his face almost touching his nose. "Call me a slut one more time Ron and see what happens." She stared at him.

"You better get your finger out of my face and back up from me." He gave her a very intimidating look.

Diana knew she was wrong for having her finger in his face because it was disrespectful and they did not do that, but at this point, she did not care.

"Or what, hit me. If you hit me, bump me, shove me, or push me in any way, I am telling your mother, my dad, and the pastor that you beat your wife." She stared him down with defiance.

Ron felt like she was playing the woman's feminine card and he could not allow her to get the best of him, especially since she was the one in the wrong. He grabbed Diana and picked her off her feet.

Diana thought he was about to attack her, so she wiggled hard trying to get out of his grasp when he picked her up and swung wildly trying to hit him.

"No Ron, stop, put me down. I am telling the Pastor you allowed the Devil to get in you." She yelled.

He carried Diana to the sofa and put her down roughly. Ron had something else on his mind. He kicked his shoes off, unzipped his pants, and then leaned forward and bit Diana's neck, and began sucking it. He ripped her dress open, snatched her panties off and started kissing her face and lips.

Diana did not expect this from him and was thrown off by his forced aggression, so she fought him. It began to turn her on and she had flashbacks of the spontaneous sex they used to have. However, she could not lay back and give in.

"Get off me Ron, I mean it, you are not going to..."

Diana never finished her sentence because she felt Ron penetrate her. His penis was rock hard, and he began slowly thrusting inside her and it felt good. He moved slowly until she was very wet and then increased his pace. He licked and sucked her neck. All this was too much, and it made her climax quickly.

"Ahhhhhh Ron I am cummiiing baby." She loved his dick stroke and aggressiveness.

After Diana climaxed, Ron pulled out and removed all his clothes and hers as well. He looked at her lying on the sofa breathing heavily.

"Stand up." He said roughly.

Diana's emotions and passions were extremely high and not sure what Ron was going to do now. He was in control too much and she did not like it.

"No, I am not." She spoke defiantly.

Ron pulled Diana to her feet, grabbed her by the hips, turned her body around, bent her over, and placed her hands on the sofa. He put his hands on her hips, kneeled, and began sliding his tongue all over her butt, and buried his face between her legs, tongue first. He licked and sucked her wetness like it would be the last time. Ron knew his wife's body well and could feel she was close to another orgasm, so he stood and slid inside her and began thrusting. The slapping of their bodies was loud, and Diana threw her body into his and looked back at him.

"Yes! This is what I want from you, fuck me Ron. Fuck your wife like you need to. Ohhhhh, it feels so good."

He slapped her butt a few times and continued thrusting.

"This will always be my pussy, say it. Say this is my pussy Diana." He pulled out, bit her butt, and slid his lips and tongue all over it. Then pressed his face deep between her butt cheeks as he gripped her hips with his hands and had his tongue deep inside her. You could hear the smacking and licking sounds of his tongue against her butt and her wetness. He smacked her butt again, stood up, and slid his hard dick inside her, thrusting deep and fast.

"Yes baby, this is your pussy Ron, all yours baby. Now fuck me like you know I need, ahhhhh Ron, it is so damn good. Fuck this tight pussy Ron, fuck meeeee. I want to suck your dick, let me suck it Ron." She moved forward and turned around and grabbed Ron's dick, licked his balls, and began sucking his dick fast, bringing him close to climax.

Ron was not ready to give in yet, so he pulled out of Diana's mouth, turned her around, and bent her over the sofa. He buried his face between her legs again while holding onto her hips. He licked all over her butt and then slid his tongue from her pussy to her ass, back and forth until Diana shook from her orgasm.

"Ohhhhhhh Ron, don't stop, lick this pussy and ass baby. Suck it Ron, ohhhhhhh suck this pussy baby. Oh Ron, ohhhhh suuuuck thisssss pusssssy, ohhhhh my goooooodness. I am cumming on your face." She pressed her butt hard against his face while her body trembled from the pleasure.

Ron licked and sucked every drop of his wife's juices and kept licking and making her scream. Afterward, he stood and slid inside her and began talking very nasty and dirty while fucking his wife the way she wanted him to. He could not hold out any longer and exploded inside Diana.

"Dianaaaa you feeeel so good, oh this pussy is good, so good."

"Yes baby, cum in me. This is your pussy, fuck me."
Ron continued thrusting inside Diana and she continued pushing back into him until they relaxed and sat on the sofa next to each other. They stared at one another and then kissed passionately, licking and sucking each other's tongues, building new passions.

"I am so sorry Ron; I am going to be good baby. I promise, but now I want some more, I want to feel your tongue deep in my ass." Diana got on her knees close to the sofa and leaned forward. "Now Ron."

Ron got on his knees behind Diana, grabbed her hips, and began kissing and licking her butt.
Diana looked back at Ron.

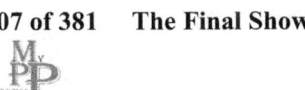

"No Ron, put your tongue in my ass baby. Lick and suck it good."

He did exactly what she asked and slid the tip of his tongue in her butt and slid his finger inside her wetness. Ron felt Diana getting wetter and more turned on as he fingered her.

Between Ron's warm tongue licking her butt and his finger inside her moving around, took Diana over the edge. Her juices began pouring out of her and she trembled hard and screamed. Ron had to hold her body in place because she shook and climaxed so hard as he licked and fingered Diana, she had multiple orgasms.

After kissing, licking, and fingering, and five orgasms later, Diana lay on the floor exhausted, and her body trembled. Ron laid next to her feeling good and assertive. All Diana could do was look at her husband and breathe heavily.

"Oh Ron!" She continued staring at him with love. The smile on her face said it all and she felt elated, to say the least. She laid there feeling great and slowly calmed down. And then, reality hit her hard. The things she said and did to Keith when she was with her mother came to her mind instantly. She thought, *oh my God, how do I ever get past what I said and did to Keith? I know he is going to tell Ron everything, with his snitching self. I acted like a different person, oh my goodness, the things I said to Keith. And Stacy, oh my God, Stacy. She is going to find out, Lord what do I do now. I am in so much trouble. Being around my mother is affecting me in a bad way, Jesus, help me!*

Diana had no clue what was about to come her way because Stacy already knew, and she was not one to play with. These two had become remarkably close over the years and had been through so much. Did Diana cross the line and make an enemy of Stacy? Diana wondered and thought the worse. Could she and Stacy talk like mature adults about all this and remain friends? Or would she see the other side of Stacy, which could be extremely dangerous? Would all this rip Ron's and Keith's friendship apart despite all they have been through? Would they become enemies and not only destroy themselves but everyone else who deeply loves them? Would the O'Neil family be destroyed from the inside out?

CHAPTER THIRTY SEVEN
KEITH AND STACY

After Ron and Diana left the Jazz Lounge, Keith left with the *Young Wolves* and rode around for a while with them because he did not want to go home, but he knew he had to. One of the *Young Wolves* took him home. When he walked in the front door and into the living room, what he saw on the floor stopped him in his tracks and caused his heart instant emotional pain. There were several large packed suitcases on the floor. Stacy walked into the living room wearing tennis shoes, snug-fitting jeans, and a dress shirt. She had another bag in her hand and placed it next to the others. Stacy was surprised to see Keith and stood there looking at him.

"I am surprised to see you. I was hoping to be gone before you got back to avoid any negative drama. Keith, we do not have to start arguing and yelling at each other, enough is enough. We have been through so much in our lives, on so many levels. We have mentally, spiritually, and physically fought so much in our relationship, and for what? For what Keith? No matter what I do, it seems like I will never be enough for you. No matter how well I treat you, pamper you, take care of you, love you, or sex you. It will never be enough. I am done Keith. And please, do not touch me." The look she gave him said it all.

Keith knew he needed to let Stacy talk, so he did.

"I know I have made some major mistakes in our relationship and caused you a great deal of pain, for which

I can't take back and I will always regret it. Yes, you have forgiven me, and we were able to move on, but we will not be able to move past this. Why? Because your heart is no longer with me, with us. You want Diana, her mother, and I do not know who else you may want. If you want them, that is your choice Keith. All of you can hang out and have regular freaky sex parties, but you will not have me at the same time, I am far more valuable than that."

He continued looking at Stacy as she talked, and his heart was in so much pain hearing these words from her.

"You are not going to give me a chance to explain? Everything is not always what it seems to be Stacy."

"There is nothing to explain Keith, I stood directly behind you, I heard and saw it all."

"Stacy, you need to listen to me as I have listened to you. Diana and her mother are operating in some sick twisted strong lust spirits. You saw how she was dressed and disrespected Ron in every way. And you know she has never done that to him."

"You are right, I discerned all that and more, and yes something evil is going on, but it always is with the O'Neil family. Everyone else gets pulled into their mess. No woman could ever love you more than I do Keith and care for you, but you have your demons to deal with. Anyway, as you can see, I am leaving tonight. You do not have to give me anything or do anything for me, I am a survivor and will take care of myself. You can have it all, the house, cars, the money, everything. I am leaving with my clothes and personal things. Please, do not make this ugly. I know you, do not have me followed or get the *Young Wolves* or whoever to track me down or keep tabs on me. I already called a taxi, when it gets here, I am out."

"Wow, you have said a lot and come to your conclusions quickly. What can I say, except you are wrong, very wrong. Let me ask you one question." He stepped closer and looked into her face. "Whatever happened to the power of prayer and the marriage vows, for better or worse?"

They both stared at each other for what seemed like hours and then Stacy looked at her packed luggage on the floor and now realized, how final things are for her and Keith. She thought about everything she heard and saw Diana do to Keith in front of her mother. It was as if Diana was another person or was trying to show off in front of her mother.

A car horn interrupted their thoughts. Keith thought to himself, *no way*. He moved quickly outside, gave the taxi driver a hundred dollar bill to go away, and ran back inside the house and stood close to Stacy but would not touch her.

Stacy was so hurt and confused. Did she want her marriage to be over, or was it too late? She began shaking her head and felt emotionally overwhelmed until tears fell from her eyes. Then suddenly, she could no longer hold it in, she balled up her fist and swung at Keith hard, he saw it coming and ducked out of the way. Stacy almost fell because she swung so hard and then stared at him and dropped to her knees, crying hysterically.

Keith stepped closer to comfort Stacy and then stopped because he did not know what to do. She told him not to touch her so would she attack him if he did? He wanted to hold her in his arms, but would she go off on him? He had no clue what to do. He looked up.

"Lord, help me. I don't know what to do." He whispered to himself, and tears came to his eyes.

As hard as Stacy was crying, the great pain she was in, and her anger, she heard Keith's whispered words to God. She fought as hard as she could not to react, but there was a force far greater at work. Stacy was bawled up on the floor crying hysterically and she raised one arm slowly in Keith's direction.

Keith was surprised at her gesture, but he kneeled beside Stacy and put his arm gently around her as tears came down his face.

For brief seconds, Keith's touch repulsed her, and she wanted to hit him as hard as she could and beat him down, but the spirit of God hit her heart and she wrapped her arms around him and screamed.

"Ahhhhhh Jesus help me pleasssss." She cried harder.

"Lord help us, please help us." Keith screamed and cried.

All they could do was hold one another and cry. They remained on the floor for an hour holding each other and crying until Keith finally stood and helped Stacy up as well. Now he did not know what to do as they stood there looking at each other trying to read one another's thoughts.

"Keith, I thank you for comforting me and I know all this is not easy for you either, but I don't want to talk right now at all. I feel very tired and mentally drained. It will soon be light outside, but I am going to take a long hot shower and take a nap. But, before I take a nap, I want you to know.

Diana is not my friend anymore and I want nothing to do with her. I saw her kiss you Keith and grab your dick out of pure arrogance and conceit and I do not want to say anymore because it will be all bad and ugly. I have to confess this to you Keith." She bent over and removed a razor from underneath one of her pants legs and held it up for him to see. "It took the hand of God to stop me from cutting your throat tonight because my pain is so great." She threw the razor across the room on the floor. "Oh God, I need time and prayer." She stared at him.

"Well, I am glad you did not cut my throat and I understand. I am going to the gym and get a workout while you are resting."

"No Keith, this is selfish of me, but I don't want you gone from the house right now. I do not want to talk, or want you touching me at this point, but I want you, close by. I can't explain it."

"You don't have to explain. I can work out downstairs."

"Thank you Keith." She walked away and into the bedroom. While taking a long hot shower Stacy prayed and cried a lot. She got out, put lotion on her body, panties on, and grabbed one of Keith's white T-shirts and put it on. She stared at the bed in deep thought and then got in and fell asleep from exhaustion.

Keith watched Stacy walk away and then went downstairs to work out. He worked out a lot harder than usual trying to release some of his frustrations. Two hours later he was finished, and felt good, but needed a shower and some food. He went upstairs and used one of the bathrooms in another bedroom, so he would not disturb

Stacy. He put on sweatpants and a T-shirt and went to the kitchen to eat something. He was in the mood to cook, so he cooked pork chops, macaroni and cheese, cabbage, and cornbread and made sweet tea. He put all the food on the kitchen table as if others were joining him and then sat down to eat. He was about to bless his food when Stacy walked in wearing his T-shirt. She looked at the food on the table and then at him.

"I woke up and smelled food. You must be hungry to cook all this. Do you want some company?" Her words were spoken calmly.

"For sure." He smiled and put another plate on the table.

Stacy sat across from him and then put her arm on the table with a gesture for Keith to take her hand. Keith had to hold back his tears as he grabbed her hand, lowered his head, and prayed.

"Lord, bless this food we are about to receive and make it nourishing for our bodies, in Jesus name, Amen."

"Lord, help us, and thank you, Amen." Stacy exhaled and they looked at one another. "Now, let's eat."

"Absolutely." Keith wanted to hug Stacy badly, but he knew it was not the time.

They began eating while looking at each other from time to time. Neither had answers to this situation but they enjoyed each other's company. Stacy winked at Keith to keep the mood light.

"Keith, the food is good, I am impressed. I must have been hungrier than I thought because I ate a lot, two pork chops. Oh, the cornbread was delicious, and the tea is not too sweet like you usually make it." She smiled at him.

"I am glad you enjoyed the food. You did a lot of smacking while eating and licking your fingers." He winked at her.

"Yes, I did because the food was good, and I am at home."

Keith stared at her and did not want to irritate Stacy, but he needed to ask.

"Are you Stacy?"

"Am I what Keith?" She looked up at him.

"Are you home?"

She stared at him trying to figure out what to say because she did not know at this time.

"Keith, I don't want to lie or mislead you but right now I don't have the answers. How do we move past all this? I have a major trust issue now with you and Diana. How do I deal with that? How do I ignore what I saw and heard from Diana? The very thought of seeing her again makes me want to punch her in the face and beat her down. And then, there is you and Ron, best friends for life. There is so much to consider and thinking about all this is frustrating, it's awfully hard Keith." She shook her head. "Life can be something." She exhaled hard and looked at him. "Keith, if Ron finds out Diana kissed you, grabbed your dick, and all that stuff she said, it's going to be bad. How can you two remain friends after that? How do you still maintain trust? I don't know Keith; I just don't know." She stared at him.

"You made some very valid points, and I can't say I have all the answers myself. This could very well end our friendship, I don't know."

"I am not trying to make things worse, but it is so hard dealing with all this. Diana kissing you, grabbing your dick, and her very arrogant words. After the kiss, your dick was so hard, and you cannot deny it because I felt it. This means, you got turned on by her touch so quickly, you wanted to fuck her on the spot. How does your wife deal with that Keith? Yes, Diana is attractive with a great body, but you have all that and more in me. Am I not enough for you anymore?"

"Stacy, it's not like that and you know it. You know how much you affect me and how much I love you."

"No Keith!" She yelled. "I don't know anything anymore. What I do know is, your dick was rock hard after Diana kissed you." She stared at him. "You wanted her so badly if she bent over a chair, I know you would have fucked her, in front of her mother. And then fucked her mother too!" She yelled and walked into the living room with tears in her eyes and sat down.

Keith shook his head and sat in his chair staring out into space in deep thought. Ten minutes later, Stacy walked into the kitchen toward Keith and looked at him.

"Slide your chair back Keith."

He looked at her strangely because he did not know what she was about to do. He thought she was getting ready to physically attack him.

"Why do you want me to slide my chair back? Are you going to get violent?"

"I said slide your chair back Keith." Spoken in a demanding tone and giving him a demanding look.

Keith looked at her because he did not know what to do but he slid his chair back.

"I don't want to talk, just do as I ask. Stand up and take your sweatpants and underwear off, and then sit down, and hurry up."

He stared at her, but did as Stacy asked and sat down looking at her hovering over him. Stacy got on her knees and began sucking Keith's dick hard and fast. When he was hard, she faced him, put her hands on his shoulders, and straddled him. When Stacy felt the hardness of his penis inside her, she started riding his dick hard and fast while looking directly at his face.

"Damn baby, you feel good." He put his hands on her waist.

Stacy frowned and then pushed his hands away.

"Be quiet Keith and don't grab me. You are not fucking me, I am fucking you. Be quiet and keep your dick hard, while I ride it." She put both hands around his neck and rode him hard. You could hear the slapping sounds of their bodies connecting when Stacy bounced up and down. She gave Keith a mean look and tightened her grip on his neck and stared directly into his eyes. "I should choke the life out of you right now while I am riding your dick." She increased her pace and could feel her orgasm coming, which made her squeeze Keith's neck harder due to her building passions.

"Stacy, you are choking me, you are trying to kill me."

"Shut up Keith. You want some pussy, well your wife, not Diana, not her mother, or anybody else, but your wife is giving you some hot, wet, tight pussy. Now be quiet and enjoy this. And maybe I won't choke you to death in the process." She rode Keith until she had an emotional and physical explosive orgasm. "Ohhhhh damn you Keith, ohhhhhh I love you and this good hard dick. Now fuck me baby, fuck meeeeee." Stacy climaxed so hard she thought she would pass out.

In the process of climaxing and her increased passions, Stacy squeezed Keith's neck harder, choking him. He pushed her hands off his neck grabbed her waist and started pushing himself into her as she climaxed. His passions caused him to explode inside her.

"Ahhhh Stacy, it's so good. Don't stop, keep riding me."

When Stacy looked at Keith and saw the pleasure on his face, it made her angry. She slapped him and leaned forward and put her arms around his neck and bit it and started sucking it hard. Stacy continued riding him with vigor and the spirit of sexual revenge. She fucked Keith hard and deep. They finished climaxing and Keith's penis was saturated with Stacy's juices. She stood and looked at him.

"I suggest you get up and take a shower and I will do the same. I will be in our bedroom lying on the bed. I need you to come and lick my ass, good." She stared at him, rolled her eyes, and walked away shaking her butt like she owned the world.

Keith looked at Stacy walking.

"She must have forgotten I run this relationship, but I'm going to do what she asks, damn the dumbness." He sat there for a while in deep thought and then ate some more and continued thinking about so many things.

Thirty minutes went by, and he realized how long he had been sitting and thought about Stacy in the bedroom. He

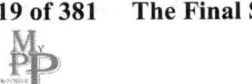

walked into the bedroom and his eyes were immediately drawn to Stacy lying on the bed wearing a negligée and nothing underneath. She pointed to the shower.

"Take a shower and hurry up and don't play with me Keith. Talking is not necessary, just take a quick shower and come out and get on the bed and do what I asked."

Keith nodded at Stacy and walked into the bathroom. Fifteen minutes later he walked out with a towel wrapped around his waist and walked to the bed. Stacy looked like she was asleep, and he did not want to disturb this peaceful moment, so he lay next to her. Stacy was not asleep, but her mood had changed. She was not feeling erotically sexual anymore but wanted Keith close. She rolled over and faced him.

"Keith, I don't want to talk but will you hold me please?"

He kissed and held her, and this was far more comfortable to his spirit and heart. It did not take long until they fell asleep.

Hours later Stacy woke up and looked at Keith asleep. Her erotic passions returned but did not want to wake Keith. So, she began rubbing between her legs, turned on her side, and caressed her butt. This felt good but she knew this would not be enough to satisfy the mood she was now in. So, she walked to the bathroom and took a quick shower and walked out naked and got in bed under the covers. She shook Keith to wake him.

"Keith wake up!"

"What's up baby, are you okay? I am sleepy."

"You can sleep later, and I am good, but now I want some lovin, so get busy."

Keith could feel his ego trying to rise because of the way Stacy talked to him but he silently prayed and looked at her.

"Stacy, I know you have a great deal on your mind and heart, we both do. However, you are not going to keep talking to me like you own me, and I am your sex slave."

She exhaled and stared at him.

"I apologize Keith, but please allow this flexibility and do as I ask." She kissed him.

He stared at her.

"I can do that."

"Good!" Stacy placed two pillows on top of each other and laid on top of the pillows so her butt would be high in the air. She looked at Keith and caressed her butt. "You have a mouth on you, so get your saliva right and start licking and kissing, and don't stop until I say so."

"Damn Stacy." For the next twenty minutes, Keith took his time and used his lips and tongue to pleasure her hips and butt. He kissed and licked her entire derriere making sure to slide his tongue slowly inside her cheeks. He placed his hands on her butt and gently spread her cheeks so he could lick her ass good and deep. Stacy rubbed her clit as he did this and screamed from the intense pleasure. Keith did all Stacy wanted and more, causing her to have multiple orgasms. Afterward, they relaxed and then showered together and laid in bed holding hands, and went to sleep.

CHAPTER THIRTY EIGHT
THE INEVITABLE

It was Saturday afternoon and Keith sat in the living room doing some research on his laptop when Stacy walked in. Both wore tennis shoes, sweatpants, and a T-shirt but Stacy's sweatpants were tight. Keith watched her all day because he wanted to make love to her, but he would not take the risk of offending her this soon, not knowing where her heart was. She sat on the sofa across from him.

"Your sweatpants are very tight. Are you advertising so you can be in someone's music video?" He gave her a mean look.

"Relax Keith, you know I do not wear baggy sweatpants and besides, you like my pants tight, and stop looking at me so mean. Anyway, you have been quiet all day, what is bothering you? It is not my pants. Oh, I know, you are irritated because I took you. I rode that dick of yours like a stallion last night and later woke you for some tongue action. You buried your face deep between my legs and slid your tongue all in my ass." She winked at him. "It felt so good baby, really good." She smiled and licked her lips.

"Yeah okay, I am glad you enjoyed it so much. You know I appreciate us talking and realize things for us will take time but inviting Ron and Diana over now, is a bad idea. I can feel it."

"You have expressed that to me several times Keith and you know I am not into dragging things out. We all need to talk and get everything out in the open and go from there. If we can remain friends, then good, if not, then we will all move on with our lives. It's that simple Keith." She thought about how things could quickly turn with Ron and Keith in the same room discussing all that happened. So, for a backup plan, she called five of the *Young Wolves* to come over.

"If you say so, but you know how Ron feels about his precious wife Diana. They were virgins when they got married, that brother paid a lot of money to get that ass. I know because I helped by giving him money to buy his big house in Potomac, a luxury car, and everything else. Ron paid millions of dollars to get that booty." He started laughing. "The only man in history to pay millions of dollars for sex. Million-dollar pussy, damn Ron."

Stacy gave him her typical, do not get hurt look and then rolled her eyes at him.

"Everything is not about money Keith. Diana said yes to marrying Ron because she loved him."

"No doubt she loves him, but she said yes after he put that expensive diamond ring on her finger. Ron would have done anything to make sure no one else got that virgin ass, you can believe that." He laughed.

Keith's comment about Diana's virgin ass irritated her and she could not hold back her feelings.

"Well, Diana is not a virgin anymore, but you sure do stare at her butt enough. Keith, keep it real with me, if you want her that badly just tell me. We can swap partners for a night. You can have Diana and I can have Ron or go all out and have a freaky foursome." She stuck her tongue out at him.

Stacy's words about swapping partners gave Keith images of having sex with Diana and he got caught up in his thoughts and felt blood flowing to his penis, at the worse time. But the very thought of Stacy being with another man, made him feel like he was stabbed in the heart and the pain gripped his brain. Without thinking about it, he got up and stood directly in front of Stacy, and stared down at her. His eyes revealed one thing, anger.

"Don't say that to me anymore about you being with another man Stacy, ever." He leaned toward her in rage and then stepped back.

The very look in Keith's eyes caused Stacy to stand up and look Keith directly in his eyes.

"Keith, I went too far, and I am sorry. You know I do not want anyone else but you. So please relax, I won't ever say it again." She put her arms around his neck and hugged him and thought, *damn, he looked like he wanted to do serious harm to me. I need to stop playing with this man, Lord.*

"I am not feeling this meeting with Ron and Diana. Not at all Stacy but we will hope for the best." He kissed her and held her hand.

The doorbell rang and Keith answered it. Ron and Diana stood there. Ron wore casual dress shoes, dress slacks, and a dress shirt. Diana wore tennis shoes, tight sweatpants, and a T-shirt. Keith looked at Ron's eyes trying to read his mood to see if he was angry, but he saw nothing.

"Come in you two and make yourselves comfortable. Stacy and I are in the living room."

"Thanks, but we won't be long, I know you are busy." Ron said.

Diana and Ron walked into the living room. Stacy and Diana always greeted each other with a hug but not now. Stacy remained seated and looked at them. Ron and Diana sat on the sofa across from Stacy and Keith sat next to Stacy.

"Let me say I prayed hard before coming over, asking God for wisdom and strength. Diana and I talked, she told me what happened with you and her Keith, what she said. I am not going to give any excuses for what was said, but I will say her mother is an extremely bad influence on her. Yes, she has love in her heart for her daughter, no question about that, but her spirit is foul, and she has an extremely strong lustful spirit, and it has affected Diana."

Stacy looked at Ron and Diana and wanted to scream. She was thinking, *are you kidding me? Once again, Ron was acting like his precious Diana was a victim, but she is far from that.*

"We all play around a lot with sexual jokes toward each other but Diana you said some nasty things and you kissed Keith on the lips hard and grabbed his penis." Stacy said with attitude.

Ron stood up quickly and looked at Diana.

"What! You kissed him on the lips and grabbed his dick. You did not mention that to me. What else have you not mentioned? I have seen the way you two look at each other," he looked at Keith. "Keith, I have noticed many times how hard you look between Diana's legs when she is sitting down and wearing skirts or dresses and how you always stare at her body when she walks. Lusting hard." His eyes revealed his anger.

Keith stood and waved his hand at Ron.

"Hold up partner, let's not get caught up in this soap opera emotional stuff. We have been through wars together, spilled blood, and weathered many storms. Ron, keep it real, we both love our wives very much and they are incredibly good-looking with a body for days. We are so blessed my friend. Now, let's relax, sit down and talk calmly."

"Ron sit down so we can finish talking, please." Diana said.

Ron turned to look at Diana and gave her a disgusting look, as if to say, shut up, and then looked at Keith and stepped closer to him.

"Oh, now you want to try and bow down because you know you are dirty. I have wondered about you, Stacy, and Diana. All three of you probably fucking behind my back," he put his finger in Keith's face. "You are foul." He stared at Keith ready to hit him.

"Don't get this situation twisted Ron, and you need to get your finger out my face and step back before something bad happens."

"It's already bad." He hit Keith in the jaw and front-kicked him in the chest.

Keith fell back but he did not fall, and he charged Ron and they began fighting hard. Throwing punches, elbows, and kicks.

Stacy and Diana tried to break them up but they both ended up on the floor.

"This is all your fault, and you know it. You and your slut mother acting like dogs in heat looking for dick."

Diana snapped and they started fighting on the floor, trading punches. The *Young Wolves* stood on the front steps of the house, and they heard a lot of noise coming from inside the house and knew something was going on. They rushed in with guns drawn and saw them fighting. They looked at each other not knowing what to do because they were close to everyone. One of them aimed his gun at the floor and shot twice.

"Stop fighting." He yelled.

All four of them stopped fighting and stared at the *Young Wolves*. Keith, Ron, Diana, and Stacy were bloody. They stood and looked at how bloody they were and started laughing. After laughing, Keith walked over to the guy who fired the shot put his hand on his shoulder, and looked at him and the other *Young Wolves*.

"Thanks, I thank all of you for coming out here. I am sure when you walked in and saw us fighting it was confusing for you. How did you all know to even come here?"

"I contacted them earlier to come over just in case. I am glad I listened to my instincts because this would have gotten much worse." Stacy said.

"Yes, it would have." Ron looked at Keith.

"So, is everything cool now, can we leave?" One of the *Young Wolves* said.

"Ron, are we good? Are we going to kill each other today?" Keith looked at him.

"No one is killing anybody today Keith." Diana said and looked at everybody.

The *Young Wolves* put their guns away and walked out of the house, got in their vehicles, and drove away.

"Now what do we do?" Diana said and looked at Ron.

Ron stared at Keith and then walked over and extended his hand to him.

Keith shook his hand and they hugged and sat down. Stacy walked to the bathroom and got some towels and a medical kit. Diana helped her and they went to the kitchen to get ice and walked back to the living room. Both wives took care of their husband's wounds, and the guys did the same for their wives. There were no broken bones, but lots of bruises from blocking blows, busted noses, and lips. After caring for one another they all sat down and stared at each other.

"Well, I guess for all the things we have been through, the fight was inevitable. Where do we go from here, is the question?" Ron said.

"No matter how many times I say it, I know it will not change what I have said and done, but I am deeply sorry for everything. I have replayed all that I did many times in my head and it does not seem like me at all. It is like looking down at yourself, hearing and seeing everything, but it is not you. We must decide are we going to remain friends or go our separate ways? Do we forget everything we have been through as best of friends or pray? I would rather pray." Diana said and looked at Ron and then Stacy.

Stacy and Diana stood, stepped to each other, and hugged tightly, and then sat close to their husbands.

"I want to say one thing Diana, you do have a nice derriere." Stacy said this to make everyone laugh and they did.

"You are something Stacy." She stared out in space and then exhaled heavily. "I don't know what to do about my mother. I cannot turn my back on her because we just started getting to know one another and she is in my life now and I cannot let that go. I know she is dealing with some spiritual bondage and deep pain, but who is not? To have my mother in my life now is an answered prayer. What do I do?" Diana said close to tears.

The doorbell rang. Sheila and Zechariah did not sleep well last night because they had Ron and Diana on their mind and spirit. So, this morning they spent time in prayer and God revealed for them to go over to Keith's house. They were casually dressed, Sheila wore a dress with flat shoes and Zechariah wore dress shoes, dress slacks, and a long-sleeved dress shirt.

"Who could that be?" Keith said and answered the door. He was surprised to see Sheila and Zechariah standing there. He sized up Zechariah quickly and thought, *this brother looks like he is getting bigger, I would not want to fight him.*

Sheila, Zechariah come on in." He said their names clearly, so the others could hear it and mentally prepare themselves.

Zechariah and Sheila looked at each other and then at Keith.

"Son, what happened to you." Sheila said.

"I am good Mom, come on in."

They walked in and Keith walked behind them. Ron, Diana, and Stacy stood as they entered the living room. Zechariah and Sheila looked at them.

"Lord Jesus, what in the world happened to all of you? Did you get into a car accident? Are you badly hurt? Somebody better start talking and tell me something." Sheila said and put one hand on her hip.

Zechariah touched Sheila's shoulder.

"Sheila, you are asking too many questions too fast. Give someone time to answer baby." He looked at everyone and then shook his head. "I already know Sheila, God just revealed it to me, but I don't know why. They have been fighting, each other."

Keith stood next to Stacy now and he and everyone else looked down when Zechariah said that.

"What! Why on earth would you four be fighting each other? Have you gone crazy? Ron, you need to start talking and tell me something, and do not lie to me boy. Everyone sit down because you look like you are about to fall anyway, don't make sense."

They all sat down, and Ron looked at Zechariah and then Sheila.

"It's too long of a story to go into details but we all had some personal relationship details to work out and..."

Sheila waved her hand in the air.

"I have heard enough. I think I know what is going on. This does not make sense, grown Christian people acting like children, fighting. So, all of you chose to fight each other instead of talking like adults and praying about the situation. I am disappointed in all of you, especially you Ron. Chosen one of God, fighting like a child would do."

"Mom, it's more involved than that, and…"

"Don't interrupt me when I am talking Ron, you are already bloody. I have one question to ask, and I want the truth," she pointed at Keith and Ron. "Did either of you two put your hands on these women?" She looked at Ron and Keith very seriously.

"Ron, did you hit my daughter?" Zechariah had a mean look on his face.

"Never that Zechariah." He looked at him and Sheila.

"No, we did not. Stacy and Diana were fighting, and Ron and I were fighting." Keith looked at Sheila and then looked down.

"So, all of you were in here fighting like a pack of wild dogs. All over who said this, who looked at whom, and who touched who. You do not have to lie to me. I did not get this age by being stupid. Let me say this to you two girls. I know you are grown woman and times have changed but you are also Christian woman, and you need to represent that in all you do. Everything you wear does not have to be up to your neck and down to your ankles, and everything does not have to be skintight and revealing either. One more thing, why does this generation think you should show everything, even their underwear in public? The only ones that should see a woman's underwear is her husband and God, not everyone else walking the streets. Pray more and you will not be fighting like animals." Sheila looked at everyone when she talked especially Diana and Stacy.

"It is the spirits of darkness and the forces of evil that try to keep us all in spiritual bondage every day, but it is the blood of Jesus Christ that has set us all free. Let us all pray and be mindful of the power of God and call on him." Zechariah looked at everyone, especially Ron. "Bow your heads."

They all bowed their heads.

"Lord Jesus, we all thank you for another day of your grace, mercy, and protection. We know the Devil is always working to divide and destroy us, but we pray you give us strength, peace, and wisdom to make the right choices. Father, we bind and rebuke every foul and unholy spirit right now that is attacking this family, in the name of Jesus. Keep us all, oh Lord, and we thank you, in Jesus name, Amen." Zechariah looked at Ron and Keith hard.

Everyone said, "Amen."

"No more fighting and I mean it." Sheila said and stared at Ron.

"Hello Mrs. O'Neil, it's good to see you and Zechariah." Stacy said.

"Hello Mom, I love you." Diana said and smiled.

"Hello to both of you and start acting like mature Christian women. You two hug each other and Ron, you and Keith do the same." Sheila pointed to them.

"Mom, we already did that."

"Don't talk back to me boy, it will not hurt to do it again."

Everyone hugged and then looked at Sheila.

"Good, now I am hungry. Zechariah and I are going to get something to eat, and you four are coming along so I can look at you."

"Mrs. O'Neil, no disrespect but I do not want to go out now looking like this, I have bruises on my face." Stacy said.

"Mom, neither do I. I cannot go out looking like this. My face does not look pretty."

Sheila looked at them and waved her hand through the air.

"Well, you both are going, so be quiet. Go put makeup on your face to hide the animal spirit you two were behaving in and hurry up because I am hungry. And do not roll your eyes at me when you walk away." She pointed her finger at them. "God don't like ugly."

Stacy and Diana looked at each other and then walked quickly to Stacy's room so they could put on makeup. Zechariah stepped to Ron and placed a firm hand on his shoulder.

"Ron, we need to talk my brother, but later." He gave Ron that, I am speaking to you as a Dad look.

"I know Zechariah, I know." He looked at him with admiration and concern.

Sheila stepped to Keith and pinched his arm.

"You know I don't like you fighting my son. What is wrong with you? Are you on drugs?" She stared him down.

"No Mom I am not but you…"

Sheila waved her hand in front of his face.

"No, don't fight my son, and I mean it." She pinched him again, hugged him, and then kissed him on the cheek and walked toward Zechariah.

Keith held his emotions in because of the great love and respect he had for Sheila. She always showed him love like a Mom. He would do anything for her. He briefly closed his eyes tightly so tears would not come.

Stacy and Diana walked back into the room.

"We are ready now." Diana said.

"Yes, we are." Stacy said.

"Good, it took you two long enough, I told you I was hungry.
Zechariah, will you and those two street fighters over there walk out first, I need to say something to Diana and Stacy."

Zechariah hugged Diana lightly and was bothered by the bruises on her body and face.

"Are you alright?"

"Thanks dad but I am okay, love you."

"I love you more. We need to talk." He whispered in her ear and then kissed her cheek.

Zechariah shook Ron and Keith's hands and they walked toward the front door.

Sheila waved at them.

"Wait a minute Ron."

Ron, Zechariah, and Keith turned around to look at Sheila.

"Ron, I am disappointed in your behavior. You need to remember this son. Your Dad did not sacrifice his life, so you could behave like an animal. He died so you could live. He died on the day you were born son. Use the power God has given you and walk in total victory." She stared at him. "Stand up my son." She yelled. "And be the man you are supposed to be." She locked eyes with Ron knowing her words were harsh and would hurt him, but she was compelled to say these things in this way.

Sheila's words hit Ron's heart like a brick, and it felt like his insides were shaking. To him, his Dad was his ultimate human hero. The bible says, *there is no greater love that a man has than to lay down his life for his friend.* My Dad laid his life down for me. Now, look at me. He shook his head and then stared out in space trying not to fall to his knees and cry out to God. Sheila's words hit him hard.

"I know Mom, you are right." He looked at her and walked out the door fighting back his tears.

Zechariah and Keith looked at Sheila and walked out of the house to talk with Ron knowing he was feeling crushed.

Diana watched Ron walk away and felt her husband's deep pain. She looked at Sheila and was thinking, *wow, that was a hard blow for Ron to take. I feel so responsible for all of this.*

Sheila looked at Diana and Stacy.

"You two come over here please."

Diana and Stacy walked toward Sheila and stood in front of her.

"I know what's going on and don't interrupt me. You two need to pay more attention to your husbands and stop all this group flirtation thing that all of you do. Do not say a word, I know you do it. And stop all this freaky sex talk among one another as well because everything is not meant for all to hear, regardless of how close you four may be.

How much time are you and your husbands spending in prayer? Diana, you and Ron keep your marriage business to yourself. Stacy and Keith do not need to know everything that goes on in your relationship and bedroom. The same goes for you Stacy. Stop all this sharing of information. Remain closer to God, the fire, and keep your husbands close as well. You start out like you can hold out, and you hold out like you started out. You keep God first, respect yourself, respect your husbands, and feed them very well. In the kitchen and the bedroom. Is that clear?" She looked at them.

"Yes, it's clear Mom."

"Very clear Mrs. O'Neil."

"Good, now let's go eat."

They all hugged and walked out of the house with Sheila in front. Diana and Stacy looked at each other when walking and Stacy leaned her head back and looked at Diana's butt as she walked, and Diana saw her. Diana smiled and shook her head at Stacy, and they winked at one another at the same time. They had been through so much and were appreciating the great friendship they shared for many years. They whispered, "*I love you*" to each other and kept walking.

CHAPTER THIRTY NINE

THE CRY OF HOPE

When Ice received the call from Martina informing her, she was diagnosed with a severe case of food poisoning, pneumonia, syphilis, and gonorrhea Ice was at Ray's house. Ice and Ray were in bed relaxing after an intense lovemaking session. They got up immediately and went to the doctor to get complete blood work done. They were diagnosed with Syphilis and Gonorrhea and the doctor gave them two different shots of antibiotics and informed them to refrain from any sexual activity for two weeks. During the two weeks, Ice or Ray would call Martina every day asking how she was doing. Martina told Ice the doctor informed her she had pneumonia for some time and had a blood infection which caused abscesses in her lungs. Her lungs were damaged, but she was now receiving antibiotics. After being diagnosed with pneumonia Martina began to understand why she was tired so often. At the time she contributed her constant fatigue to not getting proper rest. Her body was in a fragile state, and she was depressed, so receiving daily calls from Ray and Ice helped her spirits. Martina read the bible and prayed daily which made her think of her life and past activities which brought her so much sadness and pain and she did not want her life to end like this. Martina was checked regularly for sexually transmitted diseases because of her prostitution lifestyle, and she was careful. She knew her diagnoses of Syphilis and

Gonorrhea had to come from Ray or Ice, and their sexual encounters.

Ray and Ice talked about contracting their sexually transmitted diseases and concluded it came from Martina or the women they had a foursome with while in Venezuela. They promised each other to always use protection and be exclusive to one another from now on. But Ice wondered about Malone and his body because he could do whatever he wanted, to whomever he wanted at any given time, and he could not be stopped. If he wanted sex from her, it would happen. She was not about to get eaten alive by a pack of rats. She would rather deal with needles in the butt of antibiotics over rats any day of the week.

After two weeks Martina laid in her hospital bed one Tuesday morning crying tears of joy after giving her life to the Lord. She had never felt peace and joy like this in her life and was thanking and praising God for her salvation.

On the same floor where Martina was, Malone was in one of the bathrooms and in a stall wearing all black holding his cane. A picture of Martina was on the floor and Malone was tapping his cane on top of the picture repeatedly.

"No salvation for you, die slut. Years of sucking dicks, licking ass and pussy, and now you want to live for God. Not going to happen, you got to die, dick sucker. To hell you are going." He mumbled some words and tapped his cane on the picture, it caught on fire and burned to ashes.

Minutes later, Martina felt a sharp pain in her chest and her blood pressure went up and that was all Martina remembered before she went unconscious. Her heart stopped beating and a code blue was called. A team of nurses and doctors rushed into her room and began immediate resuscitative efforts. Several minutes of the team trying to restart her heart, the doctor was about to call her death, when her heart began beating. Her body began shaking violently and she had a grand mal seizure and went into a coma.

Malone was in the bathroom stall dancing.

"Martina is going to die and then go to hell, yes. Another slut baby swallower burning in hell."

A man walked into the bathroom where Malone was, and he was talking on his cell phone.

"Last night was the best sex ever. You can suck some dick lady. I hope your husband goes out of town more often." He laughed while rubbing his penis. "Oh yes, we are going to church tomorrow, you know I got to see you. God is good, all the time." He laughed.

Malone walked out of the stall and stepped closer pointing his cane at the man.

"You sorry no-good adultery-committing fool. Shame on you, having sex with another man's wife and then going to church talking about how good God is, hypocrite. I love it, but you are going to hell today." Malone pulled a sword from his cane and cut off the hand holding the phone. It hit the floor shaking.

The man opened his mouth wide to scream and Malone cut his head off and then cut the head in half and the two halves hit the floor. The man's body was still standing but shaking and Malone cut his body in two pieces and the pieces hit the floor. He put the sword back inside his cane and pointed his cane at the body parts.

"Look at you now. You will not be committing any more adultery. Your body is in pieces and your pieces will be burning in hell. Damn, I love it."

Malone heard a woman's voice through the cell phone.

"Baby, are you alright? Is something wrong? Are you still coming over next week and give me some more of that good dick because you know my sorry lazy husband ain't fucking me as he should?"

Malone got the cell phone from the dead man's hand and spoke loudly into it.

"No, he will not be coming over next week to give you some dick, you adulterer. His body is in pieces and will be burning in hell. You will too very soon, but I got some smoking hot hell dick for you now." He laughed and dropped the phone.

He tapped his cane on the floor and smoke appeared along with a pack of rats that walked around the bathroom floor looking at the body parts. Malone tapped his cane on the floor twice and the rats stopped moving and stared at him. He pointed his cane at the rats and the body parts.

"It is snack time, eat my friends, eat."

The rats began eating the body parts and all that was heard was smacking and the cracking of bones. The rats consumed the body parts and licked all the blood off the floor and looked at Malone.

"Good, time to go my hungry little friends." Malone laughed, mumbled some words, and tapped his cane on the floor. Malone, the cell phone, and rats disappeared in a cloud of smoke.

CHAPTER FORTY

STRONG FRIENDS

Before Martina went to the hospital to get checked she visited a law firm and gave them a five-million-dollar retainer for assistance in any legal matter. The law firm was listed in the hospital records for contact and Ice and Ray was listed with the firm as next of kin to Martina. When she went into a coma the firm contacted them.

Ray and Ice were on a private jet the same day headed to Vegas and the Sunrise Hospital. Later that evening they stood in Martina's room, and both were dressed nicely. Ice did not realize how much she liked Martina until now, seeing her lying in this bed in a coma looking peaceful. She thought of her own life and everything she had been through; tears ran down her face and Ray held her hand while he looked at Martina. Ray had seen a lot of hurt bodies and death from his military combat days, but he had never seen anyone so close to death look as peaceful as Martina did now. He held back his tears as he held Ice's hand.

"Lord, I know all the evil I have done, and I am messed up spiritually in many ways, but please don't let my friend die. Give her another chance, please Jesus, please." It hit Ice hard, and she fell to her knees crying hysterically because she prayed for Martina and cried out for herself as well. Ice was tired of being in emotional and spiritual pain. She spoke these words to herself, *Lord, deliver our souls, do not let the Devil kill us.*

Ray leaned over and lifted Ice and held her close to his body as she continued to cry. She looked up at him.

"I want to change Ray, but I made a horrible mistake. I want to get away from Malone, but he will not let me. He is going to kill me, I know it." She continued to cry.

"Relax and calm down baby, I got you, and don't worry about Malone or whoever, I will protect you."

"No, no Ray you can't. Malone is not just a man. He is evil personified, and he is going to kill me." She cried harder.

No matter what Ray said or did, he could not get Ice to stop crying, so he got his cell phone out and called her daughter Diana.

Ron and Diana were home relaxing and watching a movie when Ray called. Ray explained to her where they were, and why, and briefly explained the situation with her mother and Malone. Then he gave the phone to Ice.

Ice held the phone with shaking hands.

"Diana, please forgive me, I am so sorry for being a horrible mother to you. Will you, your family, and friends pray for me, please. Help me, Malone is going to kill me." She whispered this to Diana and then fell to the floor again still crying while holding the phone close to her heart.

Ray could hear Diana yelling through the phone, Mom, Mom. He got the phone from Ice and talked to Diana and then hung up, kneeled, and held Ice.

Diana's phone was on speaker while talking so Ron could hear what was being said. After Diana hung up, she was in tears and extremely concerned about her mother. She looked at Ron as tears flooded her eyes.

"Ron, please help my Mom." She stared at him as emotional pain gripped her heart.

He held and kissed her.

"Say no more." He would do anything for his wife and now, the spirit of the Lord was telling him what to do. He called Keith and the Pastor informing them what was going on.

What Ron did not know is when he talked to the Pastor, his sister Shirley was at his house visiting from Nigeria. God was speaking to her spirit for days concerning going home because her brother would soon need her. Shirley arrived yesterday, and she and the Pastor prayed together constantly, calling on God for instructions. When Pastor hung up the phone with Ron, he explained the situation to Shirley, and she nodded her head. Now she understood the timing of God wanting her to be there.

Ron also called Sheila, Sandra, James, and some others, briefly explaining the situation and asking everyone to pray. A few hours later Ron, Diana, Keith, Stacy, Sheila, Zechariah, Sandra, Luke, James, Catarina, Rick, Cynthia, Pastor Williams, Shirley, and twelve of the *Young Wolves* were on a private jet heading to Las Vegas to see and pray for Ice and Martina, although none of them were fully aware of the spiritual storm headed their way.

When James heard what was going on, he and Catarina stopped what they were doing and made several phone calls to arrange transportation and hotel accommodations for everyone, on a VIP level of course. The jet landed at McCarran International Airport at seven o'clock Wednesday morning and a bus was waiting for them.

Everyone was dressed casually except Pastor Williams and the *Young Wolves*, they wore suits. All their luggage was loaded on the bus by the *Young Wolves* and the Pastor noticed they wore guns but said nothing. The bus took all twenty-six of them to the MGM Grand Hotel. When they walked in there was a long line of people waiting to check in, but Catarina took care of this situation before they left with one phone call. The manager was at the front desk and had card keys for all their rooms on the counter. James and Catarina picked up the keys and passed them out to everyone. They all had large suites except Sandra, Luke, Pastor Williams, and Shirley had rooms by themselves because they were the only unmarried people besides the *Young Wolves*. The *Young Wolves* shared two per room. One hour later they all met in a reserved conference room and the *Young Wolves* were dressed in black combat fatigues, two gun holsters, and automatic weapons with lots of ammo on their belt. The back of their shirts read, SECURITY. The Pastor did not like them being here, but God quickened his spirit to leave them alone. He asked for everyone to form a circle and join hands, so they could pray.

"Lord, we thank you for a safe trip, now use us to do your will. Protect and guide us Lord, that you may receive the glory. Bless us not to walk in fear but power because of your mighty hand. We plead the blood of Jesus over us for spiritual and physical protection. Thank you Jesus." The Pastor said.

"Yes God, we bless and praise your mighty name above all else. Your word says every knee shall bow, and every tongue shall confess that Jesus Christ is Lord. Let thy will be done this day Father and every day after. We thank you oh King." Shirley said.

"You are King of Kings Lord and never lost a battle, we are here to do your will. Use us Lord, that the world will know, you showed up and showed out by your Holy Spirit. We will glorify your name from breath to breath, thank you Jesus." Ron said.

They walked out of the conference room with six *Young Wolves* walking in front and six in the rear. It is legal to openly carry a firearm in Las Vegas, so everyone was used to seeing people walking around with guns on their hips. People stared as the *Young Wolves* walked through the hotel with such firepower. While they were in the conference room praying, someone called the police, stating suspicious activity going on at the MGM Hotel. Five police vehicles drove up in front of the hotel with two police officers in each vehicle. The police officers walked out of their car and into the hotel as Ron and everyone else was coming out. The sergeant waved his hand at them to stop as he and all the police officers had their hands on their guns, ready to pull them. James stepped forward and introduced himself to the sergeant as legal counsel. Everyone else stopped walking and waited. James presented paperwork from the United States Attorney General's Office stating who the *Young Wolves* were, their high-security clearance and everyone in this group were under their protection. The *Young Wolves* were not to be detained or arrested and anyone failing to obey the orders in this legal document was subject to arrest and full prosecution by the United States Attorney's Office.

The sergeant read the legal document and then stared at the group. He waved at his team of officers.

"Let them pass." He shook his head, looked at James and the *Young Wolves* with an attitude realizing he could not detain them.

His team stepped aside and the *Young Wolves* and everyone else walked out of the hotel and into the bus that was waiting for them.

Before coming to Vegas James contacted the head of administration and chief security for the Sunrise Hospital to let them know he and family members were coming, along with the *Young Wolves'* security team. The bus drove to the front entrance of the hospital and the *Young Wolves* stepped out first and then everyone else. Two of the *Young Wolves* looked around the area and in the parking lot when they noticed this guy wearing all black pointing his cane at them. One of the *Young Wolves* got Ron's and Keith's attention letting them know of the weird guy in the parking lot. Ron mentioned this to the Pastor and then he and everyone else in the group looked at Malone.

Malone pointed his cane at them and then tapped it on the ground and mumbled evil curse words. He did this repeatedly.

Seeing this brought back bad memories for many of them concerning Mr. Bones and that evil woman Leticia Wilson. Now, the Devil has found another host to inhabit and control and put in its evil spirits. Everyone was on high alert and two of the *Young Wolves* waited outside to keep an eye on Malone. Everyone else walked into the hospital on guard. The hospital chief administrator and Martina's doctor met them in the lobby area and as legal counsel, James spoke with them. The administrator informed him that their presence could be disturbing for other patients in the hospital and unfortunately, their stay had to be a short one. The doctor informed James of Martina's current condition and that she could only have four visitors in her room at one time and no more than five minutes.

After Ray and Ice left Martina's room that night they went to the Bellagio hotel where they stayed. Ice was still very emotional, but Ray was able to get her to relax. He called for room service so they could eat and then Ice laid on the bed and went to sleep. Ray sat in a chair in deep thought about all of this, suddenly an old friend and his lady came to mind. Sadek Okafor and Noriko. Sadek is from Nigeria, mixed with Zulu. He is the son of Ramsey Okafor, who is the Ambassador to the Federal Republic of Nigeria. This gave Sadek the same diplomatic immunity status as his Dad. He could not be detained, arrested, or forced to testify in court but he could be expelled from the host country and not allowed to return. Sadek owns *Sadek Entertainment Company* which produced films and music videos across the globe, and he travels all over the world. Sadek had a net worth of four billion dollars. Ray remembered Sadek and Noriko informing him about their experience with a guy named, Mr. Bones. He was nice at one time until he was spiritually transformed into this immensely powerful and evil Devil incarnate. They told him of the incredible battle they went through trying to defeat him. Well, that sounds a lot like this guy Malone who Ice had been dealing with.

Sadek and Noriko were in Maui Hawaii where they had been for years. Ray called Sadek and told him and Noriko all that had been going on and the current situation. They agreed to help Ray. Sadek made phone calls to his private security team, and they were on a private plane that night to Vegas.

Two black stretch Mercedes Benz limos with diplomatic plates drove to the front entrance of Sunrise Hospital. Sadek, Noriko, Ray, and Ice stepped out of the first car along with four security guards and six security guards stepped out of the other car. The men were dressed in black suits and Noriko and Ice wore heels and form-fitting dresses and everyone had on dark sunglasses. Sadek's very presence was of royalty and strength. He held Noriko's hand and Ray held Ice's hand as they walked into the hospital with Sadek's security staff in front and behind them.

The two *Young Wolves* that stood outside were impressed when they drove up and watched them walk in. They liked their elite look and one of them called Keith to let him know.

They all stood in the lobby area watching James talk to the hospital staff. Keith tapped Ron's shoulder to get his attention.

"We have diplomats coming in." He whispered to him.

When Diana saw her mother walking in with Ray, she was elated and overlooked the rest of the crowd.

"Mom." She said louder than she wanted to, but it was too late now, and she did not care. Diana walked quickly toward her.

Sadek's security staff did not know who Diana was and her sudden movement in his direction was considered a threat. They pulled their guns out and aimed them at her. The *Young Wolves* pulled their guns out and aimed them at the security guards.

Sadek moved forward very quickly and waved his hand at everyone.

"No, the young lady is the daughter of my guest." He yelled and then looked at his security staff and they lowered their guns.

The *Young Wolves* did the same. Many people exhaled heavily, especially the chief administrator. Ice walked over to Diana and hugged her tightly.

"I am so glad to see you," Ice said and then kissed her on the cheek and looked around at everyone. "Wow, I did not expect to see so many people with you. They must love you."

"They do Mom, a great deal." she pointed to the Pastor and Shirley. "Mom, this is Shirley, the Pastor's sister. Very anointed."

"Hello, it is a pleasure to meet the mother of Diana." When Shirley shook Ice's hand and looked at her eyes, she felt the demonic spirits oppressing and possessing her.

The front doors of the hospital entrance slid open, and Malone walked in dressed in black, holding his cane and mumbling curse words. His evil presence permeated the lobby, and everyone turned to look at him. Malone stared at the crowd and his eyes turned red and then dark black. He spat on the floor and mumbled more curse words as he walked towards the bathroom.

"Die, die. Kill, kill." Malone said loud enough when he passed so everyone would hear him and then walked into the bathroom.

Sadek looked at Noriko.

"So, he is the evil one." He whispered to her.

"Yes, he is, and you can feel his demonic presence." Noriko said as her body shook.

Ray introduced Sadek and Noriko to Diana, Ron, and some others in the group. They all talked for a while to become acquainted and then Martina's doctor, Sheila, Zechariah, Ray, Ice, Ron, Diana, Keith, Stacy, Pastor, Shirley, Sadek, Noriko, Sadek's security team, and four of the *Young Wolves* took turns getting on the elevator to visit Martina.

CHAPTER FORTY ONE
PRAYER WILL

They got off the elevator on Martina's floor and walked to the lobby area. Each time the elevator doors opened, everyone on the floor stared at them as they walked out, wondering who they were and who they were going to see. The *Young Wolves* and Sadek's security team stood in the hallway lined up on both sides of the wall observing everything.

The doctor, Ray, and Ice walked into Martina's room first. She was still in a coma. The doctor checked on her and then walked out to give them some time with her. Ray and Ice stayed for five minutes and walked out. Ice had tears in her eyes and Diana hugged her and they talked in the lobby for a while. Sadek and Noriko walked into Martina's room and looked at her. Sadek touched Martina's arm.

"She has the look and feel that you and I have seen and touched many times with people that are being attacked by demonic forces. The coma she's in is caused by the powers of darkness and it will take the hand of God to deliver her."

Noriko touched Martina's arm.

"She feels so cold, when will this all end?" She and Sadek stayed a few minutes and then walked out and joined the others in the lobby to talk.

"So, my friend what do you think?" Ray said to Sadek.

"You were right to call us, and she is under heavy demonic attack, but God can deliver her." Sadek said as he looked seriously at Ray.

"Amen!" Ice said and stood closer to Ray.

Keith and Stacy visited Martina briefly. They prayed for her and then walked out. The Pastor, Shirley, Ron, Diana, Sheila, and Zechariah went into her room and stared at her. They all began to pray and then stepped back, and Pastor looked at Ron.

"Brother Ron, this is what you were called to do, so do what thus says the Lord."

Ron looked at the Pastor and Diana nodded her head at him.

"This is your call Ron." Diana winked at him.

Ron began to pray and then laid his right hand on Martina.

"I plead the blood of Jesus against every evil force attacking this soul. Devil, you have no authority here and I claim her healed by Jesus Christ's stripes and the blood he shed on the cross. Now, oh Lord, let thy will be done. In Jesus name."

Martina opened her eyes.

"Thank you Jesus, thank you Jesus." Martina started crying and praising God.

Everyone in the room began praising God and the others in the lobby area heard them and they knew, once again God delivered. Martina disconnected the needles and other connections on her body, sat up, and stood slowly. She walked out of her room with the others behind her. When the doctor saw her walking, he almost fainted and the nurses on her floor began crying and clapping their hands. Everyone was clapping and rejoicing. Ray hugged Martina and Ice, and she cried thanking God for his grace and mercy and Ice thought, *Lord, since you delivered Martina from her coma, please save me.*

Malone was still in the bathroom downstairs when Martina awoke from her coma. This infuriated him and he started cussing.

"No, hell no! She should be dead. All that praying by these ugly Christians. I hate them all and I am killing all the O'Neil's and everybody else, today! Damn these people all to hell, two times!"

Martina went back into her room and got dressed. The doctor checked her out and she was in perfect health. Not even a mark on her body from the needles that were in her arms. Martina and everyone else got on the elevators and went downstairs. Word spread quickly throughout the hospital about the coma patient waking up after prayer. Nurses on her floor were sending text messages to their friends in the hospital. Once everyone was downstairs, they talked with Martina, and many hugged her.

The Pastor was standing close to Ron and Shirley as he looked at them.

"This is not over. A battle is coming." The Pastor said.

Malone walked out of the bathroom with a serious attitude and dragged the tip of his cane on the floor while mumbling words and cussing. Everyone watched him walk away, knowing he was evil. Malone walked toward the front entrance doors and before he walked out, he turned around and pointed his cane at everyone.

"I hate you people, I hate all of you and I am killing everybody. Especially you, chosen boy Ron. I am cutting your head off and then I am going to put demonic hard dick in your wife, fake praying Christian." He spat on the floor spoke curse words and began walking slowly toward Ron while mumbling more words.

The *Young Wolves* and Sadek's security team pointed their guns at Malone. Malone stopped walking and waved his cane in the air.

"I knew all of you were coming here, but you made a mistake because none of you will live to see tomorrow. When you step out of this hospital, I am killing all of you, to hell you are going, today." He tapped his cane hard on the floor and disappeared in a dark cloud of smoke.

Others who happened to be in the lobby saw Malone disappear in smoke, they were shocked, but Ron and the others knew of such evil.

CHAPTER FORTY TWO
THE FINAL SHOWDOWN

Smoke appeared in front of the hospital parking lot and when it disappeared, Malone was standing there dressed in all black holding his cane. He was furious and looked forward to killing many people today. He pulled his sword out a little from his cane to expose it and then cut his finger and squeezed it hard and drops of blood began hitting the ground until it was a small puddle. He slid the sword back inside his cane and then took the tip of his cane and dipped it in the puddle of blood and dragged it on the ground to form a circle. Malone spat inside the circle and began tapping the tip of the cane on the ground and mumbled many curse words. Suddenly, dark clouds appeared in the sky and the ground began to shake and crack open throughout the parking lot. The shaking shook the hospital as well. Rats by the hundreds of thousands began coming out of the ground and they grew one foot long and thick, with long razor-sharp teeth. Many of the rats transformed into large wolves. All the rats lined up in front of the hospital entrance and the wolves lined up behind them. Malone stood behind the animals tapping his cane on the ground and speaking curses.

The people outside of the hospital began screaming and running for their lives. Many people inside the hospital close to the windows wanted to see what was causing the shaking. Was it an earthquake? They looked out the window and saw the ground had opened and they saw all the rats and wolves, they began screaming. Everyone in the lobby stared at this horrible scene and some people walking through the lobby looked out and saw the rats and wolves and began screaming as well. A hospital maintenance tech was in the crowd of the lobby.

"Lord Jesus." He ran and turned a switch on a wall, so the sliding doors would not open.

"Good God almighty." The pastor said as he stared at the evil scene outside.

For the *Young Wolves*, Sadek, Noriko, Ron, Keith, Pastor, and others, it was a scene reliving their past.

"Back, everybody! Move back! Run to the stairs, get out of this lobby, and hide." Sadek yelled and waved at everyone to move back.

Everyone in the lobby moved far back into the lobby and then the *Young Wolves,* Noriko, and Sadek, and his security team lined up and got on one knee and aimed their guns at the front entranceway.

Zechariah, Ron, Keith, Pastor, and Shirley stood behind them. James, Ray, Sheila, Catarina, Ice, Sandra, Luke, Martina, Stacy, and Diana stood behind Ron and the rest. Ron turned around and pointed at them.

"Ray, James, get these women out of here." Ron yelled.

"No Ron, I am staying and praying with you." Diana said.

"Diana, get out of here, now." Ron yelled louder.

"No Ron, I am staying." Diana yelled back at him just as loud.

Ray grabbed Ice's hand and then James touched Sandra, Martina, and Sheila to get their attention and grabbed Catarina's hand.

"Let's go, now." He yelled.

Sheila looked at Ron and he stared at her with pleading eyes to please leave. It was difficult to leave her only son, but she turned and looked at Ray.

"Okay, let's get out of here."

Two of Sadek's security team members gave Ray and James handguns with a lot of ammo, and then they got back in line.

Ray, Ice, Catarina, Sandra, Martina, Sheila, and James ran up the stairs to the third floor and found an empty bedroom. They ran in and began putting the table and chairs against the door.

Malone hit the ground hard with the tip of his cane and then pointed it at the animals and then the hospital.

"Go, kill everybody my friends, eat them all." He yelled.

Many of the rats and wolves ran toward the front sliding glass doors crashing into them. Ron and his team were praying hard calling on God and the glass doors did not break. Everyone in the lobby started clapping for joy. This made Malone angrier, and he grabbed one of the rats by its tail, spat on it, said some curse words, and threw it against the front doors. All the glass began to crack on the doors and then more rats and wolves charged the doors. This time, the doors crashed, and the animals walked in the lobby very slowly while snapping their teeth and foaming at the mouth and then stopped and stared at everyone.

Ron and his team continued to pray against this evil. One of the rats moved forward and looked directly at one of Sadek's security team members, snapping his teeth as if it were taunting and daring the guard to do something. He did, he shot the rat, blowing his head off.

"No, don't shoot them." Pastor yelled because he knew what this would trigger.

It did, all the wolves began howling and the rats and wolves charged them. The guards began shooting and killing them quickly, but it was far too many and they moved fast. Ron and everyone on his line held their hands out toward the charging animals rebuking their evil spirit. It was as if God put an invisible wall in front of them because about thirty rats and wolves leaped at the same time in the air toward them, but they all hit something in the air first and hit the ground. The animals could not get to them, the power of God prevented it.

The guards and security teams continued shooting and killing the animals, however, this aggravated them even more. The rats and wolves moved faster and began leaping on the guards. A rat bit one of Sadek's guards on his ankle and would not let go, the guard screamed because he could feel the rat's long sharp teeth biting and ripping his flesh. He was about to shoot it, but a wolf bit the guard in the neck and then bit off his head and the wolf ran with the guard's head in its mouth. The animals began winning because of their size, strength, speed, and numbers. They bit the guards and killed them quickly because of their powerful jaws and teeth, biting off their legs, hands, feet, arms, and head in one motion and then running away with body parts in their mouths. One guard ran away and opened the stairway door to go in, rats bit his feet off and a wolf bit his head off. Now, the door was opened, and the rats and wolves ran over his dead body and began running up the staircase by the hundreds. It was as if these animals were being guided by some unseen force. The wolves gripped the doorknob of each door on the stairway to every floor with powerful jaws and then walked in.

Malone stood outside in front of the hospital holding his cane but staring out in space as if he were in some deep spiritual trance, and he was. He knew the layout of the entire hospital and was guiding the animals on where to go and what to do.

"Run my friends run and kill everybody!" He said repeatedly.

The rats and wolves were now on every floor and in every staircase. The people screamed and ran for their lives when they saw the animals, but it did no good. The rats attacked people from low and the wolves attacked from high. No one was safe from the evil spirit-filled creatures. Arms, legs, feet, and other body parts were everywhere. It was a horror scene no matter where you looked. The wolves pushed the patient's doors open and killed anyone in the room, no one was safe, except those who prayed and believed.

One person had three church members visiting him and they prayed hard asking God for safety. Two wolves pushed the door open and attempted to come in but one of the church members pointed to it.

"In the name of Jesus, be gone Devil." He yelled.

The two wolves screamed in pain and ran out of the room.

By this time Ron and his team did the same thing, they all pointed at the animals in the lobby and spoke at the same time.

"In the name of Jesus, be gone Devils." They yelled.

The dark clouds moved, and the sun began to shine brightly. All the animals ran out of the building and the moment their bodies were exposed to the rays of the sun, they imploded in fire, and nothing was left but burning ashes.

Inside the hospital looked like a war zone and many of Sadek's security team and some of the *Young Wolves* were dead. Outside in the parking lot looked the same. Dead bodies, body parts, and blood were all over the ground. Police vehicles, fire trucks, and ambulances drove in the parking lot, but Malone was so angry he pointed his cane at them, mumbled some words, and all the vehicles blew up. Killing everyone inside.

Malone looked at the ashes of all his dead animal friends and then stared at the hospital. He was beyond furious, and his rage was going to be manifested.

Ray, James, Ice, Catarina, Sandra, Martina, and Sheila were in the room still praying. They all heard the repeated screams and horror taking place and prayed harder. Ray and Ice were ready to shoot anything that tried coming through the door. When everything became silent, they moved the furniture away from the door and Ray stepped out first with his guns in his hand. He looked around and then nodded for the others to come out. What they saw made Ice, Catarina,

Sandra, Martina, and Sheila throw up. Ray had witnessed this scene in his military career, but this was incredibly gruesome. James wanted to throw up but did not. The floor looked like a bomb exploded. Dead bodies, body parts, and blood were scattered all over the place. They walked downstairs and saw the same carnage. They greeted everyone with hugs and kisses and then Pastor pointed to the front doors.

"Look outside." He yelled.

Malone walked toward the front entrance slowly while transforming himself into an exceptionally large rat, then a large wolf, and back to himself. He did this twice until he stood in the doorway of the entrance holding his cane.

"Lord have mercy Jesus, that is evil incarnate." Sandra said.

"The powers of darkness are real, and we all have witnessed it firsthand. Have no fear, King Jesus is all power in heaven and earth." The pastor said and looked at everyone.

They all looked at Malone as he stood there staring at them with a look of immense rage on his face.

"You sorry no good church people killed all my friends, for that you will all die just as painful and very horribly and bloody, today." He tapped his cane hard on the floor repeatedly and spoke curse words and waved his cane through the air. "Wind and elements obey me. My four-footed beasts, come to me now."

The sky turned dark, the wind blew hard, and rain came just as hard. Malone took a step and spat on the floor, and when the spit hit the floor, it turned into large King Cobra snakes. The snakes rose to reveal their awesomeness in color and the death of a pending bite. There were over one hundred King Cobra snakes on the floor, waiting to strike at his command. Malone hit his cane hard on the floor and spat on it again. His spit turned into thirteen-foot-long, three-hundred-pound Alligators until it was thirty of them in line with their mouths open, ready to bite. Malone pointed his cane at the alligators and then at Ron.

"You, chosen boy Ron! I hate the very air you breathe, the day you were born should have never happened. I killed your fake praying Daddy in a hospital, just like you are about to be killed, in a hospital. I killed your fake Christian dick-sucking sister Christine too, one of my animal friends bit her head off, I loved it. Now, it is your turn, and you will pay boy. Unless you do what your sorry Daddy had the opportunity to do and bow down before me. Confess me as your Lord, Master, and God, and serve me, and I will let everyone else in this room live. Now, bow down to me, before I walk over, and demon fuck your sexy big butt freak wife to death, from the back." He spat on the floor.

The pastor pointed at Malone.

"Shut up Devil, God said, *thou shall have no other God before him.* God said, *I even I am the Lord, and beside me there is no other savior.* God said, *no weapon form against us shall prosper*, and you are the one whose knee shall bow, and tongue confess before God, that Jesus Christ is Lord."

"Never fool," Malone yelled and then pointed his cane at the snakes. "Kill the fools my serpents."

Some of the *Young Wolves* began shooting the snakes and killed them but then the snakes leaped with incredible speed and bit them in the throat. The *Young Wolves* screamed in pain and hit the floor vomiting blood and died quickly. One of Sadek's men began shooting at the alligators but two alligators somehow got behind him and bit his legs, arms, and head off.

God spoke to Ron's spirit and said, "It's your time."

Ron waved his hand at the snakes, and they all caught on fire and burned. He waved at the Alligators, and they burned as well. He pointed at Malone.

"God is giving you one last chance to repent of your sins and come to his glory."

"What! You stupid fool, I don't care if you think you are a chosen one, you are nobody fool," He yelled. "I would rather rule in hell than serve in heaven, I am God, I..."

Malone never finished his sentence because Ron pointed his hand at him, and Malone's body suddenly imploded in flames. He screamed and dropped his cane on the floor, and it caught on fire. Malone's flesh melted from his body as he continued screaming until there was nothing left but ashes on the floor. The wind blew the ashes of Malone and the cane away. Everyone clapped their hands and praised God.

As the praises continued no one saw the last wolf crouched down low in the corner. The wolf stood and walked toward Ron with saliva and blood dripping from its mouth. Its eyes were black as coal and were locked on Ron as its pace increased and he leaped toward Ron from a great distance. Its mouth was opened wide ready to bite Ron's head off. Keith saw the wolf out of the corner of his eye, and he leaped in front of Ron and shot the wolf at the same time. Keith and the wolf lay on the ground and the wolf lay on top of Keith until he pushed it off. The wolf was breathing heavily and then died. However, Keith's actions and his love for his best friend cost him. The wolf was able to bite Keith in his neck as it was shot and landed on him. Keith was now lying on the ground bleeding badly. Stacy screamed and ran to him; she was on her knees and placed her hand over the wound on his neck to stop the bleeding. The blood poured out. Ron and the Pastor kneeled over Keith trying to help him and others were close by as well praying for him.

Keith was in great pain and felt cold. He knew he was dying but he wanted to say his last words to Ron. He could barely talk as blood poured from his mouth and his voice was just above a whisper as he stared at Ron.

"Ron, my true friend. You went to prison for me my brother to protect me. You and Stacy have been my best friends. Stay focused my friend," he managed to smile despite being in great pain. "I could not let the wolf get you. A life for a life. I love you, my brother." Every word he spoke was a challenge, but he had to speak.

Ron held Keith's hand tightly and held back his tears as he looked at him because he knew his lifelong friend was so close to death.

"Keith don't talk. Hold on my brother, just hold on." Tears were in his eyes as he prayed for his friend.

Keith looked at Stacy and smiled and then looked at Ron.

"Heaven will be our home."

Stacy was in shock and her pain was beyond description.

"Keith, baby please hold on. You have so much to live for," she leaned closer and smiled. "Keith, I am pregnant."

Keith stared at Stacy and smiled and then began coughing hard and spitting up blood. He exhaled hard and died.

"Noooooo!!!!" Stacy screamed as she stared at Keith. "Noooooo!!!! Keith please baby don't die, don't die on me, please baby." She looked at Ron. "Ron, do something, pray harder, do something." She screamed at him and waved her hands frantically.

Ron was crushed as he looked at Stacy and Keith because he knew his friend sacrificed his life so he could live. Keith put his body in harm's way so the wolf would not bite him. He looked at the Pastor and then Stacy.

"Stacy, I am so sorry but there is nothing I can do. Keith is dead, I am so sorry." Tears flowed from his eyes, and he was heartbroken.

There was a sudden quiet that fell upon the place. Many stood close to Keith staring at his body and praying silently. Stacy screamed from her soul. Her best human friend, her best buddy, was gone. She was finally pregnant and now her husband was dead. She looked up and screamed.

"Nooooo!!! God, please don't let this be. Please, please Lord do not let him die, I am pregnant." She reached down and held Keith with unmeasurable love. "Please God, please."

Ron stood up and yelled with all he had within him.

"Nooooooo, this is not the will of God. Nooooooo." He kneeled and laid his hand on Keith's head as Stacy held him and cried hysterically. "In the name of Jesus for all that is Holy. Your word says *death and life are in the power of the tongue.* Jesus, you called Lazarus back from the dead, I call Keith back from the dead. All for your glory Lord, you are King of Kings, in Jesus name."

Again, there was complete quiet in the room. Because Stacy held Keith so close to her body, she did not notice the blood from the bite on his neck stopped pouring out and the wound on his neck closed quickly. Suddenly, Keith's body shook, and he coughed. Stacy thought she had imagined Keith coughing, so she looked at him and his eyes were open, he smiled as he looked at Stacy.

"Oh my God, oh my God, Keith you are alive!! Oh my God, thank you Jesus, thank you Jesus! Baby, I am pregnant, I am pregnant." She hugged and kissed him repeatedly.

"Stacy, I heard you baby, and stop squeezing my neck."

"I am so sorry baby, but you are alive, and I am pregnant baby, I am pregnant."

People began clapping their hands and praising God. Keith, Stacy, and Ron stood, and people hugged them. Keith shook Ron's hand and they hugged. Pastor stared at Ron and smiled.

"Brother Ron, this is your calling. You were chosen by God himself to do great things." He smiled at him and extended his hand to Ron, and they shook hands.

Ron looked at everyone and Diana stood close to her man and looked at her husband with unmeasurable love.

Suddenly she felt sick to her stomach and threw up. Ice moved closer and held her.

"My baby, are you sick? Are you okay?"

Diana leaned over, wiped her mouth, stood up, looked at Ron, and smiled.

"Ron, I wanted to tell you, but the timing never seemed right. Anyway, I am pregnant." She smiled at him.

Ron stared at her because he was shocked by Diana's words and so was everyone else. Tears of joy came to his eyes, and he stepped closer and hugged her tightly. All he could do was hold his wife and look up.

"Thank you Jesus, thank you. It is, My Call, oh Lord, My Call."

The praises from everyone in the lobby for this awesome victory by the hand of God seemed to echo throughout the entire hospital. Everyone was in the spirit of great joy. Except one.

An elderly lady wearing a long dress and glasses who looked as though she was a hundred years old walked close to the wall with the help of her cane. She was bent over and walked slowly from the other end of the lobby and witnessed the horrible scene that took place outside and in the lobby. The wind blew the ashes of Malone and his cane on the floor against the edge of the wall where the old lady walked. She saw the ashes and bent over slowly and retrieved the ashes and put them in an old handkerchief and put the handkerchief in her dress pocket. After looking around the lobby at everyone rejoicing over the victory, she shook her head and spat on the floor.

"People say, ain't God good. But what God? Stupid fools, hell hath no fury like unfinished plans of death and destruction. The Devil comes to steal, kill, and destroy. Diana's mother Ice, as she calls herself now, got my baby Lamont Thomas locked away in Federal prison for life. He was trying to catch that slut for stealing his money, but Lamont slipped and got caught. I hate that nasty no good, suck-a-dick-quick slut. Now, Ron's wife Diana is pregnant and so is Keith's wife Stacy." She looked over and stared at Ron, Diana, Keith, and Stacy with hate. "Very interesting indeed. Seeds have been planted, but seeds don't always grow." She looked at Diana and Stacy again with contempt. "I hate all you people, but don't worry Lamont baby, mother is going to get that slut Ice. Mother is going to get them all." She looked at the crowd again, spat on the floor, and turned and walked away. She quietly began cussing and patting her dress pocket with her hand, with every step she took. She opened the door to exit the building and looked back at the crowd of people still praising God. "Enjoy it while you can, but the spirit of Mr. Bones is not dead, and that spirit will manifest itself once again and annihilate everyone. Even those unborn babies. I hate you people." She spat on the floor and walked slowly out the door cursing as she went.

Are the evil attacks over from the forces of darkness for the O'Neil family and friends?

Can they finally relax and enjoy life?
Maybe! Hopefully! Prayerfully!

Will the old mean lady walk in the spirit of evil? Or, repent and be used by the almighty power of God…?

PRAY!

MK 9:23 - If thou can believe all things are possible to him that believe.